GREETINGS from ROCK BOTTOM

THE AFTERLIFE TRILOGY

BOOK 2

ANNI SEZATE

Chicken Taco Publishing
Phoenix, AZ

ISBN: 979-8-9870656-3-1

Library of Congress Control Number: 2023914630

Printed in the United States of America.

First printing edition 2024.

Chicken Taco Publishing

www.annisezate.com

Publisher's Cataloging-in-Publication Data

Names: Sezate, Anni, author.

Title: Greetings from rock bottom / Anni Sezate.

Description: First edition. | Phoenix, AZ : Chicken Taco Publishing, [2024] | Series: The afterlife trilogy ; book 2. | Audience: Young adult.

Identifiers: ISBN: 979-8-9870656-3-1 (paperback) | 979-8-9870656-4-8 (e-book) | 979-8-9870656-6-2 (hardcover) | 979-8-9870656-5-5 (audiobook) | LCCN: 2023914630

Subjects: LCSH: Angels--Fiction. | Guardian angels--Fiction. | Demonology--Fiction. | Good and evil--Fiction. | Faith--Fiction. | Belief and doubt--Fiction. | Families--Fiction. | Young adult fiction. | LCGFT: Paranormal fiction. | Religious fiction. | Young adult fiction. | BISAC: YOUNG ADULT FICTION / Religious / General. | YOUNG ADULT FICTION / Paranormal, Occult & Supernatural. | YOUNG ADULT FICTION / Romance / Multicultural & Interracial.

Classification: LCC: PS3619.E998 G74 2024 | DDC: 813/.6--dc23

To Charles Entertainment Cheese,
for making the best of being a terrifying giant rat.

prologue

Sheila

I spent one month in the Hurricane. One month of torture. One month of reliving the worst and ugliest of my miserable existence. He hurt me and threatened me over and over. I couldn't escape him. And I couldn't escape the sounds of the twins' crying and screaming. But if I tried to protect them, the screaming worsened, because I was a monster now. I almost gave in a thousand times. But my rage carried me through.

Amidst the torture, I was also instructed. While the Darkness destroyed me, Malum showed me how to do the same to others. I would emerge with the power to bring others into the Hurricane.

When he decided I'd suffered enough, Malum gave me his proposal: remain in the Hurricane or redeem myself. I chose the second, of course. It meant being kept on a leash, but it was better than nothing.

"Do you know what you must do?" he asked me, not even bothering to take on a form. He was a smoking darkness with a voice, in the deepest pits of the Red Zone.

Humans like to call it Hell, but it's not exactly what they imagine it to be. Most of it isn't so bad. Just the Hurricane.

"I failed to let the angel die," I said. "So I have to kill him."

"No . . ." Malum's formless dark mass caressed my face and body. "No, my child. If you kill him, he will return to the White Zone. He will have power. Don't kill him. Break him, weaken him, torture him, turn him against all he ever knew or trusted. Do it slowly and covertly at first, so he doesn't think to call for his angels. Only when he's utterly ruined must you kill him. Only then will he come to the Red Zone willingly."

"And if he doesn't?" I asked.

"Then destroy him. Throw him into the Hurricane after he dies. It will require planning, for if angels come to take him away, he may go with them. Make it so he will not or cannot. After a sufficient amount of time has passed, I will give him the same proposal as all who have dwelt in my father's presence: remain there or join me. I don't care which he chooses. If he remains, he is just another bug we have crushed. An annoyance, perhaps even a poisonous one, but not a true threat. If he joins me, though . . . he could make an interesting addition. Much like you, my precious Angel of Darkness."

His Darkness swirled around me, and I gloried in his praise.

"Yes, master," I said. "I will destroy him."

chapter 1
ROUGH START

A scream pierced the air, sharp and narrow like a claw raking my eardrums.

"David! Help me!"

I spun around in panic, recognizing the voice of my niece, Ginger. But all I could see was smoky Darkness. I jumped at the sound of gravelly breathing to my left, and I could hear the drool of some creature slowly ooze and drip to the floor. A familiar dread filled the pit of my stomach, rooting me in place. Flashes of nightmares threatened to steal my focus, but I shoved them from my mind.

"Don't touch her!" I yelled, panic making my voice higher. "Just leave her alone."

The jagged breathing caught in a laugh that sounded more like a choke.

"Ginny!" I called. "Wherever you are, cover your ears and run! Don't listen to anything he says!"

The creature laughed louder, this time sounding more like thunder. The Darkness thinned as it was slowly sucked into a man standing in the middle of my sister's kitchen. He had a deceptively unobtrusive face that you wouldn't look twice at if you passed him on the street. I couldn't place his race, hair color, eye color . . . all his features were dull and forgettable. It was the most ambiguous face I'd ever seen. Apart from the fact that he was oozing Darkness. It dripped and steamed from his nose, ears, eyes, and mouth. Looking at that face, my heart skipped a beat, and I unintentionally took a step back. But I had no time for a panic attack. With a lurch of my heart I saw what he held in his hand. He had Ginny by the throat and used his free hand to stroke her face, smudging her tears across her cheeks.

"Let go of her!" I yelled, unable to move.

Malum shrugged. "As you wish."

He tossed her aside and suddenly we weren't in my sister's kitchen, but at the top of a cliff. I gasped and leaned over seeing Ginny flailing to her death with her whistle-like scream.

A grin tugged at the corner of Malum's mouth. "Are you going to save her, or let her die?"

I stood at the edge of the cliff, contemplating the jump with trepidation. I remembered falling to my own death. The air sucking the breath from my lungs. The ground rushing up to me. The crunch of my body breaking. The pain and confusion and fear. It swallowed me up, rooting me in place, until Ginny's continued scream cut through my nightmarish musings.

I shook my head to clear it and took a breath. I was being stupid. I was an angel now, I could fly.

"I'm coming, Ginny!"

Then I stepped off the edge of the cliff.

Reality slapped me in the face as blinding pain coursed up my body. I opened my eyes and lifted my face from a bush, swearing at my incomprehensible stupidity. Above the sticks and leaves that filled my vision, the dull glow from the streetlights barely illuminated the parking lot outside Sandra's apartment complex. I looked up at the balcony I'd jumped from and groaned. What was *wrong* with me?

I sucked in air through my teeth as I tried to push myself up from the bush. The branches stuck to my borrowed flowery pajamas. My left leg flared with pain, and I fell back, landing on the small wall surrounding a bed of flowers. The wall must have caught my leg on my way down. I tried to stand but fell back again, the pain painting black spots across my vision.

"Hey, uh, Bill?" I called, hoping he was near enough to hear me. He was one of the wanderers that haunted Sandra's apartment. Though wanderers tend to live in their own little world, Bill was the most lucid. "Bill!" I called. "Can you get Sandra?" My face flamed in embarrassment. I would never live this down.

He must have heard me because the next moment Sandra's door slammed open. Her face appeared over the balcony, a coil of hair poking through the sleep cap she used to protect her curls at night. Her hands slapped her face. "David! What the hell happened?"

"I was dreaming about flying again . . ." I admitted, heat flooding my face.

"Did you *jump*?"

I gritted my teeth. "Yeah. I think my leg is broken."

Sandra's bare feet slapped down the cement staircase until she reached the bottom, her robe billowing out behind her. "Dammit, David, what are we going to do with you?"

"I don't know," I mumbled, trying not to throw up. Wouldn't that have just been the icing on the cake if I threw up on her? I didn't think I had any dignity left to lose.

"Can you stand?" She crawled around the bushes and put my arm around her shoulder, then heaved. I gasped and winced. "Come on, we need to get you to a hospital." We awkwardly hobbled around the bushes toward the parking lot. I sagged and almost blacked out when I tried to put weight on the leg, but hopping on my good leg just jostled it even more.

"We can't go to the hospital," I said weakly. "I don't have insurance. Or money. I'm not even legally alive."

"It's okay, I'll take care of it," she said, grunting under my weight.

I bit my lip as I was flooded with guilt. Could she afford my hospital bill? This wasn't fair to ask of her. But I had no one else to turn to.

"I'll pay you back. Somehow."

"Don't worry about it." She leaned me up against her car. "I'm just gonna grab my keys, so hang tight."

Shame flooded through me. Sandra shouldn't have to be responsible for me. That thought had niggled away at me for the past week. She's been the only one I could turn to since I'd been miraculously brought back to life. For eleven years I'd been a guardian angel, saving, helping, and inspiring mortals. Since my fall to mortality, I'd become nothing more than an overgrown toddler, having accidents all over the place. It's hard to adjust to a mortal body when you're used to just floating through everything.

Our hospital visit lasted for hours, and I had a feeling my mom was nearby being a total worrywart because Sandra kept shooting nervous glances across the room and saying things like, "It's fine" and "He'll be okay." Every time she did that, I shot her an annoyed look. Except for the conversation where she'd translated for me and Jake right after I became mortal, she refused to tell me when angels were nearby. I found this completely unfair, but she just kept saying that she'd been told not to say anything. Something about me being mortal and having to live by faith or something. It was totally rude.

I wanted to stay near Sandra to have at least some connection to the other side, but I kept getting this sinking feeling that I couldn't stay with her for much longer. I'd become a burden to her. Also, I was supposed to be a guardian angel. How was I supposed to help my family if I kept hiding away at Sandra's?

When we got back to the apartment, I wanted to just flop on the couch and sleep, but instead, I sat at the table and propped my crutches against the wall. "We need to talk."

Sandra sighed and pulled up a chair.

"I need to move out. You shouldn't have to take care of me. I'm a grown man. I think. Also," I squirmed in my seat uncomfortably, "I'm not sure it's right, morally, for me to be living with you."

Sandra snorted. "You are *such* an angel. It's fine! It's not like we're doing anything 'inappropriate.' You sleep on the couch. We aren't even in the same room. Plus, you're not seventeen anymore. Even if this wasn't platonic and we were sleeping together, as an adult you have the right to sleep with whoever you want. It's nobody's business but your own."

"Well . . . I don't feel right about it. And it's not just that," I said, my face burning with embarrassment. "I'm supposed to be a guardian angel. Or guardian mortal now, I guess. How can I help my family if I never go near them?"

"But how can you go near them without them recognizing you and having a total heart attack seeing their dead brother and son alive?" she countered. "I see dead people all the time and it still freaks me out."

"They might not recognize me," I said. I still didn't really know how old I was supposed to be. I looked pretty much the same as I did as an angel which was somewhere between seventeen and twenty-seven, but it was hard to tell. I did have to start shaving though, so that was new. I understood the basic concept, but after cutting myself twice with one of Sandra's pink razors the first time, Bill floated in to give me some pointers, which Sandra deigned to translate because she felt bad for me. So, a ghost taught me how to shave with a woman's razor. My life is so normal.

"You don't look that different," Sandra argued. "You still look like David. How are you going to explain that?"

"I don't know. But I think . . ." I closed my eyes and tried to focus on what felt right. "No, I know that I won't be able to help them from behind the scenes like I used to. I don't have the ability to spy on them and magically send feelings of comfort or advice. I think . . ." I closed my eyes again, trying not to let my own worries cloud my judgment, "I think what they need right now is *me*. For some reason."

"What, so you just show up at your dad's house and say, 'Hey pops! Guess what? I'm alive again!'"

I frowned and shook my head. "I get the feeling I need to start with Elena. I think she'd be the quickest to believe me. If she lets me stay with her, I can be a much better guardian angel from within her own home."

Sandra gave me a nervous look.

"What?" I asked.

"I just worry about you. You need time to adjust. I mean, look at what just happened!" she gestured to my busted leg. "I don't mean this as an insult, but you're like a little kid. You need to get used to your body."

Oh, how my pride was stinging. A flush of anger coursed through me as I thought of my predicament. I was a good guardian angel, and, surprisingly, not a terrible demon hunter! I was the one that got the closest to catching Malum. Then I made one mistake and now I was this pathetic mortal with no control over his body.

In a rush of frustration, I got up and booked it to the front door, crutching as fast as I could. My instinct to get away quickly was to just float through the door, so I forgot to open it and smashed into it with surprising force. My eyes watered as I felt a snap, disturbingly reminiscent of someone biting into a carrot.

Great. Just great. First I try to fly off a balcony and break my leg, and then I break my nose running into a door.

"DAVID, YOU IDIOT!" Sandra shouted. "Mortals can't float through doors!"

I dropped a crutch to clutch my rapidly swelling nose.

Sandra growled and tried to pull my hand from my face. "Let me see it."

"Doh . . . ibe fide." I was trying to say, "No, I'm fine," but my busted nose made it difficult to talk.

Sandra yanked my hand away, gasped, and made a gagging noise. "Oh, that's bad. How did you hit the door that hard? You're on crutches!"

"I doh doh!"

"Yeah, you are a Dodo!

"Doh, I doh *doh*!"

Sandra burst out laughing at the ridiculousness of the situation and my complete inability to speak. I couldn't blame her; we were both exhausted and sleep-deprived. I started laughing too, but that hurt my face.

After her laughing fit, she sighed and said, "All right, let's go back to the hospital. Or maybe an Urgent Care."

"Doh, ibe fide. Doh mo hospidal."

"Dude, if you don't get that looked at, it could heal wrong and cause serious breathing issues."

"Doh hospidal," I repeated, trying to bend down to grab my fallen crutch. My other crutch slid out from under me, and I fell on my butt, jostling both my broken leg and nose. I fell back against the door, laughing and crying.

I had officially hit rock bottom.

chapter 2
I AM TOTALLY USELESS

I woke with a shiver as my blanket was yanked off me, but no one was there. Two weeks had passed since my fun little escapade over the balcony, and I'd gotten used to weird stuff happening in Sandra's apartment. I mean, she lived with ghosts. Yet, a lot of this haunting stuff seemed a little malevolent and directed specifically toward me. I worried there was a demon here, one that very much hated me, that only showed up when Sandra wasn't around.

My pupils dilated as I strained to see in the darkness. All I could see was the glow of the digital clock from her microwave in the kitchen. The fridge hummed dully in the background and a tree branch rustled outside the window. A sudden clatter made me suck in a breath and it took a moment before I realized it was just the ice maker in the freezer dumping ice cubes into the tray. I took a deep breath and lay back down, trying to will my racing heart to chill out. *I must have just kicked the blanket off in my sleep. Or I was having a nightmare.* I had a lot of those since becoming mortal, which sucked because as an angel you forget how vivid dreams can be.

Just as I was shutting my eyes, a dark shape lifted from the ground, and I sat up in a panic before I recognized it as my blanket. Someone was draping it back over me. Bill, maybe? He seemed to be the only one who didn't really follow the rules of not letting me see any obvious signs from the other side. He wasn't an angel, so he didn't have to follow their rules. I was impressed, though, that he was even able to lift the blanket. Moving physical objects when you're dead is difficult.

I laid my head back on my pillow with a sigh, intent on trying to fall back to sleep, but of course that wasn't going to happen, because things can't ever happen the way I want them to. The blanket was yanked off me again and flew across the room. Then it lifted back in the air and flew back, walloping me in the face.

"Ow," I said. My broken nose was still a little sensitive.

The blanket gently draped back over me, but before it covered all of me it was yanked back into the air again.

"All right, whoever's fighting, can you guys please take it outside?" I whispered. "You're gonna wake Sandra."

At the mention of Sandra there was a moment of stillness. Then the couch started rocking back and forth. I clutched the back of the couch and the arm to keep myself from falling off as the psycho demon continued tormenting me. I had a pretty good idea of who it was, too, which made me nervous in a completely different way.

"Stop it!" I whisper-yelled. "Just stop it!"

The rocking only increased, and I couldn't help but be a little impressed by how strong she was to be able to move a whole couch with a person on it.

"Look, you have every reason to be angry with me, but if you don't stop it, you know someone's just gonna come and cast you out. I bet Bill here could even do it. I've been told he's really close to making Light now."

The couch fell back to the floor with a boom. I thought she'd given up when the pillow propping up my busted leg was yanked out from under it and smacked me in the face. My eyes watered. "Okay, *that* was uncalled for. Bill, take her out. You remember how to do it."

The room fell silent, but I knew that there was a battle going on. Demon and (almost) angel throwing Light and Darkness at each other. I waited a few minutes for more creepy shenanigans, but nothing else happened. Assuming Bill had won, I held my hand up and said, "Air five, man," imagining him returning it, and fell back asleep. You'd think I'd have trouble sleeping after being attacked by a demon, but it just shows how weird my life was that it barely phased me. Also, I was pretty sure this particular demon wouldn't actually hurt me as she was the one who had saved my life.

"David, wake up. Everyone's waiting to start the meeting."

I sat straight up and blinked blearily around, my hair probably sticking up all over. "Wha . . . huh?"

"Demon hunter meeting," Sandra said with a smile, leaning over the edge of the couch. "They wanted to have it here with you because you're still part of the team."

I rubbed my eyes. "Seriously? It's been like four weeks."

Sandra shrugged.

"Wait, they're letting you in on the meeting?" I asked. "You're not a demon hunter."

She smirked. "Yes, but I have the advantage of hearing and seeing them, and you need a translator."

"Kay . . ." I yawned. "Can I go brush my teeth real quick?"

Sandra looked back for confirmation. "Yeah, but be quick. They've been waiting for a while."

I self-consciously struggled to my feet, imagining everyone's eyes on me as I crutched over to the bathroom in my sweatpants. At least they didn't have flowers on them. Sandra had gone out and bought me some of my own clothes—one more reason I was totally in her debt.

I leaned over the sink and sighed at my appearance. My dark hair looked like shaggy carpet. There were bags under my eyes because I hadn't slept well, but at least the swelling in my nose had gone down. I hadn't had to go to the doctor after all. I grimaced though, looking at its new shape. I couldn't deny the fact that it was a tad crooked—something Sandra liked to point out as she said, "See, I told you it wouldn't heal right." I leaned in close to the mirror, lightly poking and prodding at it. It was still a little tender, but it didn't look *that* bad. Just a little bit of a bump on the bridge of my nose, and it wasn't too distracting. When I got back to The Resting Place, I could easily put it back to normal. And of course I'd lie and say I got it in a fight against a demon or something, because the truth was way too embarrassing.

I paused, leaned back, and frowned at my reflection. Was I gonna have to die again to get back to The Resting Place? As freaky as dying is, I didn't really mind the thought as much as I probably should have. I mean, if I was a normal person, I'd probably have valued my life a bit more, but this seemed to me sort of a temporary punishment that I wasn't all that happy about.

I knew I was taking forever in the bathroom, but I dreaded joining the meeting. Jake would see how pathetic I looked, and he'd never let me live this down. If only my injuries were the result of some heroic gesture. But, in true David fashion, they were all accidents. Accidents even more embarrassing than how I died because that was totally not my fault. Jumping off a balcony and running into a door . . . well, I didn't have much excuse for those.

Sighing, I squeezed some toothpaste onto my toothbrush and tried my best to make myself somewhat presentable, combing my hair around with my fingers. It didn't do much to fix the shaggy carpet vibe. This human moment of "getting ready" emphasized the divide between me and my angel friends. They didn't have to brush their teeth or go to the bathroom or even sleep. It made me feel like I was a lesser being than they were. In a way, I guess I was.

Sandra smiled at me as I made my way to her kitchen table where she was sitting. I raised my eyebrows at her before picking a spot. Living with a bunch of ghosts made me automatically check with her before sitting down anywhere in case someone was already there. She patted the chair next to her and held her hands out for my crutches, which she leaned up against the wall. Then she turned her attention to the person in the chair across the table, who I assumed was either Raj or Ying Yue. Thinking that my team was right here, and I couldn't even see them had my eyes watering, but I took a deep breath and sucked it way up.

"What are they saying?" I whispered.

"Uh . . . They're just all getting settled."

I gave her a look. "They're all talking about me, aren't they?"

She smiled apologetically. Then she turned to someone. "Don't worry, I won't."

I looked up and let out a puff of air through my nose, which was kind of stupid because it hurt my nose a little. She was probably promising not to tell me what they were actually saying, which was probably something about how pitiful I looked.

"Rajesh is just welcoming everyone and asking for updates from all the members," Sandra whispered. "Ted and Daisy are close to joining the angel hunters as undercover demons, but they're still having a hard time gaining their trust. Natalie has successfully befriended a new demon she's been trying to get information from. William and Frederick, on Hermes' orders, are starting to actually capture demons they've discovered are part of the angel hunters. To lower their numbers against us and also get info out of them."

I was so surprised by that interesting turn of events that it distracted me from my first surprise.

"Natalie's here?" I looked around the table. "I thought she quit."

Sandra smiled. "She came back."

I nodded. She probably felt bad that our team was now down two members with both of us gone.

Sandra turned back to listen before adding, "Jake has nothing new to share because he's been busy with other things."

I smirked. "Oh, has someone been slacking?"

She raised an eyebrow. "He's been watching over you,

actually."

"What?"

"He hangs around here on his off days. He and your mom switch off looking over you. He was assigned by the defender general to be your personal bodyguard when he's not watching over his own family or doing whatever else angels do. Turns out the defenders and demon hunters think you're pretty important and they're worried you'll be targeted by Malum and his demons."

My head reared back. I hadn't really thought of that . . . Being attacked by Malum while mortal would be even worse than being attacked as an angel with powers.

I gasped. "Wait, was that him last night that fought off that demon? I thought it was over really fast, especially for someone like Bill who's still new."

Sandra looked at me like I was stupid. "Bill? Bill's been doing great, but he's definitely not advanced enough to be fighting demons. Whatever happened last night, I'm sure it was either Jake or your mom who took care of it. Jake was the one who came to get me when you walked over the balcony. Well, he didn't really need to come get me, I heard him from my room screaming at you to turn around."

My face heated in embarrassment. Of course he had to be there to witness that. I could just imagine him yelling, "Turn around, ya fruit loop! David, you idiot, you're gonna fall to your death again! Why aren't you listening to me? You're gonna be cactus again, mate! Wake up!"

I smiled a little at the imagined encounter. I missed my friend. It was nice to know he still had my back.

Sandra nudged me.

"What?"

"It's your turn," she whispered. "Everyone's sharing updates."

"Oh . . ." I looked down as I felt my face flush with color. It was a little rude of them to put me on the spot like this when they knew I had done nothing but get hurt and cry and sit around the house like a total loser. I'd completely forgotten that I was still a part of the demon hunters, and I was still expected to do my job. I cleared my throat but did not look up. "Um . . . yeah, I don't have any updates. I've been a little preoccupied. Sorry. I know it's not a real excuse."

It was quiet for a minute.

"Raj says he's really proud of you and that you've surpassed all his expectations."

I laughed bitterly looking at the empty chairs across the table. "What, did you think I'd die in the first week? Because staying alive is all I've accomplished. And barely."

Sandra was quiet as she listened to the conversation. I nudged her to share, but she held up a finger. "Sorry, they're all talking at once about how upset they are about what happened to you and how unfair it is."

I smiled sadly and looked down.

Sandra's hand twitched like she wanted to pat my hand or something, but she held back. I wondered why. Was she worried I'd misconstrue her meaning? Or that I would correctly construe it? And what would be the correct way *to* construe it?

I basically just sat there feeling useless for the rest of the meeting as Sandra translated all they talked about. As they were wrapping up, Ying Yue gave out specific assignments to everyone. Then she got to me. Sandra took a while to translate, and I imagined they were all looking at each other wondering what on earth I could contribute to the demon hunters in the state I was in. All she ended up saying was, "Rest up and recover so that you're in top shape next time we hand out assignments."

I nodded glumly down at the table. Sounded about right.

chapter 3
WHINY BABY

About a week passed and little happened. I had a doctor's appointment where I learned I still had three weeks left in my cast, which was just lovely news. I did laundry and dishes and all I could to help out around the house. Other than that, I was pretty much a bump on a log. I watched TV a lot with the wanderers, but I wasn't always sure who it was changing the channels. Another demon hunter meeting happened, and I was reluctant to join in. It felt like they were including me out of pity because there was really nothing I could contribute. I couldn't understand how the Big Man expected me to still keep up with my angelic duties when I still sucked so bad at just being alive.

Toward the end of the third meeting, Ying Yue went around handing out assignments to everyone. We were all supposedly sitting or floating around the square kitchen table, but all I could see was me and Sandra squished to one side. I wondered how everyone fit, seeing as Sandra only had four chairs. Some must just be floating, or maybe they created their own chairs out of thin air. Angels can do stuff like that. In fact, sitting on an angel chair would be a lot easier than a physical one, seeing as we–I mean, they–have to concentrate not to fall through solid stuff.

Sandra was translating all the assignments handed out, then paused awkwardly, flicked a glance at me, then moved on.

"Did she skip over me again?" I whispered, barely loud enough for my own ears.

Sandra grimaced in sympathy and bit her lip. I sighed and let my cheek fall into my hand. What was I even doing here?

Sandra gave me a sad smile and patted my hand. I screamed and jumped to my foot.

"Sorry!" she said, quickly pulling her hand away.

"No, it wasn't that!" My heart was pounding, and I looked back and forth at the empty chairs around the table. For a second, I swear I saw them. All of them. I saw Jake on my right side, looking bored with his head in his hand. Natalie, leaning back with her feet on the table. Ying Yue, in the middle of scolding someone. Raj, sitting next to her and looking at me with so much compassion that I felt embarrassed. Ted, his face buried in his notes. Daisy, glaring at the floor, her arms folded across her chest. Frederick and William, in their matching colonial ponytails, having a whispered disagreement. It was the most wonderful sight I'd seen since being alive and it was over in the blink of an eye. Had I imagined it? But it looked so real. I looked at Sandra and tried to think of what might have happened to have caused it. Maybe Hermes was allowing me to see them. Maybe I was a medium too. But then, why had it gone away?

I looked down at Sandra's hand. It seemed that it all happened when she touched me. Without asking permission, I put my hand over hers and grinned. There they were again. For some reason, it seemed that being physically in contact with Sandra allowed me to also see and hear the dead like her. I beamed as I sat back down and looked around the table. Poor Sandra was very confused. Was I making a move on her? Why had I screamed and then started grinning like an idiot?

"Geez, it's like he's looking right at me," Jake said, sitting to my left. He waved his hand in front of my face, and I tried to swat it away. Of course, my hand just went right through his, but it was enough for us both to know that I saw him.

"He *is* looking at me!" Jake exclaimed.

"What is this?" Frederick asked, leaning forward. "The lad can see us?"

"And hear you," I said, holding up our clasped hands. "Looks like Sandra's some kind of spiritual antenna."

"No! Really?" another voice yelled. I spun around and saw my mom standing behind me. My eyes filled with tears. My perspective was slightly different than that of my siblings because I assumed this human experience was temporary and I'd be with my mom again soon, but it didn't change the fact that she was dead and I wasn't. Seeing her standing behind me filled me with homesickness.

"Mom!" I felt a watery grin split my face. "What are you doing here? This is a demon hunter meeting."

"As your guardian angel and your mother, I have the right to be anywhere you are." She looked defiantly at Raj and Ying Yue, daring them to challenge her. Raj sat back in his chair with his hands up in front of him, and Ying Yue looked away uncomfortably, neither brave enough to challenge my mom.

"So, what were you guys saying that Sandra was too polite to translate?" I asked, turning back around.

"I was just saying you look like a dog's breakfast," Jake blurted.

I burst into laughter. "What does that even mean?"

"You're a mess," he said, laughing with me. "Look at you sitting there all tuckered out and broken in your trackie dacks."

"Trackie dacks?"

"You know," he said, gesturing toward my sweatpants. "Trackie dacks. You go chuck on your trackie dacks."

The two of us were dying laughing. It wasn't like what we were saying was even that funny, but I could tell we both needed the release.

"At least I'm not wearing a glowing white bathrobe," I said. "I bet Beyonce can see your halo."

Jake squeezed his eyes shut and a halo popped into existence above his head. He beamed at me, and I laughed harder.

"All right, that's enough, you two," Ying Yue said, apparently annoyed and amused at the same time. "Pull it together or I'll have Sandra let go."

I snapped my mouth shut and sat up straight. There was no way I was jeopardizing losing this. All my friends and my mom were here, and I could see them.

"I'm not sure about this," Ying Yue said, biting her lip. "If we weren't given permission to reveal ourselves to him, it seems wrong to let him see us."

"You're not revealing yourselves," I said quickly. "You're not breaking any rules, and no one told me or Sandra we're not allowed to do this. Plus, if you're worried about getting in trouble, you can blame it on me. You didn't tell me the answers to the test, I just stole the answer key."

She and Raj shared a look and Raj shrugged. "Unless we're told this is wrong, I don't see why we can't let him see us. He's right, we didn't technically break any rules, they just found a loophole."

I grinned. Something about that laughter cured me of my mopiness. A little blossom of hope started to sprout inside me. Unfortunately, it wasn't long until I felt embarrassed and useless again as we moved on to the planning part of our meeting and I could feel them all holding back what they really thought of me now that I could actually hear them. Raj and Ying Yue finished handing out assignments, and they both hesitated when they were done. Ying Yue avoided looking at me and Raj wouldn't stop. What could I do as a human to hunt demons? Pray? Ask angels for help? That was pretty much it. I didn't have any powers. Even Malum didn't see me as a threat anymore because he hadn't even come after me yet.

Not that I wanted him to come after me. But at least if he did it would mean he saw me as a threat. Maybe he just hadn't found me yet—not that I wanted him to find me. But what if finding me could help out my demon hunter friends? I gasped and sat up straighter.

"Bait!" I blurted.

"Excuse me?" Raj asked.

Ying Yue was about to scold me for interrupting her end-of-the-meeting summary, but Raj held up his hand and everyone looked at me. I smiled gratefully at Raj. He always did believe in my ideas, even when they were completely insane.

"I'm no good fighting demons, but I might be able to help you find them. I could be the bait that lures the demons out of hiding. I may or may not be a target for

Malum. He probably doesn't care about me anymore. But . . . if he wanted me on his side when I was an angel, he might still. I mean, he could find some way to kill me before I earn my place back in The Resting Place and then drag me down to hell."

"David, it's not that simple," Raj said, knitting his eyebrows in concern. "No one is dragging anyone anywhere. In the end, you choose where you go, and if you don't deserve The Resting Place, then you stay there as you earn your place. When your time is done on earth, you're coming back to us where you belong."

I waved my hand impatiently. "Okay, sure, but Malum doesn't get that, does he? His whole plan when I was an angel was to turn me mortal so he could kill me and then steal my soul. Sure, maybe that's not how it works, but that was his intention. Well . . . I'm still mortal. He can still kill me and try to 'steal me away.' I'm not sure if he still wants me, but if he does, I could be useful in drawing him out. I could be your bait. Dangle me out there on your figurative fishing pole, and when he comes around to snatch me up, you all pounce on him."

Everyone looked uncomfortably at one another, probably remembering the last time an ambush depended on me confronting Malum. Even Jake didn't seem sold on the idea.

"Absolutely not," Mom said.

I spun around. "Mom, not to be rude, but you're not

exactly a demon hunter. This isn't your decision."

"I don't care! You can't just throw your life away like that!"

"First of all, my life ended eleven years ago. Second of all, he might not succeed in killing me. The point is for me to be the bait. They might catch him before he can do anything to me. And even if he does kill me, who cares? I'll get to go back home, and since I sacrificed myself, I'm pretty sure that will earn me back my spot in The Resting Place."

Raj rubbed his forehead and sighed. "I think you're misunderstanding the word 'sacrifice', kid. A sacrifice is when you give up something dear to you. Something precious. You don't seem to care about your mortal life at all, so giving it up wouldn't exactly be a sacrifice. Hermes told you that you're not welcome back in The Resting Place right now. I don't think it's because you did something wrong. I think it's because you're needed as a mortal. We can't risk your life if there's a greater plan in the works that requires you to be alive right now."

I rolled my eyes. "And what would that be? What could I possibly offer anyone?"

"Every mortal has something to offer," Ted said quietly. "Every life has meaning. You don't suddenly become important when you die and become an angel."

"Hear, hear," Frederick said.

Daisy looked at me with a softer glare than usual. "No

one else is told their purpose in life. Why should you be any different?"

Chastened, I shut my mouth. First, because they had a point. Second, because they were all looking at me like they actually cared about me and in the mental state I was in, that was a bit much for me to process. They were right, but it didn't change the fact that I felt completely useless.

chapter 4
I GET A TALKING TO

"You're dismissed," Ying Yue said.

Everyone left the meeting, disappearing just like that to travel to whatever angelic duty was waiting for them on the other side. I stared longingly after them, imagining what I'd be doing if I wasn't here. Front desk duty sounded amazing compared to this. Even dealing with a line out the door and Grandma Gertie begging me to find a dead girl to "settle down" with.

I was so wrapped up in my tortured musings, I was startled when Ying Yue said my name. She and Raj had hung back to talk to me, and I could sense Mom still behind me. Great. Now I was the problem child that the teacher had to talk to after class.

"Is this an intervention?" I muttered. "I promise I haven't become addicted to any illegal substances since becoming mortal. That's one thing I've done right."

"Look, we know you've been hurt," Ying Yue said, ignoring my quip. "You're ashamed of your mistake and you feel used and lost. But you need to snap out of this."

Defensiveness bubbled up inside me. "Snap out of what?"

"This pool of self-pity that you're drowning in. Come on, David, this isn't you. You have a duty and it's time you remembered that."

"How am I supposed to even do anything?" I protested. "I can't serve my family without them seeing me. I'm practically useless to the demon hunters except as bait. What am I supposed to be doing? Tell me, and I'll do it!"

"I don't know, David," Ying Yue said. "I really don't know. But that's what faith is for. It's time for you to relearn what that word means."

I couldn't believe her. Tough love had always been her style, but this was going too far. Why couldn't she understand what an impossible position I was in? You can't be a guardian angel if you're not an angel! It was like chopping someone's hands off and demanding they play the piano.

Raj studied my face, then said, "Give me a minute with him. I'll meet you back in the conference room." Ying Yue nodded and disappeared, and Mom followed reluctantly. Raj sat in the chair Jake had vacated and looked apologetically at Sandra. "Is there any way we could get a little privacy?"

Sandra pursed her lips, thinking, then said, "Be right

back." The second she got up and let go of my hand, Raj disappeared. I couldn't look at his face, so I just stared down at the table. After a minute, Sandra came back with some earbuds in her ears. She turned the music up on her phone, took my hand, and started scrolling through Instagram. She even turned her chair around so she couldn't see us. Her easy solution almost made me smile. It was a very Sandra thing to do.

Once Raj was convinced Sandra wasn't listening, he said, "Okay, talk to me."

I shook my head and sighed. "Why am I here, Raj? Why was I punished when so many others made mistakes and still got to stay in The Resting Place? Why just me? Was what I did really that bad? I was saving Sandra's life."

"You're thinking like a mortal, kid. Death isn't the end. She would have continued on the other side."

All my frustration at myself and my situation bubbled and boiled inside until I couldn't contain myself. I'd have stood if I wasn't tethered to Sandra. "I know that! Don't you think I know that? If I was in my right mind, I wouldn't have even considered trying to save her. I would have been excited! I'd have given her a freaking tour! But Malum was there, and he found a way to get to me, and I wasn't thinking straight. I might not have even done it if I hadn't grabbed Sandra's hand at the last minute and watched all her fears play across her mind. As much as she's familiar with it, she's terrified of death! She's afraid she'll become one of her wanderers."

Raj raised his eyebrows and sat back. "You never mentioned that last part before. That's impressive that her touch had that strong of a connection, even with a spirit." He looked at Sandra in fascination.

I nodded. "Yeah, she's really cool. And she's taking care of me and doing everything for me because I'm totally helpless. I just don't get why this is happening to me. As far as I know, no one has ever been punished this way."

"Maybe this isn't a punishment," Raj suggested, leaning onto the table. "Maybe it was supposed to happen."

"What are you talking about? Hermes basically told me I was being punished because I disobeyed orders. Which doesn't make sense because angels aren't perfect just because we're dead. We mess up all the time, and while we may get a slap on the wrist now and then, no one gets kicked out. That's just wrong. It goes against all we stand for."

I winced, realizing I'd said "we" instead of "they." It hurt too much to admit that I was no longer a part of that equation.

Raj looked at me with compassion, but in my mopey state, I read it as embarrassment and pity. He took a while to answer, likely trying not to offend me while I was feeling so sensitive. Or maybe he was pausing to listen as Hermes fed him the right words.

When he finally spoke, he asked, "Do you think it's possible that you were supposed to 'mess up'? That maybe it was all part of a bigger plan? And maybe your 'punishment' was actually a means to a greater end?"

"When you put it that way, it almost sounds like I was set up to fail."

He shrugged. "Depends on your definition of the word 'fail.'"

"Are you trying to imply that the Big Man *wanted* me to screw up? Like, he set me up and put me in a position where he knew I was going to fail as, like, an excuse to turn me mortal as punishment? That sounds kind of sneaky to me. I don't like that."

"It was Malum that set you up. I'm implying that the Big Man allowed it to happen for a reason. I'm implying that maybe there's a greater plan in the works, and for some reason, right now, you're needed in mortal form. Maybe there's something you can accomplish better alive than dead."

I didn't feel any better after my conversation with Raj. I knew that I should have because deep down I was sure he was saying something wise. But that wisdom couldn't penetrate the black cloud over me. Maybe Malum really was working on me, or at least his boss. I just had never felt so low and homesick and alone. I was thoroughly uninterested in being alive.

I wasn't suicidal or anything. It's just . . . there's a reason not a lot of people are miraculously brought back to life after being clinically dead for too long. Those defibrillators have their limits. And I think that's because once you've seen the other side, you don't *want* to come back. You sometimes hear stories about people visiting The Resting Place and then coming back to life, but I knew a guy who had the choice to go back into his body, and he chose to stay in The Resting Place. It's just so much better there! No pain or hunger or exhaustion. You don't even have to sleep. And you spend all your time helping others. You don't have to worry about yourself and your own basic needs, because other than emotional stuff like friendship and family, you don't have any needs. You can just serve people all the time and nothing stands in your way. I loved that! Most people do, they just don't know it until they experience it.

It's so much harder when you're alive to be selfless. You have to be a little selfish to stay alive and well, and it's hard to keep that selfishness contained because it just grows and grows the more you feed it. I could acknowledge that in my bitterness and self-pity I was being extremely selfish. But it was hard not to be when my problems seemed so huge.

"Hey, David?" Sandra said, from behind the couch. "Your mom wants to talk to you."

I'd been slumped on my couch-turned-bed staring

unseeingly at the TV while some ghost flipped through channels. I sighed and sat up, shoving my pillows off the couch to make room for her. Sandra put in her earbuds before sitting next to me and taking my hand. Then Mom appeared in front of me, and I couldn't help it. I broke down and cried. She was dead and I wasn't. Not only that, but there's something about a mother's penetrating gaze that's able to cut through all your crap and expose what you're really feeling. My mom just sat on the coffee table in front of me until I was done. I could see her struggling to keep her hands to herself, wishing she could wrap them around me.

I wiped my nose and glanced over at Sandra, hoping she wasn't watching me. I was sure she heard me bawling like a baby, but she gave me my dignity, pretending to be completely absorbed in her Twitter feed.

"Tell me all about it," Mom said.

And so I told her. I don't remember ever being so bitter, passionate, and angry. It was a very yucky feeling, but I didn't feel like I could help it. My mom sat and listened as the complaints spewed out of me until I calmed down enough to take a breath. I don't even remember what I said, but I did feel a little better afterward, like some of the poison had been sucked out of me.

"Are you done?" Mom asked.

I nodded, scowling at the ground.

"Well, if this is what you've been given, you know what

you have to do now," Mom said.

"What?"

"Live! Live, David!" She stood, unable to deliver this speech while sitting. "This is your second chance at everything that is wonderful and beautiful about being human. Experience it all and love it. The joy and pain. The triumphs and failures. The gains and losses. Feel it all and appreciate life so much that you enjoy it again. So much that you stop wanting to rush back to The Resting Place. So much so that the idea of dying is awful again. Learn to love your life and appreciate this second chance that none of the rest of us will ever get. And do all the things you wish you'd done that you never got to do."

My mouth popped open. I'd never thought of it that way—like a second chance. I was reminded of that day when Raj wrested out of me my reasons for joining the demon hunters. "I just want to do something with my life!" I'd said. That was my only regret—I died before I could really accomplish anything worthwhile.

Well . . . maybe this was my chance. I could finally *do* something with my life.

chapter 5
TURNING A NEW LEAF

"All right, I know it's been a while, but . . . here I am."

I couldn't exactly kneel with my busted leg, so I was sitting on the couch with my head bowed and my hands clasped together. It was quiet enough to hear all those nighttime noises that are so much louder because the world is asleep. The hum of the fridge, the furnace kicking on, leaves rustling in the breeze outside, some cricket with no concept of when it's appropriate to belt their lungs out in the shower. Or whatever the cricket equivalent to that is.

I took a deep breath. Even having been to the other side, it took a lot of faith to believe anyone was listening. I'd taken all that proof for granted as an angel. Maybe Ying Yue was right—I'd forgotten what it meant to have faith. I tried to imagine being there in the Main Office where you go to interview with the Big Man when you die.

That's when something hit me in the face.

"*Ouch!*"

The remote control lay by my feet with the batteries splayed out around it. I touched my forehead where a small bump was forming.

"What the—"

The lights flashed on and off. The microwave ran and beeped. A pillow flew at my face, closely followed by four coasters. Throwing my blanket over my head as a shield, I barely escaped a framed picture intent on slicing my head open. Someone started tugging on my blanket shield, but I held on tightly growling, "No you don't!"

Clearly, someone did not want me to pray and had sent their little minion to screw with me.

"Sheila, I know it's you! Cut it out!"

The demonic temper tantrum stopped. I cautiously lifted my head out of my blanket to find a bunch of crap she'd thrown at me littered around the living room. A minute passed and the throwing did not resume. "Thanks, man," I said, pretty sure Jake had just taken care of my little demon.

I took a deep breath and folded my hands again, trying to get back in the right mindset, and trying not to be thrown by the fact that Jake was here and I had an audience. "All right, let's try this again . . ." Folding my hands, I made my second attempt to pray.

"Okay, so I'm alive now and I need to accept that and stop wishing and dreaming that I was back in The Resting

Place. I know I'm being really stupid about this; I mean, I did always wish deep down I'd lived longer. So, I'm going to go out there and live the life I never got to live until it's time to go back, and just like every other living person, I don't know when that will be. Could be in a week, a year, ten years. Maybe you want me to grow old . . . Wow, I never really thought about that. Regardless, hopefully I'll live better for having been to The Resting Place before. I may not be dead, but I'm still a guardian angel and I intend to still act that way.

"But here's the thing . . . how do I even have a life when I'm legally dead? I can't expose myself to anyone who knows I'm dead. I can't drive because I don't have a license. I can't legally get a job. And I can't get my own place without money, which I don't have because I don't have a job. I'm gonna have to depend on Sandra for everything, and that's not fair. Unless you want me to show myself to my family . . ." I waited a moment, listening, but got no answer. "Okay, so we're still unclear on that. Seriously though, this isn't fair to Sandra. I've gotta start pulling my own weight somehow. I'm not sure if you want me to eventually go back to my family or not, but I'm gonna need some help unless you just want me to hide out here for the rest of my life. However long that may be."

A thump jarred me from my prayer. I sat up and looked around blinking. Right next to me on the couch was a backpack. My old backpack from high school. I frowned and looked up. "Um . . . thanks?" I wasn't sure what I was supposed to do with old textbooks and assignments I never got to turn in. Maybe I could turn them in to Sandra for extra credit? Maybe he was hinting I needed to go back to school? I never did graduate, but maybe I could get a GED?

Shrugging, I unzipped the big pocket, and pulled out my old binder. The cover had a Jimmy Eat World sticker next to a *Deathly Hallows* sticker and underneath that a sticker of a horrified donut with a speech bubble that said, "Where is my belly button?" Gosh, I was so lame. I chuckled with nostalgia for my younger self.

Weirdly excited to nerd out over all my old essays and notes, I opened the cover. Organized neatly into my beat-up color-coded folders were my birth certificate, social security card, driver's license, and a passport. I'd never even had a passport the first time I was alive. There were even high school transcripts. Supposedly if the Big Man was giving me these things, they were actually valid. Maybe he'd done something to the system so that if someone looked me up it wouldn't show that I'd died eleven years ago. I felt around in the backpack some more and whooped aloud when I found my glasses. I put them on and grinned at how sharp everything around me looked, even in the dark. I could actually read the time on the microwave, instead of just seeing a green blur. I hopped over to turn on the lights and whooped again as everything came into sharp focus. I turned on the TV and did a little one-legged jig when I could read everything on the Netflix menu.

It's the stupid little things that make you dance like an idiot.

"What's going on?"

I froze in my happy dance, my arms out in front of me. A yawning Sandra stood in the hallway in her satin sleep cap and taco pajamas. That girl really likes tacos.

"Hey," I said, still frozen in my happy dance.

Sandra froze and put her hand to her heart. "Oh my gosh. You look like that kid that died in a construction accident."

"I . . . am that kid." I dramatically put my hands in front of me as though approaching a spooked animal. "I'm David. Remember me? We used to hang out when I was dead?"

Sandra rolled her eyes. "Shut up. The glasses threw me, okay? You look like that picture they used at your funeral. Where did you get those anyway?"

I shrugged. "My old backpack showed up with all this stuff in it. ID's and everything. I guess the Big Man doesn't want me to hide away anymore."

chapter 6
NO MORE HIDING

"Okay, is this someone new?" I asked.

The lamp to my left flickered.

"Cool. Have we spoken before?"

The lamp to my right flickered.

I sighed. Now I had to guess their name. This usually took some creativity.

I shoved some of the tests that I was grading off my lap into a messy pile on the couch. I'd asked Sandra for more stuff to do while she was at work today and she left me some tests to grade. Midterm tests. They took *forever*. Needless to say, I'd gotten a little bored, which was why I was now playing this weird game with the wanderers in Sandra's apartment. I was trying to at least learn all their names. I mean, it seemed courteous since we all lived together. I already knew Bill, Patty, Asher, and Oliver from when I was dead, but there were at least five more of them whose names I never learned. They were taking turns making the lights flicker to answer my questions. The left lamp meant 'yes' and the right lamp meant 'no'. It kinda felt like using a Ouija board, but without the evilness.

I'd learned that there was an old wanderer named Dorine. She gave me hints by opening and closing the door a billion times until I figured out the word "door" was in her name. Now we were onto a new one. I leaned back and propped my feet up on the table, one of them a bit swollen looking. I'd recently gotten my cast off. Halle-freaking-lujah.

"Okay, first question," I said to the wanderer. "Are you a girl?"

Right lamp flickered.

"All right, so this is a dude. Do you have a pretty common name?"

Right lamp flickered.

I sighed again. "Any hints?"

After a moment Sandra's bookshelf began to shake.

"Ah, so a book name?"

Left lamp flickered. Then one of the books came off the shelf and landed in my lap.

"Hey, nice job! Carrying stuff that far is hard." I frowned as I examined the book. "*Anne of Green Gables?* Why do all the wanderers in this place have super old-time-y names?"

Both lamps flickered back and forth.

"Is that supposed to mean you don't know?"

Left lamp flickered and I smiled. I liked this guy.

"Okay, well, I never read this book, but my mom loved it, and she made us watch the TV show with her. Your name obviously isn't Anne or Marilla. Is it Matthew?"

Right lamp flickered.

"Oh, what was that one guy's name who had a crush on her? Um . . . Gilbert?"

Left lamp flickered a lot.

"Sweet," I smiled. "How old were you when you died, Gilbert?"

The TV turned on and went to channel 35.

"That's a lame age to die," I said, commiserating. "Bet you had a family, huh? Wife and kids? And they're still alive and that's why you didn't want to move on?"

The left light bulb shattered.

I pulled my feet onto the couch to avoid the glass shards. "Okay, sorry! Touchy subject."

Sandra chose that moment to walk through the door, carrying a bunch of groceries. "Hey, wanna help me with . . ." She eyed the shattered glass and the two lamps sitting next to each other on the coffee table. She looked at me amused and confused. "What were you doing?"

"I, uh, was getting to know some of the wanderers," I explained, scrambling over the back of the couch to grab the broom and dustbin, "and I sort of offended Gilbert by guessing why he's a wanderer." I quickly swept up the glass I could see and smiled innocently.

Sandra smiled and shook her head.

"Oh! Also, I had a question about number nine on Ethan's test." I moved the pile around on the couch until I found the one I wanted. "Would you count this as right?"

Sandra set her groceries down on the coffee table and took the test from me. She gave me a dry look. "He bubbled in all of the answer choices."

"I know, but technically he did bubble in the right answer."

She rolled her eyes. "No, it's wrong. He was supposed to pick one." She picked up the groceries to take back into the kitchen. "Thanks for grading those, by the way. I hate midterms as much as my students."

I followed her. "You hate your students?"

She snorted. "I hate midterms, dummy." She tried not to laugh but didn't succeed.

"Ha! Made you laugh," I grinned, shoving veggies into the fridge drawer. "Ten points to Hufflepuff!"

"Should I make tacos or spaghetti? We had tacos a few days ago, but—"

"Tacos," I said, shutting the fridge, "but only if you let me make the salsa. That canned stuff from the grocery aisle shelf is a disgrace."

"Deal," she said with a cookie in her mouth.

It only took us about fifteen minutes for the full meal.

We had a routine down by now, which made what I had to say even harder. We went through the motions of chopping, mixing, and cooking while she talked about that one kid in her class who got suspended for releasing live chickens in the hallway and I talked about my homemade Ouija board.

After we were sitting, our mouths stuffed with tacos, I bolstered myself and said, "I need to move out."

Sandra choked on her water. "What?"

"I need to move out," I repeated. "It's time."

She narrowed her eyes. "Move where? You don't have any money for your own place."

"I won't be going to my own place. I'll be staying with my family."

"They think you're dead!"

I sighed. "Sandra. You know this has to happen. They need me. Well, I don't know, they probably don't, but I know I have to see them. Starting with Elena. It just feels right. Why are you so against this?"

"The last time we had this conversation, you got so upset you ran into a door and broke your nose."

I rolled my eyes. "Yeah, I was there. I've learned now that I'm solid and can't walk through walls. Why don't you want me to move out?"

She set down her glass of water and looked down at the table. "I don't know."

I smiled sadly and scooted closer to her. Instinctively I

took her hand before I forgot that we normally only do that when I need to see dead people. She stared at our hands then back at me, and I pulled away.

"Look, I'll be okay," I said.

"I know you'll be okay," she said quietly. "Maybe I just like having you around. Maybe it's been nice for me not to be alone."

She stared down at her lap and threaded her fingers together, her face too carefully controlled.

"You're surrounded by people all the time," I said carefully. "Living and dead."

"Yeah, but that's different." She sighed and sat back. "I've spent my entire life taking care of people. My mom, my students, my wanderers—"

"Me," I said quietly.

"Yeah, but you're different. You're not selfish, you don't take advantage of me. You're my friend. Everyone else I take care of because I have to, and they need me. It's not like I don't care about them, but they don't seem to care about me. You actually listen to me. You care. And you do dumb things that make me laugh."

"I'm glad my stumbling through mortality amuses you," I said wryly. "And of course I care about you. You know I'm not leaving because I don't like being here with you, right? If I was just thinking about what I wanted I wouldn't be leaving. But I can't think about myself. I've made promises and I intend to keep them."

Sandra looked up at me. "I guess that's part of your annoying charm. All right, fine. Pack your things. I'll drive you over to Elena's in the morning. Let's hope she doesn't die of shock and beat you back to The Resting Place."

chapter 7
PLEASE DON'T KILL ME

I stood in front of a door, shaking in anticipation. This was it; I was going to see my sister!

Darkness swirled around me, and a cold feeling of dread froze my hand mid-knock. Something terrible would happen if I did this, but I could hear her on the other side. Along with Dad and Sam, all laughing loudly about something hilarious that I couldn't see. I couldn't help myself; I wanted so badly to be a part of it.

I knocked and heard quiet laughter behind me. I jumped and spun around, but no one was there. The door opened, spilling light into the dark night, and yet, my body left no shadow. Why wasn't there a shadow?

Elena's jaw dropped and her eyes filled with tears. "David?"

"You can see me?" I asked quietly.

Her chin trembled. "What are you doing here?"

"I, uh, came to see you . . . I thought you might want to see me."

Elena sighed as a tear leaked out the corner of her eye. "We've moved on, David. We don't need you anymore. I have a husband

and children and a life. Why do you have to show up here and try to reopen old wounds that have already healed?"

My face fell and I felt a twist in my gut. "I'm sorry . . . I just miss you guys and—"

"The least you could have done is bring Mom with you."

It hurt me to hear her say she'd rather see Mom than me, but who could blame her? Of course she'd rather see Mom. I wanted to see Mom.

"Maybe I can—"

"What's this?" Charlie came up behind Elena, glaring daggers at me. The guy was even bigger than I remembered. His entire shadow swallowed me up.

"I came back," I whispered. "But nobody wants me."

"Who are you?" he asked.

"It's me! David."

He shook his head. "No, you can't be David. David would never leave his family the way you did. You're an impostor." He pulled out a gun and pointed it at me. My stomach somersaulted.

"No, it's me!" I shouted, hands up. "It's really David!"

He pulled the trigger, but before it hit me, some force took hold of my arms and yanked Elena in front of me.

"NO!"

I grunted as I found myself on the ground again, tangled in my blankets. I think I'd been standing on the couch and fell over backwards. At least I hadn't jumped off a balcony. Freaking anxiety dreams. This was getting out of hand. Was I going to need a bed with railing on the side like a child? Wouldn't that just be the icing on this mortifying cake?

"I'm sure he's fine, Asher," I heard Sandra say. "Just had another nightmare, probably." There was a pause. "Oliver, that's not nice. Cut it out." Pause. "That may have been what he looked like, but that doesn't mean it's funny to act it out." The part of me that wasn't mortified was impressed by how well Sandra communicated with her wanderers who never actually spoke out loud.

I sighed and rolled over.

"You okay there, bud?" Sandra asked, standing over me tangled in my blankets. She looked like she was trying not to laugh.

"Shut up," I groaned, rubbing my face. I sighed, shaken from my dream.

Sandra held out her hand and helped me to my feet. "You okay?"

I nodded as I yawned, still rubbing the sleep from my eyes. The sun was shining brightly through the windows. I'd slept in. "Yeah, 'm fine. I'll be ready in just a sec."

I grabbed my glasses from the coffee table and headed to the bathroom to brush my teeth. I threw on a t-shirt and jeans and stared at the sleepy weirdo in the mirror. Would Elena recognize me? I looked a little older, somehow, my nose was in a different shape, my hair longer, a hint of facial hair. I was still me though, and my nerd glasses were pretty distinctive. I quickly shaved and growled as I tried to comb my hair into some kind of shape. I didn't know what to do with it. When I was alive my mom would pin me down and cut it about once a month, and when I was dead I didn't have physical hair, so it didn't grow unless I wanted it to. Now it was about four inches long and it stuck out in all directions. Sandra didn't know how to cut hair, but she lent me some product to at least make the messy look appear intentional. I squirted it into my hand and ran my fingers through my hair rubbing it around. I sighed at the result. "Good enough," I said, kicking the door open.

Elena lived about twenty minutes from Sandra's apartment, and, weirdly, Sandra and I spent almost the entire drive in complete silence. I guess we were both doing a lot of thinking. I stared at the heavy-looking overcast clouds, trying to decide if they looked gloomy or pretty. The trees along the side of the road blew in the breeze as we rushed past them.

As we stopped at the third red light, I could feel a question hovering in the air. Finally, Sandra said, "I've always wondered this, but never could bring myself to ask. Does dying hurt?"

I blinked and raised my eyebrows. It's weird to talk about your death with other angels, let alone mortals who have never experienced it. I thought for a moment before answering.

"Well, the obvious thing for me to say is duh."

"But?"

"But that's not exactly right. Dying doesn't hurt. It's whatever kills you that hurts."

The light turned green, and she glanced at me before releasing the break. "That doesn't make sense."

I looked out the window. "Dying isn't pain, it's the release from the pain. Being fatally injured—that hurts. Being terminally ill—that hurts. Being in so much pain that you wish you were dead—that hurts. But dying is when it all goes away."

"Did it hurt when you fell?" she asked tentatively. When I didn't answer right away, she rushed to say, "You don't have to talk about it if it's too personal."

I shifted uncomfortably. No one likes thinking about when they croaked, we tend to bury those thoughts down deep. They aren't usually very pleasant. I tried not to think about my fall but couldn't help reliving it as I thought on her question. In a quiet, low voice, I said, "I was pretty lucky, actually. I died almost instantly. There were like two seconds of agony and then all of a sudden, I was floating over my body. It was more traumatizing than it was painful."

"I would imagine it would be seeing your own dead body."

"Yeah. I looked . . . broken. And wrong. And empty. It

was me, but it wasn't me. And the *crunch* sound . . ." I shuddered. "I don't like thinking about it."

"Sorry," she said. "You don't have to talk about it."

"I don't think I ever have," I said honestly.

She gave me a penetrating look, like she could see me, really see me, and knew that I wasn't totally over it. "You can if you want to."

I leaned my head back on the head rest and watched in discomfort as we passed a man being lifted up in a boom lift to fix a telephone pole on the side of the road. I shuttered again, knowing firsthand how long of a drop that would be.

"I don't know. The less I think about it, the less of a deal it seems. And then you ask questions like that, and it all comes back to me, and I can't help reliving it all over again. Jake and I used to joke about it a lot—I mean who dies from a sneeze?—but it was a nightmare. I can see why so many people become wanderers."

It all came spilling out of me and I could see it like it was projecting on the windshield before me.

"After I fell, everyone was screaming my name and running to me. My poor uncle kept yelling at me, telling me to come back, and I tried, but I couldn't stick myself back into my body. And then when my family showed up . . . My dad was crying, holding Elena who was shaking, and Sam just stared at me like he couldn't process. Everyone was in shock but my mom. She screamed and ran to me, sobbing. I don't think she was as shocked as the others because she's a worrier. She feared every possible scenario of harm coming to her children, so it was less of a shock and more of a nightmare coming true. She threw herself on top of me and wouldn't let go. They had to pry her off me after a while. She was crying and I was crying and there was nothing I could do. Neither of us could let go, we were just trapped in that forever moment of horror. My Nana Maria kept telling me it was time to go, and I couldn't just leave her. But I did eventually. As short as it was, I knew my life was over."

The light turned green, and Sandra forced herself to look back at the road, her face muscles tight with concern. As much as she likes to act like she'd rather not get involved in people's lives and afterlives, she's always been a bit of an empath. Maybe that's why she didn't like getting involved—because she exhausts herself by taking on everyone's problems. She just can't help it.

After letting out a breath she asked, "How do all dead people not have PTSD?"

I chuckled humorlessly. "I think we do. That's where your wanderers come from. They're too traumatized to move on."

"Yeah, but you angels," she said, "You guys act like you don't have a care in the world. You're happy. Like legitimately happy. How? How come none of you ever just flip out after having dealt with everything you've gone through?"

I shrugged. "I don't know. When you're an angel you're too busy helping living people with their problems to really think about your own. It's great! But ever since Malum came around and drudged it all up, I've been pretty messed up by it all. Maybe I always have been, and I just ignored it."

I got distracted by a middle-aged man in a truck next to us as he tried to reach a high note while his daughter put her head in her hand and said, "Ugh, dad, you're so embarrassing!" It made me smile. It had been a while since I'd secretly rode in Dad's car, singing to the top of our lungs as he rode home from work.

I could feel Sandra look over at me as we coasted to another stop. I sighed and looked away from my distraction. "I think deep down angels all carry a little bit of old pain around with us that we just forget about because we're too busy to give it any attention. But maybe that's not the best way to be . . . Maybe if I'd had someone to talk through everything with, and actually addressed it, I never would have screwed up so bad."

Sandra patted my hand. "You didn't screw up, David. You saved my life. And I think this all was supposed to happen. But regardless of whether or not you're supposed to be here, we are here. At your sister's house, I mean. Are you ready?"

I stiffened and bit my lip as I gazed at their front lawn,

freshly mowed and freshly covered with toy trucks and kickballs. Elena's Honda Pilot stuck out of the open garage. Charlie would probably grumble about that when he got home, and then Elena would say she was just about to close it when he showed up.

Fear clutched my heart for a moment, and I shook my head. I couldn't do this. It went against all my angelic instincts. Mortals weren't supposed to see us. But who was I kidding? I wasn't a part of that "us" anymore, was I? I was mortal. But a mortal who'd been dead for eleven years. This was so not normal. The tumbling of my thoughts and fears in my brain was giving me a headache.

"David," Sandra prompted.

I bit my lip, having flashbacks of that awful dream. "You know, maybe this isn't a good idea. Maybe we should forget this idea and go home and grade some papers. You have papers to grade, right? Let's go do that. Or I can laminate that thing-y. So, yeah. *Vámonos. Tengo hambre. Debemos cocinar zapatos con frijoles.*"

Sandra tilted her head. "You speak Spanish?"

"Not at all. I think I just said we should cook shoes with beans."

Sandra, very kindly, held in her laughter. "What are you afraid of? You've been wanting this for a long time."

"I just don't want to scare her. What if she doesn't believe me? What if I reopen old wounds? What if they're all better off without me here and I just complicate things?" I didn't say it because it was so despicable to be this petty, but I also wondered if she'd prefer to see Mom, which, of course she did. That's not necessarily a put-down. Every good mother is always wanted. Obscure dead brothers? Not so much.

I sunk a little lower in my seat and said in a small voice, "Will you go in for me?" She gave me a look, so I quickly added, "Just to give her a little warning so she doesn't freak out."

Sandra stared at me with her penetrating glare, but I stood my ground. Well . . . I sat my seat.

"Fine," she grumbled eventually.

I blinked in surprise. "Seriously? I didn't think you'd actually say yes. What'll you tell her?"

Sandra didn't answer. She just rolled her eyes and got out of the car mumbling something about "puppy dog eyes." She was halfway up the toy-covered lawn when she spun around and realized I wasn't following. When I rolled down the window she said, "Get your butt over here, I am not doing this alone. You wait outside the door so I can pull you in at the right time."

It wasn't a request, that much was clear.

"Yes, Ms. Johnson," I said, scrambling after her.

When she reached the door, I moved out of sight so Elena wouldn't see me yet. Sandra rang the doorbell, and I could hear her nervous foot tapping on the welcome mat. The door opened.

"Hello?"

I gasped hearing Elena's voice so close. I hadn't realized how much I'd missed her. And not just because I hadn't seen her since becoming mortal, but also because I hadn't spoken to her since becoming an angel. My eyes watered involuntarily. My baby sister was so close!

"Hi," Sandra said. "Elena Garcia?"

"It's Elena Davis now. Do I know you?"

"Oh, sorry . . . Um, you might. I went to school with your brother. My name's Sandra Johnson."

There was a moment's pause. "Oh! Were you that girl he had a crush on in high school?"

I rolled my eyes. That was such an Elena thing to say. I could practically feel Sandra's blush. "Uh . . . sure."

"Is there something I can help you with?"

"Yes, actually. It's about your brother . . ."

I could hear by the sound of her voice that she'd turned her head in my direction, probably shooting me a nervous glare, totally regretting agreeing to do this.

Elena took a while to answer. I could imagine her giving Sandra her *you're-being-really-weird-but-I'm-trying-to-be-polite* look. "Of course. Come in."

The door shut behind Sandra, and I emerged from my hiding place to spy on them through the window. I crouched between the coiled-up hose and a pot of dying flowers and peeked over the sill of an open window just enough to see but not be seen. Elena brought Sandra into their living room and gestured for her to take the seat near the window while Elena sat on the love seat across from her. My head was blocked by Sandra's.

"So . . . What was it you wanted to talk about?" Elena asked. I heard the muffled sound of the TV from the other room and forks scraping plates. Great, we'd interrupted dinner.

Sandra muttered under her breath, "I'm gonna kill you, David."

"I would appreciate it if you didn't," I whispered through the window.

Sandra jumped and I could sense her fighting the scowl I knew she wanted to throw at me.

"All right, this isn't an easy thing to say," Sandra said. "It's totally unbelievable, but I don't know how else to say it. Your brother, David? He's alive and he needs your help."

I frowned at her phrasing. I was the one here to help Elena, not the other way around.

There was silence for a minute, and I dared a peek inside. Elena was glaring at Sandra in a dangerous way. Her face was completely devoid of emotion, which made it all the more intimidating. She continued to stare at her, and I knew she would not be the first one to talk. After all her experience interrogating naughty kids, she'd gotten the silent technique down pat.

Finally, Sandra said, "I know you probably don't

believe me."

Elena continued to glare.

"I know it's a lot to take in."

Still with the glare.

"He's right outside. I can go get him, so he can explain—"

"Get out," Elena said in a low voice. Suddenly she couldn't control herself anymore. "Get out! Get out of my house! What the hell is wrong with you? How dare you come into my house and try to mock us like this! Get out, now!"

Okay, this was not going well. I rose swiftly to my feet to jump to Sandra's rescue but fell backward over the messy coil of garden hose. I swore to myself as I pushed myself to my feet and brushed the dirt off my pants.

Of course my glorious tumble did not go unnoticed inside.

"Who's out there?" Elena demanded. "Who did you bring with you?"

"I told you, it's David," Sandra said calmly.

"David's dead!"

I took a breath and slowly opened the door, wanting to ease my way in. Of course my foot caught on the welcome mat and instead of walking through the door, I fell through it, landing on my hands as my glasses fell off my face. I'd been a mortal for like two months. You'd think I'd have gotten down *walking* by now, but apparently not.

I swore, shoved my glasses back on, and scrambled to shut the door. Slowly I turned around, foolishly hoping no one had seen that red carpet level entrance. Sandra and Elena were both staring at me.

"Hi . . ." I said lamely.

Elena looked like she'd just seen a ghost, which, in a way, she had. Her hand went to her heart, and she fell back onto the couch. She stared at me like I was some kind of nightmare. Her chin trembled.

Guilt clawed at me, and I pulled on the back of my neck. "Don't cry, Elena."

"David?" she said in a high, small voice, clearly terrified to hope.

I smiled nervously and nodded. She slowly walked toward me like I was an animal that might bite her hand off.

"Why do you look like my brother David?" she whispered, tears threatening to spill over.

"It's me," was all I could think to say.

She tentatively touched my arm to see if I was real, then squeezed the living daylights out of me, bawling on my shoulder. "You even smell like him!" she wailed, soaking my shirt with tears and snot.

I pulled her close. "That's because it's really me. And I'm sorry. I'm so sorry. I never wanted to leave you." Stupid human emotions and tears. She was spreading it to me and now my face was wet, and it was fogging up my glasses. I hugged her and rubbed her back and can't count how many times I said, "I'm sorry."

We were so caught up in our tearful embrace that we didn't notice we had an audience.

"What the *actual* hell?"

Elena and I jumped apart to see Charlie standing there in the entryway looking at me like I had three heads and cloven hooves.

"Daddy said a bad word!" Ginger gasped, peeking her head around his leg.

"Bad word, Daddy!" Rocco echoed, running through the middle of his legs. He faced his dad and wagged his finger at him. "You said bad word, you go to jail!"

"Hi, Charlie," I said nervously.

Charlie stared at me like he wanted to hit me. I gulped.

"Look, I can explain. Actually, I can't. But I didn't mean to—"

Charlie took a step closer to me and I cringed back, my heart hammering in my chest. He was so much bigger than I remembered. Despite being a year younger than me he'd always been taller, but now he was a freaking rock. He backed me up to the doorway and I had flashbacks to my nightmare, worried he'd kill me all over again. He raised his hand, and I threw my hands up to protect my face. Then he poked me in the arm so hard I was sure it would bruise.

"Ouch!" I said, moving my hands from protecting my

face to clutch my arm.

Charlie frowned. Not angry, just confused, and maybe even a little afraid. Suspicion colored his usually grinning face. He shared a look with Elena, who hugged her arms and looked down as though ashamed of herself. She'd trusted me too quickly and let her emotions get away with her. Charlie was not so swayed.

I shared a nervous look with Sandra, who I'd almost forgotten was there.

"Should I, uh . . ." she bit her lip, looking around. She seemed to be unconsciously edging toward the door.

"This is a family matter," Charlie told her, pulling me away from the door. "You can leave."

She flashed her eyes to me, and I nodded. She raised her eyebrows and I tried for a confident smile. It must have not been very convincing, because she looked back and forth from Charlie to me and bit her lip.

"It's fine," I said. "I got this."

She sighed and quietly made her escape. I looked after her, thinking about how she always pretends she doesn't want to get involved, but once she does, she just can't let go. She'd probably come check on me tomorrow if I didn't find a way to contact her.

Charlie shifted his gaze toward me, then gently, but firmly pushed me toward the kitchen. "Come on. Let's have a chat."

chapter 8
THE TRICYCLE

It was weird physically walking down the hall. I'd never been here as a live person. The house felt bigger and smaller at the same time. Bigger because there was a lot more walking to do, smaller because the walls were all in the way. I had to hold myself back from taking the route I normally took. In through the ceiling, down the cobwebbed attic, circle around the kitchen, through Ginny's door, through Rocco's wall, and on to the master bedroom. No barriers, just straight to the person that needed me. Now, I had to concentrate to not smash into things that were right in front of me. And the toys! I never realized what a tripping hazard they were. I slipped on a toy truck on the way to the kitchen and caught myself on the counter.

"Just, uh, wait here," Elena said, not meeting my eyes. She gave Charlie a look and he nodded.

"Want to watch a movie in our room before bed?"

Charlie asked the kids.

He was greeted with jumping and cheers.

"Can we get eye cream?" Rocco asked.

I assumed he meant ice cream and not some kind of topical ointment. Elena gave him a stern look. "After you eat *all* your dinner. I'll set down a towel on the floor and you can finish your spaghetti in there."

Oh geez, this was serious. Eating in Mom and Dad's room was definitely not a normal thing. The last time she let them eat in her room was when she found out Mom died, and she didn't want them to see her fall apart. She could have turned on the TV in the living room for them, but they'd be more contained in their mom's room without open access to the kitchen.

Elena gave me one last nervous glance before herding the kids into her bedroom, while Charlie collected their plates, his back to me.

I leaned against the side of the counter tapping my foot and drumming my thighs. Eventually I slumped in a chair and rested my forearms on my thighs. I felt like I'd done something wrong. Even after the hug, those dark, guarded looks they gave me concerned me.

Eventually I sighed and sat back, looking around. The kitchen was changed from what I remembered. Gone was the rectangular wooden hand-me-down table that had stains and scuffs even before they added children to the mix. That had been replaced by a purposefully distressed dark wooden table with black metal legs. I assumed the distressed look was meant to hide the accidental scrapes and stains sure to come. The brand new granite countertop stretched in an L shape around the kitchen, matching the island in the middle. A pink plastic plate of eggs and toast sat forgotten on the countertop next to a tipped over sippy cup that was slowly dripping orange juice onto the gray tile. The sink was full of dishes and the cabinet doors were all missing, showing the organized chaos of plates, Tupperware, and cereal boxes inside. It seemed they were redoing their entire kitchen. Elena had been wanting to fix it up for a long time, but she wanted to wait until Charlie was home. It felt strange being out of the loop with what was going on with them. I was used to just popping in whenever I wanted.

The smell of spaghetti distracted me, and I eyed the pot on the stove. I was on my way toward it before I noticed I'd gotten up. I frowned and paused. One side of me wanted to grab a fork and start eating out of the pot, since it was my sister, and she should expect me to steal her food. Another part of me felt like I was in a stranger's house, and that would be super awkward. I sighed and left it alone. Maybe they'd offer some to me later.

Elena and Charlie walked in after a whispered conversation in the hall. They glanced at each other, then came to stand in the middle of the floor.

"Take a seat," Charlie said, gesturing toward a chair.

"Uh . . . am I in trouble?" I asked. Neither of them answered. They just stared at me until I sat down, looking up as they loomed over me. I felt like I'd been sent to the principal's office for getting into a fight.

Neither of them moved. A long buried part of me was disoriented by the fact that they could even see me. After eleven years of invisibility, a direct glare made me feel like I was naked in the street. I tried to decide which of them would play good cop and which would play bad cop. The obvious answer was that Charlie was the bad cop, but he had a sensitive side that often got the better of him. And Elena hadn't gotten so far in her career by backing down and playing nice.

I folded my arms and tried to feign confidence I didn't feel. "You don't believe me."

Charlie folded his arms. "Would you?"

"No."

Charlie studied me longer, then sat down in the chair at the head of the table, while Elena sat on his other side. Charlie leaned forward. "You claim to be David, but David died. A bunch of people saw his body, which is now buried in a cemetery. So there are only two options here: you are David and you faked your death, or you're an imposter."

"Not sure how you think I'd have access to a dead body that looks exactly like me," I said. "I mean, it was pretty damaged, but my face was still recognizable."

Elena winced and Charlie clutched her hand. "That one's a long shot, I'll admit."

"So, you're leaning more toward the second option in which I actually did die and the person before you is some kind of imposter trying to impersonate a high schooler that died eleven years ago with zero prospects, and maybe a hundred dollars in his bank account."

He frowned. It did sound pretty stupid. Who would want to be me?

I sighed. "Look, I never meant to hurt anyone, and you can't begin to know how sorry I am. I never would have left if I had any choice in the matter. All I ask is that you just . . . try to believe me. If you really focus on what feels right, you'll know I'm telling the truth."

Charlie studied me with a frown, thinking. He looked back at the front door, then at me again. "Who was that girl earlier?"

"Sandra Johnson. I sort of . . . washed up on her doorstep and she was nice enough to help me out for a while."

Charlie's eyes lit up. "Sandra Johnson? I remember her. Weren't you super into her? Didn't you draw a heart around her face in your yearbook junior year?"

"That wasn't me!" I blushed. "That was *you*. And everyone teased me about it forever."

He put a fist to his mouth, trying to cover a chuckle.

Elena turned on Charlie. "You're starting to believe

him."

Charlie shrugged and held up his hands. "You did too at first. I don't know, it just . . . feels like him. And he knew about the hearts in his yearbook. That's such a random specific thing. There's no way a real imposter would have been that thorough."

I rolled my eyes. Of course it would be something lame that convinced Charlie that it was really me. But I was over the moon that he seemed to believe me. Who'd have thought I'd win Charlie over faster than Elena?

I gave him a grateful smile. "I'm sorry to dump myself on you guys. I just wasn't sure where else to go."

Charlie and Elena looked at each other, but I wasn't fluent enough in Charlenaese to know what it meant. They appeared to be arguing, though I wasn't sure who was winning.

"Look," Charlie finally said, turning back to me, "if you're really David, you're always welcome with us, but you have to tell us what happened to you. I mean, what the hell?" He held his hands up like he didn't have words for what was happening.

"If you are my brother, where have you *been*?" Elena asked suspiciously.

"Are you in some kind of trouble?" Charlie chimed in. "Is this going to endanger our family? We're not going to throw you out on the street, but you've gotta tell us what we're up against."

I closed my eyes trying to listen in case some angel or Hermes was nearby whispering in my ear. I felt nothing. What did that mean? Was nobody listening? Or did they just trust me to say the right thing?

"I don't know if I can explain," I finally said.

"Can you at least tell us why you faked your death?" Charlie asked. "FBI? Witness protection? Escaping conviction?"

"It's nothing like that," I said.

"Then why did you leave?" Elena asked.

I gulped, wiping sweat from my neck. Why did it feel like it was suddenly a million degrees in here? I felt like I was in an interrogation chamber.

A feeling of calm washed over me—a delayed angel whisper?—and I felt that I should tell them the truth, or the watered-down version, at least. They may or may not believe me, but that was their problem, not mine.

I sighed and rubbed the side of my face. "I'll tell you the truth—or as much of it as I can—but it's up to you whether or not you want to believe me. If you trust what I say, great. If not, you can jump to whatever conclusion you want, and we'll just agree to disagree."

"Yeah, okay, just tell us what happened," Charlie said impatiently.

"I died," I said simply.

There was silence.

"I didn't fake my death. That actually happened," I

said. "You know it did. How could I have faked my death? Uncle Richard saw me fall and you all saw my body. This may sound kinda hokey, but I've been an angel for the past eleven years. I'm just back for a little while because . . . well, I don't really know why. And I don't know how either. It's all really confusing, and I don't understand it all. There's a lot of complicated stuff going on on the other side and I got caught up in some of it, and kinda messed up a few things and . . ." I trailed off, noting how I was totally blowing their minds. "That was probably too much information."

Charlie was looking at me like a three-year-old listening to someone explain the Pythagorean Theorem. "What?"

"I died, but I'm back for a little while," I summed up. "Don't ask me how it happened, I have no idea. But the Big Man is all powerful so I guess if he wants someone to be alive again, he can make them alive again."

Charlie narrowed his eyes like he was starting to doubt me again. He poked my arm, making sure I was real. Then he stood and yanked me to my feet, circling me and lifting my arms, inspecting my body.

"I mean . . . you definitely look like David," he said. "But you're taller. Why would you return older than when you left?"

I shrugged. "I don't know, man. Nobody really sat me down and explained it to me."

He frowned at my face. "What happened to your

nose?"

"Um . . . I got into a fight?" I tried.

Charlie smiled and raised an eyebrow.

"Okay, fine, I ran into a door . . ."

Charlie threw his head back and laughed. "Okay, it's definitely David."

I sighed and flopped down into my seat. "Can we stop pointing out how lame I am?"

He just chuckled and sat back down, putting his arm around Elena, who still did not look convinced.

"Little quiet over there," I said. "You okay?"

Her face flipped back and forth from fragile little sister to complete boss lady. "Well, I'm trying to decide whether to believe your ridiculous story. Dead people just don't come back to life."

I raised an eyebrow. "All right. I'll prove I'm David." I started listing facts on my fingers. "Your first name is Maria after Nana Maria. She says hi, by the way." I didn't know if she said hi, but it sounded good. "You lost your first tooth biting my arm because I threw your Bratz doll in the toilet. When you were seven, you were so nervous before your soccer game that you peed your pants and tried to pretend you spilled lemonade." Red-faced with embarrassment, Elena tried to interrupt me, but I was on a roll.

"When you were nine you went to Jessica Sanderson's birthday sleepover next door, and they watched *The Ring* when her parents went to bed. You got so scared you walked home all alone and came into my room sobbing in the middle of the night, begging me not to tell mom and dad. Which I never did."

I looked up at the ceiling. "Let's see . . . what else would only I know? Oh, I got one. I met Charlie in wood shop class before I even knew you two were dating, and we hit it off. We went to go see one of the Harry Potter movies together once and he asked if he could bring his girlfriend with him, and I didn't know it was my sister until you showed up. It was weird, but after a little while the three of us became our own little awkward friend group. And then after I died, you two broke up for a little bit and it was really sad because I felt like it was my fault. I think because a lot of the memories you associated with Charlie had me in them . . ."

I felt myself getting emotional, thinking about all those days when no one could see or hear me. I loved being an angel, but it was hard in its own way. I was witness to so much pain that I didn't have the power to take away. I felt alone a lot of the time. In some ways I was kind of like a reverse orphan. My family was alive, and I was dead. Not as difficult as if they were the ones that died and I was alive, but still difficult. I couldn't talk to them or ask for their help or get any kind of emotional support when I needed it. Not even one little hug. That's why I'd been so happy when my mom died. Suddenly, I wasn't alone anymore. Though, the rest of my family didn't see it that way.

I took a breath, reminding myself that I was here now, with my sister before me, and I searched for more I could say to convince her that I was her brother, and I was and will always be here for her. "Ever wonder where Rocco and Ginny get all their prank ideas from? Totally me. As an angel I was always whispering in their ears. And yours, Elena. I was there when you were crying alone in your room, and when you had nightmares. Telling you I was here and that it would all be okay. I promise I didn't abandon you, Elena. I've always been here. You just couldn't see me."

Tears streamed down Elena's face, and I wasn't surprised to see tears in Charlie's eyes either. "I want to believe you," she said in a thick voice, "but I'm afraid. I don't want this to be a dream and be crushed when I wake up again."

She clutched Charlie's arm and let out a sob. The poor girl was being confronted by a deep loss. Unable to stand her tears, I walked around Charlie's chair and knelt next to hers, taking her hands in mine. "This was the worst part about being dead. Not being able to hug you when you cried."

She sobbed and threw her arms around me, burying her head on my shoulder like she used to when we were younger. "I missed you so much," she whispered, her words muffled by my shirt. "Oh, David, I missed you!"

I shoved my glasses off to wipe my eyes. "I missed you too."

Charlie joined in on the hug, sniffling in my ear. "Dude, you're back! Now we can finally discuss *Endgame*. And *The Last Jedi*. And *The Deathly Hallows* Parts 1 and 2. And *Tangled*!"

Elena lifted her head for a moment to give me a watery smile. "Charlie was almost more broken up about you than I was. He hasn't had a nerd to talk to in a long time."

I chuckled, unable to wipe the tears from my eyes with my arms wrapped around them. I felt safe and at home for the first time in a very long time, here with my sister and my friend. The old times of the three of us laughing and razzing each other didn't seem so far away. The two of them made an amazing bicycle, but once upon a time we were a tricycle, and I wasn't always the third wheel. Sometimes it was Elena, when she didn't get whatever obsession Charlie and I were discussing. Sometimes it was Charlie, when Elena and I were having a sibling moment and laughing about memories he wasn't a part of. The point was, the trio was back together, and for the first time I was genuinely glad to be alive.

chapter 9

I GO ROGUE

The next day I woke up to a small child leaning over me, her little kid morning breath blowing in my face.

I jolted awake, my heart flying to my chest. I closed my eyes and took a deep breath. Once my heart started beating normally again, I sat up noting how the air mattress I'd slept on had lost most of the air during the night. That explained why my back felt so stiff. My butt was practically touching the floor. The plastic made loud folding sounds every time I shifted an inch. At least the floor was soft. They'd placed me in their makeshift workout room, so most of the floor was covered in those squishy puzzle piece mats.

I found my glasses and shoved them on my face. Streaks of light from the blinds set stripes across Ginny's face.

"Uh, hey there, Ginny."

Ginger blinked. "How do you know my name?"

"Because I'm your uncle." It was so weird for her to be talking back to me. I felt the need to either whisper in her ear or shout, expecting her to ignore me, but she was staring me right in the eyes. The part of me that wasn't weirded out wanted to squeeze the daylights out of her. I'd never hugged her before. She was my niece and I loved her, and I needed a hug! Though I doubted she'd appreciate that coming from some random guy she'd never met.

"Sam's my uncle," she said matter-of-factly.

"I'm your other uncle. David."

"He died. Mommy told me."

I frowned. What on earth was I supposed to say to that? I turned to face her, sitting cross legged in the middle of the deflated air mattress. "Well, I'm not dead anymore."

She unconsciously picked at a loose string on her blue nightgown. "Like Ana from *Frozen?* Or Flynn Ryder from *Tangled?* Or Meg from *Hercules?* Or Wesley from *Princess Bride?*"

"Yes," I said. "Exactly like that."

She frowned and blinked. "Okay!" Then she ran off, her little feet pitter-pattering on the tile floor in the hall.

Well, that was easy.

I groaned and got up. Tomorrow night I'd just ask for a sleeping bag, because this mattress was not created for human use. I grabbed Sandra's light purple duffle bag she'd lent me and took it to the bathroom to get ready.

The countertop was a mess, and it made me smile how lived-in it looked. A race car toothbrush teetered on the edge of the counter next to a puppy toothbrush, still with a gob of toothpaste on it. There were little hair ties and barrettes scattered across the countertop, and dirty clothes and undies littered on the ground. I had to shove a yellow step stool out of the way to get to the sink, which for some reason was plugged with a decapitated barbie head. I frowned and pulled it out by the frizzy yellow hair with my finger and thumb and tossed it aside.

I had a weird feeling as I was brushing my teeth that I needed to call Sandra. It persisted until I was finished and dressed. Trusting that feeling, I chucked my duffel back in their spare room and went looking for Elena. I followed the sounds of loud cartoons and clanking pots. I found her in the kitchen making pancakes and humming to the annoying theme song playing on the TV.

"Hey, can I borrow your phone?" I asked her.

She screamed and flipped a pancake onto the floor. "David!" she gasped. Then she sighed, throwing her hand over her chest. "Don't just sneak up on me like that!"

"I didn't sneak up on you. I was just walking. I'm sorry I didn't put on my jingly cat collar this morning."

She rolled her eyes, pulled her phone from her pocket, and tossed it to me.

"Thanks," I said.

I paused before walking away, realizing how quickly

we'd jumped right back into our sibling banter. She smiled, seeming to have had the same thought.

"The passcode is—"

"I got it," I said, putting the phone to my ear with Sandra's number already dialed.

She frowned at me.

I grinned. "I know all your passwords. Dead people are great stalkers."

She gasped as I spun on my heel and walked away. "You can't just say stuff like that and walk away!"

I chuckled as I made my way back to the makeshift guest room. It only took one ring before Sandra picked up.

"Finally," she said. "Raj says good job."

"Huh?"

"He was the one who told you to call me, and you listened. So he said good job."

"Oh," I said. "Cool. So, what's up?"

"Demon hunter meeting right now. Thought you'd want to be involved."

"Can you come pick me up?" I asked.

"Already here."

I was past being Mr. Mopey, but I still didn't know why they went through the charade of including me in their demon hunter meetings when I had no role to play. I was glad they did involve me, and I tried to stay upbeat and positive, but I couldn't help leaving every meeting feeling a little useless. There had to be a reason I was here, but for the life of me, I could not think of a single way I could actually help the demon hunters. And it wasn't like they were going out of their way to give me a job—they didn't know what to do with me either. They were also super swamped. I think they tried to hide it from me, for some reason, but they all seemed ridiculously overworked, like things were worse off for the angels than they let on.

After Ying Yue handed out assignments and subtly didn't give me one, I sighed. Jake frowned at me, pursed his lips like he was trying to think of something I could do, but I just smiled and shrugged like I didn't care.

"All right, you're dismissed," Ying Yue said. My team popped out of existence one by one until only Ying Yue was left. She floated up to Sandra. "A word?"

Sandra tried to hide her look of shock that she was being addressed by Ying Yue. She didn't generally participate in meetings as she wasn't technically part of the demon hunters. She was only there as an interpreter for me.

"Um, sure," she said. "What's up?"

Ying Yue looked around the room at the wanderers floating around. Bill and Gilbert were subtly listening in on the meeting while Asher and Oliver flipped through channels on the TV. Other wanderers were in various stages of simply staring off into space or senselessly knocking objects over with their minds. "Do you believe these wanderers are trustworthy? These meetings are meant to be confidential, and yet they are privy to every word we say. Could you not make them leave while we meet?"

Sandra's brows furrowed. "No, I can't make them leave. I'm not their master, they're just lost souls who need a place to stay. You don't need to worry about them. Most of them aren't coherent enough to even listen in."

Ying Yue nodded her head toward Bill and Gilbert, who quickly looked away and tried to pretend they hadn't been listening.

Sandra spun around and said, "Hey, Bill. Gilbert. You won't tell anyone what you hear, will you?"

Gilbert nodded and Bill floated forward uncertainly. He opened his mouth and closed it a few times, squeezing his eyes shut. He exerted an enormous effort to do something, but I wasn't sure exactly what he was trying to work himself up to do.

"I . . . won't . . . tell," he whispered finally.

Sandra's jaw dropped, then she spun around and smiled at me. "I've never heard him speak before!" She spun back around. "Bill! That was amazing!"

Bill blushed and shrugged.

Ying Yue sighed. "I suppose my only choice is to trust you. Thank you for offering up your residence for our meetings. It's the only confidential place we could think of where both you and David could be involved. Goodbye." She disappeared.

Sandra gave me a look.

"Ying Yue is very direct, and sometimes a little short with people, but she's a total boss and she means well," I said. "She's kinda like Asian Professor McGonagall."

Sandra rolled her eyes. "You *would* say that. I just don't like people looking down on wanderers, or when they talk about them like they're not there."

"Isn't that what we're doing right now?" I asked. I looked back at Bill and Gilbert, still subtly angling themselves to hear us without looking like they were listening. I was pretty sure they were listening to the entire meeting. They knew valuable information. Maybe we could use that . . .

I leaned in close to Sandra and whispered, "Hey, what if we did involve them somehow? Remember my idea back when I was dead and tried to teach them how to make Light and recruit them as demon hunters?"

Sandra leaned back in her chair, considering "I don't know, David. The stakes are higher than they were before, and I don't think Ying Yue would go for the idea. She doesn't seem to think too highly of wanderers."

"Well Raj said I could last time. And maybe we don't have to tell anyone," I said slowly. "We could put together our own team of wanderer spies."

Sandra tilted her head. "You're suggesting lying? You,

the former angel?"

I shifted uncomfortably at her phrasing. It still twinged to be called a "former" angel. She had a point, and I don't understand what exactly came over me, but I felt an oddly rebellious desire to take matters into my own hands. The demon hunters wouldn't give me a job to do, so maybe I could find one on my own and show them that I was still useful, even as a mortal. I probably wanted to prove it to myself more than anyone. I had to believe that there was some reason I was mortal and that I could still make a difference. I couldn't bear the thought of being the forever honorary demon hunter who was only involved so his feelings wouldn't get hurt.

"If you think about it, all spies are liars, especially when they go undercover," I said. "'Demon Hunter' is a misleading name. We're mainly just spies. We—they—can fight demons when necessary, but that job falls more on the defenders. So, yeah, creating our own team and not telling anyone would be lying, but it's kind of my job to lie. And if it works out, no one will care."

"What if it doesn't work out?"

I sighed. "I don't know. Worst case scenario I screw everything up and everyone dies or gets captured and curses my name for all eternity."

Sandra blinked a couple times. "That escalated fast."

"Yeah, well, I'm used to screwing everything up. But every now and then I have an idea that actually works, and

I think this could be one of them."

Sandra pursed her lips as she considered, then turned around and said, "What do you guys think?"

Bill blinked and looked around like he was confused she was talking to him.

Sandra rolled her eyes. "Oh, don't pretend you weren't listening."

Bill shrugged, chagrined, then looked at Gilbert and nodded toward us. They floated over and sat across the table.

"What do you guys think? You wanna make our own group of demon hunters?" I asked. "No offense, but people don't really pay attention to wanderers, so you guys would really make the best spies. The demons wouldn't worry if a wanderer heard what they were talking about, because you guys don't usually talk." I eyed Bill suspiciously. "Unless you're thinking about moving on? Which would be super awesome if you did."

Bill shook his head vigorously. I wasn't surprised, but I still held out hope for the guy. He wasn't ready yet, but I could tell he was starting to remember who he was, even if he was still in denial.

"Wait," Sandra said. "How would the demons they spy on know they're wanderers and not angels in disguise?"

"Angels glow, wanderers don't. And demons radiate Darkness. Wanderers are the only dead who don't have an aura."

She considered. "Why didn't you guys ever go undercover as wanderers?"

I frowned. "I'm not sure how well we would be able to pull that off. Angels can create Darkness to cover up their glow, but I don't think they can get rid of the glow altogether. I'm pretty sure being a wanderer is a mindset you can't fake. As a wanderer, you lose all sense of self and reality. I think that's why they don't talk, because what you say and the way you say it is part of who you are, which they're trying to ignore. If angels were able to get into that mindset enough to completely snuff out their glow, I think they would literally become a wanderer, and that would be a whole new problem."

"But you can make Darkness?" she said skeptically.

I rubbed my forehead. "I don't know. I think that's because everyone has Light and Darkness inside them. Angels try to focus more on the Light, but that doesn't mean we don't still have Darkness in us—I mean, them. Whereas wanderers are so lost they don't have access to either one."

I looked guiltily over at Bill and Gilbert. It was weird picking apart what they were right in front of them. I hoped they weren't offended.

"Should we see if any others are interested?" Sandra asked, looking around at the various wanderers chilling in her living room and kitchen.

I thought a moment. "No. Pardon the comparison, but

if you want a cat to come to you, you ignore it. It comes when it's ready and when it's curious enough about you to approach. I think the same concept will work better with these wanderers. Right, Bill?" I asked with a smile.

He nodded. That was basically what happened with him and Gilbert. We ignored them during our meetings, and they got curious enough to listen in.

Bill held up his hands, then gestured to him and Gilbert. I frowned trying to interpret what he was saying. It seemed like he'd used up all of his talking energy for the day. "Uh . . . are you asking why I picked you two?"

He shook his head and let out a sigh. Then he held his hands up again in a sort of "what" gesture. Then he pointed to me. He made a grabbing gesture with his palms up. I was pretty sure that was "want" in sign language. After that he pointed to him and Gilbert and did little walking fingers on his hand.

"Oh! What do I want you to do?" I asked.

He nodded with a look of relief.

"Great question." I sat back for a second, considering. I'd never really taken charge of a group before. I mean, some school projects I would end up kind of leading everyone, but only if no one else did anything, and that was nothing like creating my own rogue group of demon hunting wanderers. This was actually important and super risky. It was weird for people to be turning to me for direction, but also, I wanted to take charge. Which was also weird.

I couldn't give them an important mission too early on. We needed to give them something easy to test them. Also, they didn't talk, so anything they heard would likely stay locked in their brains until Bill got better at speaking. Maybe they could just locate where demons hung out so that me and Sandra, innocent and oblivious mortals, could do our own spying.

"Okay, here's all I want you to do," I said, leaning forward. "Find out where lots of demons hang out. Places where they gather for meetings or just to chill. But a place where it wouldn't be weird for mortals to show up. A place that Sandra and I could go to without looking suspicious. You think you can do that?"

Bill and Gilbert looked at each other, then Bill looked back at me and nodded.

"Awesome! You guys will do great! Go ahead, when you're ready, and get back to me when you find someplace."

Bill disappeared, closely followed by Gilbert.

Sandra looked at me with an unreadable expression. "What's this about you and I going somewhere where demons hang out? Are we going to go spy together?"

"Yes?" I said uncertainly. "If you're okay with that." I wasn't sure how she'd take it. She might feel like I was using her for her powers. Or that I was putting her in danger. In a way, both were true. Though that wasn't the only reason I wanted her around.

Sandra grinned, pumped her fist, and said, "Yes!"

"Seriously? Didn't you say from the beginning you didn't want to get involved?"

"That was before things got interesting. You've sucked me in, and what person doesn't secretly fantasize their own James Bond or Nancy Drew moment?"

"I've been a spy for over a year, and I've never felt like James Bond."

"No . . ." she said slowly, "but your Evil David alter ego wasn't terrible. You fooled Sheila. Speaking of Evil David, I see you're joining the ranks of all men in their twenties and experimenting with facial hair."

"Is it bad?" I asked, self-consciously rubbing my stubbly jaw. I was too lazy to shave over the weekend.

She shrugged casually. "I kinda like it."

I smiled. Then startled at a throat clearing sound behind me.

"*Hijole!*" I shouted as I spun around. My mom stood there with her arms folded looking suspiciously between me and Sandra.

"How long have you been standing there?" I asked nervously. Had she heard my plans for going rogue?

"Facial hair," she said. Then she smirked at mine and Sandra's clasped hands.

I breathed a sigh of relief. She hadn't heard anything important.

"Elena's taking Rocco to Urgent Care because he got a toe ring stuck in his nose," Mom said without preamble.

"A *toe* ring? Where did he find a toe ring?"

"Do people still wear toe rings?" Sandra asked.

My mom sighed impatiently. "Ginger found it on the ground. Now—"

"Hold up," I said, "She found it on the ground? How did it end up in Rocco's nose?"

"Focus!" Mom said, snapping in my face. "Charlie isn't home yet, so Elena had to take Ginger, who's crying because she's afraid Rocco is going to die and that it's all her fault. You two should meet them there and take Ginny back to Elena's house so she can just deal with the child who's got a large object lodged in his nose."

"Yeah, okay," I said, leaping to my feet. "You okay with that, Sandra? Sorry, I just don't have a car."

"Of course," she said, grabbing her purse. "Let's go."

"Thanks, Mom," I said as we ran out the door. "You're doing great as a guardian angel!"

"Of course I am, I'm a mother," she said. "Now, go!"

chapter 10

DAVIS FAMILY DRAMA

"Is he gonna die?" Ginger wailed as Sandra drove us back to Elena's house. I was in the back seat as she squeezed the life out of me while bawling her eyes out.

"He's not gonna die, Ginny. I used to get stuff stuck in my nose all the time when I was little, and I never died."

Sandra shot me a smirk through her rearview mirror, probably amused at the thought of me sticking crap up my nose.

Ginny pulled back and sniffed, looking up at me with heavy, wet lashes all clumped together. "Yeah you did. You said you died and then came back to life."

I opened my mouth and then closed it, backpedaling. Sometimes talking to kids is like wading through a minefield. "Well, okay, yeah, I did say that, but my point is I never died from getting something stuck in my nose."

"How did you die?" Her eyes were all big and shiny from crying and it simultaneously broke my heart and made me smile at how sweet and innocent she was.

"I fell very far," I told her quietly.

Ginger's face was horrified, and she burst into tears. "Rocco falls down all the time!"

"Oh boy," I muttered, sharing another look with Sandra. Maybe I should have lied this whole time and said I'd gone on a trip instead of being honest about having died. Or maybe she deserved honesty. Was being a parent like this all the time, just trying to wade through difficult conversations as you explain how the world works?

I decided to shut up and just let Ginny soak my arm with her dramatic tears. As much as I didn't want her to cry, it made me feel special that it was me she clutched tightly. Like her mom used to. I wondered if that was some kind of complex I had. I wanted to feel needed. It seemed a little pathetic when I thought about it. I should help others because of the way it makes them feel, not because of the way it makes me feel.

When we got back to the house, Ginny wasn't crying anymore, but she was still sniffling and wiping her face. I decided that was enough of that. I went to Rocco's room and found a fake snake.

"Hey, Ginny! Wanna do a prank? We're gonna need some string."

Immediately her sniffling stopped, and she ran to the junk cabinet to the right of the sink for some yarn. She grinned as she handed it to me. Her smile looked so pitiful with the tear stains down her cheeks. "What are we gonna do?"

I cut off some of the string and tied it to the snake's head, then nodded for her to follow me to the garage door. I tied the other side of the string to the doorknob, then I put Ginger on my shoulders so she could place the snake on the thin ridge above the door.

"There," I said as I set her back down. "When your mom or dad comes in the door, the snake will fall on their head, and they'll scream."

She grinned and ran around in a circle, giggling evilly. "I like pranks! One time I tied a rubber band on the faucet and sprayed Mommy! She screamed!"

"I know," I smirked. "I was there."

It was Charlie that the snake attacked first. He was so tired he didn't even scream, which was a disappointment because he has a really funny scream. He always does this big gasp before he lets out a yell, sounding like a reverse donkey *hee-haw*. But he just yawned and shook his head, then flopped onto the couch. He was obviously exhausted and my old guardian angel instincts kicked in.

"Want me to make dinner?"

"It's fine," he said, flipping through Disney Plus with Ginny. He looked like he was about to conk out.

"You're letting me live in your house for free. I'm making dinner."

"I'll help," Sandra offered. So, we fell into our regular routine of cooking together and cleaning up the kitchen. We made tacos again, because they're easy, and there was a bunch of hamburger meat in the freezer. Oddly enough, it kinda made me a little homesick for Sandra's place.

It took longer than I expected for Elena and Rocco to make it back home. By then, Sandra had left, and the three of us had fallen asleep on the couch watching a movie. It was nice. I took a moment to just be happy to be with my family, my niece fast asleep in my lap.

I woke up when Elena got home. I was too sleepy to actually open my eyes and get up yet, so I just listened as she walked to Rocco's room and shut the door. I guessed he'd fallen asleep, and she was putting him down for the night. Then I heard the weight on the other couch shift. Charlie groaned awake, then whispered, "Everything go okay?" I could tell by the way he was talking that they were really close to each other. She was probably lying on top of him.

"Yeah, he's fine," Elena said, yawning. Then, apropos of nothing, said, "How would you feel about having another one?"

"Another what?"

"Another trip to Urgent Care," she said sarcastically. "Another kid, Charlie."

"Oh . . . Uh, I think I'm good. Two's enough for me."

There was a pause.

"Really? Because if we tried for three, we might end up with a genius or something. Third time's a charm."

"Three's uneven," he pointed out.

"Yeah, but remember when they were babies? They were so cute, and they didn't talk back. Imagine having another baby. What if you could actually be around for the birth this time?"

His voice hardened. "What's that supposed to mean?"

"I just mean if we timed it right, you might be able to be there."

Charlie sighed. "Look, you know I was on the fence about kids when we first got married, and it was for this very reason. I don't get to be around to be their dad all the time. I wasn't there when either of them was born, and Rocco didn't even know who I was last time I came home. I hate being the stranger dad who's never around. Or worse, what if something happens to me while I'm gone, and they're all messed up because they don't have a dad anymore? I'm glad we have the kids that we do. You were right, it's worth it. But two is my max. I don't want another one."

I winced. If I was dead, I'd totally be whispering better things for him to say. It was annoying that I couldn't anonymously put ideas in people's heads anymore.

There was another pause, then in a strangled voice Elena said, "It's good to know you feel that way. I'm going to bed. Goodnight."

The couch groaned as she rolled off and got to her feet, then practically ran from the room. The door to their bedroom slammed shut.

"Oh, Charlie," I said, shaking my head once Elena was out of earshot.

"Whoa, I thought you were asleep."

"Nope, heard the whole thing. You didn't handle that well, man."

He sat up, looking very confused. "Handle what well? What was all that about, even? We were talking about Urgent Care and all of a sudden she's bringing up having another kid?"

"Dude, she's pregnant."

His head reared back. "What? No, she can't be, she's on the pill."

"I don't think it works one hundred percent of the time."

"How would you even know that?"

I shrugged. "You learn a lot of stuff when you're dead and the majority of your job is to just watch and eavesdrop on people."

Charlie put his hands to his head. "No. That's crazy, she's not pregnant. Why would she just be telling me now?"

"She probably just found out," I said. "I'm sure they can do pregnancy tests at Urgent Care. Maybe she's been feeling sick, so they just did a test while she was already there."

Charlie stood and started pacing. "Seriously?" He froze and swore. "I just went on and on about how I don't want any more kids. She's probably thinking I'm gonna ditch out on them or something."

I nodded and smiled sarcastically. "Yeah, way to catch up."

"What do I do?" It was funny how he had so much more life experience than me but was looking to me for advice.

"Go talk to her, stupid. She's probably crying in her room right now because she thinks you don't want your baby."

He swore and raced from the room.

"Well, that went well," I muttered to myself.

Ginny shifted and looked up at me with sleepy eyes. "Daddy said a bad word . . ."

I smiled down at her. "I'm glad you caught the important part of that conversation."

She yawned and flopped back on my chest.

The next morning, Charlie barged into my room, looked around nervously, and shut the door.

"Dude," I said, sitting up. "Knock."

"You were right," he whispered, sitting on the edge of my bed. "She's pregnant."

"Yes, I'm very smart," I said sleepily.

"Glad you caught on, because I probably would have just gotten annoyed that she was so hung up on this baby thing and made her even more upset."

I nodded. "It's nice to be acknowledged for saving the day. Usually, I'm screaming in people's ears and they either don't hear me, or they think they came up with the idea all on their own. So, did you fix it?"

"Well, I think so. I mean, after we talked, she was so emotional she just latched onto me, and we ended up . . . you know—"

"La la la!" I said, putting my hands over my ears. "I don't need to hear about it. She's my sister, you sicko."

Charlie grinned. "Oh my gosh, I just realized. You're still totally innocent, aren't you? I mean, you obviously died a virgin, and we both know you haven't seen any action since then. Unless you and Sandra . . . I mean you did live with her."

"Okay, not that it's any of your business, but no. And we're done talking about this."

Charlie stood and grinned wider, "You gotta get out there eventually, man. The field is ripe."

"Get out of here," I said, chucking a pillow at him.

He ducked out the door chuckling.

chapter 11
EASTER

I sat there for a minute as another aspect of mortality fell on my shoulders. *Dating.* Not that I was going to "get out there" anytime soon. It would be pointless because I wasn't even sure how long I'd be alive. I'd just focus on doing my job. I wouldn't think about how the only girl I ever asked out or kissed was a demon. I also wouldn't think about that time when Sandra was trying to hint that I should ask her out to the school dance, and I was too stupid to realize it. Nope. Not something I needed to deal with right now.

Of course that's all I thought about the rest of the day. Stupid Charlie.

Apparently while Charlie was razzing me about dating, Sandra had dropped by with a bunch of applications and pamphlets for various scholarships and colleges she took from the high school guidance counselor's office. I guess she had some kind of event she was supposed to attend, so she didn't stick around.

"Hey, Sandra just dropped this stuff off for you," Elena said, spilling the shiny brochures and papers on the counter.

"Oh," I said. "Thanks."

"That was nice of her," Elena said smiling. "I mean, she came all this way . . ." She looked at me mischievously.

"Oh my gosh, not you too," I grumbled.

Charlie chuckled as he made himself a cup of coffee.

"You two are the worst." I looked pointedly at Elena and paused. "What about you? Is there anything you want to tell me?"

She smiled and pointed to her belly. "I'm gonna get fat again."

"That's awesome," I grinned, coming around the island to give her a hug. "Congratulations!"

"I wish people would tell me congratulations every time I got fat," Charlie said with his mouth full of bacon.

I rolled my eyes. The guy was a muscular rock sculpture.

Elena slapped his arm. "You're not supposed to agree that I'm fat!"

"I didn't say you were fat. *You* said you were *going* to get fat."

She made a petulant pouting noise. "But you didn't contradict me. You're supposed to say, 'No, you've never been fat, Elena. You were just growing a human child in your womb.'"

Charlie got a mischievous glint in his eye. "Yeah, but other parts of you got bigger too, and I liked that."

"Oh, so now my boobs are too small?"

"*What?* How did you get *that* from what I said?"

I tuned out Elena's hormonal temper tantrum and spent the rest of the morning looking over all the crap Sandra left for me. It got less exciting and more stressful the deeper I delved into them.

Around lunch time, Elena made food for the kids and scooped mac-n-cheese into a pink plastic bowl for Ginny. "How's it going there?"

I groaned and let my forehead conk on the counter, a bunch of applications and pamphlets strewn around me in addition to the billions of tabs up on the screen I'd been staring at. I closed Charlie's junky ten-year-old ThinkPad he found under his bed. Luckily, I'd already taken and passed the GED back when I was living with Sandra, so at least that was out of the way. I didn't study, because the last time I studied for a major test I died. This test was super easy though. One of the perks of being a total nerd is that you're usually a little smart.

Unfortunately, I did not see myself winning any full-ride scholarships, even with a good application, so I needed to find a job first so I could earn some money, and then probably take out a few student loans. Except none of the places I'd applied to were hiring. Why does being mortal cost so much money? And explain this: you go to college to get a degree so you can earn more money, but you can't go to college unless you already have money. It's like when you apply for a credit card for the first time, and they turn you down for not having enough credit. *What?* That's why I want a credit card! To build up credit!

The garage opened and Charlie walked in with his arms full of groceries. "Any luck with that mess?" he asked as he dumped all the food out on the counter.

I shook my head despondently, regretting it because staring at the screen so long had given me a headache. "No one wants to hire a dead guy. It's pretty alive-ist if you ask me."

"Don't make up words," Elena said.

I shrugged and started helping with the groceries. Elena kept opening her mouth like she was going to say something, then thought better of it. I was pretty sure she knew I was aware of her reluctance and was just waiting for me to ask, but being the annoying brother I was, I just ignored it and waited for her to bring it up herself.

Eventually she set down the orange juice she was putting in the fridge and spun to look at me.

"Hey, so we're going to have the Easter egg hunt over here this year. So . . . you need to decide if you want to tell the rest of the family if you're alive. Otherwise, you're gonna have to hide out in your room the whole time."

"Wait, why here? Why not at Dad's?" I asked.

Elena sighed. "Apparently his backyard is under

construction with a giant hole in it. He's putting in a pool."

I grimaced. "He hates swimming. Why is he putting in a pool?"

"Midlife crisis," Charlie said under his breath.

"And mom's not around to talk him out of it," Elena added sadly. "He probably thought it would be fun for the grandkids or something, but it's just been this giant hole for months."

I sighed and let my head fall in my hands. "I'm supposed to be helping him. That's my job. Now he's freaking out and I'm not around to do anything."

"Why don't you let him know you're alive? Come to the party. Personally, I think they all deserve to know."

I looked down, considering, listening in case someone was nearby to give me a little nudge in the right direction.

SAM IS NOT READY.

I startled and looked up incredulously. "Hermes?"

SAM IS NOT READY, he repeated.

My mouth popped open. It was totally Hermes! I heard his voice in my mind, just like I once did as an angel.

"Uh, David . . ." Elena said. "Who are you talking to?"

I ignored her, focusing on Hermes' voice.

Why can I hear you?

ALL MORTALS CAN HEAR ME IF THEY CHOOSE TO LISTEN. THEY LIKE TO CALL ME THEIR CONSCIENCE.

Seriously? Like, I could have heard you all along?

YES. THE MORE YOU LISTEN, THE MORE I CAN SPEAK

TO YOU. WILL YOU CHOOSE TO LISTEN?

Uh, yeah. Don't show myself to Sam. He's not ready. Got it. Do I get to ask why?

He chose that moment to stop communicating with me. I guessed that it was Sam's business why he wasn't ready to see his dead brother return from the dead. Honestly, I was surprised Elena hadn't run out the door screaming by now. She had accepted this all way too easily. They all had. That had me worried something was bound to blow up soon.

The demon hunters offered to hold another meeting on Easter, so I'd have a reason to be out of the house. Sandra even offered to go see a movie with me. It was sweet of everyone to care enough to distract me, but I wanted to be there, even if it hurt me to not be able to be with everyone. Though a part of my brain regretted turning down Sandra.

Rocco and Ginny hung out with me in my room while we waited for everyone to show up. Then the doorbell rang, and they scampered out to go play with Little David and baby Gloria. I quickly shut the door behind them. I sat with my back against the door with my eyes closed and listened to my family. Laughter, footsteps, chairs scraping, the smell of food, squeals of babies, some game on the TV. Even though I couldn't leave the room, listening in was such a gift. I felt almost content. It was like being an angel again when I'd attend family gatherings and watch from above. Except, there's a greater intimacy to being physically present. Even though I couldn't see them all, I felt so close to them.

And then I heard them all travel outside and watched like a creeper through the window as the kids hunted for easter eggs. Dad looked a little spaced out, but he smiled whenever somebody talked to him. Sam looked . . . haggard. I hated not being in the know about everything that was going on with him. I worried about him. He wasn't always the best decision-maker. The good news was his new girlfriend Jessica was there holding his hand, so they must still be together. And when Little David ran up to him with an egg Sam smiled and congratulated him instead of ignoring him. That was a plus.

Part of me wanted so badly to go out and join them. Another part of me cringed inward at the very thought. Even if Sam was ready, I wouldn't have been able to bring myself to do it. I didn't want to get too attached. It would be so much harder when I left again. And I did still want that to be soon. The Resting Place was infinitely better than here, but . . . it was also nice to be with my family again. I had been a loner on the other side for so long.

After lunch time, everyone trickled out until Elena knocked on my door and said it was safe to come out. The house looked like a house after a family get-together. Plastic cups with half drunken soda were left on almost every surface. A forgotten pacifier was on the counter, along with one child-sized shoe. Two Easter baskets were knocked over on the living room floor with candy wrappers littered around them. I got to work putting the house back together.

"You don't have to do that," Elena said, carrying a conked-out Rocco to his room. "You weren't even here."

I shrugged. "I don't mind. I like having something to do."

The front door suddenly opened, and I dashed to the hallway bathroom before whoever it was could see me.

"Hey! David left his shoe," called Sam.

I heard the little one run down the hallway calling for his shoe. Elena said, "Oh! I think I left it on the counter somewhere." She yelled it much louder than she needed to, probably trying to warn me that someone was coming. Elena and Sam were in the kitchen now, complaining about their children leaving things everywhere they go, and I had a sudden realization. If I returned back to The Resting Place, I'd never get to complain about my kids leaving things places. I'd never have kids. As a teenager, that wasn't such a terrible sacrifice, but for the first time, that thought was incredibly depressing. I'd never have a Charlie freak-out moment when I discovered my wife was pregnant. Or even have a wife, for that matter. I'd never attend get-togethers with the family where my kids could play with their cousins. For the first time, I wanted that.

Maybe staying here wouldn't be such a bad thing...

The pitter-patter of little feet neared the door. I cringed as the doorknob turned and I realized I hadn't locked it. In came Little David. He paused when he saw me.

"Stranger!" he whispered, pointing at me. Not in a terrified way, but more in the way a kid would say, "Dog!" or "Horsie!"

I bit my lip, hoping he'd just go away, but that would be ridiculous. I'd have to say something to him. I knelt down in front of him and smiled. He had Sam's brown eyes and Chelsea's strawberry-blond hair. Yet, the face itself did look quite a bit like his namesake. The thought made me oddly emotional.

"No," I whispered. "I'm not a stranger. I'm David."

"No, I David," he said, patting his chest with his chubby little hand.

"Yes, you're Little David. And I'm Big David," I said, patting my own chest.

"You David? Wike me?"

"Yes," I grinned. "Just like you."

He laughed like I'd just said the funniest thing and then his dad called from the other room. "David! Where are you? It's time to go."

He patted me on the head, trying to be funny or nice, but his fat little palm hit with more of a smack. I chuckled as he ran off down the hallway, humming something totally unintelligible.

Once I heard the front door close behind them, I sighed and leaned back against the bathroom cabinets. This was all so complicated. I hated that I couldn't know my nephew because I already felt a connection to him. And I missed Sam too. And my dad. And I'd never even met baby Gloria. I didn't want to want these things because that would mean I was getting attached to this life, and I didn't want to get attached. I was leaving soon, and I couldn't bear to leave again without saying goodbye. And I didn't want to think about the things I'd be giving up if I died too soon again. Like being a husband, or father. Actually *doing* something with my life.

Elena ran to the bathroom and asked, "Did Little David see you?"

I nodded.

She bit her lip. "It's probably fine. He makes things up all the time. No one will believe him if he tells . . ."

"Hope so," I whispered.

She took in my face and smiled sadly. "Emotional day?"

I nodded again.

She sat next to me on the ground. "Life is complicated."

"What gave you that idea?"

We sat there together for a while. It was nice to be together without talking. I wasn't sure I'd have been able to put my feelings into words anyway.

chapter 12
NOT ENOUGH

Sheila

It was a risk to ask for help, I knew that from the start. Asking for help showed weakness, something Malum despised. I might even be thrown into the Hurricane again, but this task he'd given, while important, was obviously impossible. I was starting to feel that the task itself was a punishment. This made me more determined to prove that I was equal to the challenge. I would not show weakness.

Malum, in human form, paced around me as he questioned me.

"What have you done to destroy him?" he asked.

"I've sent him nightmares of you. He's never been as terrified by anything as you. And thank you, Master, for sharing his fears with me. It's made his nightmares more effective."

Malum froze and spun around to glare at me. "That's

it? Nightmares?"

I blinked, taken aback. "You said to start small so that he doesn't suspect—"

"That won't destroy him! You must think bigger—"

"I've attacked him as well!" I said, foolishly interrupting him. "But every time I get close a stupid angel shows up and casts me out! How am I supposed to work around that? He's protected!"

Malum floated up into my face and his breath of Darkness swirled around my head. "Get creative," he hissed. "They can't protect him always. Those angels have other duties than watching over the boy. Find him when he's alone. And do more than just send him nightmares! You need to pull the rug out from beneath his feet. Remove his strength. Make him question all he knows and believes. Fill him with anger and desperation. Fill him with *fear*. Fear is a good man's worst enemy. Only when his fear is greater than his foolish love will he join us."

"Yes, master," I said through clenched teeth.

He dissolved into a cloud of Darkness that surrounded me in a miniature cyclone, a reminder of the Hurricane. A threat. "The next time you report, you will have something better to share than nightmares."

He disappeared in a puff of smoke, and I stood there simmering in Darkness. That stupid boy was the reason I'd been punished, and it was time to punish him back. .

chapter 13
DADS AND DEMONS

I started getting a feel of when angels were present or when they weren't. I was no Sandra—I couldn't see or hear them—but part of me could sense them. I wasn't sure if this was just a result of paying attention and being aware of how the afterlife works, or if it was a sort of extra sense I had because I had been an angel once. Regardless, I'd come to really appreciate showers. Angels never hang out when you're in the shower because of privacy. Don't get me wrong, I appreciated the angels in my life, but I was kind of self-conscious that my life was on display for everyone to see. Most mortals get to go through their lives blissfully ignorant of the fact that dead people are watching them all the time. It's kinda creepy when you think about it.

It was about a week after Easter, and I still hadn't gotten a job interview anywhere. It's like no one had even seen my amazing resume, which was actually kind of a disaster. I felt bad about it, but I definitely lied. Just like when I applied to the demon hunters, all I had to include was that one summer camp job and Hot Dog on a Stick, so I added that I'd been a receptionist for ten years at a company I completely made up. I mean, come on, I wasn't going to let that front desk work in The Resting Place go to waste. The other lies were the references at the bottom. I made up the names and put in Elena, Charlie, and Sandra's numbers for the contact info. They all agreed to lie for me if someone called. I'll admit that was wrong, and I was sure mom did not approve.

I was stewing about what I was going to do as I showered off when a shocking chill ran down my spine. I frowned, hoping I was wrong in my assumption. Nothing happened, so I squirted shampoo into my hand and rubbed it in my hair, relaxing as the warm water ran down my back, erasing the memory of the sudden chill.

The lights shattered, spraying glass and electric sparks everywhere. I screamed as I was showered with glass instead of water. The bathroom was pitch black without the lights on because the window was blocked by a storage shed outside. I panicked, trying to reach the faucet, when I heard it turn on its own and the water burned scalding hot. I tried to step away from the water but stepped on glass which slid out from under my feet. Grabbing for dear life, I caught hold of a small soap shelf as my feet tried to find purchase on the glass-shattered bathtub floor. It felt like rubbing them against serrated knives. The water was fire, the floor was glass, and all I could think to do was launch myself out of the shower, getting entangled in the shower curtain as I fell. The worst thing was, I knew there was a demon behind this, but I was too mortified to call for an angel. I was naked with sudsy shampoo in my hair, tangled up in a shower curtain on the floor. Just when I caught my breath enough to sit up, a drawer shot open, clipping me in the forehead.

"Ow!" I yelled, clutching my head. "GET OUT OF HERE, STUPID DEMON!"

I scrambled to my feet and, despite the fact that I felt like my life was in danger, I fumbled for a towel to throw around my waist before grabbing at the doorknob. I'd rather be attacked by a demon than have my niece see me naked and run away crying because she saw my junk. Just as I found the doorknob, something scraped down my back, and I yelled out again. It felt like a razor, and it *burned*. Finally, I found the doorknob and threw open the door, limping on my cut-up feet into the hallway. Luckily, or maybe unluckily for me, no one was home. I'd forgotten that Elena and Charlie took the kids out to see a movie. I'd declined because I wanted to do more job hunting. That was, apparently, a very stupid decision.

Pictures on the walls shook, and I yelped. It was following me! "Hey!" I yelled. "Hermes, you wanna send someone down here to take care of this?" I was sure Mom and Jake were both busy with something important or they would have already caught her. It seemed my demon had been watching and waiting for a time when no one was looking.

I found the hallway closet and shut myself inside. My logic was that there wasn't anything in the closet that could really hurt me. If I'd run to the kitchen, there was plenty in there that could be used as a weapon. I hid for about five minutes, dripping water and blood until I was sure the demon was gone. Shakily I let myself out of the closet and sat down in the hallway to inspect my feet. There were still tiny glass shards in them. I'd need tweezers to pluck them out. Unfortunately, tweezers were in the bathroom, and I was too scared to go back in there at the moment.

Of course the doorbell rang right then, and I swore, remembering I was supposed to let in the AC repair guy. There was no way I was answering the door like this. They rang again, and guilt gnawed at me. I told Elena I'd let the guy in. "Just a sec!" I yelled. Quickly, I hobbled to my room, wincing at the glass in my feet, and tried my best to towel the leftover shampoo out of my hair. I wiped some of the razor blood off my back and threw on whatever clothes I could find. I shoved on my glasses, which I'd luckily not taken to the bathroom with me, just as the doorbell rang again.

Limping as fast as possible, I raced to the door and threw it open.

"Sorry I was in the show . . . er." I froze and my jaw

snapped shut.

Crap, crap, crap, crap!

"D-David?"

Nope, not the AC repair guy. It was Dad with an empty cake pan in his hand, probably stopping by to return it. His face paled and the pan clattered to the ground.

My heart thudded in my chest, and I can't quite explain why, but I was one hundred percent terrified. More terrified than I'd been when I'd been attacked by the demon. I loved my dad, but I loved him from afar. That's how our relationship worked. I'd tried to maintain that while mortal so I wouldn't have to rip open old wounds and hurt him again when I left. That wasn't just it though. It would hurt me just as much to leave him. To give up my dad. I didn't want to deal with that. Not again. Now, eleven years after my death, we stood face-to-face. I felt exposed. What could I say? I couldn't lie—he'd already recognized me.

Dad's eyes filled with tears as he leaned in closer to look at me. "Is it really you?"

I gulped and nodded.

He threw his arms around me. "My son!"

I wanted to be concerned for his mental health. He just saw his dead son alive and didn't even question if he was mistaken. He didn't think, "Maybe this is some guy that just looks like my son." He didn't even ask me where I'd been or how I was here. Elena was so guarded and unbelieving at first. Was my father so desperate for some happiness in his life that he would latch on so quickly to such a ridiculous idea that his son had returned from the dead?

Later I stewed over all of that, but in the moment, I just let him hug me, needing it right then just as much as he did.

I let him in, and we sat on the living room couch, just staring at each other.

"What happened to your head?" he asked.

I reached up and felt the dried blood. I'd completely forgotten about the demon attack just minutes before.

"Um, I hit my head on a drawer," I said. "Look, Dad, I can explain about everything. No, actually, I really can't. I'm sorry, but—"

Dad held up his hands and smiled, his tears still wet on his cheeks. "I don't want to know. It's just enough that you're here."

My jaw dropped. This was insane! How could he believe this so quickly and not even care about an explanation? My father had finally snapped!

Dad put his hand on my shoulder and stared at me with a fatherly look of concern. "Are you okay?"

Okay, first, you need to know something about my dad. Growing up, my dad was always ultra positive, to the point that it was kind of annoying. Don't get me wrong, I appreciate it when people can see the bright side of life, but Dad was optimistic to the point of not allowing anyone to have feelings. The glass was *always* half full, and if you couldn't see that, you needed to change your attitude. Even if you were dealing with an actual crisis. It's why I always turned to my mom for advice, and why Elena always cried to me.

So, for the first time in my life, my dad was seeing me, really seeing me, and noticing that I was having lots of feelings, and instead of telling me to "cheer up" he asked me if I was *okay*.

That did it. I dissolved into a fit of tears with sobs and snot galore. I don't know what it is about someone recognizing when you're not okay, and then asking you about it that makes a person so emotional, but that happened to me. Also, this was my dad. My dad who was finally seeing me. My dad who was finally giving me permission to have feelings. My dad who I'd missed too much to even acknowledge. I always acted like hanging out with him as an angel was just as good as being physically with him. I'd convinced myself that it was better, that nothing had really changed. But deep down, I was devastated. It wasn't until that moment that I let myself feel how much I'd missed him over the eleven years I'd been without him.

There was a knock and a scruffy guy with curly, shoulder length hair in a flannel shirt stuck his head through the door we'd left wide open. "Um, is now a bad time?"

It was the AC repair guy. Of course. Fantastic timing. I wiped my snot on my sleeve and let him in, trying to explain to him the problem while tears were still slowly dripping down my chin and blood was trailing from my feet.

Geez, I was a mess.

My dad patched up my forehead and helped me get all the glass from the bottoms of my feet. He bandaged them up with gauze, then made me sit on the couch in the family room while he, I kid you not, made me some chocolate milk like I was three. I let him. I suspected taking care of me made him feel just as good as it did me. At least he didn't put it in a sippy cup. He still didn't ask suspicious questions, like why the bathroom looked like a horror show, or why I was too shaken to go back in there yet. It was almost like he thought he was dreaming and just accepted every wild, ridiculous explanation, because in dreams we're never aware of how insane it all is.

"Dad," I hedged nervously, when he joined me on the couch and flicked on the TV. "Are *you* okay?"

He frowned. "Why wouldn't I be okay?"

"Because! I d-d- . . ." I couldn't bring myself to say it. "I was gone. And now I'm not. That's not normal, Dad. You shouldn't be so calm about all this. Elena accepted it too quickly too, but even she was suspicious at first.

Dad sighed and turned off the TV. "Let me explain it to you then. Are you a liar?"

"No," I said quickly. Then I worried that was a lie, so I added, "I mean, not usually. I've lied before, though. But only because I felt like I had to—"

My dad cut me off. "A liar isn't someone who lies a little here and there because circumstances call for it. A liar is someone who lies so much you can't trust anything they say. Are you a liar?"

"No," I said.

"Do you like to hurt people?" he asked.

"No!"

"Are you one hundred percent in control of everything that happens to you?"

"Definitely *not.*"

"Have things been easy for you?"

"*Definitely* not . . ."

He nodded. "So, if you are truly my son, and you aren't a liar, and you don't enjoy hurting people, and you aren't in total control, then the most logical explanation is that when you left us, you either didn't choose to, or you did it for a good reason. And if you aren't a liar, then if you had the choice, you would have already explained it all to us. So, there's no point in me demanding an explanation you can't give, especially if, as you said, things haven't been so easy for you. You're home now. That's all I care about."

I blinked in surprise. He really didn't care. He was just happy I was here. I wondered if he thought I'd left for some dangerous reason, like Charlie thought, and that I faked my death. Or did he believe that I really had died and now I was back from the dead? But I guess his point was that it didn't matter. Whatever happened to me, he accepted it as something I had no control over and didn't blame me for it.

Elena, Charlie, and the kids came through the garage just then, and the tornado of my niece and nephew swept through the house trailing popcorn and M&M's, Rocco reenacting some fight that happened in the movie, and Ginger crying because she lost a toy she brought with her. Elena saw me and Dad, and I grew defensive. "I thought he was the AC guy!"

Elena grinned knowingly and my eyebrows rose. "You knew! You told dad to come at that time because you knew I'd open the door!"

Elena nodded smugly. "I'm a genius."

I rolled my eyes and fell back onto the couch, too exhausted to even be angry. It had been a *long* day.

"Holy hell!" Charlie exclaimed from the bathroom. "What *happened* in here?"

"Ew! Why is there blood on the carpet?" Elena added, finally seeing my trail.

I groaned and threw my arm over my face, just done with everything for the day.

chapter 14

WHO SAYS YOU CAN'T GO HOME?

I told Elena and Charlie the truth and they promptly kicked me out. I didn't blame them. I wouldn't have wanted a guy haunted by a demon to be staying in the same house as my kids. I shuddered at the thought of Sheila getting anywhere near them and I doubted she was above using children to get to me. It was all pretty convenient timing, actually, because Dad wanted me to move back in with him. I wasn't opposed to the idea. I think the poor guy was lonely and probably needed me more than I needed him.

So, I packed my things and said goodbye. I wasn't banned from visiting, they just didn't want me living there. Ginny cried and hugged me and asked if I'd ever come back, so I told her I'd bring her ice cream and watch a movie with her sometime. I'd bring Sandra with me so we could make sure there was an angel nearby who could fight off any demons that showed up.

So, the next phase of my mortal life began. I moved

back into the house I grew up in. The house I lived in before I'd died. I made my dad let me out in the driveway so I could come in through the front door. I don't know why; I just wanted the feeling of officially stepping into my house. I found the hidden key under the red patio chair pillow and felt a ritualistic sense of nostalgia as I fit it through the lock in the door.

When I walked through the front door with my backpack, it felt exactly the way it always had. It even smelled the same. The entryway side table still had two large family pictures—one picture was the last one we all took as a family, the other was the most updated one they'd taken that still had Mom in it. Between those were pictures of me, Elena, and Sam. Elena's and Sam's were now updated with pictures of them with their families, but mine was still from my junior year. I couldn't help but compare it to my reflection in the large mirror hanging above it on the wall. Not only did I look older, but the look in my eyes was completely different. In the picture, I looked uncertain and insecure, but in an optimistic way, like I really believed there were great things to come. I felt a weird sense of compassion for the kid who still thought he had his whole life ahead of him. He had no idea he was going to die. The me in the mirror didn't look so naive. I looked wiser but also . . . haunted. I frowned, concerned that this was the face I was displaying to the world.

With a shake of my head, I moved on to the open living

room and kitchen as my dad came in through the garage and hung his keys on a peg. It was all very clean. My dad had always been very neat and methodical about where he kept things, but you could see the absence of mom in the dust on the TV stand and wall decor. The sectional had a slight dent on the end where dad usually watched the news, his reading glasses sitting on the end table next to an empty mug. The couch was only a few years old, but when I peeked under it, I found a soda stain I made when I was six. It made me smile.

There were other things around the room that took me back to the good old days when we were all a family here. A family album in a drawer in the TV stand with embarrassing pictures of kids in the bathtub; a chipped pottery vase Elena made that Sam and I accidentally knocked over when playing tag; little doilies Grandma Gertie made before I was even born. I'd been in this house plenty of times since dying, but physically being there and interacting with it filled me with a bittersweet melancholy for the past I'd left behind.

I crossed the room to look through the curtained windows, raising an eyebrow at the aforementioned giant hole in the backyard covered with a tarp. Piles of dirt still lined the perimeter of it. Mom's precious vegetable garden along the wall was covered in brown, wilted sticks, either through neglect or from the dust and dirt from the pit.

"How long have you been working on this?" I asked

Dad, who'd been hovering behind, watching me curiously.

Dad gave a noncommittal grunt. "A little while." He avoided my eyes and walked down the hall. Sore subject? I wondered what that was all about. Obviously "a little while" meant since mom died. I wondered if one day he just got so upset he went outside and started digging to get out his frustration. Then to cover it up, he decided to have the yard demolished and put in a pool.

I shrugged and made my way up the stairs and down the hall, smiling at the crayon drawing pictures and elementary school photos still hung on the walls. I passed Elena's and Sam's rooms, which had been turned into a guest room and storage room since they moved out. My room was the smallest room at the end of the hall, because Elena and Sam would have complained if it had been any other way. It was petulant of me to still be annoyed by that, but something about being home made me feel like a kid again.

I knew what it looked like, but I still hesitated before turning the knob and stepping inside. My room hadn't been left the same. I did lots of angel whispering after I died to convince my family to get rid of my stuff. I think it hurt them too much to see it exactly the way it was— bed unmade, my clothes all over the floor—and not expect me to walk right back in the door and flop on the bed. It was now a guest room with different decor and different bedding.

Dad came in behind me and said, "Sorry all your stuff's gone. We didn't think you'd be coming back."

"No, Dad, I wanted you to get rid of it. It was better that way."

"There's a box in the closet over there with some of your old things." He eyed my backpack and frowned. "Looks like you already found some of it though."

I opened my mouth to try to explain, but he held his hands up and said, "I don't need to know."

He left quickly then. I wondered if when he said he didn't need to know he actually meant he didn't want to know. Elena and Charlie interrogated me. I think they would have continued asking more and more questions the longer I lived there. Why didn't Dad want the truth? I mean, I was fine with it. It was a lot easier for me that he just accepted things without needing an explanation, but why didn't he want one?

The next morning, I was woken by Dad stomping down the hall singing *Bohemian Rhapsody*.

He threw my door open and waited for me to sing it back.

"No . . ." I groaned, rolling over.

He repeated the last part he sang over and over until I grumbled the lyric in my scratchy morning voice. Dad shut the door and continued singing down the hallway.

I groaned, but smiled as I sat up and stretched. The

stupid *Bohemian Rhapsody* call-and-response was how Dad used to wake us up when we were kids. He wouldn't leave us alone unless we said the "Galileo" part back so he could know we were actually awake. It was annoying. But also kind of comforting because it had become routine.

I went to the bathroom to get ready and felt weird that I didn't have to shove Elena's makeup and crap to the corner of the counter. I kept expecting Sam to pound on the door and yell at me to hurry up. They were annoying things I had to deal with, but I felt homesick thinking of those days.

I closed the door while I went to the bathroom, but quickly opened it back up again after washing my hands. Looking around, I whispered, "I'm just brushing my teeth and stuff. If anyone's there, you can come in . . . Please." As much as I appreciated privacy, I was kind of afraid of being alone in the bathroom and I hoped an angel was nearby. I felt stupid for being afraid of the bathroom, but yesterday freaked me out. It's not super fun being attacked by something you can't see.

Dad was making scrambled eggs when I made it downstairs and was watching the morning news.

"Hey," I said.

"Morning! Want some eggs?"

"Sure."

He set a plate in my old spot at the table. Then he set down a phone and a pair of keys.

"What's this?" I asked.

Dad sat with his plate of eggs and said quietly, "Well, no one's using them anymore, so I thought someone might as well get something out of them. Haven't canceled her phone plan yet."

Looking closer I recognized them as Mom's old phone, and the keys to her Honda Accord. "Oh . . . Um, are you sure?"

He shrugged. "She's not coming back to use them. Is she?" He met my eye for just a second, and I saw his carefully concealed desperation.

I gulped and shook my head. He just nodded and started eating his eggs. I pretended not to notice when he sniffed and wiped his eyes. I decided it was good that I was here. He shouldn't be alone in his grief. He tried to hide it in public, but here it was easy to see that he was not okay.

"She's okay, you know," I said quietly.

Dad nodded, chewing, and I could almost see his thoughts play across his face. *She may be okay, but I'm not . . .*

I wasn't sure what to say or do. I was familiar with comforting my family in their grief, but the situation was usually them mourning me, so I'd just try to let them know I was there. I had no idea what to say to someone when they could actually hear and see me. Especially when I could not completely relate. It sucked for me that my mom was dead, but not nearly as much as anyone else—I still saw her sometimes. For Dad and everyone else, she was gone for the rest of their lives.

As familiar as I was with death, especially having experienced it, I'd never really dealt with it as a mortal. Grandma Gertie died when I was really little. The only death I had ever been affected by was Nana Maria. That was awful. But it was different than my dad losing my mom. I didn't see Nana often, so her death didn't necessarily change anything about my life. I had no idea what my dad was going through losing his wife, or Elena and Sam losing their mom. I took a moment to be grateful that, even though mortality had been rough, I could still see my mom.

"Hey, are you looking for a job?" Dad asked suddenly.

I blinked. "Uh, yeah, actually."

"I go to church with someone who works for Chuck E. Cheese. Says they're hiring."

I made a face. "Chuck E. Cheese?"

He smiled. "Beggars can't be choosers, son."

I sighed. "I guess. Well, if they'd hire me, I'd take it. I literally have zero dollars."

"I'll let him know I know someone who's interested. Put in a good word for ya."

"Thanks."

I'd been with my dad for one night and already I had a phone, a car, and maybe a job. Why didn't I come to my dad to begin with?

When I got to my room, someone was already in there. I screamed and for some reason threw my phone at him, but of course, it just went right through him and hit the wall. He flickered, uncertainly.

"Oh my gosh!" I said, shutting my door. "You scared the crap out of me."

It was Bill. It turned out wanderers didn't worry much about following the rules of not revealing themselves to mortals. I could see him very clearly floating above my bed.

"What's up?" I asked, finally.

He didn't say anything.

"Did you find a place?" I asked.

He nodded.

"Great," I said. "You can go back to Sandra's. I'll text her and then you can show us where this place is."

Bill nodded and disappeared.

"Freaking ghosts are gonna be the death of me," I muttered as I put Sandra's number into my mom's old phone.

Me: Hey, it's David. Bill says he found a place. Are you home?

Sandra: Oh my gosh! Where have you been? Whose phone are you using? What happened???? There's a demon hunter meeting right now and everyone's freaking out about your demon attack! Where are you??? I texted Elena's phone and she said you weren't home.

Me: Oh . . . sorry. Things have been a little crazy.

Sandra: Ya think?!

Me: Calm down. Haha. I'm fine. I'll be there in a sec.

Sandra: You don't need me to pick you up?

Me: I'm borrowing my mom's car.

Sandra: ???

Me: I'm over at my dad's. Long story. I'll explain when I get there.

Sandra: You're gonna die and it's going to be all my fault! You never should have moved out! If you'd stayed with me I would have seen your stupid demon before she attacked you!

Me: Careful there. You're starting to sound like me. Just chill, lady. I'll be there in a sec. You can yell at me then.

I found my dad falling asleep watching an old recorded *60 Minutes*.

"Hey, Dad, is it okay if I borrow the car?" I asked.

He startled awake and said, "Sure. Where are you gonna go?"

I hesitated. "I'm meeting some friends."

He gave me an odd look, so I said, "You and Elena aren't the only ones who know I'm alive."

Dad frowned. "Will you be safe with these friends?"

I nodded. "Yes. I'll be very safe. These friends know everything, and they've been looking out for me."

Dad hesitated now. I could see him tempted to ask more but stopped himself. "Okay. Just be careful."

"Will do." And, while it wasn't something I normally used to do, I hugged him before I left. You never know when it's going to be your last chance. It surprised him, but he hugged me back tightly, then continued being unusual by saying, "Love you, son."

In my raw, emotional state, those words almost made me cry again. How do mortals go about their lives without crying all day every day? I'd been an emotional wreck since I reentered mortality. Though, I will say, my version of mortality was a bit more insane than most.

chapter 15
OVERPROTECTIVE ANGELIC BABYSITTERS

It took me a while to get up the stairs to Sandra's apartment because my feet were killing me. They were wrapped in gauze inside my shoes, so it felt like walking on marshmallows, but some of the cuts were still raw. When I got to Sandra's door, it flew open, and she threw her arms around me. Then she pulled back and gently touched the butterfly bandage on my forehead. I'm not gonna lie, I kind of enjoyed the attention.

"I'm fine," I said.

She let go and slapped my arm. "You're like a pet dog that keeps escaping and running into the road! How many dangerous situations do you have to get into in a week?"

I held my hands up. "I'm sorry. I don't much enjoy it either. I'm a little bit incompetent at life."

"This wasn't incompetence! You were just taking a shower!"

She sighed in a way that sounded more like a growl and took my hand, pulling me behind her. I tried not to wince as I walked on the cuts on my feet. Once she took my hand I could see my team pop into existence, everyone arguing over each other. Bill and Gilbert hung out in the corner of the room, secretly listening.

"He's here!" Sandra announced.

Suddenly their arguing voices changed direction from yelling at each other to yelling at me.

"All right, everyone calm down!" Raj said.

Slowly everyone shut up as Sandra and I sat down at the table.

"I am so sorry!" I didn't realize my mom was there until she flew at me and tried to hug me. "I would have been there, but Sam was going through something really hard. He's not doing good . . ."

"What happened with Sam?" I asked.

"Apparently he'd had symptoms for a long time but never told anyone. He was feeling numb and weak and was having trouble seeing, so Jessica took him to the hospital. They haven't diagnosed him officially, but they think it's Multiple Sclerosis. He didn't take the news well. He was yelling and raging, and the doctors tried to explain to him that he can still lead a normal life. Eventually I was able to help calm him down, but he's still angry and scared because it isn't curable and progressively gets worse."

"*What?* If he's been dealing with this for a long time, I should have known! I was his guardian angel!"

"Well, you're not anymore, that's my job, and clearly

you were doing much better than me. Two of my boys hurting on the same day!" She was crying angel tears that disappeared after they fell from her chin, and I felt terrible.

"Mom, things that happen to people are not your fault. You can't prevent bad things from happening, they're supposed to happen. You're just there to help. And you can't be in two places at once. I'm glad you were with Sam instead of me." The selfish part of me was lying about that, but the unselfish part of me knew it was the kind of lie that should be true and needed to be said.

"It was my fault you were attacked," Jake said with a sigh. "I was on bodyguard duty. I was in the house, but then Hermes called me off to go help my cousin who was thinking about suicide. I talked him out of it and got his mate to go check on him, but I should have made sure someone was watching you before I left. I just didn't think anything would happen to you in the shower of all places."

"Dude! The cousin thing was way more important!" I said.

Everyone was talking at once again, trying to take the blame for not checking up on me until I stood up and said, "Oh my gosh, everyone shut up!"

They quieted and looked at me. "Look, it's really touching that you guys care. But first of all, you guys aren't in charge of me. I have one guardian angel, and she was doing an amazing job and helping the son who needed her most. You guys all have your own people to look after.

You forget I was once one of you. I know how busy it is and how you can't take care of everything. I remember having front desk duty and demon hunter meetings on top of keeping tabs on all four members of my immediate family who were all going through a bunch of crap at the same time. No one is to blame. You guys have been really overprotective since I've become mortal."

"You're part of our team," Daisy said, her arms folded. "We'd take down any demon that attacked you."

"Can you blame us?" Jake said. "You almost die on a weekly basis."

"That's an exaggeration," I said.

"It's not," he said grimly. "You don't see everything your mum and I fight off."

Ying Yue also stood, looking guilty, then poofed a whiteboard into existence with a really intricate chart scrawled across it. "Daisy's right. You're one of us and we should be looking out for you. I've devised a system that makes sure one of us is always watching over you. I tried to coordinate it with all your schedules, but if there are any conflicts, please—"

I started laughing in exasperation. It was so loud, everyone looked at me. "Guys! This is ridiculous! Look. If it was important enough for all of you to come running to my rescue, Hermes would have told you. Let's just all cool it, okay? Don't change your routine."

"I think he's right," Raj said quietly. He gave me an

apologetic look. "We all have enough on our plates without this added duty. We need to focus on the bigger picture."

"Thank you," I said, holding my hand out, then I sat down. "By the way, who did end up fighting her off?" I asked curiously.

"That would be me," Mom said darkly. "As it should be. Nobody touches my son."

The rest of the meeting was pretty normal. Each team member went around sharing information they'd learned while undercover, and Raj shared things he'd learned from other task forces. It seemed that demons were banding together more than ever. Angel hunters were now planning coordinated attacks on angels. Sometimes this involved using mortals as bait. One angel was almost captured. A demon attacked his son, and when he went to cast out the demon, he was ambushed by ten demons waiting for him. The guy was told by Hermes to abandon his son and return to The Resting Place immediately. He obeyed, but it was obviously difficult. Luckily once he left, the demons lost interest in his son, since they were only there to capture the angel.

"That's why we need to be vigilant," Raj explained heavily. "Do not be taken in. If you sense a trap, get out of there immediately. Who knows, maybe the attack on David was an ambush to capture Jake, who was on duty."

I grimaced. "Crap, I didn't even think about that. Yeah,

no one try to save me!"

"I'm not leaving you out of my sight," Mom argued. "Not unless Jacob is on bodyguard duty."

"I think the attack on David was separate," Ying Yue said. "This specific demon has a personal score to settle with him. In fact, I don't think she wanted any angels around. It's possible she had a hand in the things that pulled Jake and Gloria away."

"That's terrifying," I said under my breath. I'd been trying not to become paranoid, but this was making it kind of difficult. "Either way," I forced myself to say, "Raj is still right. Jake and my mom did the right thing by doing what Hermes told them to do. Believe me, you do *not* want to ignore Hermes . . . I did that once. It was stupid. Bad stuff happened."

Sandra glanced at me, and I realized how that might have sounded.

"Not that I regret saving you!"

Sandra just shrugged. "I'm grateful, but I don't argue that it was stupid."

"Um, you're welcome?"

"So, no to the chart?" Ying Yue asked, gesturing toward her beautiful, complicated bodyguard schedule. She looked a little disappointed.

"No to the chart," Raj said softly. "Sorry, David. If we're nearby, we'll obviously help. I hope you know how much you mean to all of us. Of course we don't want any harm to come to you. But unfortunately, we can't get so focused on guarding you that we let our other duties fall to the wayside. I hope you understand."

For some reason the apology made me more embarrassed because everyone was looking at me with pity again. I shoved my defensive feelings away and tried to focus on the fact that they cared about me. I nodded. "Yeah, of course. That's what I've been saying. Is there anything you guys want me to do? Anything I could do to help?"

Crickets.

Raj and Ying Yue looked at each other, then back at me. "We'll let you know," Ying Yue said, and my shoulders slumped involuntarily. My question was sort of a test. If they gave me a task, I might have abandoned my secret group of demon hunting wanderers. As it was, I was even more determined. I didn't know what it was, but I just felt like I was supposed to be doing *more*.

"You're dismissed," Raj said. One by one they appeared to just pop out of existence. All but Jake and Raj. Jake was apparently on guard duty, but Raj looked intent on having a little talk with me. Oh boy. This would be fun. Jake subtly floated out the front door, giving us some privacy.

Raj came around the table to sit next to me. "Look, kid. I'm sorry things have been tough for you, and I'm sorry I don't have all the answers. This situation is unprecedented and we're trying to figure it out, but it's tricky."

"I know," I said. "Believe me. I don't even know what to do with myself. There's not much I can do to help you."

"Maybe not in the field," Raj said. "But we are one hundred percent open to your ideas. We still want you on the team, just more as a consultant now. Give us insight on what you're seeing from the outside. Give us the mortal perspective. And if you have any crazy schemes cooking up in that weird brain of yours, please share. I mean it. We could use some David-level thinking."

It was my turn to look at Raj in pity. "You and Ying Yue seem a little stressed."

He barked out a laugh. "That's the understatement of the century. You have no idea. Well, I'm sure you do, it's just a different kind of stress. Things are hard on all of us right now, so it's important we stick together as a team, all right?" He looked at me seriously and I wondered if he knew about my plans to go rogue.

I just gulped and nodded. I knew I probably should have told him, but I was afraid he'd tell me not to.

He sighed. "All right, well, stay safe. I mean it as a compliment when I say that I hope you don't join us for a long time."

I made a face. "You think I'll just stay mortal for the rest of my life and die old?"

"That's how it's supposed to go," he said with a sad smile. "You were deprived of the long life you could have had. Might as well enjoy it while you can."

"You don't look like you were very old when you died. What were you, late thirties?"

He smiled, then transformed into an old man, with folds and wrinkles all over his face and just a tiny tuft of white hair left in the middle of his head. "Oh, I lived to a ripe old age," he rasped. "It was a beautiful life full of love and heartbreak and tragedy. It wasn't easy, but it was worth it. I'm glad for the experiences that I had. They made me into the person I am." Then he transformed back into the face I knew him by. "I just feel the most me in this form."

I was shocked. Raj was so cool. I never realized he was an old guy. But age on the other side is super arbitrary. It doesn't mean anything, and you can look like whatever you want to look like. It did give me further insight into who he was though. It also made me consider the benefits of growing old. Maybe that was why he was so wise and collected all the time. I could probably use some of that.

Raj left soon after that and Sandra and I waited a few seconds until we were sure he was gone. I twisted around in my chair. Our secret wandering spies were, for some reason, creepily floating with their backs against the ceiling and their eyes staring at nothing. I wondered if this was a conscious choice in order to throw off the angels and make them appear like they weren't aware enough to be listening in. Or maybe they were just really that weird.

"Uh, Bill? Gil?" I tried.

They blinked and looked at me.

"Do you wanna share what you got?"

They slowly floated down and sat themselves at the opposite end of the table.

"You still want to go through with this?" Sandra asked.

"I don't know . . . Maybe let's just see if they found anything?" I wondered if Bill would talk for us again, but his mouth remained firmly shut. I think I scared him with talk of crossing over.

Bill made a drinking gesture with his hand.

"Um . . . are you thirsty?" I asked.

Sandra slapped my arm. "Don't be stupid, he's dead. That means getting drunk."

"You think we should get drunk?" I asked.

Bill shook his head. Then, embarrassed, he stood— floating in the middle of his chair—and started . . . dancing? Nothing crazy, he just put his hands into fists, bent his arms and moved his arms around in front of him. It was so unexpected that I threw my head back and laughed. Bill cracked a smile and chuckled. It was the second time I'd heard his voice. Even Gilbert snorted and rolled his eyes.

"Um, that was beautiful," I grinned.

He nodded his head, smiling and blushing.

"Drinking and dancing," Sandra said. "Are you telling me and David that we should go clubbing?"

He shrugged and held up his hands.

Me and Sandra looked at each other. "What do you think?" I asked.

"I guess," she said with a shrug.

"Probably don't want to drink though," I said. Not that I had ever drunk before. I died at seventeen, and I was a goody two-shoes rule follower. "We need to keep our heads if we're going to get any spying done."

Sandra nodded. "We could get away with that if we danced a little and didn't sit at the bar too long. It would look kind of weird though if we just sat there and neither of us drank. In my experience, demons love to gang up on the DDs. If neither of us drank it would attract their attention, which would be bad if we're trying to be covert."

"Was there a place you had in mind, Bill?" I asked.

Bill took a breath and closed his eyes. Then, in his low voice, said, "Nightlife."

I tried not to smile and make a big deal out of it, but the guy was seriously progressing. He'd even shown a little bit of personality earlier, dancing and getting embarrassed about it. I wondered when Gilbert would start catching on.

"What do you think?" I asked Sandra.

She shrugged. "It's up to you."

I sighed. "Okay. Next Friday."

Bill looked at me questioningly, probably wondering

what I wanted them to do next.

"How about you guys come with us? Four spies are better than two, right? And you guys can watch our backs."

Bill nodded, then smiled.

"All right, so we have a plan!" I said, trying to sound enthusiastic. "Let's hope I don't screw this one up."

Knowing me, I'd probably just jinxed it.

chapter 16

I AM GARBAGE MAN

Dad's house was silent in the morning, and I missed the noise. I missed waking up next to a creepy blinking baby doll and running Rocco to the bathroom when he pooped his Pull Ups and getting my makeup done by Ginger. Dad's house was so quiet you could hear the birds outside and someone mowing the lawn. No Doc McStuffins blaring or children whining or little feet slapping against the tile. Living with Elena was living with a family. The house didn't feel as full with just me and dad.

I had to remember, though, that as lonely and quiet as it felt here to me, it was more so to my dad. He lived alone with no sound but the TV and the thoughts in his head. It probably would have done him good to live at Elena's house and be around his grandkids all the time. And Elena could always use a babysitter. I'd have to suggest the idea sometime. I doubted my dad would go for it. He'd probably see it as pity and was a little too prideful to accept that he needed people, but if I could do it, why couldn't he?

I supposed the quiet wasn't too bad, but I could only take so much of it. I got myself a bowl of cereal, sat on the couch, and pulled my feet under me against the cold. Then I flipped on the TV. It may have just been me, but it felt like there was a lot more crime on the news than usual. A kid was kidnapped from his home, a woman abducted and raped on her way to her car, a family killed by their dad setting the house on fire. This stuff had all happened in the past couple of days. It seemed like the demons were working overtime lately. What was their game? Was it Malum working them harder than usual? Tempting mortals was fun for demons, but it seemed like it was still some level of work. I was pretty sure even demons took breaks from destroying lives every now and then. Angels took breaks from saving them, though we did it in organized shifts, so no one was neglected.

Dad rumpled my hair and sat in his armchair with a glass of orange juice. "Since when do you watch the news?" he asked.

I shrugged. *Since Malum escaped and set his demon followers on a crazy killing spree.*

"Hey, I talked to that guy from church. He says they're hiring and would probably take you if you applied. You can use my computer if you want."

"Okay," I said, tossing him the remote. I'd had enough

of the depressing news. He handed me his laptop and I started my application. About ten minutes later I got a call asking me to interview that afternoon. These guys were apparently desperate. It made me wonder if this particular location had some special challenges that caused a lot of people to quit, but I wasn't really in a position to be picky.

Dad drove me to the interview. I could have driven myself, but he wanted to come for "good luck" and then celebrate with dinner afterward. He was pretty confident I would get this job, which was comforting, because I was weirdly nervous. I'd gotten a position with the demon hunters of all things with my only work experience selling corn dogs. I'd hoped that I could land a job designed for high schoolers and broke college kids.

I'm sure there's some nice Chuck E. Cheeses out there, but this one smelled like feet. The cheap, red carpet was covered with stains and the closest arcade game to the door was flickering and periodically buzzing, crying out as it died a slow and painful death. There were no customers but a crying five-year-old with her elderly grandmother who was trying to get her to eat some pizza.

A blond teenager in pigtails bounced up to me and said, "Welcome to Chuck E. Cheese! I'm Piper! How can I help you?" Her smile was so happy and genuine I had to smile back.

"Hi," I said. "Um, I'm here for an interview?"

"Finally!" she whispered under her breath. She

gestured for me to follow her and said, "I've been working double shifts since our last manager left and it's killing me! And then Jessica and Trish went off to college, and Patrick died—"

"I'm sorry, what? Someone died?"

She waved her hand nonchalantly. "It's fine, he was old. Anyway, unless you totally screw up your interview, you definitely have the job because we're dying."

"Literally, apparently," I said darkly.

She giggled loudly. "You're funny! Okay, Preston's office is just down there. Word of advice," she lowered her voice, "don't make yourself sound too smart, or he gets intimidated and mean. He has no idea what he's doing, but he gets super mad if anyone says anything about it. Suck up, and he might be nice to you. Just know, the hours suck because we're understaffed, and you *have* to wear the Chuck E. costume. It's required for everyone at all the locations. Good luck!"

She scampered off to welcome the parents of a group of children who had just burst through the doors and immediately scattered.

"Okay then . . ." I said to myself.

Nervously, I walked past the humming drinking fountains to the office down the hall with the open door and awkwardly peeked in. The freckle-faced redheaded frat boy sitting at the desk looked younger than I was. Not that I actually knew how old I was. His desk was covered with piles of papers, a greasy Burger King bag, and miscellaneous junk.

"Uh, hi. I'm here for an interview?" I cleared my throat and tried to fix my posture.

"Yeah, whatever, sit, I guess," he said. His voice had a lazy, but annoyingly nasal sound to it.

I repressed an eyebrow raise and obeyed.

He held his hands up and said, "So, who are you?"

I forced myself not to start with an "um." "My name's David Garcia. Thanks for seeing me. I'm really interested in a position here."

"Cool," he said sarcastically. "Why should I hire *you?*"

Because you're desperate . . .

I tried not to let his attitude throw me off, but it was hard. Especially when, even at a job like this, I felt weirdly unqualified. Anytime I was asked that in an interview, my internal response was, "You shouldn't hire me. I'm kind of incompetent. I don't know why anyone would hire me." Luckily, I was pretty good at BS-ing answers. I'd also gotten better at lying since becoming a demon hunter.

"I think I'd be a great fit because I love kids and I have a lot of energy. I'm a quick learner and do really well in fast-paced environments. And I'm great under pressure. I have a lot of experience coordinating activities for large groups, but I can also think fast on my feet when situations arise." Most of that was a total lie, so I paused a minute, hoping for him to interrupt me so I wouldn't have to go on.

He just sighed. "Yeah okay. Can you start today?"

I blinked. "Wait, today?"

He raised his eyebrows and leaned forward, speaking loudly as though I was hard of hearing. "Yeah. Today. Can you do that?"

"Uh . . . yeah, that would be great!"

And that's how that night I found myself stuck in a ball pit, fishing out some kid's pants, in a rat costume that smelled like dirty laundry and Taco Bell farts.

Dad took me, Elena, and Rocco out to dinner after I finally had a night off work. Charlie and Ginger were at a daddy daughter event at her elementary school, so it was just the four of us. Well, four and a ninth of us? I wasn't sure if she'd told anyone yet, so I didn't mention anything about the baby.

"I want nuggies!" Rocco said for the fifth time. "I want dino chicken!"

Elena rolled her eyes, trying to smooth his kids' menu in front of him and sending a couple of crayons rolling off the table. "Rocco, I told you, this is a noodle place. They have spaghetti and meatballs, not chicken nuggies."

"I don't like basketti!" he said, clenching his fists and standing up on his chair.

"Meatballs are good for you," Dad said. "It's protein. And the sauce has tomatoes in it. That's good for you too."

Rocco folded his arms and plopped onto his butt. "No!"

I leaned across the table conspiratorially and whispered, "Thor eats meatballs. That's how he gets his muscles. They're stuffed with meatballs!" I flexed my unimpressive arm and pointed to my bicep. "See that? There's meatballs in there. I ate them and they turned into muscles."

Rocco's eyes widened. "There's meatballs in your arms?"

I nodded. "Grandpa has lots of meatballs in his arms!"

Dad flexed his more impressive bicep and Rocco gasped. "I want meatballs!"

I folded my arms and leaned back, smirking at Elena. "You're welcome."

"Oh, be quiet. I could have made him eat his meatballs."

I raised an eyebrow, and she stuck out her tongue.

A waiter took our order and soon came back with various steaming plates of cheesy, tomatoey pasta. Rocco ate his spaghetti and meatballs with a little too much gusto, getting sauce all over his face and hands. Throughout dinner Dad kept smiling between me and Elena, clearly enjoying us bugging and griping at each other. He even bought dessert, which he never would have done before I died. He never really believed in indulgence.

When the chocolate lava cake came out, I heard and felt a loud breath against my neck, but when I jumped and spun around, no one was there. Paranoid, I gripped the edge of my seat, looking around myself with wide eyes.

"Why so jumpy?" Dad asked.

I shrugged and shook my head.

Elena gave me a sharp look, then looked at Dad, likely wondering if another horror show like the bloody broken bathroom had occurred at Dad's house yet. I wished she hadn't seen that.

"Tell us about your new job," Dad said.

"It's fun," I said. "I like working with kids."

Elena raised an eyebrow. "You sound really enthusiastic."

"It's good, really!" I said, trying to be positive for Dad. "I get free pizza and help kids have good birthdays."

"And?" Elena prompted.

"Okay, so it's really not a bad place to work. The only thing is my boss."

"Everyone hates their boss," Elena said with a nasty chuckle. She was a market researcher for Nordstrom and had had her fair share of difficult bosses along the way.

"Not everyone," Dad said.

"I've had great bosses. And I know you're a great boss," I added quickly. I knew dad was really proud of his plumbing business and didn't want to offend him. "You actually care about the people you work with. This guy . . . does not. And he doesn't really know what he's doing. The only way he got this job was nepotism."

"I've had nothing but wonderful experiences with every boss I've had," Dad said. "A person wouldn't be made the boss unless they were qualified and able to do a good job. Bosses look out for their employees. You just have to try to see things from their side."

Elena and I shared a look. Dad loved to act like everything was always perfect. I loved the optimism, but the lack of sympathy was annoying. My manager really was terrible, I wasn't just having a bad attitude.

"Dad, I asked him where we kept the napkins, and he told me to go . . ." I glanced at Rocco, "*fork* myself. He also likes to tell the girl employees, both to their faces and behind their backs, that they're a nice piece of *ash*. Oh, and he ranks them based on how nice their . . . *ash* is. He likes to nudge me and laugh as he says these things like he expects me to join in. I told him once to knock it off, and he made me wear the Chuck E. costume for three hours straight. You normally only wear it for like thirty minutes at a time. And that thing is so hot and smells like death." I paused, horrified. *Oh my gosh, did Patrick die in that suit?*

Elena bore her fangs. "Get that kid fired."

"Sounds like the boy's father didn't teach him proper respect," Dad grumbled, thoroughly upset now.

The light above me flickered and I felt another breath

on the back of my neck. I squirmed in my seat, clenching my hands into fists and pulling my shoulders up near my ears. A sense of foreboding filled my gut, and I bit my lip. It had been a while since I'd been physically attacked by my demon, which meant my guardian angel and bodyguard were doing an amazing job. But they had a lot to do, and there was bound to come a moment when neither of them was with me. At the moment I regretted turning down Ying Yue's plan to have someone watching me at all times. There's nothing quite so terrifying as being attacked by something you couldn't see. And in a public place no less, with my family around.

"Are you okay?" Dad asked me. "You look a little jumpy."

Elena gave me a sharp, questioning look.

"Excuse me, I need to take this," I squeaked, pretending my phone was ringing. There was no way I was gonna let this demon mess with my family, so I had to lead her away. Which was obviously her plan, getting me alone, but I didn't care. I quickly slipped out of the booth and hurried outside, trying to draw her away. The lights leading to the exit flickered as I walked, following me. I increased my pace. I figured outside would be safer than inside where there were lots of knives and electricity around.

When I got to the door, I couldn't open it. It kept locking every time I pulled on the handle. Frantically, I spun around, looking for another exit. There was a back door down the hallway to the bathrooms and kitchen. Trying to keep myself from running, I hurried past my family again and toward the back exit. I didn't have time to worry about what they thought about me acting like a lunatic. Lights flickered as I passed them, but when I got to the back door, it didn't lock on me. I threw it open and quickly shut it behind me. I scanned the area around me for dangerous objects. There wasn't much to the left—an old shopping cart and empty asphalt leading to the parking lot. To the right were a stack of wooden crates, metal trash cans, and a dumpster across the way.

I started toward the parking lot when I heard the sound of loud, deep barking coming from that direction. From the sound of the bark, it was a very large dog. I froze, hoping it was not coming toward me. Of course it was though. Within a second a rottweiler turned the corner and skidded to a halt. It lowered its head and growled deep within its chest, looking directly at me.

I forgot how to breathe for a second. It took me a second to realize it wasn't looking quite at me, more at the empty space above my head. I was pretty sure Sheila was floating above me, making the dog think I was part of her demonic Darkness. I put my hands to my head, panicking because dogs go *absolutely insane* around demons. Holding my hands up I tried to slowly back away, but the dog just growled louder.

"Uh, nice doggie," I whispered in terror, gulping.

It lowered its head further and growled louder.

I tried snapping at it, going, "Tss, tss!" like the Dog Whisperer, but it didn't do anything but make me look like an idiot.

I continued to back up until I got to the back door of the restaurant. Trying to plan out how I could get inside as quickly as possible and without turning my back on the dog, I slowly reached behind me for the doorknob.

Of course it was locked now.

An old brick fell from the roof and clipped me on the shoulder, and I yelped. That was enough to set the dog on me. It lunged toward me, and I screamed, spinning around. I knocked over one of the trash cans in a clatter of metal, trying to slow the dog down, then climbed up on one of the wooden crates. They were stacked in a sort of misshapen pyramid, so I continued to climb until one of them collapsed in on itself, throwing me tumbling to the ground. The dog barked in a way that sounded more like a roar as it jumped over the trash can and crates to get to me.

Gritting my teeth and ignoring the multiple scrapes and bruises from the wood and asphalt, I got to my feet and sprinted for my life toward the dumpster. I had no doubt that the dog could outrun me, so my thinking was that I needed a hiding place. I could hear his paws behind me, drawing closer as it barked and panted. I'd just reached out for the top lip of the dumpster when the dog clamped down on my pants leg, just barely scratching my calf with its teeth. My legs came out from under me, and I fell forward, clipping my chin on the asphalt hard enough that my teeth clattered together. I tried to blink the disorientation away and reached my hands in front of me, trying to find purchase on something as the dog dragged me away. Whimpering pathetically, I tried to shake my leg free, but the dog had a very firm grip on my pants. Desperate, I somehow kicked off my shoes, unbuttoned my pants and shimmied out of them. I crawled to my feet and glanced behind me. The dog roared in frustration and tossed the pants to the side. With a yelp I took the last three steps to the dumpster, gripped the edge of it, and hopped inside with a magnificent splatter.

The rottweiler barked and put his paws up on the edge of the dumpster, and I crouched in the garbage, praying he wouldn't jump in. It continued furiously barking and scratching at the dumpster for some time until something made it yelp. I peeked over the edge and saw it run away with its tail between its legs.

"Thank you," I said weakly to whichever angel had just scared it off. I let out a breath I'd been holding in and leaned my head back against the dumpster wall behind me. I closed my eyes and took a moment to slow down my racing heart, filled with gratitude that I hadn't just become puppy chow.

And then I realized my predicament. I was in a

dumpster with no pants.

I hoped that the angel who saved me wasn't Jake, or he'd never let me live this down. I was about to hop out when the back door of the restaurant opened.

"Yeah, okay!" some guy yelled right before a giant bag of trash walloped me over the head, shoving me deeper into the slimy mess of crap all around me. It took all my willpower not to make a sound, because I could not let anyone see me like this! I didn't know if I even wanted to know what was dripping down my hair and through the neck of my shirt.

The door closed and I peeked my head over the lip of the dumpster. When I was sure no one else was coming, I jumped out and quickly yanked my pants and shoes on. I groaned looking down at myself. I was covered in spaghetti sauce, chunks of pasta, and a bunch of other stuff I wasn't even sure about. My left pant leg was ripped. I tried my best to get all the garbage off of me, but the end result was a very sticky, stained, mortified David. Luckily, I'd driven myself to the restaurant, so I could possibly sneak around the building to my car and drive away before anyone saw me.

I shot Dad a quick text.

Me: Work emergency. I'll meet you back at home. Tell Elena sorry. 😑

Dad: it's Elena. where are you?? why did you run away?

are you okay???

Me: Why do you have Dad's phone?

Dad: dad texts like an old person and i got to it first

Me: I'm fine. Tell him I got called in to work.

Dad: called in? like you're a doctor or something?? you work at chucky cheese!

Me: I just don't want him to freak out like you are! Chill!

At that point she called me. I rolled my eyes and answered. "Elena, I don't want you talking about this crap in front of dad or Rocco."

"I'm not by them, I stepped away. What is going on?" she demanded. "Did something happen again? Do you need help? Just because I don't want the danger around my kids doesn't mean I won't help! Are you hurt?"

"I'm fine, I promise," I said. "There's just a lot of stuff going on and I don't want to drag anyone into it."

"Do we need to call you an exorcist or something? Seriously, I'm worried about you!"

I snorted. "No, I do not need an exorcist. They're useless without the help of angels and take all the credit. Super annoying."

"I'm serious!" she whisper-yelled.

I sighed. "What do you want me to tell you? Yeah, I'm in danger, but I've got some help from the other side, so I'll be okay. I'm not hurt, I promise. Just don't say anything to Dad. He doesn't want to know what's going on and, frankly, I'm not sure he could handle it. I've already told you way too much. Stop pressing me, all right? Just chill and eat your meatballs."

I hung up, which probably infuriated her, but our conversation was getting nowhere. I furtively peeked around the corner of the building and located my car. I glanced around, ready to book it before anyone saw me, when an old lady leaving the restaurant noticed me and started walking my way. She had wispy white hair, bifocals so thick I honestly didn't know where her eyes were and carried a tiny little wallet purse in front of her with both hands.

Crap.

I tried to pretend I hadn't seen her, but she kept shuffling toward me until she was standing right in front of me.

"Um, hi," I said.

She took my hand, put some money in it, then closed my fingers over it, patting my hand kindly. "You're too young to have fallen on such hard times. I hope this helps you get yourself back on your feet again."

"Oh, no, no!" I said quickly. "I'm not—"

"It's all right, deary. Let that be the start to a whole new life for you!" Then she shuffled away.

I had just been mistaken for a homeless person. Wonderful.

I opened my hand to see how much money she'd given me. It was two dollars. The way she was going on, I thought it would be enough to at least buy a sandwich.

Not the point! Get out of here!

I shoved the money in my pocket and tried to force myself not to run through the parking lot. Looking around myself, I unlocked Mom's car and scrambled inside, hoping nobody had seen me. I tried to keep my back and head from touching the seat. At least my pants weren't covered in garbage soup. Because, you know, I literally took them off in an alleyway behind a restaurant. That's a totally normal thing to do.

I leaned my forehead on the steering wheel and sighed loudly. Hopefully Sheila was long gone by now, because I did not want to find out what it was like to drive with a demon in the car. I had a moment of regret thinking about my time undercover with Sheila when we terrorized kids at a haunted house. Sheila was having the time of her life, and I was almost having fun too. Now that I knew what it was like to be on the mortal side of that equation, I felt horrible at the nightmares I probably caused those kids. At least I wasn't trying to actually hurt them though. I was starting to think Sheila was legit trying to kill me.

"I know it's kinda against the rules," I whispered, "but if someone's there, can you give me a sign? I'm just a little freaked out right now and I'm afraid to start the car."

I sighed again when nothing happened.

Hand shaking, I shoved the keys in the ignition and started the car, jumping at the rumble of the engine. The first song that came on was one I had definitely not been listening to when I was driving to the restaurant and didn't remember ever adding to my music. All on its own, the song skipped forward to the chorus, where the singer was crooning, *"dry your eyes, mate."*

I started laughing, more than a little embarrassed by my audience, but comforted I wasn't alone.

"Thanks, Jake," I smiled. And then I talked to him the whole drive home, the way Dad used to talk to me. I felt good, and it was comforting to know that Dad must have felt the same way.

chapter 17
SECRET MISSION

I stood in front of the shower for a full five minutes before I got up the courage to get inside. I needed to really scrub to get all the garbage stink off me, but I had been avoiding long showers since the bathroom incident. After what happened outside the restaurant, I was extra jumpy and more than a little shaky. It was embarrassingly childish, but I couldn't stop myself from saying, "Uh, Jake, if you're still here . . . do you mind sticking around in the bathroom? I'll take my clothes off in the shower and throw a towel on before I come out."

My face heated in mortification. A guy in his twenties afraid of the shower . . . And yet, I was too much of a coward not to ask for a bodyguard.

After cleaning up, I went to my room and sat at the edge of my bed, too keyed up to just sit there, but unsure what to do. Eventually I jumped to my feet and grabbed my keys. I didn't want to be alone, and there was only one living person who I could actually talk to about all of this. I shot Sandra a quick text and jumped back in the car.

She opened the door before I even knocked. I was waiting for her to lecture me on how I need to be more careful, but she just hugged me.

"Thanks," I said, quietly.

"Jake was here," she said, still not letting go. "He wanted me to tell you that he has a meeting with the defenders and your mom's working the front desk, but they're pretty sure no one's going to attack you while you're here. Your demon seems to like attacking you unseen, and with me she can't do that. But he said if you need anyone, just call for help and Hermes will send someone."

I nodded and pulled away, afraid to admit aloud how scared I was.

Sandra took my hand and pulled me behind her. "Come on, I made some cookies and they're actually edible this time."

"Oh good," I said, "Because the last time you said that you tried to feed me rocks and I chipped a tooth."

"Shut up."

We watched *Parks and Recreation* and ate her edible cookies, and even though I had no need to see ghosts, I took Sandra's hand and held it the whole time. She glanced at me with an unreadable look, but she didn't pull away, so I assumed she was okay with it. It was just nice knowing she was there, and especially after being dead for so long, physical touch can be a really comforting thing.

Eventually we were interrupted by Asher and Oliver messing around with Sandra's Roku. They kept switching it over to Disney Plus, which I just realized she probably only paid for so those two child wanderers could watch it. I mean, I'll watch Disney movies without the excuse of having kids around, but all I ever saw Sandra watch were rom coms, intense dramas, and boring documentaries. Disney Plus obviously wasn't for her. I quirked a smile at her, thinking about how sweet she was. She smiled back and raised a questioning eyebrow.

We were interrupted by Bill standing in front of us in the middle of the coffee table just staring at us. When you're a baby and you need attention, you cry. Apparently, when you're a wanderer, you stare creepily.

"Hey Bill," I said, tearing my eyes away from Sandra. "What's up?"

Bill shrugged his shoulders.

"Do you need something?" Sandra asked.

Bill shrugged and pointed to the top of his wrist, like he had a watch there.

"I'm not sure what you're asking," I said.

Bill glared at the ceiling, then started doing his white guy arm dancing before pointing to his wrist again.

"Oh, are you wondering when we're gonna go on our secret mission?" I asked.

He nodded.

I looked over at Sandra. Then she said, "I don't have any plans tonight. And there's no school tomorrow."

I frowned, considering. "All right, let's do it."

We found the club Bill was talking about online and got ourselves onto the guest list, then we had a quick meeting on what to do and what to look for.

"Me and Sandra will be moving around a lot, trying to look like we're dancing and having fun," I told Bill and Gilbert. "You guys can snoop around and guide us to places we can listen in on demon conversations happening. But, also, like, let us know if any particular demon shows up that we're trying to avoid."

"It won't be a problem," Sandra said. "I told you; she likes attacking you when you're alone and can't see her."

"How do you know?" I asked.

She folded her arms. "I haven't seen her since that time she possessed me when you were still dead. Trust me. She hasn't shown up near me since then. She doesn't want you to see her."

That comforted me a little.

"I'm gonna go get ready," Sandra said suddenly. "It's already late and I'm wearing sweats."

She ran to her room, and I sat watching some anime show with who I assumed was Ash and Oliver until Sandra came out of her room. She looked amazing. She did something to her hair to make it bigger and curlier. She had glossy maroon lipstick on and silver hoop earrings. She wore a tight blue crop top, black high-waisted pants, and chunky heels.

I looked down at myself feeling like I should have worn something nicer. Back when I was living with Sandra, she'd bought me a bunch of clothes in all different styles because she didn't know what I liked. I didn't know either. I hadn't picked out clothes for myself in eleven years. Even when I was undercover as a demon hunter, Jake put my whole outfit together. I'd never had an eye for that kind of thing, which is why in high school I just wore the same thing every day: a T-shirt, jeans, and my old Vans.

I was currently wearing one of the sportier outfits she put together for me: a gray hoodie, stretchy black sweats that were tight and baggy at the same time, and white high top athletic sneakers that were way too cool for me and I honestly had no business wearing.

"Well, I feel underdressed now," I said.

Sandra flashed a smile, "That's okay. Unlike with peacocks, the lady is supposed to be the fancy one. You ready?"

"I guess."

Sandra growled and rolled her eyes. "Why are you here?"

I blinked, shocked and a little hurt. "I mean, I can go if you want."

"I wasn't talking to you, David." She quickly grabbed my hand so I could be included. Her aunt Tamara had shown up, standing with her arms folded.

"I think this is a good idea, and David needs help. I'm not just gonna say no," Sandra said.

Her aunt shook her head. "This could be dangerous for you. You aren't a demon hunter. You shouldn't get involved. This is a job for angels who are trained in undercover work. What makes you think you two will do better?"

I felt uneasy and guilty that I was involving Sandra this way. Her aunt had a point. Also, she was Sandra's guardian angel, so for all we knew her orders were coming straight from Hermes.

"She's right, Sandra," I said quietly.

"Be quiet," she snapped. "Tamara, no. You don't have the right to tell me how to live my life. I thought I'd made it clear that I don't want you around."

Her aunt sighed. "You need to get over this grudge, girl. I am here to help you."

"I don't want help from you!"

After a deep breath, Tamara said, "Okay. You're free to do as you wish."

I suddenly felt nervous that she was going to tell on us. If Raj or Ying Yue found out we were doing our own secret mission, I knew they wouldn't be too thrilled.

"Um, you're not going to tell anyone, are you?" I asked

nervously.

Tamara looked at me for a long time. "No. I'm not in charge of you. Though I think you should know better than to lie to your team."

And then she disappeared.

I looked at Sandra. "What's up with you and your aunt? You act like you hate her."

She let go of my hand to angrily press her hands to her temples, then smooth her hair back. "I don't hate her, but I don't like her, and she has no right to tell me what to do after what she did to me and my mom."

I waited a beat, then cautiously asked, "What did she do?"

Sandra's eyes snapped to me. "She's the one my dad cheated on my mom with. She's the one who ruined my mom's life and sent her on a downward spiral."

"Whoa, your dad cheated on your mom with your aunt?"

Sandra gritted her teeth. "Yes. I have cousins who are also half-siblings. And we're done talking about this now." She pulled her keys from her clutch purse and stomped toward the door, her heels clomping loud enough to disturb the neighbors below her.

The car ride was pulsing with tension. I wanted to ask her more about the family drama she just spilled on me, but I could tell she didn't want to talk about it. Being Sandra's friend, I was definitely on her side, but having been a guardian angel, I felt a little bad for her aunt. Sandra didn't make it very easy for her to do her job. If she was an angel, it meant she was trying to be better and fix her mistakes. Angels aren't perfect, but they do have to have good intentions.

"You ready?" Sandra asked quietly when we got there.

I blinked out of my thoughts. "Yeah, sure."

The first ten minutes or so were a whirlwind of me not knowing what to do and how things were supposed to go. The word NIGHTLIFE was emblazoned in pink and purple neon on a dark building with lights flashing through the windows to the beat of the music. I could feel the base pulsing beneath my feet as we walked to the doors. A large man checked some kind of list, asked for IDs, then stamped our hands when we got there. I fumbled and dropped my driver's license as I tried to shove it back into my wallet. Sandra pulled me aside before I could get trampled by a stampede of people. I was suffering from sensory overload from the flashing lights and the music that literally shook the ground. Before I could adjust, Sandra took my hand and towed me into the mob of people jumping and dancing in the smoky, epileptic nightmare of flashing lights. What were these people even doing with their bodies? Was this how people danced? How did I replicate that? Did I even want to replicate that? I suddenly understood why someone might want to be drunk for this.

Sandra certainly had no problem moving with the music. She seemed to actually be enjoying herself, and she looked good dancing, which made me even more awkward. I sort of stood there, just barely bouncing to the beat. Some preppy dude wearing a blazer with shorts came up to Sandra and tried to grind on her which made me mad, so I pulled her away and started dancing more like I meant it. After the first song ended, she spotted something ahead and pulled me to the edge of the dance floor. Now that she was holding my hand, I could see her destination. Three slightly translucent people stood at the edge of the dance floor laughing and arguing loudly.

"Stop looking at them!" Sandra said in my ear.

I nodded. Good spies don't look like they're spying. Unfortunately, they were right by the speakers, so it was hard to tell what they were saying. I only caught bits and pieces.

". . . think he will get to the president?"

"No chance . . . hate Malum . . . not as scary as he thinks he is . . ."

". . . wouldn't let him hear you say that. I've been to the Hurricane. It's no joke."

". . . supposed to be for angels. . ."

". . . catch any?"

". . . last week. . . two, I think. . ."

". . . bored. Let's go."

They disappeared then to go tempt some dancing mortals. I didn't quite understand their conversation, but I had an idea and it made me want to go home and hide under the covers. Unfortunately, one of the demons chose Sandra and I to relieve his boredom. He floated around my head, telling me to grab Sandra, pull her close to my body, touch her, kiss her, pull her to a back room and seize the moment. What did it matter that we were friends? She was beautiful and right in front of me. She'd want it too, wouldn't she?

I shook my head and let go of Sandra's hand, hoping that it would be easier to ignore the demon if I couldn't see or hear him. It wasn't any better. He continued whispering in my ear until I felt like his words were my own thoughts. I felt like we should get some drinks. Maybe this party would be more fun if we were drunk. Then maybe this stupid demon would leave me alone.

I shook my head. That was the demon too. He wanted us drunk, so we'd be easier to manipulate. But we needed to stay sober so we could keep our heads and spy. I was sure Sandra could hear everything the demon was telling me to do, so I was surprised she didn't pull us away to go dance somewhere else. When I looked at her questioningly, she just raised an eyebrow and I frowned. Was this a test? Was she seeing if I could resist the demon on my own? I scowled and pulled us deeper into the dancing. The demon reappeared and was now laughing and clapping.

"Yeah! Show her who's boss!"

I growled and ignored him, wondering why he was so focused on me and not Sandra. Then I realized he was whispering in her ear too. "You guys need a drink. This guy is so stiff. He needs to loosen up. Go get yourselves a drink."

Sandra frowned, then nodded behind me. I turned around and saw a few more demons congregating around a table. We made our way toward the outskirts of the dancing so we could listen in on their conversation. Unfortunately, our annoying demon followed us.

"These guys aren't listening," the guy told his buddies around the table. "Maybe they need more encouragement?"

The other five demons laughed and all floated around our heads, urging us in all different ways to go get a drink. They somehow knew we wanted to stay sober tonight, and I worried they knew the reasons. Did they know we were trying to spy on them? Did they know we could hear them? It got so distracting that at one point I leaned in and whispered to Sandra, "Maybe we should just do it. Then maybe they'd leave us alone."

Sandra shook her head, then whispered back, "They're targeting us. That doesn't mean we should do what they say. If we were just having fun, I wouldn't see any harm in a drink or two, but—"

I nodded and said, "We're on a mission and we need to stay focused. Right."

I was embarrassed she had to remind me of our purpose here. It was just so hard to concentrate with all of them swirling around our heads, shouting at us and laughing. I considered letting go of Sandra's hand, but I was worried I'd be more tempted to do what they said if I couldn't see that the idea came from the demons and not myself. They continued alternating between whispering and yelling at me and Sandra.

"Come on, kid! Just one drink!"

"Look at that body. . ."

"You worthless piece of. . ."

"Idiot!"

". . . be a man for once, you piece of. . ."

"No one cares about you. Might as well live it up."

"Take control for once in your useless life!"

I let go of Sandra and threw my hands over my ears, squeezing my eyes shut. This wasn't as bad as Malum or Sheila tormenting me. They knew me personally and understood exactly how to hurt me. These demons were strangers, and their words were just general things they'd tell anyone they chose to torment. That didn't make it any easier to ignore.

Sandra yanked on my hand to get my attention. I opened my eyes, and she was pointing upward where the demons had been circling our heads. They were gone.

"Look," she said, pointing behind me.

There were Bill and Gilbert, looking stunned. Bill was looking down at his hand as though it had just caught fire. He looked at us and the demons who had just scattered like bowling pins.

One of the demons bared his teeth. "There's an *angel* here."

Six demons converged on Bill, who disappeared just in time, leaving Gilbert behind looking shocked and confused. He quickly adjusted his expression to look vacant like a wanderer. The demons threw Darkness at him, but it had no effect whatsoever. I guess that's the plus of being a wanderer. If you hide deep enough in your own mind, no one can touch you. Eventually the disappointed demons swore and left him alone to go seek out someone else to torment.

Sandra and I looked at each other.

"What just happened?" she asked, bewildered.

"Let's get out of here," I said. "We'll talk in the car."

"But why did they think Bill was an angel?" Sandra asked as we were driving home.

"I know that expression. He just made Light for the first time. That's why the demons scattered. He threw Light at them."

"So, is he an angel now?"

"I don't know," I murmured, lost in my own thoughts.

My definitions of angel, demon, and wanderer were getting all tangled up and confused. Angels were creatures of Light. Demons were creatures of Darkness. Yet, as a demon hunter, I learned that angels could make both. Could demons? Could a wanderer? If the ability to make Darkness didn't necessarily make someone a demon, could it be true that anyone could make Light? I doubted a demon could make Light, because it required faith and good intentions, and demons, by definition, had evil intentions. But what really counted as an angel anyway? Someone who lived in The Resting Place? What if someone had faith and good intentions, but just didn't want to go there? Could they have access to Light?

And Bill . . . he was a confusing one. I didn't learn how to make Light until I had been in The Resting Place for some time, and he'd never even been there before. Usually, a rescuer angel's goal is to get wanderers to cross over, *then* they can learn how to be an angel. Bill was learning how to be an angel *before* crossing over. Also, most wanderers didn't talk until after they crossed over.

All of that was overshadowed when I came to a sudden realization. I gasped, and hit the dashboard, finally taking in what one of the demons had said.

Sandra jumped and hit my arm. "Oh my gosh, what is wrong with you? Don't do that!"

I covered my face with my hands. "We need to have a demon hunter meeting *right* now."

chapter 18
KEEPING SECRETS

I asked Hermes to send Raj my way, and once he was available, he rounded up the demon hunters. Usually, we only had meetings when Raj and Ying Yue held them, but sometimes members of the task force could call for one if they had important enough information. Luckily everyone was available right now.

"Um, when were you guys gonna tell me that angels are already being captured?" I demanded, as soon as everyone had arrived at Sandra's house.

They all looked nervously at each other.

"We didn't want to worry you," Raj said. "You've had a lot on your plate."

"I told you he deserved the truth," Ying Yue said through clenched teeth.

"Yeah!" I said. "If we really are a team, you guys can't keep things from me. We just talked about this, Raj! You said you wanted to keep me on the team because I gave valuable feedback and ideas. How can I even do that if you don't tell me everything that's going on?"

Raj shook his head and held his hands up. "Try to remember what it was like to be an angel, kid. Our job is to protect mortals and keep them safe. We're the silent spectators to all their hardships and struggles, and I know things haven't been easy for you. I'm sorry if my mindset has shifted toward you since you've become mortal, but I feel a greater need to protect you than I did before. I'm sorry. I should have told you what was going on, I just didn't want to add to your burdens."

I blinked and gulped uncomfortably. That was certainly not what I expected him to say. I just yelled at him only for him to tell me that he cares about me and wants to protect me.

"It wasn't just him, mate," Jake said. "Those first few weeks you were pretty pathetic. I don't think you could have handled the stress of all that was going on. No offense."

I frowned at Jake. "Thanks."

He shrugged, unphased. If you ever want an unabashed truth storm, look no farther than Jake Williams.

"So how many angels have they captured?" I asked. "The demons we heard mentioned two. I think they were recent. They said something about last week."

Everyone winced.

"Those would be new ones then," Ying Yue said. "The

last capture we heard about was three weeks ago."

"How many?" I repeated.

"It hasn't been many," Raj said. "Four angels, including the two you heard about. We don't know much about how he's doing it or where he's taking them, because he only does it when no one else is looking. The only reason we know some have been captured is that they've disappeared. Even Hermes can't find them."

"You don't know anything about the angels he took?" I asked quietly.

"I knew one of them," Daisy said. "She trained me to be an usher."

I raised my eyebrows. "You're an usher?" Generally ushers have a very calming presence, like Ted, who are good at bringing frightened souls to the other side. Daisy didn't necessarily strike me as calm. Her default expression was a scowl.

Daisy floated up in my face. "You don't think I can be a good usher?"

I held my hands up and shrunk into the back of my chair. "I'm sure you're wonderful."

"Focus up," Ying Yue said. "Tell us about what you heard and how you heard it." She glared at Daisy until she reluctantly returned to her seat.

I hesitated. I didn't want to tell them about our secret mission, but not telling them was gnawing at me from the inside. So, I told them all about my idea and how we'd involved Bill and Gilbert and the nightclub we went to. I even told them about what happened with Bill making Light.

Raj and Ying Yue weren't happy with me for doing all of this behind their backs. Apparently, I should have run it by them, and had an angel on stand-by just in case, and blah blah blah. I wanted to roll my eyes, but they were right. We didn't accomplish much, and in the end, we were targeted by a bunch of demons to the point that a wanderer had to come to our rescue.

"It might have been worse if they knew who you were," Natalie pointed out. "You're kind of famous among the demons."

That wasn't comforting. "What about Bill?" I asked. "He made Light. Have you ever seen a wanderer do that?"

I looked around the circle and everyone shook their heads.

"It's strange," Ted said. "I worked as a rescuer for a while before I was an usher, and you don't usually see wanderers progress until they decide to cross over. Bill's progressing as an angel without being trained. He probably doesn't know what he's doing."

"Can we talk to him?" Jake asked. "Maybe he can join the team."

I looked to Sandra for advice. These wanderers always seemed like a part of *her* team, and she was very protective of them. "If he wants to talk, he's free to talk," she said.

"Just don't push him, please."

We turned around to where Bill and Gilbert were hiding behind a fake tree like creepers.

"Hey, Bill?" I said. "Can you join us for a sec?"

He looked behind his shoulder and pointed to himself.

"No, the other guy named Bill lurking in the corner." I smiled encouragingly and waved him over. "Gilbert, you can come too."

Gilbert shook his head, content to stay where he was. Tentatively, Bill crept closer, nervously looking down at his hands.

"Hello, Bill," Raj said. "How are you?"

Bill made a face like he couldn't understand the question. Likely he didn't get asked that very often. Raj moved on.

"We noticed you listening and heard that you've been helping David. Would you be interested in joining the demon hunters?"

Bill understood that question and shook his head vigorously.

"That's all right. Is there any information you would like to share with us?"

Bill opened his mouth, then cringed and shook his head.

"He doesn't talk much," I said. "It's hard for him."

"Could you tell us a little about yourself?" Ying Yue asked.

For a second Bill lost his far-off look as though fully lucid for the first time in a long time. It was followed by him clutching his head and shaking. "No!" he moaned. A look of agony scrunched up his face. Then slowly his face smoothed out, his mouth fell open, and his eyes glazed over.

"What the heck was that?" Jake asked.

"He was remembering," Frederick said quietly. "He has memories he cannot confront. That is why he has reverted to this absent state of wandering."

I really felt for the guy right then. I hardly knew him, but from what I'd seen, he seemed like a really nice guy. I wondered what horrors he went through before he died that made him want to forget everything.

"Hey, Bill," I said gently.

He blinked and looked absently in my direction.

"That night club might not have worked out very well for us. Did you find any other places for me and Sandra to scout around? A place with demons we could spy on?"

He nodded, looking a little more like himself. He held his palm toward me, then mimed hammering a nail.

"I hammer?" I asked, confused.

Bill shook his head.

"Hit the nail on the head?" Natalie guessed.

"Construction work?" Ted asked.

Bill shook his head and tried some other hand movement, looking around the circle of angels.

"That's ASL," Daisy said. "He's asking if we sign."

"How do you know sign language?" Jake asked.

"My parents are deaf," she said.

Before any of us had the chance to ask her about that, she signed something back to Bill. He shook his head and made a "little bit" gesture with his thumb and index finger.

Daisy nodded. "I'm guessing he learned some in high school and forgot most of it, so he's using a combination of ASL and charades."

Bill nodded and smiled. Then he bit his lip, thinking hard. He nodded and held his palm out toward me. Then he uncertainly put his hands into fists and hit his wrists together a couple of times.

"David's work?" Daisy asked. "Are there a lot of demons at Chuck E. Cheese?" She snorted as she said this.

Bill smiled and nodded.

Raj looked back and forth between Bill and Daisy, a slight smile on his face. "How about this? Bill, why don't you and Daisy scope around there and report back to us?"

I wondered why he wanted Bill to go with Daisy. Daisy didn't need Bill to scout around. Maybe because Bill already had some background information on some of the demons there. Or maybe Raj was hoping that being around Daisy would help Bill to open up more.

Bill backed away and shook his head. He quickly signed something to Daisy.

"He doesn't want that," Daisy said. She turned back to

him. "You don't have to join the demon hunters. We'll leave you alone. But will you go with me to David's work to show me what you were talking about?"

He nodded.

"Thank you, Bill," Raj said.

Bill tipped an imaginary hat and disappeared.

Bill and Daisy shadowed me at work the next day. I couldn't see them, but they told me they'd be there. I hoped their presence meant my mom and Jake could get some time off of guard duty for a little bit.

"David!" Piper was just leaving when I arrived at work. She ran up and hugged me.

"Hey, how was the party last night?" I asked.

"Ugh, it sucked," she said, and skipped out the door without saying bye. That's all you need to know to get an idea of Piper. She loves everyone and has the attention span of a butterfly.

There was a birthday party in full swing and the Chuck E. costume was out. I was pretty sure Joanna was in there. It was confirmed when she motioned me closer to her and whispered, "I will slit your throat."

I took a few steps back and put a hand to my chest with a horrified look. We stared at each other for a long time with some pop song blaring in the background. I bit my lip, trying not to laugh but all I could see was Chuck E. staring at me. I broke first. I snorted and I heard her giggling inside.

"I won!" she said.

"This time," I said, walking away. "Next time I will defeat you! Hey, Jorge, how's it going?"

Jorge was at the cash register today and grunted a greeting. That was the most I'd ever gotten out of him. I was mainly on cleaning duty today, so I made my way down the back hallway to the cleaning closet. I double-checked the schedule on the door. Bathrooms first. I grabbed the mop bucket and rolling cart of assorted bathroom cleaning products. As I was rolling it all down the hallway, I heard the manager, Preston, having a conversation with someone in his office. It sounded like Tala, another one of my coworkers around Piper's age.

"I was just wondering if I could have tomorrow night off?"

"Why? Are you finally gonna go get those eyebrows waxed?"

There was silence for a moment, and I could picture Tala's bottom lip quivering, trying not to cry. "It's for my grandma's birthday party." She ran out of the office in tears, her hands over her eyebrows. I started to go after her, but she ran straight into the girl's bathroom. I stood there fuming in the hallway when Preston came to his door to shut it.

"What are you looking at, four-eyes?" he snapped at me.

"Four eyes?" I said, arching an eyebrow. "What, are you getting your insults from kids TV shows?"

He cussed me out and slammed his door.

Here's the thing. I'm very much a keep-your-head-down-and-don't-cause-trouble kind of guy. I don't like confrontation, and I don't like hurting people's feelings. But even a nice person will lash out when enough buttons get pushed. Preston pushed *all* of my buttons, and every interaction we had I couldn't help but throw insults back at him and make everything worse. It wasn't a problem I usually had, so I didn't really know how to deal with it.

Fuming, I set to work cleaning the boy's bathroom with a vengeance, until it was squeaky clean. Then I knocked on the girl's bathroom. "Is anyone in there?"

"Yes . . ." Tala croaked.

I paused, not sure what to do. "Can I come in?"

"Okay."

She was standing by the paper towels, blotting at her eyes. "Do you think I have a unibrow?"

She did kind of have a unibrow, but I obviously wasn't going to say that. "Just ignore Preston. He's a jerk."

"Am I ugly?"

I didn't know Tala very well, but my big brother instincts urged me to hug her, so I did. She cried on my shoulder, and it broke my heart. "You are not ugly. And Preston's opinion doesn't matter because he doesn't care about you. Think about the people that care about you.

Would they call you ugly?"

"No," she said, her voice muffled in my shirt.

"Well, there you go. Theirs is the only opinion that matters."

Tala nodded and let go, grabbing a few more paper towels to dab her eyes. "Thanks, David."

"Anytime," I said. "You gonna be okay?"

She nodded and walked out of the bathroom with her shoulders slumped.

Freaking Preston.

Later, after fishing a diaper out of the ball pit, I heard him call Jorge "fatty" again. Except this time, he called him, "*el fat-o*," which was not only racist, but also incorrect. Fat in Spanish is *gordo*. Duh. And so what if Jorge had a little bit of a belly? He was a big dude. It only made sense for him to have a *pansa* to go with it. Nothing wrong with that.

Growling, I spun around and said, "He has a name. Do you literally not know the names of your employees, or do you just enjoy insulting everyone?"

"Of course I know everyone's names," Preston said, pointing to the employees he saw as he called them out, starting with me and Jorge. "Fatty, Four Eyes, Asian Chick, Hottie, Unibrow. Oh, and Mole Face is over there."

I stepped forward wanting to deck that stupid smirk off his face, but the fact that I was holding a used diaper reminded me I was at a kid's party place, and I probably shouldn't be fighting. Also, I didn't know how to fight, so I'd just end up getting beat up. Now if I were an angel and he was a demon, that would be a different story. I was the inventor of the demon killer bullet. I could definitely do some damage.

"Hey!"

I looked down and a kid next to me was doing the pee-pee dance.

"Where's the bathroom?" he asked.

"Just down the hall," I said, gesturing with the diaper. *I really should throw that away.*

By the end of the day, I was exhausted. Not from working. I actually didn't mind my job, as lame as it was, and I really liked my coworkers. I was exhausted from holding myself back from attacking Preston's stupid face. His sexist, racist comments only got more derogatory throughout the day. As I put the cleaning supplies away, I stood staring at the duct tape on the shelf, daydreaming of slapping some of it over his mouth and taping him to his chair. It made me feel a little better, in a sadistic sort of way.

I worked until closing that day, cleaning and working the ticket booth. It took some pointed hints to get the last of the kids and their parents out of there, but eventually everyone left. I locked up and headed for the Dairy Queen across the street where I was meeting with Daisy and Bill to discuss what they found. Our translator, Sandra, was already there when I walked through the doors. The first thing she said when I sat down next to her was, "What happened to your head?"

"What are you talking about? Nothing happened to my head."

She gestured to my forehead. "What's with the band-aid?"

I felt my forehead and, indeed, found a band-aid. "Yeesh!" I flung it away from me and shook out my arms and legs. "That wasn't mine."

"Then how did—"

"I had to fish a diaper out of the ball pit today. I fell in a few times. It must have gotten stuck to me then. That pit is a cesspool . . ."

Sandra grimaced and scooted away from me, which made me feel disgusting. I was very aware of my lame polo shirt tucked into my black pants.

"So, have Daisy and Bill shown up yet?" I asked, changing the subject.

Sandra grabbed my hand and Bill and Daisy appeared across from us.

"Hey, how'd it go today?" I asked.

"So, two things about your boss," Daisy said without preamble. "One, he's got a LOT of demons. They hang around him all day tempting him and telling him he's worthless. Even after Bill and I cast them out, they just came back with more and ganged up on us until we had to leave. So, there's that."

"Why does he have so many demons?" I asked. *Maybe because he's a piece of crap who's asking for it.*

She shrugged. "Demons don't like hard work, and Preston's really weak right now. They gang up on him because he's easy prey."

"Easy prey? The guy's a jerk! He makes people cry!"

"He is a jerk. I hate him and I don't even know him. But that's not the point. Speaking of crying, that was the second thing I was gonna say about him. He cries in his office."

I frowned. "We all thought when he was in there with the door locked, he was watching porn."

"Maybe that's been true before, but today he was crying like a little baby."

"Why?" I asked. "What's the matter?"

She shrugged. "How should I know? I've only followed him around for one afternoon."

Bill signed something to her.

"Really?" she asked.

He nodded.

"Well apparently Bill's followed him around a lot. He came to work with you once and was curious about Preston, so he followed him home a few times."

"What do you know about him?" I asked Bill.

He and Daisy signed back and forth. It took a while

because Bill clearly didn't know how to sign everything he was trying to say and often had to improvise. I had no idea what they were saying, but at one point I think Daisy did the sign for "sad."

Eventually Daisy turned back to me. "He says you should ask Preston yourself."

Bill gaped and held his hands up.

I gave Daisy a wry look. "He did not say that."

"Okay, fine, I'm saying that. The guy's an a-hole, but he's an a-hole that's falling apart and he needs some help. You don't get to be a behind-the-scenes guardian angel anymore, David. You get to be an in-person one. So, stop whining about everything and go do your job."

With that she took Bill's arm and they disappeared.

"Well, that was harsh," Sandra muttered.

"No," I said, sitting there blinking. There are times in life when you need a good kick in the pants, and Daisy was the only one I knew that was direct enough to tell me exactly what I needed to hear. "Daisy's right. My job is to help people, not make their lives harder. As disgusting as the idea is, I need to befriend Preston." I shivered with the heebie jeebies and resisted gagging.

chapter 19
DON'T GO IN THERE

My dad was watching all the grandkids the next day for a huge, chaotic sleepover. I wasn't sure if both Elena and Sam had plans, or if Dad just offered to take them for the night. The kids were like a tornado from the second they walked in the door. I had to listen to it all from my room until Sam left. Little David was screaming for his "foopy," whatever that was, and Gloria was laughing really loudly at how upset he was, which I thought was hilarious. Her baby laugh sounded like a banshee.

"Come on, David!" I heard Ginger say. I had to remind myself she wasn't talking to me. "Let's go look at the pit in the backyard!"

"No going in the backyard!" Elena said. "It's under construction. Dad, when are you gonna fill in that swimming pool?"

"One of these days," Dad said evasively. "Hey, hey! No pulling hair."

One of the kids screamed and started crying. Baby Gloria continued laughing.

"Good luck, Dad," Sam said with a chuckle. "Let us know if you need a break."

"Hey, Rocco and Ginny. Look at me," Charlie said. "You be good, okay? Listen to your grandpa."

"You sure you're okay doing this?" Elena asked. "It's gonna be like this the whole time."

"I'll have some help," he hinted quietly.

"Is someone coming over?" Sam asked.

Dad cleared his throat. "I meant the help of this."

Ginny screamed with delight, and I wondered what toy or treat he'd brought out for bribery.

Eventually the front door shut, and I heard Dad whisper, "Go get him!"

Little feet slapped down the hallway to my room and a bunch of children tumbled through the door. I was tackled by Ginny and Rocco and literally fell on my back. Ginny squeezed the life out of me, and Rocco smothered my face with his Pull-Up clad bum and bounced. I was laughing and wheezing at the same time.

"All right, that's enough," Dad said in the doorway. "Let Uncle David breathe."

Ginny crawled off me, but Rocco had to do one last bounce on my face before laughing and screaming down the hallway.

"I'm gonna get you!" I grinned. Ginny, Rocco, and

Little David screamed, and we ran around the house until I bumped into a vase Elena once made in pottery class. It teetered precariously back and forth, and before I could catch it, it hit the ground and shattered.

"Crap," I said.

"David said a bad word!" Ginny announced.

"Everything okay in there?" Dad called from the other room.

"Shh!" I said to the kids, holding my finger to my lips. "Don't tell Grandpa. It's a secret."

Little David giggled and copied me. "Sssss! See-kwet!"

I sent them into the other room while I covertly cleaned up the mess before Dad saw. When it was time for dinner, Dad plopped Baby Gloria in front of me on the ground so he could whip up some Mac n' Cheese. She just sat there and stared at me. Was she seriously old enough to be sitting up? When did that happen?

"Hi there," I smiled.

"Ah bah!" she said.

"Your cousins are crazy, you know that?"

She blew a raspberry and smacked the ground.

I picked her up and almost cried. I'd wanted to hold Baby Gloria since she was born, but I was either too dead, or too busy pretending to be dead to do so. She was so chubby! I gave her a squeeze and closed my eyes, smushing her head to my cheek. She smelled like formula and that smell that is just specifically "baby." Then she smacked my face and grabbed my glasses. I wrestled them out of her grip and shoved them in my back pocket.

Ginny ran into the room and grabbed my shirt, pulling me into Elena's old room to hide from the boys. I guessed I didn't count as a boy, and I wasn't sure if I should be offended by that. We played with Elena's old Barbie dolls, and Ginny did my hair with old barrettes and clips, which Gloria liked to pull out with big chunks of my hair and laugh at me. It was a weirdly enjoyable abuse.

"Food's ready!" Dad called.

The girls and I went to go join the boys for dinner and Dad held his arms out to take Gloria from me.

"Mine," I said, holding her closer. "I want her."

"Well, if you need a break—"

"Nope. I've only just met her, and I don't know when I'll see her again. She's mine."

Dad shrugged and I spun Gloria around before giving her a squeeze.

I kept true to my word and held her until she squirmed away. Even then, Gloria got a lot more of my attention than the other grandkids that night, which maybe wasn't fair, but the kids were having so much fun playing with Grandpa that they didn't mind.

I let Dad take her eventually so I could go shower and get ready for bed. I had my phone blasting some music while I was in the shower, which made my cowardly self less scared of the bathroom but used up almost all of the battery. I was in the middle of brushing my teeth when I got a text from Piper.

Piper: david hey!!! 😁 so srry to bug u!!! but u said to text u when the d bag says something earlier he said i yap like a pomeranian when i talk and now evry time I try to say something to him he just barks at me and laughs and its rlly rude! 😨 😠

Me: You don't sound like a Pomeranian. If he's gonna be a d-bag every time you talk to him, just avoid him. When I get in tomorrow I can yell at him for you.

Piper: thx, david! your so sweet 😊 but srsly, I dont know—

My phone decided to die right in the middle of reading Piper's text.

"Shoot!" I muttered. What a crappy time for my phone to die. Piper was really sensitive, and I knew if I didn't respond right away, she'd be offended. I quickly threw on my sweats and booked it for the kitchen, where I was pretty sure I'd last seen my charger. As I was hurrying down the hallway, toweling the remaining dampness from my hair, I got this really weird feeling that I shouldn't go in the kitchen. I brushed it off. What bad could come from going out to get my charger? Was it going to electrocute me?

I paused for a minute. *Could Sheila do that?*

I shook my head. She wouldn't attack me with all the kids around. She only came after me when I was alone. It was just a charger. What was I supposed to do? My phone was dead, and Piper was sitting there waiting for my response.

DO NOT GO IN THERE!

Was that Hermes? Nah, it was probably just my mind playing tricks on me. Why would Hermes tell me not to get my charger if it would allow me to help a friend in need?

The charger wasn't on the counter where I left it. It was likely moved out of the way when Dad made Mac n' Cheese.

"Hey, Dad, have you seen my charger?" I called.

"David?" someone gasped.

I spun around and froze. The kitchen was one of those open-concept kitchens, so it was open to the family room. Dad and the kids were gathered around his laptop on the couch, FaceTiming with their parents before bed. On the screen across the room, I could see Sam's slack-jawed face as he stared right at me.

My first reaction was to drop to the floor and crawl away. I was looking back to see if they could still see me, so of course I ran into a wall and rolled over like a cow that had been tipped.

Elena yelled, "We can still see you, dummy!"

"What's going on!" Sam demanded.

I jumped to my feet and sprinted away clutching my head. It didn't matter though, he'd already seen me, and I had to be stupid enough to run away, making me look even more guilty. I couldn't imagine how I was going to fix this. This was all my fault. I'd ignored that first angel whisper, and I'd ignored Hermes. Had I seriously learned nothing?

chapter 20
OH SHIRT

My dad found me hiding in my room ten minutes later. I was sitting on my bed with my arms around my knees while my brain chased itself in panicked loops.

"The kids are all watching a movie in sleeping bags," he said. "What are we going to do about Sam?"

"I don't know," I said in a strangled whisper. "He wasn't supposed to know."

Dad sat down next to me on my bed. "Is it that big a deal? Maybe it's good that he knows you're alive. I'm glad that I know. Elena's glad. All the grandkids are glad."

"Dad, you don't understand," I said, my hands in my hair. "Sam wasn't supposed to know. I was told specifically he wasn't ready. The last time I did something I was told not to do, this happened!" I said, gesturing to myself.

"Well, we can't undo it now," Dad said. "When you ran away, I told him it was you."

"*Why would you do that?*"

"He'd already seen you. Trying to cover it up with another lie would have just made it worse."

I groaned and rubbed my face. "Why am I so stupid? Why didn't I listen? I felt like it was a bad idea to go in there and I did it anyway. What's wrong with me?"

He put his arm around my shoulders. "It's going to be all right. Just breathe. We'll figure it out."

There was a bang and we both jumped.

"Was that the front door?" Dad asked.

Feet stomped down the hallway and suddenly my bedroom door slammed open. And there was Sam. Huffing and puffing and looking like he was about to blow the house down. The part of me that wasn't terrified was blown away by how happy I was to see him. The fear of seeing him again had distracted me from the fact that I'd missed my brother more than I wanted to admit. My heart was pounding with both fear and excitement.

"You're alive?" he demanded. His face was contorted to the point that I wasn't even sure what emotion it was showing. Probably a combination of them all?

Jessica ran after him. "Sam, what's going on?"

"Where have you been?" he yelled, spraying a little bit of spit.

I stood up. "It's hard to explain. I'm sorry for not telling you, but it's complicated."

He stared at me and his eyes watered. He took a step

closer, and I started to hold out my arms, thinking he was going for a hug. But then I saw the look on his face and ducked just in time to avoid getting punched in the face.

"I can't believe that worked," I said when I came back up. After getting hurt so much since being alive again, it was a nice victory. And then Sam tackled me. We landed on my bed, which was nice, but then rolled off and hit the ground pretty hard.

"You selfish piece of shit!" Sam yelled as he rolled over on top of me. "Do you have any idea what that did to us when you left?"

"It wasn't my choice," I panted, trying to squirm out of his grip. "I didn't want to leave!"

I kicked against the wall, shoved him over and pinned his hands to the ground.

"Does Elena know you're alive?" he spat as he tried to wriggle free.

"Yes," I said, "And *she* didn't attack me when I told her, you psycho!"

"What about Mom?" he growled as we rolled and hit the wall. "Did she know you were alive all this time? Or did she die before you got the chance to tell her?"

"I wasn't alive all this time! I really died."

Sam stood up, yanked me to my feet by my shirt, and slammed me against the wall. "You are so full of—"

Suddenly Charlie was there, ripping me and Sam apart. I guessed he and Elena booked it over here right after that

FaceTime call, knowing Sam would freak out like this. Charlie shoved me at Dad while he restrained Sam.

"What is wrong with you two!" Charlie said.

Sam was red in the face, wriggling like crazy trying to escape Charlie's grip. "You all lied to me!"

"I wonder why?" Charlie retorted.

Elena's hands clenched into fists, and she stepped toward Sam. "You're missing the point, you idiot."

"The point of *what?*"

"We have our brother back!" Elena said, gesturing toward me. "Doesn't that make you happy? Didn't you miss him?"

Sam froze, his anger giving way to hurt. He looked at me with tears in his eyes as though he really did miss me. But instead of saying so, he muttered, "We were better off without him."

Ouch . . .

I looked down, feeling my shoulders slump. Sam yanked out of Charlie's grip and stormed out, Jessica scrambling after him.

I don't think Sam knew how deeply he'd cut me, so I tried to forgive him. He didn't know how worried I'd been about ruining my family's lives. He was hurt, and his first reaction was to hurt me back. And from what I'd seen on the other side, he wasn't very good at ignoring the demon whispers. Someone was probably telling him to say that.

We all hurried after Sam down the hallway, and I tried

to catch up with him. "Look, I'll tell you everything. Just calm down and listen for a sec."

"Too late," he said, bursting into the family room. "Come on D-David," he said to Little David as he scooped him up, visibly regretting the name he'd given his son. Little David started crying about staying the rest of the night.

"Now there's no need for that," Dad said. "He can stay. Just because you're upset with your brother—"

"Grab the baby, Jessica," Sam said tonelessly. "We're leaving."

Jessica, obviously frightened and confused by Sam's behavior, hurried and took Gloria out of the portable crib and grabbed the diaper bag. She rushed after Sam who had already blown through the front door.

"Wait!" I yelled, running after them. "Will you just listen for once!"

Sam spun around and glared at me after buckling Little David into his car seat. "Why? So you can lie to me some more? Why does everyone keep things from me? Why do you all act like I can't be trusted?"

"It isn't always about you!" I said. I tried to fight it, but anger was bubbling up inside. Not just at what he'd said and done that night, but at all the times he'd flipped out and hurt someone like this. All the times he made everything about him. When Elena got pneumonia and we had to cancel our trip to Disneyland. When I ran away after we got into a fight and Sam had to cancel a date to help look for me. When he found out Mom and Dad went to couples counseling. Any time something was going on with someone else, all he ever did was yell and complain about how it affected him. I'd suppressed those memories, but they all came flooding back in that moment, and I was just so sick of it.

"I'm the one that died!" I yelled. "Not you!"

Sam glared at me a moment longer. Quietly fuming he said, "But we're the ones you left behind."

Baby Gloria cried as Jessica buckled her in. Sam revved the engine impatiently while she hurried to the passenger's seat and then they drove off, the car screeching as it turned out of the driveway.

I flopped onto the couch and let my head fall into my hands.

Elena tentatively sat next to me. "He'll come around. He's just going through a lot right now."

"I ruin everything," I said into my hands. "You guys were better off without me, and then I came along to complicate everything."

Elena rolled her eyes. "Don't be so dramatic. That's Sam's job."

Dad sat down on my other side. "I know he didn't really mean what he said. You're his brother and he loves you."

"He missed you so much and he blames you for going away," Elena said. "He doesn't understand that it wasn't your fault. He thinks you just abandoned us."

I didn't answer.

"Why are you sad?"

I lifted my head to see Ginny, standing worriedly in front of me in her Disney princess nightgown. I'd almost forgotten she and Rocco were still here. I didn't know how to answer her, so she just shoved her way into my lap and hugged me. I smiled and held her tight. As much as I felt I'd ruined things for my family, I couldn't regret the way being alive let me feel this little girl who loved me hugging me because I was sad.

"It's gonna be all right, man," Charlie said from behind the couch. "It's late. Go to bed and sleep on it. It won't seem so bad in the morning."

Ginny ran past a conked-out Rocco—who had somehow slept through all of this—to her sleeping bag and grabbed her teddy bear. She shoved it into my hands and said, "Nana Gloria gave that to me. It helps me sleep. You can use it tonight."

"Why is everyone being so nice to me?" I whispered. I was mortified that my eyes were welling up with tears again.

"Because we love you, weirdo," Elena said with a smile. "And we're glad you're back."

So, I followed Charlie's advice and went to bed, hugging a teddy bear my mom had given my niece.

chapter 21

GINNY'S BIRTHDAY PARTY

I woke up the next morning to two children quietly giggling as they climbed up on my bed. I was kind of annoyed at being woken up, because I was having a really weird dream. My brother was on the run because he stole a Pomeranian, and we were all chasing him down on tricycles. I was kind of bummed I didn't get to see where it went.

I dramatically opened my eyes and gasped dramatically. "What are you doing?" Ginny and Rocco ran away screaming and giggling.

I held my phone up to check for messages, but it was still dead. The night before ran through my head again for the billionth time and I wondered if I'd ever see Little David or Baby Gloria again. You may think that's dramatic, but I know my brother—he knows how to hold a grudge.

I dug around in the nightstand drawer for my back-up

charger and plugged it in. Once the phone was fully on, five messages from Piper popped up. I was right about her freaking out.

Piper: thx, david! your so sweet 😊 but srsly i dont know wat to do i love this job but i dont want to work for the d-bag i might quit
Piper: or not i dont know
Piper: are you mad at me? srry i said id quit 😐 i know everyones working double shifts
Piper: srsly are you mad?
Piper: r u ok??? pls txt so i know yr ok and not mad!

I quickly texted back a reply.

Me: Piper! I'm so sorry I disappeared last night!!
Piper: did you die???

I smirked, thinking how I would respond if I was being completely honest.

Me: My phone did! The poor guy . . . Just petered out while we were texting. He tried so hard to stay alive. Gave a really valiant effort! But in the end, it was too much for him . . .
Piper: oh no poor phone 😆

Piper: u working today

Me: Yeah I'll be there at opening

I wondered for a second if it was inappropriate that I was texting a high schooler. I was pretty sure I was like a decade older than her. Maybe. But all we ever texted about was work stuff. We had a group text, but some of the girls texted me individually when Preston was being a jerk. I'd kind of taken on the role of big brother with all the youngins because I felt bad. They didn't deserve to be treated that way.

I watched *Paw Patrol* with the kids while Dad made them breakfast. They begged me to play with them until Elena came to pick them up, but I had to get ready for work. They took that as an invitation to play in the bathroom while I brushed my teeth and shaved.

"Ooh, what's this?" Ginny asked, squirting some shaving cream on the mirror. Rocco laughed and took it from her, spraying it in her hair. Ginny laughed and rubbed my deodorant all over Rocco's face.

I took it from her quickly. "Ew, Ginny, you don't know where that's been."

"Where has it been? On your *bottom*?"

She and Rocco giggled as they kept making toilet jokes that didn't make sense. I smiled and rolled my eyes. I missed living with the shenanigans of these two. Soon to be three, I remembered. I wondered if Elena had told anyone yet.

Sandra called me while I was driving to work.

"Hey, demon hunter meeting right now," she said. "Can you make it?"

"I have work," I said.

"Anything you want me to pass along? They don't want to reschedule because it's been hard to find a time when they're all available."

"Uh . . ." I thought about what Daisy had said about my evil boss and all his demons. "Did Daisy or Bill see a guardian angel with Preston at all when they were there? I was just wondering because they said they tried to fight off some of the demons, but there should have been an angel there for at least some of the day."

"Hang on, let me ask." It was quiet for a second, then she said, "They think his mom was one of the angels that was captured."

I winced. Double whammy there. Not only was his mom dead, but she was one of the angel hostages, probably being tortured as we spoke. I felt an inkling of sympathy for Preston, but quickly smothered it. None of this excused the way he treated people. My mom was dead too, and I didn't go around tearing people down. Mind you, I did still get to see my mom, but that was beside the point. He was a garbage human, and I did not want to feel bad for him.

"Uh, David, you still there?" Sandra asked.

I blinked. "Yeah, sorry. Any info they want to pass on to me? Anything they want me to do?"

Sandra listened, then said, "They were wondering if you had any bright ideas. They're all stretched really thin and are at a loss."

I frowned and bit my lip. "I'll have to think about it. The problem is there aren't enough angels, and I can't think of how we could solve that unless a bunch of people died and went to The Resting Place, and we don't want that. I did have that idea of recruiting your wanderers, but the only ones that have really shown interest are Bill and Gilbert, and their progress has been pretty slow."

"Last time we talked, the rescuer commander said we're doing great with them and should keep it up," Sandra said.

"The rescuer commander?"

"I told you a long time ago I was in touch with the rescuers. I've been an honorary member since they discovered me when I was sixteen."

I did remember her saying something to that effect. Wow, she was way more in touch with the other side than I was. She was helping the rescuers and the demon hunters. I had a feeling if she was an angel she'd climb the ladder so fast she'd be like Hermes' personal assistant within a couple of months.

"I wonder . . ." she said, trailing off.

"What?"

"Nothing, it's a stupid idea."

"I'm full of stupid ideas. Sometimes they work."

"I need to think about it first. Good luck at work!" She hung up on me.

"Well, fine then," I said, frowning at my phone.

I parked and sat in silence for a few minutes, watching a little twittering bird hop through the rocks in front of my car. This job was a combination of fun and torture, and I needed a minute to psych myself up for it. I sat there for a second wondering if this was just my life now. I was, maybe, twenty-seven years old, with no degree, living with my dad, working at Chuck E. Cheese, and with no legit plan for the future. This wasn't exactly what I had in mind when I'd said I wanted to do something with my life. Even when I was dead I had a cooler job than this.

"At least I have a job," I said to myself as I got out of my car and pasted on a smile before walking through the doors.

"Hey, Liam," I said, when I passed him working the cash register. Liam was a little closer to my age, but he only worked weekends. He was studying to be a history teacher, like Sandra. "How's it going? Did you start your student teaching this week?"

He frowned. "Yeah. Turns out two of the kids that work here are my students."

I winced. "Ooh, that's weird."

"I feel like a creepy stalker. I've been in the same room as Joanna since 7 am. She's been avoiding me, but Caleb came up to me in the middle of serving pizza and asked if I would give him an A on the quiz he failed since we work together."

I chuckled. "That is so awkward."

"Shut your faces and get to work," Preston said when he passed us on the way to his office. We both glared daggers at him.

When Preston was out of earshot, Liam said, "This morning, he made some stupid racist comment, then he was all, 'Ooh, Indian burn!' and laughed at himself for like five minutes. That's not even the right kind of Indian—my parents are from Mumbai. He thinks he's being insulting, but he just makes himself look stupid."

I gritted my teeth so hard I was surprised I didn't crack a tooth. I honestly just couldn't anymore with Preston. I'm not sure if I'd ever genuinely hated anyone before. Sheila was annoying and scary, but I didn't hate her. Part of me still wanted to believe there was some good in her because I could tell she had limits. And Malum . . . well my feelings toward him were more terror than hatred. But Preston . . . . He made me want to break something. Preferably his nose. If Daisy thought I was going to befriend him, she was insane.

I immediately got this feeling that I needed to fix my attitude.

As I walked over to the ticket counter I muttered under my breath, "Mom, if that's you, I do not need a lecture right now."

I wasn't sure if it was just my imagination, or if I was sensing her, but in my mind I could totally see her folding her arms and raising her eyebrows at me, and it made me smile.

While on my break—which I took without Preston's permission, because he didn't believe in breaks—I got a text from Elena. I was hiding in the Chuck E. closet where we go to change into the costume.

Elena: hey, so Ginny's birthday party is next week. she really wants you to come, but Sam says he's not coming if you're there . . .

I rolled my eyes.

Me: He can go then. I wouldn't want Ginny to miss out playing with her cousins.

Elena: but she really wants you to be there! she's gonna cry if you don't come!

Me: Me too. I've been to every single one of her birthday parties since she was born. But I don't want to cause drama.

Elena: have you tried calling him?

Me: Yep. Straight to voicemail. Hasn't answered any of my texts. I think he blocked my number.

Elena: 😠

Me: Yep.

Elena: he's going through a lot right now, so I feel bad, but he's being a butthead about it. did you know Chelsea got remarried this week?

I sighed in frustration that I didn't already know this. Back when I was dead, I was in on all the gossip. I knew everything that was happening with my family, sometimes stuff they probably wouldn't have wanted me to know about.

Me: No, I didn't. I'm sure that's been rough. How's he feeling? I heard something about him having MS or something.

Elena: he's okay. I think he's just kind of achy and tired. at least that's what Jessica was saying. argh, I really wish you could come to the party!!! this is all so stupid!

I looked up at the Chuck E. costume hanging on the wall and pursed my lips.

Me: I might have an idea . . .

The week leading up to Ginny's birthday party, I did my best to work through my feelings with Sam. As annoyed as I was with him for not even giving me a chance, I tried to have compassion for him. I was sure it was hard for him knowing Chelsea had moved on. Sam was with Jessica now, but I'm sure it still hurt. He and Chelsea had been high school sweethearts and had two kids together. I don't think those kinds of feelings just magically disappear once you're divorced. Not to mention the fact that he was just diagnosed with a degenerative disease that he knew very little about. I did some research online and apparently there was such a thing as remission. Some people's symptoms go back and forth getting better and worse, while others just progressively get worse until the person's in a wheelchair or confined to their bed. I hoped Sam was the first kind.

I was already in that stinky costume when they all showed up. We decided to have Ginny's birthday party at Chuck E. Cheese, and I scheduled it for a time when I would be in the costume. That way I could be there without Sam knowing. I still think someone might have died in that costume, because the smell was so bad that *I* wanted to die. They ordered their food and sat around a table as they waited for their pizza. I took that as my cue to do the whole Chuck E. act. I'd never really been a performer before, but you learn fast when you have a costume on.

I dramatically ran up to my family and jumped up and down like I was so happy to see them. Little David started crying, but Rocco and Ginny laughed and clapped. Even baby Gloria in Sam's arms gave me a tentative smile and I wanted so bad to give her a squeeze! She was my new favorite person. Sam looked . . . tired. Jessica kept rubbing his back and looking at him with concern, while trying to smile through her worry. I was glad he had her.

"It's Chuck E. Cheese!" Ginny yelled and ran up to me holding her arms out. When I knelt down and hugged her, she whispered, "Is that you in there, Uncle David?"

"Of course it's me, silly. Think I'd miss your birthday party?"

She grinned and patted my masked head, then ran back to the family. Elena winked at me, and Dad waved.

I danced around as they sang "Happy Birthday" to Ginny, and then did the Chuck E. dance when the music came on. After that I had to meander and give other kids the chance to see Chuck E. It either made their day or freaked them out. I saw two little girls arguing over who got to throw the last Skee-Ball and got their attention. I pointed at the ball excitedly, then at myself. The girls reluctantly gave me the ball and I earned them 500 points. Not terrible, but these little girls had only gotten 300, so I definitely won them more tickets than they would have on their own. One of them hugged my legs and thanked me. The other ripped the tickets from the machine, kicked me in the shins, and stomped away.

As I grabbed my shin, I heard someone chuckle. Charlie was playing a racing game with Rocco and had witnessed the whole thing. You're not allowed to talk in the Chuck E. Costume, so I gave him a rude gesture, which just made him laugh more.

"No flipping people off in the Chuck E. Costume, or I'm gonna have to chop your little mousy fingers off."

Of course Preston was right behind me. "Sorry," I mumbled.

"No talking either, idiot," he snapped. "Gosh you're useless. Freaking deadbeat."

I counted to ten and reminded myself that I had actually made a mistake and Preston was right. But still . . . what right did he have to call me a dead-beat? I worked just as hard as anyone else here. *More* than him.

Be nice to him, I reminded myself. *He needs a friend.*

But then he caught a look at Elena pulling Ginny along behind her and he whistled quietly. Under his breath he said, "I'm not usually into moms, but that Mexican chick is . . ." He trailed off as he leered at her back side.

"Dude, that's my sister!" I said, punching him in the arm.

"Oh, sorry," he said, quickly looking away and blushing as though embarrassed. I raised an eyebrow. That was an almost human reaction. He must have sensed my surprise because just as suddenly he had that stupid sneer back on his face. "I said no talking!"

After he walked off, I stood there baffled for a second. Did the guy have multiple personalities? Or was he just trying really hard to be someone he wasn't? Why would someone try so hard to be such a jerk? I still wanted to deck him for looking at my sister like that . . .

I shook my head and returned to all the laughing and screaming children. For the first time since working there, I was glad Preston made me wear the stupid costume for so long. It's only supposed to be thirty minutes max, because it gets really hot, but it was rare we were allowed to take it off before at least an hour had passed. As stinky as it was, I was glad about it because I got to be there for Ginny's party and didn't have to worry about Sam seeing me. I wore it a little longer than necessary, just so I could see them out the door. Ginny and Rocco both hugged me. I even got a chuckle out of Little David when I purposefully tripped on my own feet. Okay, it wasn't on purpose, but I tried to make it look that way by jumping up and bowing. Elena even handed Baby Gloria to me, so I got to give her a squeeze after all.

chapter 22
DEATH OF THE RAT

It had been a long day, and I was exhausted from preventing myself from lashing out at Preston. His sexist, racist, disrespectful comments got even worse as the day wore on, as though he was trying to make up for having a human moment and apologizing to me. This guy was frustrating and confusing in the extreme. The only good thing about that day was that I got to see my nieces and nephews. The other plus to that day was that I was the first one on the schedule for that stupid costume, so I didn't have to wear it for the rest of the day.

I was so ready to go when my shift was over, but when I went to clock out, I thought I smelled something burning. Frowning, I poked my head around the corner and saw smoke coming through the crack in the door of the closet where we kept the Chuck E. costume. I ran to the closet and threw the door open to one of the oddest sights I'd ever seen. Chuck E's pants were on fire.

"Oh crap!" I spun around to go grab the fire

extinguisher from the kitchen, but the door slammed shut on its own. The light bulb exploded in a burst of sparks. The only light came from the burning costume, the flames flickering dark shadows all around me.

"Not now, Sheila!"

Here's the annoying thing about that closet. It had a lock on the doorknob you can use so no one bursts in on you when you're changing. But there was this one pervert who used to work there that learned how to pick the lock, so that kid was eventually fired, and they installed a deadbolt on the door that wasn't as easy to pick. Unfortunately, the idiot that installed the lock did it backwards, so the latch to the deadbolt was actually on the outside of the closet. It still hadn't been fixed, and of course when I tried to escape the closet, I heard the deadbolt click. I was trapped in a closet with a burning rat costume.

How the fire got started in the first place, I didn't know. Though based on Sheila's sadistic track record, I was sure she was the cause of it. Maybe she possessed someone or convinced someone to commit arson. Maybe someone was so offended by the smell of that ugly rat that they took matters into their own hands. Regardless, I was trapped in a closet with a rapidly spreading fire. The entire costume was in flames by now, and I was pretty sure that image of evil flaming Chuck E. would be forever imprinted on my brain. The flames were now caressing the shelf above it, encouraging the fire upward in flickering lurches.

I pounded on the door, screaming for help, but nobody heard me, and the room was slowly filling with smoke. Remembering basic fire safety from elementary school, I went down on my hands and knees where the air was a little cleaner, but I was already coughing up a storm.

"Help!" I yelled, pounding on the door.

Still, no one came.

The fire alarm in the hallway went off, screaming to the whole world that there was a fire. Unfortunately, no one came running to the closet. Probably because they were doing the right thing and evacuating the building. Wished I could join them.

I'd seen a movie once where they pulled the hinges out and opened the door from the other side. It turned out, that didn't work in real life. I scanned the walls and ceiling for vents I might be able to climb through. Nope. Even if there had been a vent big enough to climb in, I'd have needed a screwdriver to open it.

The carpeted floor was starting to catch fire, so I did my best to stamp it out. I did not want to be standing on a floor of flames. Breathing, however, was a very real issue. My head was starting to feel fuzzy. I went down on my stomach and tried to breathe clean air through the crack at the bottom of the door and it helped a little.

Panicking, I turned around to assess the size of the fire.

The whole back wall was in flames, and despite my efforts, the floor was eagerly catching fire as well. If that wasn't enough, the costume cleaning supplies on the shelf were apparently very flammable, and a few bottles exploded, spraying fire in all directions. Some of it hit my shirt, some hit my face. There wasn't enough room to stop, drop, and roll with the floor on fire, so I climbed up and crouched on the chair in the corner of the room as the fire slowly inched its way toward me.

The stress of it all only increased my heart rate and need for more oxygen, which only made me breathe in more smoke. If I didn't cough my lungs up, I was going to pass out.

I let out a pitiful moan and leaned my head back against the wall. "Help!" I croaked. But there was no one around to hear me.

Hermes! Please send someone to help!

Still, no one came.

So, this is how I'm going to die, I thought. *Sheila wins and I fail again.*

Finally, blessedly, the door opened, and smoke billowed out around a blurry figure. The figure coughed, and when some of the smoke cleared I saw Piper make eye contact with me and scream.

"What the—"

Preston ran to the doorway and his jaw dropped

looking at the wall of flames. Then he saw me, and his eyes widened. I almost didn't recognize him, because I'd never seen him without his stupid sneer, or his face scrunched up from laughing at someone else's expense. All of a sudden, he was in a situation he couldn't just laugh or sneer at, and he knew it. This was real.

He swore and spun around. "Hey! Someone grab the fire extinguisher. Piper! Don't just stand there! Go get the fire extinguisher! Jorge, call 911! Get everyone out of here!"

He stepped into the closet and yanked on my arm, forcing me to my feet. I was too weak to really walk, though. Once we were out of the closet, I collapsed on the blessedly cool tile. He grabbed me under my armpits and started dragging me down the hallway. I was only vaguely aware of what was going on, but eventually realized he was talking to me.

"Dude, you better not be dead. If someone dies on my watch, I'm definitely fired."

"Not . . . funny," I wheezed. I regretted speaking. It sent me into a coughing fit that really hurt. But I was still so sick of his stupid face, I couldn't stop myself.

Preston sighed and said, "I didn't mean it like that. I was joking."

I shook my head weakly. If I could talk, I'd have really given it to him. I'd have told him that his jokes were awful, and they hurt people's feelings. I'd have told him how he was a jerk, and everyone hated him. But I'd just spent the past several minutes inhaling smoke and fumes. My everything felt like it was on fire.

Preston must have noticed my mouth open. "Don't try to talk, man. You sound terrible."

I detested that it was Preston I had to depend on right now. There was no one I wanted less, but I didn't really have a choice. My body was completely useless.

"I found it!" Piper yelled. "Oh my gosh, it's spreading a lot!"

Preston set me down and ran to Piper.

"Give it to me," he demanded. "Get out of here!"

I heard her sprint down the hallway while Preston ran back toward the fire. I heard the comforting sound of the extinguisher putting out the flames, before it gurgled and petered out. Preston growled. "This is why we failed the stupid safety inspection. Piece of crap!"

He cursed colorfully and threw the expired extinguisher at the wall. Then he ran back to me, looking absolutely terrified. He started dragging me again, but it wasn't working very well. "Think you could help me out a little?" he grunted. He let go of me and wheezed, his hands on his knees.

I sat up, but I was suddenly nauseous and before I could stop myself, I threw up all over the floor. My throat burned and I groaned, falling onto my hands.

"Lovely," Preston said dryly, shaking some of it off his

shoes as he looked behind us. "We really gotta get out of here. It's spreading. Think you can stand without blowing chunks again?"

I nodded, even though I wasn't sure. He pulled me to my feet, and I immediately collapsed onto him. He caught me and pulled one of my arms over his shoulder. Stumbling, we made our way toward the exit.

"Did you start that fire?" he demanded.

I shook my head and grunted. For real? He thought *I* would do something like that? "Already . . . on fire . . ." I croaked. Ouch. Oh, why did I try to speak?

"How the hell did you end up locked in a closet on fire?"

I considered how to answer. I couldn't say someone locked me in there, because then it would look like a coworker tried to hurt or kill me, and that wasn't true. I could have just played dumb and acted like it was my fault, but there was no possible way I could have locked myself in there when the lock was on the outside. Instead of answering, I opted to close my eyes and go to sleep. That sounded a lot nicer than worrying about all of this.

All my weight fell on Preston, who stumbled into a wall. "Dude, wake up!"

I forced my head up and groaned as I made myself stand. I'd never felt so weak.

"Who did this to you?" Preston demanded once we were walking again. "You were locked in there!"

"I . . ." I coughed so violently it felt like one of my lungs came up.

"Never mind," he said, looking nervously from my face to the fire behind us. "We'll talk about it later."

We continued our pathetic stumble to the exit. Why did the hallway feel like it was getting longer? My throat and chest hurt so much; I might have cried but I felt like the fire had burned all the moisture from my eyes. I must have moaned or something, because Preston said, "You're gonna be okay. We're almost there. Just think about something else. Like how you'll never have to wear that costume again."

I didn't respond.

"Come on. Tough it out. You're not that burned."

I shot him a glare.

He grimaced. "Okay, you do look a little crispy around the edges."

I pushed him away so I could stop for a moment and lean against the wall. I slid down to my butt, panting. I was exhausted, my head was pounding, and as hard as I was breathing, I just couldn't get enough air.

"Come on!" Preston said desperately. "We're almost there."

I shook my head.

Preston groaned. "Are you gonna pass out again?"

I nodded. And then I did.

I woke up on a stretcher with an oxygen mask on my face, which really hurt because part of my face was burned. My chest felt like someone had been stomping on it. All these EMT's were rushing around and behind them I saw coworkers staring at me, wide eyed. It was humiliating. I didn't want them to worry though, so I gave them a thumbs up before they shoved me into the ambulance. As far as I could tell, I was the only one on a stretcher.

The building didn't look on fire anymore, so at least there was that. The firefighters must have put it out pretty quickly. Either that or I'd been passed out for a while. I wasn't sure which.

"Where is he going?" someone asked. "I've got his dad on the phone."

I looked past my feet. Preston had his phone to his ear, nervously biting his lip. The EMT told him which hospital they were taking me to, congratulated Preston on the CPR, then slammed the door shut.

My mind was foggy with confusion. Preston called my dad? I didn't think he even knew I had a dad. He must have gotten his number from my emergency contact form. And did that EMT lady just say Preston did CPR on me? Oh, that was why my chest hurt. I was so glad I was unconscious for the mouth-to-mouth with my boss.

The EMT started talking to me, but I couldn't really understand what she was saying. I was too busy sinking back into the enveloping darkness of unconsciousness.

chapter 23
CRISPY AROUND THE EDGES

I woke up to the sound of my own heart monitor. I was lying in a hard bed, and there was some annoying obstruction on my face. I squinted as I opened my eyes. The lights were too bright, which didn't help my insane headache and sore eyes. I was in a white hospital room. Dad was sitting next to me tapping his feet and scowling nervously out the window at the cheerful, puffy clouds that contradicted both of our moods completely. I must have made a sound or something, because his head snapped around, and he leaned closer to me.

"You're awake! How are you feeling?" He gave a pained smile.

I groaned as I pulled off the oxygen mask to talk. "How do I look?" I whispered, sounding like a smoker.

"Not great," Dad said quietly. "I'm just glad it wasn't worse. David, what happened? They said something about being trapped in a burning closet? How—"

Dad's phone rang and he rolled his eyes. "That'll be Preston. This is the fifth time today. He wants to know what started the fire. Are you up for talking?"

I just held out my hand and took the phone. I held it to my ear and winced as I'd touched the phone to my bandaged, burned cheek. Holding it further away, I croaked, "Hello?"

His voice wasn't as gentle as I would have expected for someone talking to a person in a hospital bed. "You have to tell me who did that to you!"

I sighed. "No one."

"Dude, you were locked in there from the outside. Someone locked you in! There's an investigation going on and they're gonna blame you for starting the fire if you don't fess up."

I was suddenly angry. "Why would I have started a fire in a room I was locked inside of?"

"That's what I've been trying to explain to the arson investigators. They thought it was suicide, but you couldn't have locked that door from the inside. But right now, they don't have any leads on who did it. Other than it had to have been an employee or a customer that was here today. Please tell me if you know who it was. Someone needs to get fired and arrested for arson and attempted murder!"

What on earth was I supposed to say? I couldn't tell the truth, because no one would believe that. But I couldn't lie, or an innocent person could lose their job and possibly go to jail.

"I don't know who did it," I said finally. "All I know is that it wasn't anyone we work with. They'd never do something like that, so please don't fire anyone." I had a panicked moment of stupidity all of a sudden. "Crap, who's taking over my shift? Please don't make Piper do it. She has an exam tomorrow and needs to get home to study for her test."

Preston actually started laughing. "Wow, I must be horrible if you're worried about your shift after almost getting killed."

"You really are," I said honestly.

He sighed. "Don't worry about it. We're shut down for the rest of the day. I will personally take your shifts for the rest of the week, or however long you need to recover. If you want, I'll even clock in and out for you so you can still get paid."

I scowled suspiciously. Was this actually Preston talking to me? Was he being possessed? It was just as well I had nothing to say, because I had a very intense coughing fit right then. When it was over, I fell back on my pillow, exhausted. "Um, thanks. That's really . . . nice of you?"

He sighed again and muttered something unintelligible.

I hated saying anything nice to Preston, because a part of me still hated his guts, but I forced myself to say, "Hey, you did a good job back there during the fire. I've never seen you take charge like that."

"Thanks," he said icily. Then he hung up and Dad shoved the oxygen mask back on my face.

The doctors did a bunch of tests and x-rays on me after that, and then they let me sleep again, which was the most wonderful gift I could imagine. Just breathing was exhausting.

Someone was holding my gauzy, padded hand the next time I woke up. I opened my eyes to see Sandra looking down on me with big, worried eyes, her hair hanging down toward my face. She smiled with half her mouth, the rest of her face scrunched up with concern. As crappy as my situation was, it was one of the better ways I'd woken up. It almost made it all worth it to see her look at me like that.

"Hey," I said sleepily, pulling off my oxygen mask. "How did you know I was here?"

"Elena told me," she said quietly.

"You guys talk?"

She shrugged. "I think she thinks I'm your girlfriend, so she thought I'd want to know you were in the hospital."

"Oh," I said awkwardly. Part of me wanted to ask her if she was my girlfriend, another part of me wanted to ask if she wanted to be, and another part of me doubted she liked me that way. It was all very junior high, and I'm embarrassed to admit that I decided not to say anything.

"How are you feeling?" Sandra asked before I could reach the end of my mental argument.

I shrugged. "I'm fine. They want to monitor me overnight, but I'll probably be out of here by tomorrow. I'm just super tired."

"We need to implement my schedule!"

I jumped and looked around, recognizing Ying Yue's voice. She, William, and Daisy were floating on the left side of my bed.

"Oh, hey guys," I said. "We having a meeting?"

"Not officially," Ying Yue said. "We just came to check on you. Unfortunately, everyone else is occupied at the moment."

"The schedule might be a good idea. He's definitely gonna die if we don't give him more protection," Daisy said bluntly.

William shook his head. "You both know we cannot provide more protection than we are already giving him. Or are you unaware of why everyone else is occupied at the moment?"

"Why?" I asked, sitting up. "What's going on?" I clutched my head and tried to ignore the way the room spun once I was upright.

"Simple," Daisy said. "We don't have enough guardian angels to keep watch over you mortals. We're losing more than we're getting."

"What do you mean?" I asked.

"The ratio of angel to demon generally favors the angels. At least it has for most of history," Ying Yue explained. "Angels have a high turnover rate with some of us moving on to the next place, while others join us when they die. Generally, the number of angels in The Resting Place stays almost constant, and that amount has always been greater than the amount of demons. More people go to The Resting Place when they die than . . . the other place. The Red Zone, I believe the demons call it. Here's the issue: the demons don't have a 'next place.' They don't move on like we do. So, while our numbers stay the same, theirs are slowly but constantly growing. I believe that we've reached the point that there is an equal number of angels and demons."

"If it's equal, how are there not enough angels?" I asked.

"It won't stay equal for long," Ying Yue explained. "Angels are still moving on, but we aren't gaining enough to make up for the loss. Fewer people these days are becoming angels when they die. The rescuers are at their limit dealing with all the wanderers. And that's not to mention the angels Malum has captured. We're only at five now—one more was captured yesterday— but if he continues at this rate . . . I don't want to think about that."

"You guys are still using the buddy system, right?" I asked quietly. "No one's going anywhere alone? I don't want anything to happen to any of you."

She nodded. "We're trying. But I doubt two angels would be much of a challenge for Malum. If he found two angels on their own . . . what's to stop him from taking both?"

Ying Yue looked genuinely scared, which scared the crap out of me. I was already worried about my team, but I just assumed they had it more together than what I saw. It turned out they were even more vulnerable than I imagined. I was terrified something would happen to my angel family and there was nothing I could do about it.

Unfortunately, when people are scared, their heart rate spikes, making them breathe faster and harder, and my lungs weren't really up to that. I could hear my heart rate increasing on the monitor, which made me even more panicked, which made it even harder to breathe. My eyes widened with panic and my hand flew to my chest. I was hyperventilating and I didn't know how to stop, which made me even more panicked.

"Whoa, lay down," Sandra commanded me, pushing me back down. She shoved my oxygen mask back on my face and put her hand on my cheek. "It's okay," she said soothingly. "Just breathe."

Easier said than done, I wanted to say.

Sandra glared back at Ying Yue, William, and Daisy. "Stop scaring him. He needs to rest."

I looked at Sandra and focused on the air coming in and out of my lungs. She nodded encouragingly and I continued to focus on her eyes. Her irises were so dark brown they were almost black, and the color was pure and consistent throughout. No flecks of other colors, just these beautiful deep brown eyes framed with long wispy eyelashes. I marveled for a minute at the fact that those eyes were staring down at *me* with a mixture of concern and possibly something else. Why would anyone look at *me* like that? Eventually the heart monitor slowed down and the crease between her eyebrows lessened slightly.

Once I felt up to it, I took the mask off again and tore my eyes away from Sandra to look at Ying Yue. "You guys need to stop worrying about me. You have bigger problems than me to deal with."

"You're just so pitiful and we're worried about you," Daisy said, which was both insulting and sweet.

"You are one of us and we need you," William confirmed.

"Then stop worrying," I said. "Because if something happens to me and I do die, you'll have one more angel on your side. It's a win-win."

"It is not a win-win, dummy!" Sandra said angrily. I think she might have slapped me if I wasn't so pathetic looking. "If you die, then *we* lose you. Us living people."

"We were friends when I was dead before," I said. "What's the difference?"

She glared at me and didn't answer for a long time. I couldn't blame her. There was a big difference, I just didn't want to acknowledge it.

"What about your family?" she said quietly. "Do you want them to lose you again?"

Guilt welled up inside me. She was right. This wasn't a win-win. It was more of a lose-lose. It was bad either way.

A nurse came in to check on me, knowing somehow that my heart rate had gone haywire for a second. My angel friends disappeared before the nurse was done fussing and I didn't get the chance to say something more encouraging. They should have been more worried about themselves than me. It was angels Malum was capturing, not mortals.

Weirdly enough, I wasn't scared when it was time to go home. Usually being alone freaked me out because that's when Sheila liked to attack me, and there were plenty of opportunities for her to attack me at Dad's house. But for some reason I wasn't afraid. I'd realized that I really didn't have control over anything that happened to me. All I had control over was how I acted, and the rest was out of my hands. I was weirdly at peace with that. I think it was Sandra and I talking about win-win and lose-lose situations. Things were going to work out and suck either way.

I spent a day taking it easy. It was still hard for me to breathe, and I was still coughing a lot. The medication made it a little easier though. The main thing was the boredom. Elena took all my books after I died, and Dad stopped paying for Netflix after Mom died, so there was nothing to do. I'm not very good at relaxing, so I did the dishes and cleaned out the fridge. I stopped after vacuuming though because the dust sent me into a coughing fit. I wished I had some papers to grade. The boredom was mainly why I went back to work the next day, even though I'd been given the rest of the week off.

I frowned in the mirror as I got ready the next day. I had a burn on my lower jaw that I had to change the bandages on. It was pretty gross looking. It wasn't very big, but I was pretty sure it would scar. There was also one on my chest from where my shirt caught fire, and my hands from trying to pat it out. I sighed. I went seventeen years without any broken bones, stitches, or scars. Now, after only three months of being alive my face had visible damage. My nose was just a little crooked and I had a burn scar on my jaw.

Dad helped me cover my burns with ointment and gauze and tried to discourage me from going to work. I thanked him for the help, but promptly kicked him out of the bathroom so I could get ready. Doing my hair was kind of hard to do with gauzy hands, so I just didn't even try. I took one last look at myself and laughed. I looked ridiculous. I had the worst bedhead I'd ever seen, and blue circles under my bloodshot eyes because I spent the whole night coughing. If it hadn't burned up, I might have volunteered to wear the Chuck E. costume just to hide my disgusting face.

Apparently, I looked just as pathetic as I felt because the second I walked through the door at work, a little kid looked at me and hid behind his mom's legs.

"Oh my gosh, David!" Tala said when I walked past the cash register. "Are you okay? I thought you were at the hospital! Preston said you'd be out the rest of the week!"

"Nope, I'm good," I said with a smile. My rough voice kinda contradicted what I was saying.

"What the hell are you doing here?"

I spun around and saw Preston in the middle of exchanging fifty tickets for a cheap light-up pen. The kid gasped and Preston swore, realizing he just said "hell" in front of a seven-year-old. Then he just glared up at the ceiling, realizing he'd made it worse.

After the kid left, I walked up to the ticket counter. "No swearing in front of the kids, idiot. Quick, who do I sound like?"

"Shut up," he grumbled.

"You're seriously taking over my shift?" I asked. "Don't you have manager stuff to be doing?"

He shook his head and slumped against the wall of prizes, staring at his feet. "Honestly, I don't know how to do most of it. I shred all the forms I don't understand and just act like I never got them. There's like 200 unread emails in my inbox. And with inventory and stuff I just make up numbers. Jorge actually does a lot of the stuff I don't get. I should probably give him a raise or something."

I raised my eyebrows and blinked. "You suck at your job, man."

"Yeah, I know. Oh hey, there's something I wanted to show you." He left the ticket counter and motioned for me to follow him down the back hallway. The walls touching the Chuck E. closet were blackened by the fire. I let Preston pass me and froze where I was at.

"Um," I said with a gulp. "I don't really want to go over there."

Call me a baby, but returning to the place where I almost asphyxiated to death didn't sound very fun to me. I also didn't exactly trust Preston to not lock me up in there just for a laugh.

"Well just look from over there then," he said. He got to the closet and pointed to a hole where the dead bolt used to be.

"A peep hole?" I said with a glare.

"No, idiot. I'm fixing it so the lock is on the inside." He gestured to the screwdriver on the ground and the lock he'd removed. He looked surprisingly proud of it.

"Oh . . ." I said. "Cool. Yeah, that was a problem."

"Yeah, you would know," he said, kicking the blackened door shut with his foot. If he was smart, he would have just had someone replace the whole door, but I didn't say anything. He walked back and paused, giving me a really weird look like he was hoping I'd compliment him for doing the bare minimum. Why was he seeking *my* approval?

I sighed. "What do you want me to say? Good job? You're a great boss? You're not. You've done a lot of damage here. That fire incident might not have even happened if you'd fixed the lock a long time ago and actually made sure the fire extinguisher was up to date. I almost died because of your carelessness."

"I know," he said, shoving his hands into his pockets. "I'm . . . trying to be better."

It kind of freaked me out to see him so vulnerable. The evil side of me—or maybe even some demon whispering in my ear— wanted to kick him while he was down. I forced myself not to listen.

I made sure he was looking me in the eye before I said, "Look, I don't know why you act the way you do and treat everyone around you like garbage. I don't know if you picked it up from someone, or if that's how you were taught. Maybe you just have some really crappy friends. Wherever you got the idea, it needs to stop or you're gonna wind up all alone with nothing but your regrets to keep you company. Life is short. Take it from someone who knows."

He gulped and nodded, looking down at his feet.

"The thing is," I continued reluctantly, "I don't think that's who you really are. I feel like you're trying to be something you're not, and I don't know why. You can be so much better. Look at what you did the other day. You took charge and saved my life. Without you—and Piper, who actually found me—I'd probably be dead. So . . . thanks."

He nodded awkwardly and shifted his weight. I frowned, freaked out that I'd just sounded like Raj for a second.

"David!"

I spun around and saw Chuck E. running down the hall toward me. I croaked out a strangled screamed and flattened myself against the wall.

Preston valiantly held back a laugh and motioned for the rat to back up a couple paces. "It's just Piper. She's trying out the new costume they sent us."

"Are you okay?" Piper asked from inside the costume, throwing her furry arms around me. I tried not to squirm away. I couldn't get that image of the flaming rat out of my head.

Before I had a chance to respond, she ran away, probably afraid Preston would yell at her for talking while wearing the costume.

"Really though, are you okay to work?" Preston asked. "I don't want to tire you out when you're still recovering."

"Don't make me wear the rat costume," I said firmly.

"Deal."

"Also, I'm not supposed to be around smoke or do stuff that makes it hard to breathe. So probably no kitchen duty."

"I'll just keep you at the ticket counter," he said. "Let me know if you get tired and need a stool or something."

He left me to go finish fixing the lock. I decided to let him be and went back out to the ticket counter where I worked for the next six hours. I must have looked tired, because after I took a quick bathroom break, there was a stool in there waiting for me.

chapter 24
SANDRA'S PSYCHIC TV SHOW

After the fire incident, it took Dad three days to work up the courage to bring up what happened. In the middle of our nightly ritual of watching TV while eating dinner, he set down his fork, took a breath and said, "David, what's going on?"

I didn't know what he was talking about at first. I gestured at the TV. "Peralta, Boyle, and Gina are in a hostage situation, but Jake is geeking out because it's just like *Die Hard*."

Dad blinked in confusion. "What? No, not the TV show. With you. I've tried to trust you and give you some space to figure out whatever's going on, but I'm worried about you. I feel like there's something . . . haunting you. I know that sounds strange, but these accidents that keep happening to you don't feel like accidents."

I looked away from the TV and stared at Dad nervously. His usage of the word "haunting" definitely caught me by surprise. I always knew he was more in tune with the other side than most mortals. I just didn't realize his awareness was this strong. He was no Sandra, but he definitely was more aware than I thought.

I procrastinated responding by swirling some of the fettuccine around on my fork. I really didn't know what to say. Elena already knew too much, and I knew it stressed her out. Also, early on my dad seemed to not want to know about all of this. Like he'd rather just live in blissful ignorance. I was fine with that. There was no need to drag him into my insane, dangerous world.

Dad misinterpreted my silence. "I'm sorry. That sounded nuts. Forget I said anything."

"No, Dad, it's not nuts." I sighed, setting my fork down. "I just don't think you want to know."

Dad frowned. "I'm sorry if I gave you the impression that I don't care. You're my son and I want you to be safe. You can tell me what's going on."

"I can, but I'm not sure if that means I should."

"Why shouldn't you tell your father the truth?"

I leaned my head in my hand. "Because the truth is dangerous. You've got some idea of what's happening to me. I don't want that to happen to any of you. I really shouldn't even be living with anyone I care about. It puts you at risk. You could be used to get to me." Though, now that I thought about it, Sheila had been very specific to only target me. She hadn't yet used anyone in my family to hurt me. She might have been evil, but not enough to hurt innocents. That was comforting.

"And what makes it right for you to risk yourself and wrong for anyone else to?" Dad asked.

"Because I'm a . . ." I trailed off and looked at him. *Guardian angel . . .*

"You're a what?"

Should I tell him?

I closed my eyes and listened. I got this impression that I should. That it would be good for me, specifically. That it was okay to share my burdens. It wasn't selfish, it was a sign of trust. I wondered if that was Mom whispering in my ear, because those thoughts definitely didn't come from me.

"You're listening," Dad said quietly. He smiled when I looked up at him with surprise. "I can tell. I do that too. What impression did you get?"

"That I should tell you," I said quietly. "That it would be good."

He leaned back and held his hands out, gesturing for me to begin.

And so I did. I tried to keep it as general as possible: I died, became a guardian angel, an evil demon escaped, I joined the team to capture him, then I was sent back to mortality for saving Sandra's life when Malum tried to kill her. Dad was a good listener. He didn't interrupt with questions, he just sat there taking in everything I said. It was both terrifying and relieving to talk about it. He had a great poker face, so I had no idea what he thought about it all.

He had one question at the end. "So now this Malum is haunting you?"

"*Yippie kayak, other buckets!*"

We both jumped and looked back at the TV, while Charles Boyle had his Bruce Willis moment. I snorted, and Dad turned it off. He looked back at me seriously, waiting for me to answer his question.

I sighed. "I don't think he's haunting me directly. I'm pretty sure it's Sheila. I didn't tell you about her. Sheila's a demon I pretended to date when I was undercover. She works for Malum and hates my guts. But she doesn't usually attack when there's a guardian angel around. Odds are Mom or someone is nearby, because she isn't trying to kill me right now."

Dad blinked. "Your mom? You really think she's here?"

I smiled. "I can't be sure, but I think that was her I was listening to earlier. I think she wanted me to tell you the truth."

Dad stared down at his cold chicken alfredo, completely forgotten during my story. "So . . . you've seen your mother since she died?"

I nodded. "A few times while I was still dead, and now every once in a while, with Sandra's help. Mom's with you all the time, Dad. She worries about you."

Dad stood up suddenly. "I'm gonna go . . . think."

I sighed watching him walk away. The thing was, we spent this whole time talking about me, and the conversation still turned to my mother. She was who my dad was always going to be thinking about, no matter what else was going on. I didn't resent that, I just felt sorry for him because being without my mom was always going to hurt for him. I was sure it would get easier with time, but I doubted the hurt would ever go away completely. He just missed her so much. And he couldn't see her again until . . .

I gasped and pulled my phone out to text Sandra.

"I'm sorry for using you like this, I know you're not just a tool, but—"

"No, I don't mind," Sandra said, closing her car door. "Honestly, I'm happy to help."

I smiled and instinctively took her hand as I led her inside my dad's house. It hurt because my hand was burned and covered in bandages, but I wasn't paying attention to that. I was weirdly proud of Sandra for that response. I knew I wasn't in charge of her or better than her in any way, but from the beginning, she never wanted to get involved in other-side drama. Now, she almost welcomed it. I wondered what had changed.

We waited in the living room and watched TV until

Dad came out of his bedroom. We didn't want to intrude on his alone time.

"Oh, hi there," Dad said, stopping in the hallway.

"Dad, this is Sandra," I said.

Sandra stood up and shook his hand. "It's nice to meet you, Mr. Garcia."

Dad gasped and pulled his hand away as though he'd been given an electric shock.

"Are you okay?" Sandra asked knowingly.

His mouth hanging open, Dad shook his head and forced himself to look away from the empty space behind Sandra. "Yes, I'm fine. I thought I just saw . . . Never mind."

I almost snorted thinking about how often this must have happened in Sandra's life. I'm sure she'd shaken plenty of hands in her life, and each time that happened, if there were angels or demons nearby, the other person would have momentarily seen them too. And Sandra didn't even know the effect of her touch until this year when we started using it to help me communicate with the demon hunters.

"Who did you see?" Sandra asked gently.

Dad gulped. "My wife."

"Would you like to talk to her?"

Dad's eyes watered and he nodded.

They sat at the table, Sandra put in her AirPods, and then put her hand on my dad's arm. I went to my room to give them some privacy, but I could hear him crying before I shut the door.

They talked for a couple hours, and then Sandra came to my room to say goodbye. Her eyes were red.

"Are you okay?" I asked.

She nodded and plopped down on the edge of my bed. "They just love each other so much! I wasn't eavesdropping, but I couldn't help but see the way they made each other smile and laugh, and the concerned looks they gave when the other one cried."

"Do you think it was a good thing?" I asked. "I mean, I hope it wasn't just reopening closed wounds."

"I don't think this wound was closed in the first place," Sandra said softly. "I think it was good for both of them. Her death was an accident, so they never really got closure in the end. There were things they both needed to say to each other."

I nodded thoughtfully, understanding the closure issue more than she probably realized.

"So, are you gonna have one of those TV shows now?" I teased after the silence lasted too long. "You know, with those psychics who go to people's houses and say things like, 'Oh yes, he's here! I'm seeing the color blue! Did your son have any connection to the color blue?'"

Sandra pretended to cry and said, "He once had a blue crayon in his crayon box!"

I gasped. "It's a sign!"

She laughed and shook her head.

It was quiet for a minute, and I was very aware of our clasped hands and how she was sitting right next to me. We looked at each other and I wondered if I should . . .

"Oh, were you two having a moment?"

"*Hijole!*" I gasped as Sandra and I jumped. Mom had just popped into existence right in front of us.

"Hey, Mom," I said, somewhat annoyed.

"I'll leave you two alone," she said with a smile. "I just wanted to say thank you again, Sandra. It was so nice to finally talk to him."

"Any time," Sandra smiled.

"You're lucky," I said to Mom with a wry smile. "When I was dead, I never got to talk to anybody. I just shouted away, and no one could hear me."

My mom's hands looked like they were itching to wrap themselves around me. "Oh, my poor, lonely boy!"

"Mom," I grumbled.

She put her hand on her hip. "Don't you *mom* me for having compassion on my boy."

She disappeared after that.

chapter 25
THE PLAN

Sheila

He dangled me over the pit by the throat as the red mists swirled around me. Harsh, deafening wind blew my hair around my face, carrying the cries of the miserable wrenches below. I fought to focus on the demon before me and not the images of the past that flashed across my mind. I couldn't afford to be compromised at this moment.

"Have you destroyed him yet?" he hissed. Drool dripped down his chin as though he'd forgotten to leave the beast behind.

"I'm close," I said, trying not to struggle or show weakness. "I just need more time."

"Time? Is that it? You don't need another plunge into the Hurricane?"

"No, Master," I said, firmly. "I have a plan. It will work. I promise. Angels are predictable. I will use their loyalty against them."

Malum's boring, forgettable face frowned. The only

thing terrifying about his human appearance was the Darkness that didn't just radiate from him, but oozed and gushed, pooling at his feet, like he couldn't contain it all.

"Tell me," he whispered.

I gave him every detail of my plan, outlined each word I would say, while I dangled just above the Hurricane. Seconds away from the inescapable torture. Malum nodded and even grinned as I shared my plans.

"I like your thinking," he said, finally pulling me away from the pit. He didn't let go of my neck. "Do you know what will happen if you fail?"

"I return to the Hurricane," I said.

He paused and created a cloud of Darkness that encompassed us both. He let me go, but I was trapped just the same. His voice echoed around me, and I didn't know where he was. "I'm disappointed that you think me that merciful," he hissed, slithering past me. A sudden flap of wings flew by my face, and I gasped, spinning around. "No, you will not just return to the Hurricane," he whispered, in a low gravelly voice. "I know your true fears. If you fail me, I will make all your wildest nightmares come true . . . The things you see in the Hurricane will become a reality that you cannot escape."

"No," I whispered.

"Yes, they will! Unless you do what?"

I gritted my teeth in pure hatred. "I must utterly destroy him."

chapter 26
KISS OF DEATH

As I was pulling off my face bandage the next morning, I frowned at some of the stubble growing in. I'd been too scared to shave with part of my jaw all raw and nasty. I could have just shaved around the bandage, but even the skin that wasn't disgustingly burnt was still sensitive, and it seemed too dangerous. Curiously I wondered if hair would grow on the burn once it healed. I didn't think hair grew on scars. Which meant if I ever wanted to experiment with facial hair again, I'd probably get some really weird patches.

Sandra called me, and I put her on speaker phone as I brushed my teeth and pulled off my chest and hand bandages. The chest burn was probably the worst, and the creepy part was that it had the faint outline of a hand from where I'd patted it down.

"Ow. Gross. Ow!" I said, trying to lightly dab the gross smelling ointment on my chest. I should have left the hand bandages on before doing this, because my hands were also stinging.

"What are you *doing?*" Sandra asked.

"I'm suffering the aftereffects of almost-death by flaming rat."

"Do you need help?"

"No, it's just really gross. Do you wanna see a picture? The top layer of my skin is gone."

"No, I do not want to see a picture, you nasty. There's a meeting happening over here in thirty minutes. You coming, or not?"

"Yeah, I'll be there soon, I just need to—Ow!"

I could imagine her raised eyebrow as she said, "Yeah, sure you don't need help."

A loud knock on the door startled me and I instinctively threw a strip of gauze at the door and leaped into the shower. Not sure why that was my instinct. The gauze floated lightly to the ground, mocking me in its pathetic-ness.

"Everything okay in there?" Dad asked.

"Yep!" I said, my heart pounding out of my chest. I climbed out of the shower and cautiously opened the door. "Don't knock so loud. I have bathroom-related trauma."

Bathroom-related trauma?

Dad eyed the gauze all over the floor and the ointment all over my fingers. "Do you need help?"

I sighed and sat on the edge of the tub. "No, but since everyone around here thinks I do, then fine."

I heard Sandra laugh on the phone and say, "Hi, Mr. Garcia!"

"Hey, Sandra," Dad said. "And the name's Sam. Mind if I intrude to help David with his 'bathroom-related trauma?'"

I groaned and covered my face as they both laughed at me. Why did I say that?

"Don't forget, I'm going on that camping trip today," Dad reminded me. "Are you going to be okay on your own? Sure you don't want to come?"

I definitely did not want to come. It was a big neighborhood camping trip. The neighbors knew me as a kid, and some would definitely recognize me.

"I have work tomorrow," I said. "And yes, I'll be fine. I can take care of myself."

He gave me a look, but let it go. He helped patch me back up again, and in five minutes I was on my way to Sandra's house.

I got to Sandra's before most of the demon hunters got there. Daisy had somehow managed to physically tip one of the chairs back so she could sit with her feet up on the table. She looked a little proud of herself for that feat. Bill was the total opposite. He floated through the middle of a chair, not even bothering to try to look like he was sitting. Gilbert hung back, but I could tell he was still listening curiously. Sandra and I sat together across from Daisy and Bill. I drummed my fingers and Sandra checked her phone as we waited for everyone else to show. Nobody was talking, so the only sounds were anime characters screaming from the TV show Asher and Oliver were watching. The room had that feeling of awkwardness you get when it's just the wrong combination of people. Nobody was starting a conversation, and the silence became more uncomfortable the longer nobody spoke.

"So, Bill," I said finally. "What did you used to do for a living?"

Sandra tried to signal for me to shut up. It was risky asking him questions about his past. Anything could trigger him, but I was genuinely curious. Also, I was about to die from the awkward silence.

He signed something and Daisy said, "He owned a store."

"What did you sell?" Sandra asked, jumping into the conversation despite herself.

Bill mimed opening a book. He didn't seem to know how to charade the next word, so he finger-spelled it to Daisy. There was a slight smile on his face.

"He sold books and plants," she said.

"In one store? That's interesting. What was the store called?" I asked.

Bill looked down at his hands, seemingly frustrated that

he didn't quite know or have the energy to sign it. He opened his mouth and sighed. He pursed his lips and closed his eyes, then whispered, "Leaf . . . Leaf . . ."

"Leaf, leaf?" I asked.

"Hush," Sandra said, absentmindedly swatting at me. "He wasn't finished."

Bill took another deep breath and said, "Leaf Me Alone, I'm Reading."

I chuckled. "That's punny. I like it."

Ted showed up suddenly, looking around wildly. "Daisy! Why did you leave without me? We're supposed to keep with the buddy system! Don't you understand how dangerous it is to be wandering alone?"

I'd never seen Ted so agitated before. He was usually such a quiet, calming presence that you forgot he was even there.

"What's the big deal?" Daisy said. "We were all going to meet here anyway. I wouldn't be alone if everyone would actually show up to the dumb meeting."

"The meeting's canceled," Ted said. "There have been more disappearances."

Daisy let the legs of the chair fall back to the ground as she lost concentration. "Any we know?"

He shrugged. "Not as far as I know, but we don't know who all was taken. Hermes is putting The Resting Place on lockdown until we get a headcount of all the angels to figure out who was taken."

"Lockdown? But what about . . ." she trailed off, looking at me and Sandra.

"Go," I said, urgently. "Don't worry about us."

Daisy nodded and disappeared. Ted looked around the room as though expecting something to pop out. He pursed his lips and looked at me nervously. "Be careful, David. I'm worried she might take advantage of this."

"Who?" I asked, already knowing who he meant.

He looked around, taking another sweep of the room. "Just be on guard." He disappeared, leaving us in silence.

Sandra and I looked worriedly at one another. Who had been taken? Was it any of ours? I didn't think I could handle someone I cared about in Malum's clutches.

I also worried about us mortals. If the angels were in lockdown in The Resting Place . . . were we on our own?

I hung out at Sandra's for the rest of the day, partially because I wanted to spend time with her, partially because I was worried, and she made me feel better. I helped her grade papers like the good old days, and we made tacos. I didn't go home until late that night, when Dad was already asleep. I slowly crept to my room, trying not to make any sounds that would wake him up. Then I remembered Dad wasn't home—he was on that camping trip.

"I'm stupid," I laughed, shutting my door behind me and turning on the light.

Someone was in my room.

I froze, and my heart tried to jump out of my chest. She sat there on my bed, fully visible, and cloaked in Darkness.

"Hello, David," Sheila said.

"You," I whispered, frozen in place.

"Me," she agreed, tonelessly.

Why didn't I stay over at Sandra's? That was so stupid! She never shows up at Sandra's!

I hadn't seen her since she saved me. It was hard to reconcile her with all the horrors she'd put me through. When I saw her face, I couldn't not think about the girl I dated for a while. The one I would often find staring off into the distance with that unreadable expression on her face. The one who tried to warn me not to join Malum. Then I thought of all she'd done to me. The nightmares, the attack in the bathroom, the murderous dog, the fire. I felt like it was all happening all over again. Falling in the darkness, smoke filling my lungs, pleading for help. I couldn't stop myself from shaking where I stood.

I tried to force my voice not to quaver but didn't quite succeed. "What are you doing here?"

"I'm waiting."

"For what?"

She grinned and I slowly backed away.

"You don't have to run away," she said. "I won't touch you, I promise. Just do whatever. I'll be here. It's really sad it's taking this long. Security's gotten really pathetic with you guys."

Hermes! She's here! Help!

Sheila laughed. "Did you just call for Hermes to send help? That's perfect. It'll speed things up. I won't have to wait as long."

"For what?"

"Nothing," she said, waving me away. "Go brush your teeth or do whatever you mortals do, I'll still be here when you're done."

I stood there rooted in place, unsure of what to do. Sheila was here in my house. I knew it wasn't the first time she'd been in my house, nor the first time she attacked me, but it was the first time she showed herself to me. Why would she go unseen for so long, just to reveal herself to me now? I considered hopping in my car and running away, but what was to stop her from following me? And I wouldn't endanger Sandra by leading Sheila right to her. The last time they were in the same room Sheila possessed her. What was I supposed to do? I had no defense against her, except to call for angelic help, which was apparently in short supply tonight. Hermes had called for a lockdown. Did that mean no help was coming?

There was nothing I could do to make her leave, so, strangely enough, I did as she said. I brushed my teeth, put on my pajamas, and got ready for bed. True to her word, she did not follow or attack me. She was still in my room when I returned, sitting on the edge of my bed.

"You can go to sleep if you want," she said, gesturing

to the bed. "Don't let me keep you up. Like I said, I won't touch you. You'll be safe from me tonight. I kept my promise earlier, why would I break it now?"

I cautiously sat near my pillow and glared at her, my mind going a hundred miles an hour trying to figure her out. What was her game? She said she was waiting. But waiting for what? For me to go to sleep? Why would she need to wait until I was sleeping to attack me? And why show herself to me now, if she wasn't going to attack until I was asleep? It didn't make sense.

She sighed. "This is taking too long. I thought my presence would be enough, but I guess it's not anymore. Sorry, but I'm going to have to break my promise."

Too late, I realized we were waiting for the exact same thing. "No, don't touch me!" I pleaded, scooting back against the headboard. I knew that if she did something, help would come. And that's exactly what she wanted.

"This is gonna hurt," she warned me, floating closer. "If it's any consolation, it's gonna be just as uncomfortable for me as it is for you."

Hermes, don't send anyone!

"Desperate times call for desperate measures," she said, seeming to psych herself up. "And I know this will get a response."

Then she disappeared.

Something hit me and I collapsed sideways onto my pillow. It was like I was a puppet, and someone had cut all my strings. I couldn't move, I couldn't think, I couldn't even breathe. Darkness filled me up with despair and hatred, like smoke slowly filling up a closet. My mind clouded until I completely forgot who I was. I wasn't a twenty-something kid named David. No, I was a vengeful demon who hated, absolutely *hated,* David. I had to kill David and I had to do it now. Nothing else would make me feel better. If I killed David, he'd get what he deserved, and then I'd finally be free.

Without my volition, I jumped to my feet and ran to the kitchen, laughing as I ran. I took a knife from the knife block and gripped it in my hand so tightly that my knuckles turned white. The worst part about it was I couldn't even scream. I grinned and laughed like a maniac. I lifted the knife and directed it toward my heart. Inside I knew this was bad and I'd die, but the freakiest part was that I *wanted* to do it. I *needed* to do it. It would bring me so much pleasure!

The knife flew from my hand, and something hit me in the chest again. A ripping sensation had me crying out in pain. I fell to the floor and started shaking, flapping my arms and legs around as the *thing* took greater hold of me. An even sharper pain shot me in the chest, and I stopped my twitching long enough to gasp. I screamed my lungs raw as the ripping sensation intensified to a blinding agony.

And then it was gone. Panting, I sat up, only to flop

back down again.

Sheila floated not far from me, looking almost as bewildered and disgusted as I was. She was still, her arms behind her back, as though someone was holding her. Slowly her evil grin returned.

"You angels are so easy. I knew that would get your attention," she said. "Now show yourself to him. I want him to see this."

"Whoever's there, get out!" I yelled. "It's a trap!"

Glaring at the knife on the ground, Sheila floated it up until it was pointing it at my chest. "I just want to talk," she said. "But I want David to be able to hear it. Show yourself, so he can witness this for himself." She rolled her eyes and shook her head. "I don't think you understand. I have a knife. David has a beating heart. I will plunge this serrated kitchen knife into that heart unless you reveal yourself. It's super dull too, so it'll take a long, painful time for it to work its way into his chest."

Jake appeared, glowing like a true angel, his face contorted with fury. He held her in a chokehold. "Leave him alone," he growled.

"Oh, I'm not here for him," Sheila said softly.

She wiggled and squirmed, then disappeared, reappearing only a foot or two away. Jake formed a gun and held it to her head. With the other hand, he held actual handcuffs, marbled with Light and Darkness. "Let me explain what's gonna happen here," Jake said in a low voice. "I'm going to shoot you with a demon killer bullet, which will stun you long enough for me to get these handcuffs around you. Then I'll drag you to The Resting Place kicking and screaming where you'll be imprisoned for a very long time."

"That's very cool of you to outline your entire plan for me. Is that like your defender version of reading me my Miranda rights? I'm sorry to break it to you, but none of that's going to happen. I have you exactly where I want you."

Then she did something neither of us expected. Ignoring the gun, she leaned in close and kissed him. It wasn't just a peck, but it wasn't a true kiss either. There was something very *wrong* about it. Her hands went around his throat as she did it. At first Jake was stunned, then he fought, trying to push her off him, but he slowly lost his strength. He dropped the gun and it vanished. His eyes widened in fear and started to glaze over. It was like she was feeding him Darkness from her mouth, putting her own twisted spin on Malum's favorite form of torture. Panicking, I held my hands in front of me and tried to make Light to throw at her, but I couldn't do it. I was completely helpless. Eventually Jake stilled and froze completely.

"Good boy," Sheila said, patting his horror-stricken face with her hand. "Say goodbye to your bodyguard," she said to me, waving Jakes' hand for him since he was literally frozen in terror. "This was pathetically easy. I'm kind of disappointed. But that's fine, because here's the fun part. Do you want to know who I'm going to capture next, Dave?" She paused. "Well, I'm not going to tell you. I'll just let you agonize and lose sleep over it, knowing that whoever it is, it's all your fault. You let Malum go in the first place, and you made an enemy of me. Literally none of this would have happened if it weren't for you. I'll see you soon. I wonder which of your precious angels I'll capture next . . ."

Then, with her hand still around Jake's neck, she disappeared.

chapter 27
RIDDLES

I screamed. I kept screaming until I couldn't scream anymore. I gave a backhanded punch to the cabinet next to me and kept hitting until my hand felt sprained. Eventually I groaned and leaned my head back against the cabinet. My whole body was shaking, still stunned and disgusted at being possessed. I couldn't believe she'd done that. I knew she hated me, but . . . this went beyond what I thought she was capable of. She used me to get to Jake, but if I was her target, why didn't she just kill me? Why target him if I was the real enemy?

Killing me would have been too easy, I realized. I'd just become another angel to fight against her, and I'd have power. Maybe I wasn't as powerful as other angels, but I'd been the dark horse Malum didn't expect. Maybe he actually saw me as a threat, and that's why he wanted to destroy me, and used Sheila to do it. He wanted me to turn dark, so that when I died, I'd join him.

But I wasn't a threat. I was pathetic. I was nothing but some kid stumbling his way through stupid plans and schemes that never worked and endangering everyone I cared about. Now Jake was captured, and I didn't even want to imagine what torture he was experiencing now.

"I can't do this!" I yelled in a broken voice. "I just can't! Why did you send me here! I've almost died so many times, why not just let it happen? At least dead I'd be some help to the angels!"

No one answered. Somehow, I wasn't surprised. What good had faith done me so far? I prayed and believed and kept trying even when things didn't make sense, and still I was left with nothing. He'd forgotten about me. I was alone. No one was listening. What an idiot I'd been to believe.

I held my head and cried like the pathetic child I was.

Liar. Coward. Stupid. Useless. Naive. Weak.

"*Begone,*" a voice whispered.

Startled, I lifted my head and saw Hermes sitting next to me, glowing like the sun. Then I saw the demons around me who'd been feeding off my despair, whispering in my ear, kicking me when I was down. A burst of Light scattered the demons, sending them wailing and swirling through the air until they disappeared though the walls. But even without them, my pain was still there.

I was too exhausted to even be surprised Hermes was revealing himself to me.

"I can't do this anymore, Hermes," I whispered. "I can't just stand by as a useless mortal while my friends are captured right in front of me."

"You will," he said, unwavering. "You must."

"Can't I come home yet?" I said, my voice breaking. "Haven't I been punished enough?"

"You aren't being punished, David."

"You said I was no longer worthy of The Resting Place because angels don't sin, and I screwed up big time."

He frowned and tilted his head slightly. "I don't believe I used those exact words."

I waited, too torn apart inside to even care that Hermes was almost showing a sense of humor.

Eventually, he sighed. "I said what you needed to hear, David. The larger plan would not have made sense to you."

"So, you lied?"

"No. You know The Resting Place is not the final stop. Mortality tests us, but it does not perfect a person completely. The Resting Place is where we go to finish up what mortality started. When an angel makes a mistake, that does not mean that they are no longer welcome there. If that were the case, there would be no angels left. All unperfected beings make mistakes. In fact, they must make mistakes in order to grow and learn. The only qualifications for residing in The Resting Place are that one must be dead, have a true desire to be there, and have good intentions. You still met all those qualifications, even after saving Sandra."

"Then why was I kicked out?" I exploded.

"You were not 'kicked out'. You were simply reassigned. The Big Man has his reasons, and even I do not know all of them. I gave you the reasons I understood at the time. I have since been corrected. You were not sent here as a punishment for saving Sandra's life. That was merely an excuse to make this 'reassignment' just, and to throw off Malum. Generally, when an angel breaks their contract, they are simply stripped of their duties for a while. The Big Man asked me to give you this highly irregular consequence for a purpose beyond what I understood at the time. I know now, but unfortunately, I cannot tell you."

In a softer voice he said, "I do not enjoy watching you suffer through mortality and blaming yourself for your sufferings, but such is the case with all angels. We are spectators to mortal struggles, and even I am required to have faith sometimes."

My brain short-circuited. Did he just admit to not knowing everything? I wasn't sure how to even process that. I thought he was perfect.

"Almost," he whispered with a smile.

"If you know now why I'm here, then why can't you tell me?" I asked.

He stared at me, visibly struggling to keep a neutral face

and tone. "You would not react well . . . Also, in the words of your comrade Daisy: *No one else is told their purpose in life. Why should you be any different?*"

I took a breath, trying to calm myself, but I just couldn't let go of the frustration. Still, nothing I said or did was going to change Hermes' mind. I figured I might as well ask him my questions while he was here.

"Other than it went against the plan, why was it wrong to save Sandra?" I asked quietly.

Hermes studied me for a while before answering. "It was wrong because you went against an order that was given by a perfect being who has a plan and knows what he is doing. Sandra was needed in The Resting Place. She still is. Just as you are needed in mortality."

My heart skipped a beat for a second. "Wait a minute . . . You said she's *still* needed in The Resting Place? Is . . . is Sandra still going to die? Did I just delay her death? Did I save her for nothing?"

"I doubt she thinks it was nothing," Hermes said.

"Is she going to die, Hermes?" I said through clenched teeth.

"You know I cannot reveal when mortals are going to die. But I will say this: the Big Man takes you when he says it is time. Sandra's time was three months ago."

"She can't die!"

"Why?" Hermes asked.

"Because I . . . care about her! She's been with me this

entire time and she's one of the best people I know. She doesn't deserve to die. She's too young! And without Sandra, how can I be a demon hunter? I can't see or talk to them without her."

Hermes didn't answer.

I clenched my fists and screamed again. Was everyone I cared about going to leave me? How was this *not* a punishment? All the worst things that could possibly happen to me were happening!

I stood and started pacing, hands clenched in fists, fury coursing through my veins. "You say I'm needed here. That there's some purpose to it all. For some reason I'm supposed to struggle through mortality like any other mortal. No signs, no direct contact with angels, just living purely by faith."

"Yes," Hermes said.

"But I'm not like any other mortal!" I yelled in frustration. "I'm a demon hunter and a guardian angel. How the hell am I supposed to fulfill those duties as a mortal? Those are jobs given to *angels*. Because angels have the power to actually do it! Expecting me to do this is like expecting a toddler who's barely walking to start doing backflips. A demon hunter chases down demons. I can't do that in a mortal body! I can't even defend myself!"

Hermes waited patiently until I stopped to take a breath. "Are you finished? I have an answer, but I do not appreciate being interrupted, so I suggest you consider if there is anything else you would like to scream at me before I speak."

I was too upset to speak, so I just waved my hand, gesturing for him to proceed. I'd never dared speak to Hermes like this, and the part of me that wasn't boiling in fury was ashamed. He was showing me more patience than I deserved.

"I have discussed this with the Big Man," he said, "for I have shared your concerns on this matter. He is willing to grant a compromise."

I froze in my pacing and gasped, wide-eyed. "You changed his mind?"

He shook his head. "Perhaps compromise was the wrong word. One does not change God's mind. Sometimes it appears that way because he often waits to be asked before he grants a particular blessing. I made this request on your behalf, and he has granted it."

I slowly sat down cross legged, giving him my full attention.

"Your mortal body has limitations. There are things you may be asked to do that are impossible to do in a mortal body. So . . . you will be given three opportunities to leave it. You will not die; your body will be left in a comatose state during the time your spirit leaves it. Listen very carefully to the terms: You will choose when you wish to use one of these opportunities, so choose carefully. As I said, this may only happen three times.

When out of body, you will have all the capabilities of an angel. You will temporarily be just as you were before you reentered mortality. While you may choose when this occurs, you may not choose how long it lasts. On behalf of the Big Man, I will choose when it is time for you to return to your body, so use your time wisely. I also suggest you be careful with where you leave your body, because while you are not in it, you will be completely defenseless. Do you have any questions?"

My head was reeling. I had too many questions to even pick one. I settled on the stupidest one. "Is this for real?"

Hermes nodded. "This is 'for real'. As I said, do not take this lightly. This is a very rare gift for him to grant. You are needed as a mortal during this time, but he does not wish to leave you defenseless."

I was too busy gaping to even say anything. I sat there for a long time as Hermes let me process. My brain was so full of feelings and directions and questions I didn't know what to think.

Eventually Hermes said, "I am needed elsewhere. I must leave you now. You will likely not see me in person again until you are called home."

"Wait! Hermes!"

He turned to look at me.

"When *will* I come home?" I knew the answer before he told me, but I couldn't stop myself from asking.

"I cannot answer that."

"I just need to know if it's safe to put down roots, or if I should be preparing myself and my family for me to leave again soon."

"I'm sorry, but I am not permitted to tell you that. Except in the case of terminal illness, no mortal may know when they will die. All must live their lives with the knowledge that each day may be their last."

I sat up on my knees. "But we've discussed this! I'm not a normal mortal! I'm a demon hunter. I've been to the other side. Because of Sandra I talk to the dead all the time. You just gave me the ability to leave my body! I just want to know if I'm gonna be here a while, or if this is just temporary."

"All moral life is temporary."

I clenched my hands into fists. "Please. Just tell me if there's a chance that I'll live longer than last time."

He gave me a look I couldn't identify. In a softer voice he asked, "Is that what you want, David? You've expressed interest in returning home to The Resting Place. Now you are asking if you will live longer. Which is your true desire?"

I considered. I'd never really let myself think about how long I wanted to live, I think because I was afraid to want it. I'd spent most of my mortality griping about how it was so much harder than being an angel. And yet, a secret part of me wanted it badly. I got to be with my family. We got to talk and hug and laugh with each other. And my future was filled with endless possibilities. I wanted those possibilities. I was just too scared to grip onto that desire because I was afraid it would be snatched away at any moment.

"I do want to live," I said finally. "I want to live for a long time. I know I've complained about being mortal so much it doesn't seem like it, but it's only because I thought I was being punished, and I'd been asked to do an angel's job in a mortal's body. If that were taken out of it, and if I'm being totally honest with myself, this is what I want. I've always felt like I died too soon, and I want to live. For a long time. I want to . . . do something with my life. Last time I died too soon to even know who I was yet. I'd like the chance to figure that out, and I want to do that with my family by my side. Is there at least a chance I'll live long enough to do that?"

Hermes sighed heavily before answering. "There is a chance you will live a very long life with many joys and sorrows and a family that grows. There is a chance you will make your mark on this world, beloved by all who had the privilege of knowing you. There is a chance you will one day look into a mirror and see a face full of wrinkles and a head of white hair. There is a chance you will live so much life that when it is your time, you will leave content with how you left this world. There is a *chance*."

I gulped. My heart swelled with hope. "How do I make that happen?"

"With a choice."

"A chance . . . with a choice? One choice? What does that even mean?"

"I cannot say more. You will understand someday. Do not think too much on this, David. Paranoia never helped anyone. Do not worry about *when* you will die, but *how* you will live."

I sighed. I was so sick of these stupid riddles! Just give me a direct answer! And yet, in my heart I knew Hermes was telling me exactly what the Big Man wanted him to tell me. If I were to rage and scream, I'd be doing it against the Big Man himself, and I couldn't find it in myself to do that. I took a deep breath and forced myself to trust that he knew what was best for everyone, not just me. He had his reasons, and I would be okay as long as I just did what he said.

It still didn't take away the pain and confusion I was feeling. Even with all Hermes had told me, it didn't change the fact that at this moment I was falling apart.

"I know you do not want to hear this," he said quietly, "but this is not the end of the pain. There is more to come. So, brace yourself. And when you think you've reached the worst of it . . . unfortunately you will be wrong. Always be on guard and keep your faith strong. For as it is with all mortals, life only gets harder. But if you hold true to your faith, you will always be equal to your challenges, even as they increase."

"That's all very comforting," I said sarcastically.

Hermes went to touch my shoulder, then remembered he couldn't do that. "I know it hurts, but you are not alone. You are not forgotten. You are not only remembered, but you are loved. Always remember that. Many people look to you for hope, David. You have a far greater impact on those around you than you imagine."

And then he left, leaving me alone in the middle of the night. I'd just been possessed by a demon. My best friend was captured. Sheila promised to capture more. And I didn't know when, but someday Sandra was going to die.

I fell asleep right there on the kitchen floor and had nightmares of the last time Sandra was going to die. How she pleaded for her life. The part of me that wasn't riddled with pain and self-pity thought of Sandra, and I was determined not to tell her. As much as it hurt to die without closure, and as much as I'd just begged Hermes to tell me when I'd die, I knew he was right not to tell me. There are reasons mortals aren't usually warned when their time comes. They often don't have the strength to carry on. Sandra's days may have been numbered, but she didn't deserve to live with the fear of knowing it.

chapter 28
DEMONS LOVE ME

I woke up at three in the morning on the cold tile with a crick in my neck. The house was completely dark except for the light from the microwave clock and a dim streetlight.

filtering through mom's faded yellow curtains. I was achy all over. I didn't know if it was because I'd fallen asleep on the tile, or if it was some kind of aftereffect of getting possessed. Probably a combination of the two. Feeling like an old man, I slowly pushed myself up and groaned. My brain replayed everything I saw and heard that night. I didn't need the reminder—my dreams had been a constant loop of Jake being captured and Hermes' conversation with me. Achingly slow, I made my way to my room and flopped on my bed. If I wasn't so exhausted, I'd have been concerned that with one of my bodyguards gone, Sheila would have more opportunities to get to me. Also, my mom would be in greater danger. I didn't feel right about her going up against Sheila alone.

"David! Wake up!"

I groaned and rolled over, squinting at the bright light shining through the blinds in stripes on my bed. When my eyes adjusted, I saw Dad frowning down at me in concern.

"Don't you have work?" Dad asked.

I sat up so fast I saw black dots. "What time is it? I thought you were camping."

"I felt like I should come back early. Are you all right? It's almost eleven a.m. I found you passed out on your bed with your clothes on."

I jammed my hands over my eyes like that might keep them inside my head. I felt like someone was squeezing my brain and my eyes were about to pop out.

"I'm fine," I whispered, sliding off the bed. When I landed, my knees almost gave way and I fell into my dad.

Steadying me, he said, "Maybe you oughta stay home today?"

I was so weak and dizzy I'd almost forgotten why I felt this way. Sheila. Jake. He was captured. Gone. And it was my fault. I had to warn my friends.

"I gotta go," I said, yanking my shirt off and rushing to my closet for a fresh one. I pulled it on as I hurried to the bathroom to brush my teeth. I barely glanced at the mirror, but what I saw was not encouraging. Bags under my eyes, insane hair, scruffy 5 o'clock shadow from yesterday, partially covered by an old bandage. I didn't smell too great either, but I didn't have time for a shower, so I heaped on the deodorant and called it good.

"Son, you don't look too good," Dad said nervously in the bathroom doorway. "I think you should call in sick."

"I can't talk right now," I said, rushing past him. "There's something I gotta do."

I was gone before he had a chance to question me.

The phone rang three times before Preston picked up.

"Hey, I might be late today," I said without preamble. "I'll be there as soon as I can."

"Whoa," he said. "You sound kinda crazy."

"I am crazy," I muttered honestly.

"Well, hurry up. I don't have anyone to cover for you and you're supposed to start at eleven."

"I'll be there when I can," I said.

"Dude, what's going on?" he asked.

I hung up, unable to deal with him right now. Not that he was being rude or anything—if anything I was being rude—but I didn't really have it in me to care.

Next, I called Sandra, and of course she didn't answer because she was teaching. But I didn't feel like this could wait. Luckily, I was already on my way to her school. It only took me about five minutes until I was pulling into the parking lot by the office. I flung my car door open, shut it without locking it, and booked it to the office. Out of breath and looking like something the cat dragged in, I stopped at the front desk where my mom used to work.

"Can I help you?" a middle-aged lady asked. I knew I'd seen her before, but I couldn't remember her name.

"I'm here for Ms. Johnson. I'm volunteering in her class today," I lied.

"What is your name, sir?" she asked skeptically.

"David . . . Green," I said, not wanting to give my real last name. If she knew my mom, she'd have known about her dead son who would have the last name of Garcia.

She raised her eyebrows and lifted her reading glasses to look through a binder. "Ms. Johnson doesn't have any volunteers today."

"She must have forgotten," I said, impatiently. I truly understood the skepticism and the security measures at a high school, especially one that had experienced a shooting not too long ago, but I didn't have time for all that right now. What a pain that I couldn't just invisibly fly through the school and float into Sandra's classroom.

"One moment," she said as she checked her directory and put her phone to her ear, dialing Sandra's number. "Ms. Johnson?" she said. "I have someone in the office saying he's here as a volunteer. Says his name is David Green." She paused. "I'll send him right down."

I let out a relieved breath as the front office lady handed me a visitor badge and made me sign in on a clipboard. "Room 208," she told me.

"Thanks."

I walked through their metal detector and through the hallway door as soon as she pushed her button to unlock it.

Part of me was startled by the déjà vu of walking through these echoey, fluorescent lit hallways from my high school days. It must have been a passing period, because the hallway was filled with teenagers laughing and shoving, while the invisible ones ducked out of the way and walked with hunched shoulders. I paused as I passed the library. The last time I was in there, I learned that my mom had died. And I was happy about it, because I was dead too. I froze for a second when I passed my cousin Dani. I spun around to look at her, which unfortunately made her notice me. She made a creeped-out face and signed something to her boyfriend Tyler as they turned around and kept walking. I was stunned. I used to watch over her all the time. It was weird that she didn't know me.

"Focus!" I reminded myself, spinning back around and booking it for Sandra's classroom. Once I found 208, I peeked in the window. There were only a few students in there, either stragglers from her last class, or overly punctual students waiting for the next period. I knocked and waved when she saw me, and she hurried out into the hallway.

"What are you doing here?" she hissed.

"I used to visit you here all the time," I protested.

"Yeah, when you were invisible!" she whispered, looking around nervously. "What if someone recognizes you?"

"Who's gonna recognize me?"

"You used to go here. Your mom used to work here. Some of the teachers we had in high school still work here."

"None of that matters right now!" I said louder than I meant. A few girls eyed me and Sandra, then looked at each other and covered their mouths, giggling. One of them pushed them along I was sure they were about to go tell all their friends that they just watched a teacher get dumped in the hallway.

Sandra's face fell, realizing how upset I was. "What happened?"

I opened my mouth to tell her, but even if this was the right place, I just couldn't do it. "I'll tell you later. We need to call a demon hunter meeting ASAP. Please, if you see anyone, can you tell them to tell Raj and Ying Yue that we need to talk? I'm coming over immediately after work. I gotta go now."

"David, what the heck?" she yelled after me.

I shoved my way back through the hallway and out the office doors, forgetting to sign out or return my visitors badge to the front office.

Now that I'd delivered my message, my urgency faded away, giving way to a deep sense of hopelessness. Everything was so far from okay, I doubted anything would ever be okay again. I didn't have the energy to fake being happy, so I didn't even try. When I got to work, someone waved at me in the Chuck E. costume, and I just nodded and walked away.

"Hey, what's up?" Joanna asked behind the cash register.

"Hey," I said quietly, without stopping.

Part of me worried that I was being rude, but another part of me was just too tired to care. When I clocked in, I passed Jorge, who said, "hey" to me. I barely looked at him. I couldn't focus on anyone or anything around me. All I could think about was how angels were being captured, how my best friend was one of them, how it was my fault. I couldn't find my way out of this pool of despair where I felt like nothing could ever get better. How could it? The demons were winning.

Not to mention my disastrous personal life. My own brother still wouldn't talk to me, and somehow it was up to me to fix that relationship even though he was the one being an idiot about it. What could I say? He would never believe me. I didn't think he'd even want to believe me. He loved holding his grudges.

And what about my family? I'd comforted myself so far by believing that Sheila had limits. In a way, she was predictable. She only attacked unseen when I was completely alone. This last time, she not only revealed herself, but she waited until I *wasn't* alone. She would hurt everyone I loved, and I wouldn't be able to do anything about it. Unless I used that weird gift Hermes discussed . . . But I was still too wary to think about that.

I'd been so lost in my thoughts, going through the motions at the cash register, that I didn't notice Preston talking to me at first.

"What's up with you today?" he asked. "You're so mopey, Joanna came up to me and asked if I'd been mean to you."

I shrugged.

"Dude, you're literally the only person here who's talked back to me. Something must be wrong if Joanna thought she had to come tell me off."

"It's nothing," I mumbled.

"It's not nothing," he said persistently. "You're acting all depressed. You look like a nerdy Eeyore."

I sighed. "First of all, I'm allowed to not be happy all the time. Second of all, if you want to know why someone's upset, you say, 'What's the matter?' or 'Are you okay?' You don't insult them more." I was annoyed that it had somehow fallen to me to teach Preston common courtesy. That wasn't my job, but nobody else was brave enough to do it.

What he'd said wasn't actually that rude, but the thing

about calling me a nerdy Eeyore sounded like something Jake would say, and that just had me spiraling down that hole of depression again.

"Fine. Sheesh," he said, holding his hands up. "You just didn't seem like yourself. I was trying to . . . pay attention to the employees, like you said."

"Well good job, but I don't want to talk about it."

He looked a little crestfallen, which was annoying because I hated feeling bad for Preston, especially when I didn't do anything wrong. The way I was acting was nothing compared to how he usually acted.

"Let me know if you do want to talk about it?" he said uncertainly.

I just nodded and waited until he walked away. Ever since the fire, he weirdly kept coming to me for advice on how to be a nice person, and I didn't feel like being Preston's mom. That thought immediately filled me with guilt. His mom was currently in the Hurricane, along with my best friend who'd worked so hard to protect me.

I halfheartedly tried to smile and be chipper for the customers and for my coworkers, but I did a horrible job. An hour into my shift nobody was talking to me. I tried to remind myself that not everything had fallen apart. I still had my family and my team and Sandra. I had a job and a car and a phone. I just couldn't rid myself of the guilt. I felt like it was my fault Jake was gone. I literally just sat there and did nothing while Sheila took him away. It was Malum's escape all over again. This entire mess was my fault. None of this would have happened if I'd stopped him in the first place!

When I got to Sandra's house after work, the first thing she did when she opened the door was back away from me.

"What the . . ." Her eyes widened and she looked behind herself. "I don't normally condone fighting, but someone needs to take care of this."

"What?" I snapped.

"Just hang on a sec," she said, looking back and forth at people I couldn't see.

"Are you seriously *not* going to let me in?" I said in a tone I'd never used with Sandra before.

Sandra pursed her lips and folded her arms. "I'm going to forgive you for speaking to me like that, only because I know you normally wouldn't. Just trust me and hang on a sec."

I felt stupid and annoyed just standing in her doorway, but slowly my anger ebbed, and I felt bad for how I'd snapped at her.

"Better?" she asked.

I nodded, just beginning to understand what was going on. I felt like I could finally breathe again. Things were still crappy, but that didn't mean I had to be a jerk about it.

Sandra took my hand and I saw my whole team floating

protectively around me, still on guard in case another enemy showed up.

"You were surrounded by demons," Sandra explained. "There were a ton of them all over you. Was it like that all day?"

I shrugged. "I wouldn't have been able to see them, but probably. It was a pretty crappy day."

She led me to the table, and we all sat down.

"Why were there so many of them?" Sandra asked.

"Demons like to kick a man when he's down," Daisy said darkly. "Something must have happened."

"That shouldn't matter," Ying Yue said. "Gloria is clearly occupied with another family member, so Jake should have been there to fulfill his bodyguard duties. Where is he, by the way?"

I let my head fall into my hands and couldn't bring myself to move.

"Oh no . . ." Ted whispered.

"What?" Natalie asked.

Raj's face fell and his hands went to his hair. "Not our Jake."

"What?" Natalie demanded.

I lifted my head and forced myself to say, "He was taken. By Sheila. I saw the whole thing."

I didn't want to relive that nightmare, but I told them the whole story from Sheila appearing to me in my room, to her possessing me, to her paralyzing Jake with fear using her own disgusting version of Malum's biggest weapon and dragging him away.

"Is there any way to find him?" I asked desperately when I was done. "It's not hard to track other angels, you just think of them and show up where they are."

Raj shook his head slowly. "It's been tried. This Hurricane is as untraceable and elusive as Malum. Even if we could find it . . . the angel that got there would probably be captured as well."

I pounded my fist on the table, then let my head fall into my hands. Everyone was silent until I lifted my head again. "I'm sorry, but I think you should all stay away from me so she doesn't capture you too."

"She could kill you," Ying Yue said worriedly.

I shook my head. "She's not trying to kill me. She never was. If she wanted to kill me, she could have easily done it before Jake arrived. She's trying to destroy me. She wanted me to see her taking Jake because she knew it would kill me inside. And she threatened to take one of you next. I don't know if it's just some revenge thing, or if Malum is ordering her to tear me apart, but she's trying to break me, and she'll use you all to do it. If I had to choose between being attacked by a demon, and someone I care about being captured, I choose the first one."

"How could this have happened?" Frederick asked, angrier than I'd ever seen him. "Hermes put us on lockdown in The Resting Place until he had a head count of all the angels. Our entire team was present for that, Jacob included."

"We were meant to stay in lockdown until the headcount was complete," William said softly. "Likely, our young friend left once he'd been counted, worried David would be in danger without him."

"Hermes didn't say anything about that, but you're probably right," I mumbled.

"Hermes?" Raj asked urgently. "You spoke with Hermes? He appeared to you?"

I nodded and gave them the gist of that conversation. Not all the personal parts, but the part about this apparent new ability I had. They all looked either confused or impressed. I couldn't help but think of how Jake would respond. He'd say something blunt and funny to relieve the tension and make me feel like this was something really cool I could do.

"How are you going to use it?" Daisy asked.

I shrugged. "I hadn't thought about it yet. But if Sheila comes near any of you, I *will* be joining the fight."

"Three opportunities," Ying Yue mused. "We could use this. We're down a member, and if necessary, David can join us for any coordinated attacks. We should schedule this out carefully."

"Wait a minute," Raj said, holding his hand up. "This is David's gift, not ours. It should be his choice when and how he uses it."

"Of course I want to use it to help you guys," I said. "You just let me know when you need me back as angel David, and I'll be there."

"How does it work?" Ted asked curiously.

"I don't even know," I said. "I think I just tell Hermes when, and then I float out of my body or something."

Raj smiled. "This is an incredible gift, kid. I know you'll use it wisely."

I smiled back, not even sure why. I wasn't happy, or even that hopeful, but somehow just the motion of smiling made me feel a little better. Just a tiny bit.

All the angels left, leaving me and Sandra with the wanderers. Patty lay despondently on the couch. Asher and Oliver were rattling and knocking things over on the counter. Dorine floated around aimlessly. Gilbert floated where he was, staring off into space. Bill pretended he wasn't looking interestedly at me and Sandra. I thought about Sandra's fear and how she worried she'd become one of them one day. I didn't believe it. She had too much drive in her to just give up.

I wasn't sure if it was because I'd gone crazy, or that I had mortality on my mind. Sandra could die any time, and I could, too, if I didn't make some important choice. I was not going to leave this life again with regrets. Though I knew this would complicate things if something happened, I couldn't stop myself. Once everyone had left the meeting, I turned to Sandra and said, "Will you go out with me?"

She blinked and reared back. "What did you say?"

My first instinct was to take it back, worried she wouldn't respond the way I wanted her to. But that was the old David, high school David. That wasn't me anymore. I'd learned since then that good things are almost always on the other side of fear. So instead, I pretended to be brave and looked her in the eyes and said, "I like you. Will you go out with me?"

She smiled very slowly, though I thought I saw a tinge of nerves behind her eyes, mirroring my own. I could see her wavering, but her hopeful smile won out. "Yes, I'd love to."

I let out a relieved breath and tried to act casual, and not like my heart was hammering a million miles a minute. "Cool. We're going to dinner Friday at 7. I don't know where yet, but I'll come pick you up."

I felt ridiculously giddy, because I'd never picked a girl up for a date before. And I had money to pay for our dinner. My first date was with a demon, and we didn't need cars or money. The thought of picking Sandra up made me feel like I was adulting. This was one part of growing up that I never got to experience my first time around.

I gathered up my keys and Sandra walked me to the door. On my way out, I passed Bill and Gilbert. Bill was doing a goofy happy dance and Gilbert gave me a thumbs up.

"Shut up," I said, trying not to smile.

See, not everything is bad.

Weirdly enough, that simple act of doing something brave made me want to be braver. I knew what I had to do next.

chapter 29
NO REGRETS

I knocked for the fifth time on the door and still no one answered. I frowned, staring at the beveled designs in the dark wood. I felt like a salesman. Honestly, I probably would have had better luck if I was. I sighed and walked aimlessly in a circle as I waited. The front lawn was actually pretty nice, probably because Sam could afford landscapers. Their grass was neatly trimmed, and there was a huge pine tree shading a patio swing. Flowers grew perfectly in little bricked-off areas around the perimeter of the yard. The wind carried a slight chill that had me folding my arms, wishing I had more than my plaid flannel for warmth.

The door cracked open, and I spun around. "Hey," I said, hurrying up to the door, "is Sam home?"

The door opened all the way and Jessica walked out, shutting the door behind her. Her wavy, strawberry-blonde hair was pulled up in a frizzy ponytail, the fly-aways blowing in the wind. I wondered if they tickled.

She squinted at me, then blinked in what looked like an

intrigued surprise. "You're David, right?"

"Yeah, and you're Jessica, right? Nice to meet you." I held my hand out and she shook it.

"You too," she said with an uncertain smile. "I'm sorry, but I don't think Sam wants to talk to you."

"I know," I said quietly. "But I need to talk to him. I need to fix this. If I ever have to . . . leave again, I can't stand the idea of leaving things the way they are between us."

She looked at me with what looked like concern, which was odd. I'd have thought Sam would have talked enough crap about me for her to be totally turned against me. Maybe she'd talked to Elena or my dad since that fiasco at my dad's place. I wasn't even sure if she knew Sam had a brother before that.

She sighed. "I'm sorry, but this probably wasn't the best time for you to pop into his life again. He's in a dark place right now, and this whole situation seems to be dredging up a lot of painful stuff from his past. Maybe it's best if you both just go your separate ways."

"Come on, Jessica," I said with a raised eyebrow. "I know you're not as cynical as that. I think you want us to patch things up."

She tilted her head and folded her arms. "You don't know me."

I just smiled. "Am I wrong?"

Jessica chewed on her lip. I nodded to the porch swing.

"If I can't talk to him, can I talk to you? Just hear me out. If you think I'd be a bad influence on his life, you can throw me out and I won't come back."

After a pause, Jessica nodded and led me over to the swing and sat stiffly at the very edge, though she looked at me with tentative curiosity. She probably didn't know what to make of me. I think part of her hoped that reconnecting would be good for Sam, but another part still felt protective of him. I mean, I had to be bad if Sam's first reaction was to attack me.

"Why did you leave?" she asked.

"I didn't want to," I said firmly. "I was taken away."

Her eyebrows pulled together, and her mouth popped open. "Were you kidnapped?"

"Eh . . . sort of?"

She leaned forward. "Who took you?"

I gave her a nervous close-lipped smile and pointed up. Jessica glanced upward and frowned. "Oh, come on, you don't actually expect me to believe you died."

I shrugged. "I don't expect you to believe anything. What you believe doesn't change what actually happened. I died. Sam saw it. There was no way I could have faked that, and no reason I would have."

She seemed to struggle within herself. "Faking your death does seem a little far-fetched . . ."

I barked out a laugh. "As far-fetched as a long-lost brother returning from the dead?"

She smiled. "I guess not."

A little bird twittered above us, and we both paused to look as the breeze blew a few pine needles from the tree. They danced across the ground.

"He's never going to believe you," Jessica said finally. "Whether it's true or not. He doesn't believe in an afterlife, and, like any sane person, he doesn't believe in zombies or resurrected beings or whatever you claim to be. If you know Sam at all, you know you can't change his mind once he's made it up. And even if you do, he won't admit it. He wants to hate you, so that's what he's going to do."

I rolled my eyes. "Yeah, that's nothing new. He always wanted to hate me. I think he thought I was self-righteous 'cause I'd call him out on his crap when no one else would. He loved to shove it in my face whenever anything bad happened to me like it was proof that I wasn't better than him. I'd trip, he'd laugh in my face. I got a D on a test— he'd laugh in my face. I got scolded by Mom—he'd laugh in my face. I resented him for that, but I never thought I was better than him. I guess I just always expected more of my big brother. I hated that I had to be the responsible one. The decent one. The good example for Elena. Not that he *wasn't* those things. He just . . . wasn't to me."

I blinked and looked up, startled that I'd said all that out loud. "Sorry . . . I didn't mean for it to come out like that. I know you care about him."

Oddly enough, she seemed sympathetic. Maybe she had a sister she had similar feelings about. She gave me a sad smile. "I know Sam, and I love him. He's a good man. But he is . . . difficult. I've chosen that difficulty because it's part of the man I want to spend my life with. But if your relationship is so rocky, why are you trying so hard to shove your way back into his life? It seems like you two only butt heads."

I shrugged. "I don't know. Because he's my brother and I love him, and I know that it's right."

She smirked. "I can see why he thought you were self-righteous."

I grinned. "Well, I was an angel for a while."

I bit my lip, not meaning to have said that bit out loud. Jessica raised an eyebrow like she couldn't decide if I was being ironic or serious.

"He's never going to buy that," Jessica said slowly. "So . . . if you want to eventually talk to him, we need to come up with a realistic explanation for why you left."

"What, lie to him?" I asked. "Isn't that why he's mad at me in the first place? He thinks I lied about dying. Why would I make it worse by lying even more?"

She sighed. "I'm just saying, it's the only way you're gonna talk to him. Like I said, you can't change Sam's mind. He has to choose for himself, and it seems that where you're concerned, he's not going to choose to forgive you anytime soon, especially if you keep 'making up' stories about what happened to you. So, we need to come up with a lie that sounds like the truth, so when you tell it, he'll feel like you're actually being honest with him. If we come up with a really sad, dramatic story, he might even feel bad for you."

I nodded. She had an even better understanding of Sam than I did, which made sense, I guess. And I figured I'd rather build a relationship with him on a little technical lie than never talk to him again. He'd understand one day. Maybe. "Okay, what do you think we should say happened to me?"

Luckily the day warmed up as the sun came out from behind the clouds, because we sat there for a long time as we came up with this ridiculous story about my fake death. I'd somehow witnessed a terrible crime, and someone tried to kill me so I wouldn't blab. After falling from the scaffold—which had been tampered with—I did die temporarily but was revived at the hospital and immediately placed in witness protection. I didn't tell my family because I thought it would be harder to stay away from them if they knew I was alive somewhere.

We kind of had fun coming up with the story, and it was odd because Jessica and I had never spoken, but she felt like someone I could be friends with. We kept going back and forth saying, "Oh, and what if . . .?" or "Yeah! And then . . ." The story was insanely unlikely, but in Sam's eyes it would still be more realistic than the truth.

While unlikely, the lie wasn't impossible.

When we were done both of us smiled at each other, then slowly looked away and frowned.

"This isn't going to work, is it?" I said.

She shook her head.

"I have to make myself look bad, don't I? Screw it. I'll just say what he thinks happened. I walked out on everyone because the pressure was too much or something. I got into drugs and . . . Crap, that still wouldn't explain how I was able to fake my death. What the heck does he think happened?"

She shrugged. "I don't know, but I still think you should try. Don't say you walked out on everyone though. No one who knows you would believe that. This is the first time I've spoken to you, and I don't believe that. Just go with the original story. It probably won't work, but it's your best chance to at least get his attention."

I smiled gratefully. Jessica suggested I write it all down in a letter for him, like we lived back in the stone ages. Her reasoning was good though. He'd never agree to see me or look at my texts or emails. He definitely wouldn't listen to a voicemail. But a letter was a physical thing. If she subtly left my letter on Sam's desk, he'd eventually read it for curiosity's sake, if nothing else. Jessica and I exchanged numbers so I could let her know when the letter was ready, and she could give me a heads-up when he read it. Honestly, she should have been a little more wary of me.

For all she knew I was a total creep and a liar. I figured Mom was whispering to her as well, urging her to trust me.

"Thanks, Mom," I whispered as I walked back to my car.

Jessica waved from the doorway.

chapter 30
BELATED SENIOR YEAR

It was at work that Friday that I got the idea for mine and Sandra's date. Part of me was in deep denial about what Hermes said about Sandra and how she was needed on the other side. I actively ignored the thought with stubborn defiance. Another part of me deep inside was trying to prepare for the possibility of that actually happening. That's probably what made me act so impulsively about this stupid date. You never know how much time you have. I waited too long to ask her out in my first life, I wasn't going to do that again.

"Good luck! Take pics!" Piper said when I clocked out.

"Thanks," I grinned. I waved to Jorge as I walked out, and he seemed relieved I wasn't being mopey anymore.

I checked the time on my phone and tapped my foot as I stood with my hand on the car door handle. I'd really have to book it to make this work. I got in the car and texted Sandra.

Me: Hey, change of plans. What's the earliest you're available?

Sandra: Probably around 4. Why?

Me: I'm picking you up at 4.

Sandra: What are we doing?

Me: You'll see

This is so stupid. It's stupid, right? She's gonna laugh. This is dumb.

Those thoughts didn't stop me from following through with my plans. After a ridiculously fast shopping trip and some time spent in the bathroom making my hair look somewhat nice for a change, I folded my garment bag over my arm and hurried back to the car to get Sandra.

I waited outside her apartment door, tapping my foot nervously. She answered the door in her slippers with her hair in a scrunchie. She looked adorable. I smiled and said, "Hold out your hand."

"What?" she asked.

"Just do it."

She held her hand out like she expected me to kiss it and I knelt down on one knee.

"I'm not proposing," I said quickly. "I'm just being dramatic."

Sandra raised an eyebrow and quirked a curious smile. "Okay?"

I pulled the corsage from behind my back and put it around her wrist. "Sandra Johnson, teacher of teenagers, maker of delicious tacos, and keeper of the ghosties, will you go to prom with me?"

She blinked. "I'm sorry, what?"

"Adult prom," I clarified, standing up.

"That's a thing?"

"Apparently. Piper was telling me her aunt and uncle are going, so I got us tickets. I never got to go to prom, and I couldn't care less about that, but I regret never asking you to a dance. This is me making up for being stupid and literally dying before asking you out. So, will you go to prom with me?"

"Okay," she grinned.

"Sweet," I said. I squeezed her hand and said, "Let's go."

"Wait, now?" she asked, looking startled.

"I didn't know about it until today, and the dance is tonight, so the first part of our date is going shopping and getting you a dress. I already found myself a really cheap tux." I started pulling her along.

"Wait," she said, letting go of my hand, "Let me grab my purse!"

"Okay," I said, "But I can help with the dress. I live with my dad, so I don't have a lot of expenses. I've got some money saved up."

"Money you should be saving for college!" she yelled

as she raced to her room.

"I just feel bad for springing this on you," I said when she returned with shoes on, and her purse slung over her shoulder.

She locked her door and took my hand. "Did you buy the tickets?"

"Yeah," I said.

"So, I'll buy the dress."

I shrugged. "Fair enough."

My mom clearly wasn't with me as we were shopping. The difference was night and day. I felt worried and depressed and angry as the demons followed me around and whispered in my ear. Sandra tried waving them away and saying, "Shoo!" It obviously didn't help, but it did make me laugh a little, which I definitely needed. It was like this huge net of dread had fallen over me and was trying to pull me to the ground. I kept pushing my way forward, but the dread and self-hatred only seemed to get heavier as I walked. Eventually I let go of Sandra's hand. It was easier to ignore the demons if I couldn't see and hear them. Sandra's face fell when I let go, probably thinking I just didn't want to hold her hand, but I was so focused on not curling up into a ball of misery that I didn't take the time to explain.

It was a little easier to bear once Sandra started trying on dresses. It was an entertaining distraction. She had her own little fashion show in the dressing room, walking down the hallway like it was the red carpet. At one point she tripped over the front of her dress and ran into the wall, which made me laugh so hard I think I scared the demons away. I felt a lot better after that.

I told her she looked great in everything like I was supposed to, but my favorite was this emerald green dress she tried on with a slit up to her thigh. We found her some heels and then found me a tie to match her dress. Having made surprisingly good time we ended up having time to grab a quick dinner before hurrying back to Sandra's so she could get ready.

All I had to do was change, so I just hung out with invisible wanderers while we watched *The Floor is Lava*. I wasn't sure who chose that particular show, but everyone seemed to like it, because the TV wasn't flipping back and forth between shows like it normally did. There must have been an angel around because I didn't feel the demons anymore. I usually assumed it was my mom, but at Sandra's house it could be anyone. Lots of dead people hung out there. For all I knew my friends were following Ying Yue's schedule of babysitting me despite what a terrible idea it was. Especially since Jake . . . well, I couldn't think about that.

Eventually Sandra came out. Her hair was smooth and wavy, no trace of her cute, bouncy curls. Her makeup made her look like a model. Her eyes were huge, and her lips were red. Her skin was completely flawless with a slight shimmer on her cheekbones. I almost didn't recognize her, but then she snapped at me and told me to stop staring and I saw Sandra behind her cosmetic layers.

"Ready?" I asked, standing and holding my arm out.

"I suppose," she said, suppressing a smile.

And I finally took Sandra to the prom.

By the end of the night, we were both loopy and tired. Neither of us were big party animals and all the dancing really sapped our energy. I didn't mind though. I got to hold Sandra close to the slow songs and dance like a lunatic to the fast ones. I honestly don't remember much of the dance because I was too busy obsessing over Sandra. Part of me saw danger in this. If she was going to leave someday, wouldn't this be harder if I got attached? Another part of me said, *Shut up and dance.* So I did. We were laughing our heads off on the way home, reliving that moment when I stepped on her dress and we both fell over. It was nice to have someone share in my clumsiness for once.

When we parked, I walked her back up to her apartment.

"Thank you for doing this," I said. "I know it was dumb."

"Took you long enough," she said, leaning forward slightly.

Crap . . . she wants me to kiss her, doesn't she? But what if she doesn't and I freak her out? Why would she want me to kiss her anyway? And what if I do and it gives us both false hopes and one of us dies? Shut up, stupid! Just do it! But what if I'm not a good kisser? The last and only person I've kissed was Sheila, and it was horrible. I literally barfed Darkness for like five minutes after that.

Sandra bit her lip. She nervously looked down and back up again. Her eyes definitely inviting—even pleading—me to do it. I cleared my throat and fiddled with my keys. I tore my eyes away from hers before I exploded from nerves. When I finally looked back up, my eyes locked in on her lips, which definitely tipped the balance. I didn't just want to kiss them, I needed to. I'd hate myself forever if I didn't.

Before I could talk myself out of it, I put my shaking hands around her waist and pulled her toward me.

"Can I?" I choked out. I swallowed, unable to finish. Sandra put her arms around my neck and closed her eyes, making her ginormous eyelashes rest like butterflies on her face. Weirdly, her closed eyes gave me more courage. She couldn't watch my face and neck blush red as a tomato.

I pressed my lips against hers and it was nothing like kissing Sheila. It felt both right and terrifying. Safe and dangerous. Nothing else mattered, and all my problems completely vanished for a few seconds.

Our moment of bliss was interrupted by a, "What the

fart?"

We pulled apart and spun around. Asher and Oliver were gaping disgustedly at us. Sandra and I gaped back at them.

"Asher?" Sandra asked incredulously. "Did you just talk?"

"You guys are nasty!" he said.

"Yeah," Oliver said. "This is *our* house! No kissing! Sickos!"

They both disappeared.

After a disbelieving silence Sandra said, "They've been here for five years, and I've never heard them speak!"

"I should have kissed you a long time ago," I said.

We kissed again but were interrupted when Bill popped up next to us and whispered, "Finally." He smiled and gave us a double thumbs-up, looking like an embarrassing dad.

We jumped apart again, but before we had the chance to get anything else out of Bill he disappeared too.

Sandra grinned and said, "Okay, next time you come over we'll just, like, make out on the couch and see how many wanderers start talking."

I grinned back. "What a noble sacrifice we'll make in the name of rescuing wanderers."

"Such a noble sacrifice," she said.

I snorted and we both laughed awkwardly, both wondering how much of this was a joke and how much was us making a joke out of something real. Did she really like me in that way? If so, how much did she like me? Were we more than friends now, or was this a one-time thing?

As I shuffled in the doorway I said, "So . . ."

She was apparently wondering the same thing. "So are we dating, or . . ."

"Yeah," I said, trying to be bold. "If you're cool with that. I really like you, Sandra."

She smiled radiantly. "I really like you too."

"Just one more for the sake of saving wanderers," I said, taking her face in my hands.

We weren't interrupted this time.

chapter 31
JAILBREAK

I came home smiling ear to ear and didn't hear my dad when he asked me how the date went. I was reliving our kiss, almost running into walls in my euphoric daydreams. I put on some music while I got ready for bed and danced like an idiot while I changed into my PJs. Of course, I fell over for the second time that night, because you can't exactly dance with only one leg in your pants.

When I went to brush my teeth, I was too busy singing *The Way You Make Me Feel* in my best Michael Jackson voice that I almost didn't see the literal writing on the wall. At first, I was confused. I blinked, my singing slowly trailing off. Then I froze as the rug was pulled out from beneath my feet. There was a message written in shaving cream all across the mirror: *I GOT HER!* There was a heart for the dot in the exclamation point.

Heart trying to beat out of my chest, I sprinted to the living room. "Dad, have you been in my bathroom?"

"No."

"Has anyone else been in the house since I left?"

He shook his head and frowned. "Just me. Why do you ask?"

My hands went to my head, and I would have sunk to the ground if I wasn't so full of adrenaline. My dad asked me something, but I was too busy sprinting to my car. I slammed the door shut behind me and was tempted to just bust through the garage door as it slowly opened foot by foot. I called Sandra as I cut someone off and sped down the road fifteen over the speed limit. I sped up to twenty when a light a quarter mile off turned yellow, and I shot through it just as it turned red.

"Hey, long time no see," Sandra said when she picked up. I could hear the smile in her voice. I was relieved that the "her" the mirror referred to wasn't Sandra, but I never really thought it would be.

"Are there any angels there?" I demanded.

"No."

I gripped my steering wheel tighter. "How can we get one there?"

"You'd know better than me. You were an angel. How did you know when people needed you?" she asked.

"I didn't! I just sort of took turns checking up on people. If it was a big thing, Hermes would send me someone's way."

I swore as the car in front of me slowed to a crawl in

order to turn right, and the car in the left lane was driving the same speed as me so I couldn't switch lanes to go around them.

"David, what's going on?" she demanded.

I couldn't answer. I didn't want to put my fears into words.

"Look, if it's a big deal, maybe Hermes will—"

She cut off.

"What?" I asked.

"Raj just showed up. He wants you here as soon as possible."

Finally, I veered right into Sandra's parking lot and shot to the closest empty space, not bothering to stay within the lines.

"I'm here," I said, throwing open my door and taking the stairs two at a time. I barged through her door without knocking, only momentarily dismayed that she hadn't locked her door. I ran up to Sandra and hugged her tightly. She'd changed into pajamas but was still in full prom hair and makeup. The part of me that wasn't freaking out was distracted by how my heavy breathing caused her fly-away hairs to blow back from her face.

"What's going on?" she asked, her voice muffled against my shoulder.

I let go of her and snatched her hand. The whole team was there, floating around the table, not even bothering to act human by sitting in chairs. Their faces were drawn and grave and no one would meet my eyes. They kept glancing at me, then looking away.

"Who was taken?" I whispered, barely loud enough to hear.

No one answered.

"Who!" I yelled.

Raj swallowed and said what I'd been fearing deeper than anything I'd ever feared.

"Your mother."

I gripped the table with my free hand until my knuckles turned white. Sandra flinched as I squeezed her hand too tight. Everyone cringed, looking away, not knowing what to say. Somehow sensing even before I did that I was about to blow up.

"Now, lad," William said cautiously, "we've all lost people—"

"Shut up!" I yelled. "Don't try to make this okay! She took my mom! And it's my fault!" I kicked a chair over and stood there huffing, unable to contain all I was feeling.

Daisy said, "It's not your—"

"Yes, it is!" I screamed. "All of it! From the very beginning!" I could feel my face burning red with rage.

"David, you need to—" Ying Yue started to say.

"EVERYONE JUST SHUT UP AND LEAVE ME ALONE!" I released Sandra's hand so I wouldn't have to listen to them and ran out of the room, slamming the laundry door shut. I took a gallon of laundry detergent and threw it against the wall, watching it splatter all over the cabinets. With a scream, I punched the door, then leaned against it, closing my eyes and breathing heavily. There was a part of me that wanted to sink to the floor and sob, but I was way past crying. I was done. I'd had enough.

This would end. Today.

Something clicked inside me. I'd been worrying and agonizing over what to do for so long I felt like I couldn't breathe. Suddenly all my concern was washed away, pushed out by a single-minded fury and determination that not only made me feel capable, but dangerous.

Sandra knocked on the door. "David?"

I ignored her and looked up. *Hermes. Now.*

Sandra came in and I kicked the door shut behind her. *ARE YOU SURE?*

"Now!"

Then my body fell off. It was like someone was holding onto me by my clothing, and I simply slipped out of it, leaving the clothing behind in their hands. Except instead of falling down, I fell up. I saw myself crumple to the ground as my body lost purchase of my spirit. I had a hideous moment of reliving my original death, while another part of me let out a relieved sigh. You don't realize how heavy and exhausting a human body is until you shed it. I felt light and free, and probably would have grinned under normal circumstances. As it was, I felt more like a soldier donning a uniform and gearing up for battle.

Sandra saw my body fall and my spirit lift, and she screamed, falling to her knees. "David! No, not now!" Tears sprang to her eyes and her hands went to her head.

"I'm not dead, Sandra," I told her, my voice oddly expressionless. "This is temporary. I have a demon to track down."

Quietly I evaluated my powers, testing if I could still create Light and Darkness. It took a few flickering tries, but soon I had a huge ball of Light and Darkness in either hand. Once upon a time that would have been difficult for me, but after my demon hunter days it was like muscle memory. I nodded with grim satisfaction. I created a gun and filled it with a few demon killer bullets, which I stashed in a pocket I created in my robe.

"I'll be back," I told Sandra. "Watch over my body, and don't tell anyone I left. Tell them I fainted or had some kind of accident. Shouldn't be that hard to believe."

She stared at me, open-mouthed, her eyelashes sparkling with tears. "David, what—"

But I was gone.

As an angel it's not difficult to track people down, living or dead. If you know the person well, it's even easier. You simply think of them and appear wherever they are. The better you know them, the closer to their location you appear. It didn't work with Malum—he was somehow able to hide—but Malum wasn't the only demon that knew about the Hurricane.

I thought of the demon I wanted, and before even looking at my surroundings, my hand was around her throat with a demon killer bullet to her head.

"Tell me where they are," I said in a low voice.

Sheila's eyes bugged out of her head "Da—*What? How?*"

"TELL ME!" snarled. The hand around her throat sparked with Light and she twitched like she'd just been given an electric shock.

"What do you want?" she yelled. "I don't know who killed you, but it wasn't me!"

I didn't bother to correct her that I wasn't dead. "You can haunt and torment me all you want. Scare me, hurt me, kill me for all I care! But you do *NOT* touch my *mother!*"

She laughed darkly, but I could see a tinge of fear behind her blasé manner. I took satisfaction in that. "Guess I hit a nerve. Well, I had to change tactics because angels kept saving you. Then I realized I could just take out your bodyguards. Then if I couldn't kill you, eventually you'd just kill yourself out of despair. Is that what happened? Did you finally kill yourself?"

I leaned in so close, our foreheads were almost touching, "Where. Are. They."

"You can't intimidate me," she growled. "Your little bullet will hurt me, but it won't make me talk."

It was true, I couldn't make her do anything. Well, no . . . that wasn't quite right, was it? I couldn't make her do anything without stooping to her level. In order to hurt a demon, I had to think like one. I thought quickly about moments of weakness or fear I'd seen in her. Back when she saved my life, she mentioned something about hating me as much as she hated *him*. I had no idea who "him" was. It could be Malum, the Big Man, literally any male being living or dead from the beginning of time, but whoever it was had power over her. It was a flimsy bluff, but I'd already thrown her off by showing up as an angel. For all she knew, maybe I did know her nemesis.

"If you don't tell me, I'll take you to *him*," I said through my teeth.

"Who?" she asked uncertainly.

"You know who."

Her eyebrows came up and color drained from her face. "No. *Please,* no."

Part of me was distracted by the fact that she didn't question whether I knew who "he" was. This horrible nightmare of hers had to be someone that I knew.

"I will do it right now." I released the gun to her head and reshaped it into a chain of Light and Darkness that I shackled around her closest wrist. Only then did I let go of her throat. "I'll take you to him. I'll drag you there like you dragged Jake and my mom off to whatever hellish torture you threw them in. Now you tell me how to find them, or I'll do it!"

Sheila gasped and tears filled her eyes. "Fine! I'll take you there, but you'll never get them out. No one escapes the Hurricane unless Malum lets them out."

Hermes. Distract Malum. I need time for a jailbreak.

We hadn't discussed this before, and Hermes usually didn't interfere directly with mortal or angel affairs, but he was all I had. He had all the defenders and demon hunters at his disposal and the ability to speak to all their minds. Also, when he saw fit to use it, the guy was crazy powerful. Surely he could whip up some kind of distraction. I didn't wait for his answer.

It was only then that I took in my surroundings. We were in a neighborhood Sheila and I hung out in once when I was undercover. I'd found her here looking in at a family she was planning to torment, just like last time. Those teenage girls and their grandparents. She looked back at the house and paused.

"What are you waiting for?" I demanded. "Let's go."

Sheila yanked on her chain and transported us, dragging me behind her. In a second, we were at the edge of a bottomless pit. I couldn't see into it, but I could hear the screams, the cries, the wails. It was the sound of torture and hopelessness. Of wanting to die, but already being dead. And above that a deep, resonant, all-encompassing *breathing* that swirled around us like the wind in a storm. It carried with it the screams of the damned, whipping our hair and clothes around us like a hurricane of despair.

I didn't have time to be scared. "How do we get them out?" I yelled over the wind.

"You don't. Only Malum lets you out."

I frowned. "How do you know only Malum can do it? Has anyone ever tried pulling someone out before?"

"I don't know," she said. "I doubt anyone's been stupid enough to try. They'd get sucked in too."

"Well, there's a first time for everything," I said grimly. I sat at the edge of the pit and squeezed my eyes shut. I couldn't think about it, I just had to do it. "Hold on to my hand and don't let go." I didn't give Sheila the chance to protest before I jumped in.

I thought I'd be prepared. I'd had every nightmare in the book, and they always got more terrible and creative than the last. Almost all of them had to do with my family and not being able to save them. Yet, there was one person whose salvation I'd never questioned. Not because of arrogance, but because the thought was too terrible to even dream up.

Despite the many souls in the Hurricane, there was only one Presence I could feel. It was deeper and darker than Malum. It was hate and agony on a level that threatened to tear me apart. Like trying to swim through a tidal wave, there was no chance to fight it.

I could see nothing, and then the Presence stood above me, looking down in his righteous indignation. I knew him, but my mind protested what I saw because he was all wrong. I'd met the Big Man, and it was him that I saw shining in the Darkness. I gasped and knelt on nothing, and then I heard him speak.

"You have disappointed me," he said quietly.

I gasped. I'd feared, but never believed he'd say this. But it was true. I'd failed him over and over. How could he not be disappointed in me? I moaned and covered my face. "I know."

His voice was cold. "You have failed me. You have shamed me. This I cannot forgive."

"No!" I looked up in terror. He couldn't be saying what I thought he was saying.

He stared down at me, unfeeling. "Grace can only extend so far. Look at what you have done. You have destroyed everything. Your family was better off without you. How foolish of you to think you could save anyone when you can't even save yourself. You were never going to be good enough and you know it. You always have."

I gripped my hair and sobbed. "But I tried! Please! Forgive me!"

"I cannot."

"But I have to come back home! I have to! Please!"

"Never again," he whispered harshly. "I don't want you anymore."

"No!" I screamed, wishing I could tear myself apart.

"You were never good enough, you miserable wretch. You are lost and I wash my hands of you."

And then he disappeared, and I was left in the Darkness.

"*NO!*" I screamed.

I never imagined this kind of agony. Never. I wanted to stop existing.

Suddenly I could see all the lost souls like me caught in the red mists of the Hurricane. Weeping and moaning in their own personal torture. The sound seeped into my heart, and I became one with it. In the smallest part of my mind that was still me, I was aware that I had a mission and that I hadn't truly seen the Big Man forsaking me, but the sight of it shook me to my very core. The whole exchange was less than a minute, but it was enough to completely unhinge me. The scene played over and over in my mind until I was sure that it was real, and I was truly lost forever. My screams joined the screams of the other forsaken wretches as I joined their ranks of eternal torment.

And then I felt someone squeeze my hand.

Who was that? Why was someone holding my hand? My first thought was Sandra, but that couldn't be right. She was too good to end up down here with someone like me. It wouldn't be her holding my hand. Something in my mind vaguely remembered telling someone not to let go, but it was a faded and fuzzy memory. I was supposed to be doing something. What was it? Was I saving someone? How could I save someone when I was lost myself? But not completely . . . someone was still holding on to me.

They squeezed again.

Sheila! I gasped as the memories flooded back and I remembered what I was doing here. I couldn't believe that Sheila hadn't let go of me. She could have been rid of me. She could have left me down there like she did Jake and my mom when she threw them into the pit. But for the second time, I was saved by a demon.

Though I remembered my identity and purpose here, I still hadn't succeeded. The red mists of misery caressed me as I agonized over how to find my mom and Jake in this pit of torture without letting go of Sheila. How would I get them out of here? And how could I leave everyone else in their torment? I wouldn't wish this on my worst enemy.

"Help me!" I prayed, tears streaming down my face as I dangled from Sheila's arm. *"How do I save them?"*

LIGHT.

I squeezed my eyes shut and thought of where Light comes from, pleading and praying I could make it in this Darkness, but it wouldn't come. All I could produce were little flickers that were quickly eaten by the Dark. It was hopeless. Everything was hopeless. I couldn't do it!

HAVE FAITH, DAVID. REMEMBER WHAT I TOLD YOU:

YOU ARE NOT ALONE.

I'd never tried so hard to have faith in a position as hopeless as the one I was in. Oddly enough, it was my experience with Malum that carried me through. When I met him during that failed ambush, I had to talk to him without him freezing me with fear and discovering my identity. I learned how to shove that fear aside and replace it with something else. With a giant mental heave, I expelled my fear, believing with all my heart even though it didn't make sense. It didn't matter if I was strong enough, the Big Man was stronger than everyone and everything and he hadn't left me. I had to believe that.

Yelling in defiance I gave it another almighty effort and Light burst from me, shining from my entire body and filling the space around me. I gasped at the brightness and how far it reached. I didn't just illuminate me, but everything around me. I'd never done this before, not even when I was an angel.

The trapped souls cringed away from the Light, some wailing in pain, but others hesitated, squinting at me with the smallest wisp of hope on their faces.

"Come on!" I yelled. "Take my hand; I'll pull you out!"

No one moved. They either couldn't or wouldn't come near me.

"Mom! Jake!"

I scanned the crowd, cursing the fact that I couldn't just let go of Sheila and go searching for them myself. But

I knew that if I let go, I'd become lost as well. I could feel the red mists trying to pull me back under, and gritted my teeth, redoubling my efforts to keep my Light burning bright. I closed my eyes and tried to locate them the way I'd found Sheila. I took a deep breath and when I opened my eyes, they locked in on a crumpled heap in the Darkness. I wouldn't have recognized him if I hadn't had that extra sense. He wasn't glowing, and his emaciated face would haunt me for a long time after that. The red mists formed into little skeletal arms, pulling and tugging at his hands, feet, robe, even his eyelids. He was completely oblivious, eyes half shut, staring into oblivion. My heart sank. His glow was gone. It looked like *he* was gone.

"Jake!" I yelled.

He didn't react to his name.

"No," I moaned. He looked like a wanderer. Hopelessly lost, with absolutely no sense of self left. It was no wonder since he'd been down here for days. I'd been down here for less than an hour, and it was enough to scar me forever.

"Come on, Jake!" I yelled.

There was still not even a flicker of recognition.

This was impossible! I couldn't let go of Sheila or I'd never find my way out again. But Jake wasn't coming, I had no idea where my mom was, and I didn't know how much longer Hermes would allow me to stay in this form.

"Mom!" I yelled, looking frantically around me. *"Mom!"*

A dead-eyed woman grabbed my arm and I flinched.

"Uh, not my mother, but okay . . ." I pushed her up to Sheila, who took hold of the woman with her other hand and pulled her out.

"MOM!" I yelled again when the random lady was free. "STOP IT! STOP IT!"

I gasped. A tortured soul shifted out of the way and there she was—legs pulled up to herself, hands over her ears, rocking back and forth. She was still glowing slightly, but it was dim and flickering. The red mists surrounding her formed into hands and faces, shoving her remaining Light into their mouths. They were eating her Light! I thought I'd explode from the conflicting feelings of fury and devastation. I didn't know if I wanted to cry or scream.

"Mom, I'm right here!"

"MAKE IT STOP!"

My broken heart ripped farther because she thought I was another nightmarish illusion. She was hearing her son pleading for her and being unable to go to him.

I couldn't solve this with panic. I couldn't yell for her down here. Screams belonged in this Darkness, and we belonged to the Light.

"Gloria, open your eyes," I said softly.

I'm not sure how my voice reached her through the

cacophony of screaming and moaning, but Mom startled and hesitantly opened her eyes, then shielded her face from the blinding Light coming off me.

"Mom, it's okay," I said. "It's me. I'm getting you out of here."

She lifted her head and blinked. Slowly recognition crossed her features. She gasped and ripped her arms free from the red misty hands trying to tie her down. It looked like it took all her remaining strength, but once free, she flew at me, throwing her arms around me. "My boy! My boy! What happened to you? Why are you down here? Did you die? How did you get captured? How are you glowing so bright?" She was sobbing so hard she was practically unintelligible.

I hugged her back tightly with my one arm, squeezing my eyes shut. I knew we had to move, but I needed to take in this moment because I didn't know when I'd get another opportunity to hug her. "Time to go," I whispered eventually. "Can you get Jake?"

She nodded and let go reluctantly Slowly, she approached Jake, kneeling in front of him. "Jacob? Honey, it's time to go." He didn't move.

"Just grab him!" I said. "We don't have much time. Malum could show up any minute."

I regretted saying his name because my mom flinched like I'd just said Voldemort. She took Jake's hand and pulled him behind her. He just let her drag him along, not even noticing he was moving. He looked so terrifyingly *wrong*.

My mom and I pushed Jake up to Sheila, who pulled him up with her other hand. Then I did the same for my mom, hanging behind for any last-minute stragglers.

"Come on!" I said, looking around at the hoard of tortured spirits screaming and tearing their hair out. My heart twisted knowing exactly how they felt. I didn't know which of them were angels or demons, but I didn't think anyone deserved to be in this hole.

A few approached me hesitantly. Flinching at my slightest movement as though I'd hurt them.

TIME'S UP.

"Hurry!" I shouted beckoning the prisoners toward me. One of them floated up to me, stared at me with glazed over eyes, and took my hand. I pushed him up and three more followed.

"Come on!" I urged the rest of them, still cringing away from me.

MALUM IS ON HIS WAY.

But there are still so many—

YOU CAN'T SAVE EVERYONE, DAVID. FOCUS ON THE ONES YOU CAN.

It was one of the hardest decisions of my life to leave the rest behind in that pit of horrors, but I knew Hermes was right. I sighed and reached up with my free hand for Sheila's and she pulled me out. It felt like being pulled out of a river I'd been drowning in. I slumped to the side and breathed a sigh of relief, finally free of that oppressive Darkness.

"You are such an idiot!" Sheila yelled, slapping me. "That was the stupidest thing I've ever seen anyone do. And you roped me into it!" She glared at me with a look that could kill. Darkness swirled in her eyes. "You don't actually know who *he* is do you?"

I shook my head.

"For an angel you do a lot of lying!"

I smiled. "For a demon you do a lot of saving."

She growled and shoved me away. I was immediately caught by my mom hugging me again. It was weird, because I kept expecting the squeezing to make it hard to breathe, but I wasn't exactly in my body at the moment and couldn't feel physical pain or discomfort.

"Mom, you need to get out of here," I said, pulling away. "Take Jake with you back to The Resting Place where you'll be safe."

"You're coming with us!"

"I can't."

"Yes, you can!"

I pulled mom aside and whispered low so Sheila couldn't hear. "I'm not dead. I'm having an out-of-body experience or something. My body's in a temporary coma. There's no time to explain. Just go!"

She squeezed my arms. "I love you so much! Please be

safe!" She gave me one last worried glance, took Jake's arm, and disappeared.

I couldn't return to my body until Hermes put me back, so for some insane reason I decided to stay a few more minutes with Sheila, only feet away from that awful pit.

Sheila and I awkwardly looked away from each other, but when I looked back, I had a crazy urge to smile again.

"What?" she demanded.

"I knew there was good in you."

"There isn't!" she hissed.

"You're not evil," I said stubbornly. "I may have been acting when we dated, but you weren't. You were nothing but yourself and I just know the real you is so much better than what you're trying to be."

Sheila's face hardened and her aura of Darkness expanded. The silence smoldered and I took a step back from her. "You want proof of what I am? That I belong down here? You asked me once how I got on Malum's good side in the first place." She leaned in closer. "Do you want to know what I did?"

I nodded nervously, Sheila in front of me, the pit behind me.

She leaned in close to my ear and whispered, "*I* was the one who set him free."

Before I had time to puzzle out how that was even possible, the devil we spoke of appeared. Malum, with his bland, featureless face, barely containing all the Darkness inside.

Before he could react, I elbowed Sheila and whispered, "Push me into the pit! So he doesn't know you—"

She kicked me in the stomach so hard I flew backward and fell into the Hurricane, the Darkness and red mists blocking out all light and sound. Despite the horror of falling back into the Darkness, I couldn't help thinking, *Wow, no hesitation there.* I didn't know why I was trying to protect Sheila from Malum's wrath or why I'd offer to take the fall for her, but it was still hurtful she'd throw me in the pit without even a second of guilt. She didn't know I wasn't dead. For all she knew, I'd be stuck down there for all eternity. I guess she really did hate me.

The Darkness became a pressure, squeezing me from all sides as I fell. I tried to cover my ears and shut out the voices, but it didn't work. The voices—well, one voice in particular—was loud and clear.

You failed too many times.

There is no forgiveness.

You can never come back.

I closed my eyes, covered my ears, and held onto the Light inside me. "*Hermes. Please—*"

Before I hit the bottom, I was yanked to the side and dumped back into my body.

chapter 32
A SILENT JAKE

I gasped loudly and stood up, my head spinning. Then I collapsed onto Sandra who fell over beneath me.

"Oh my gosh! David! What the *hell* just *happened?*"

"Sorry, sorry!" I said as I groaned and rolled off her. I lay on the floor for a minute feeling every ache and pain all over my body. Somehow, I was in the living room, and I'd just fallen from the couch. How the heck did Sandra get me up there? Did she drag me? Maybe that was why I felt so achy . . . But it was more than that. It took so much work just to *breathe* in and out. I felt things pop and crack. The soft carpet felt like stabby little knives on my face. It also smelled like dust. After my brief break from the land of the living, my body was going through sensory overload.

Sandra knelt next to me and rolled me over, so my face wasn't in the carpet, and I moaned pathetically.

"Are you hurt?" she demanded. There were mascara

streaks down her cheeks. I felt awful remembering how I'd left her there with my body looking like I'd just died.

"No, mortal bodies just suck," I muttered. "I hate that transition."

"What just happened?" she demanded.

"I did the thing. I left my body to go save Jake and my mom."

Her jaw dropped. "Did it work?"

I nodded and grinned, feeling unbelievably relieved and triumphant. "Yeah. Yeah, it actually worked."

She looked behind herself worriedly and I felt my smile melt away.

"What's happening?" I asked.

She didn't seem to have words. She just shrugged. "I don't know, I've been over here with you the whole time. They were just having their meeting and then something happened and now they're all freaking out."

I held out my hand and Sandra helped me up. I wobbled a little, so she steadied me and pulled me toward the commotion in the kitchen. My team was all still there, but they weren't sitting around the table, they were all gathered around something, frantically crying or shouting.

"What's going on?" I demanded.

They all stopped and looked over at me and I saw my mom and Jake in the middle of their circle. Mom was crying silently, and Jake was still staring blankly at nothing.

"Ah, Jake . . ." I said, slowly walking up to him, towing Sandra behind me. Guilt clawed at me from the inside. His eyes were haunted, but his face was completely devoid of emotion. "Why didn't you take him back to The Resting Place?" I asked my mom quietly.

"We're not supposed to," she said. "It's against the contract to bring anyone in who doesn't choose to be there. W-wanderers aren't coherent enough to choose."

I sighed, remembering that little detail. You can't bring anyone into The Resting Place by force. They have to make the choice. The only exception is when demons are brought to trial or are imprisoned, and even then, you have to have permission from the Big Man.

"We know Jake," Natalie said. "He would want to be there. He already chose it."

"So did I," I said with a shrug. "Not the same situation, I know, but still. Things can change."

"And I don't think shouting and crying at him is helping much," Sandra muttered. The angels backed away with chagrin. I could understand how upset they were though. Jake had always been so loud and vibrant and obnoxious in a way that you forgave because he had this annoying habit of making people like him. A silent Jake was just wrong.

"All right, it's time someone explained what happened," Raj said, folding his arms. He looked at my mom. "How on earth did you two escape?"

My mom pointed at me. "He saved us."

Everyone looked at me and I shrugged, uncomfortable

with all their eyes on me. "I had help."

Raj narrowed his eyes. Then sighed and shook his head, running his hands through his hair. "We're idiots. How did you . . . That was so dangerous! I should have realized. I should have followed you!"

"Will someone explain what's happening," Daisy yelled, literally stomping her foot. Though, being incorporeal, it didn't have much impact.

"The boy did not faint," William explained. "He left his body and went on a solo rescue mission."

Ying Yue pointed to the table. "Sit. Explain. Now."

I sighed. The story felt too heavy to tell. I didn't want to relive the nightmare. Sandra, noticing my distress, squeezed my hand in support, which just reminded me of Sheila squeezing my hand as I dangled in the Hurricane. How could such opposite people make the same thoughtful gesture? Why didn't Sheila, who'd tried to take everything from me, just let me fall? Why did she help me rescue them? On another note, how on *Earth* could she have set Malum free? How did she even get into The Resting Place? She had to have been imprisoned herself, but if Malum—the Son of Evil—couldn't break out, how could she have done it? There was no way she could have broken out without all the angels hearing about it. Hermes would have sent the demon hunters after her, but I'd never even heard her name until I was undercover.

I looked around, realizing I'd been silent too long. The team settled down around the table, Mom hovering protectively by me and Jake floating to my left. Natalie took Jake's hand and pulled him into a chair to make him feel more a part of the meeting. He likely didn't even notice, but it made me feel better. I smiled at him just in case he noticed, feeling like I was trying to talk to someone in a coma.

After taking a calming breath, I told the team about how I left my body, tracked down Sheila, then threatened her so she'd take me to the Hurricane. I explained how she lowered me in and . . . I had to pause for a minute in my telling. I skipped to the part where I lit up really bright, deliberately leaving out the horrors I saw and heard.

Raj gasped and cut me off. "You lit up? Like this?"

I couldn't see it, because Sandra's gift didn't allow me to, but I could see the effect on the other angels. They squinted and shielded their eyes like he was too bright to look at.

"Yeah, like that," I said.

Raj looked meaningfully at Frederick and William. Everyone else looked confused.

"What?" I asked.

Raj smiled with pride. "It means you're an archangel now."

I looked around at the other confused angels around me. "What does that mean? I've never heard of that."

Raj looked at Frederick. "How does this work if he's mortal now?" It was odd to see Raj deferring to someone else, but I guessed Frederick did have seniority. He and William were flippin' old.

"Still confused over here," I muttered. "Why are you three the only ones not confused? Are *you* guys . . . archangels?"

"It means, lad, that you have been gifted greater power," Frederick explained. "There are other implications as well, but that is a conversation that you must have personally with the 'Big Man,' as you like to call him. Most angels will reach this milestone before they move on, but not everyone, and generally not for many years. And to answer your second question: yes. William, Raj, and I are also archangels, but it is not something we're meant to discuss. Angels have no rank, and if we brandied our status about, that would not bode well for a rank-less system based on unity and equality."

"What about Hermes?" Natalie asked.

"Hermes is far more than an archangel," Raj said, and left it at that.

"Okay?" I said, still confused. None of this made sense, and even if it did, it didn't apply to me. I wasn't even an angel. I was just a mortal now.

"So, about you literally jumping into the Hurricane . . .?" Sandra said pointedly.

I took the hint to move on and finish my story. I explained how we pulled a bunch of angels and demons out and how Malum showed up, so I told Sheila to throw me back in. Then Hermes put me back in my body.

"So, you *broke* into the Hurricane and *saved* a bunch of angels and somehow came back in one piece?" Daisy summed up.

"Yeah," I said, confused by the harsh tone in her voice.

It was silent for a while as everyone processed that. Natalie opened her mouth once, then thought better of it. Ted sat with his arms folded, an unreadable expression on his face. Frederick shared a glance with William, then frowned down at the table. Ying Yue just stared at me in disbelief, while Raj winced looking at Jake. Daisy was scowling, though, being her default expression, that scowl could have meant anything.

I couldn't figure out what everyone's problem was, but they didn't seem pleased. Part of me was actually offended. I thought they'd be happy, or even grateful. Maybe even a little awestruck. I'd actually done something kind of heroic. I brought a member of my team back from the Hurricane, something that nobody had done before, and instead of congratulating or thanking me, they all just frowned and looked away uncomfortably. Confused and dejected, I slumped a little in my chair.

It was Ted who finally spoke. "We could have saved them all along."

I blinked, startled, as I realized that it was shame that made them all so sullen. They weren't disappointed with me; they were disappointed in themselves. They were ashamed that they hadn't been brave enough or smart enough to do what I had done sooner. And, to add insult to injury, it was the mortal, the weakest of the group, who succeeded where no one else had even tried.

"No," I said quickly, unable to accept my team treating themselves the way I often treat myself. "It's nobody's fault this hasn't been done before. You would have been crazy to try. You couldn't have found it without Sheila. Sheila's like Malum's right-hand woman, so he's let her in on a lot of his secrets. Even taught her how to paralyze angels . . ." I glanced at Jake then back down at my lap.

"So, we should have thought of finding her and using her like you did!" Natalie said.

"I'm glad you didn't," I said. "She'd have done to you what she did to Jake and my mom. The only reason she didn't do it to me was because I surprised her. She didn't expect me to show up. I also sort of know her weakness, and I used it against her. I feel kinda bad about it . . . Whatever it is, she's terrified."

"What's her weakness?" Daisy asked hungrily. "We can use it too."

I scowled. "I'm not gonna tell you. I don't even know what it is. There's just a thing that scares her and I implied that I knew what it was."

"And?" Natalie asked.

I shook my head. "No. I'm sorry, it just feels wrong to use her like that. We're angels. We're supposed to be better than that."

"*You* did it," Daisy pointed out. "I'd rather hurt one

bad person to save a bunch of innocent people than just let them suffer."

"They weren't all innocent," I argued. "I'm pretty sure I saved a few demons."

"That's not the point!"

"Enough," Ying Yue said. "Raj and I will discuss this later. Right now, we know all we need to know. Angels have been saved, thanks to David. We're lucky to still have him on our team. Now our focus needs to be on preventing further capture and discovering if there were any angels left behind. If there were, we can plan another rescue mission. There are other ways to find the Hurricane than threatening a dangerous demon." She looked expectantly at me.

"Oh . . . Yeah, I guess I know how to get there now too. And all the other angels that escaped."

"Exactly," she said. "After we've reclaimed all the captured angels, we can focus back on how to capture Malum. Luckily, we know where to find him now, though we still have no way to actually capture him. We will need to do further research, which means more undercover missions."

She finished the meeting by handing out assignments. When she came to me, she said, "What would you like to do, David?"

I blinked. "You're asking me?"

"You're more aware of your own capabilities than we

are."

I shrugged. "I don't know. Maybe have Hermes do another head count. If there are angels that still need rescuing, I want to come. I mean, I don't *want* to—there's probably nothing I want to do less than go back there—but I should come so I can show you how we did it."

She nodded and smiled at me with respect, which felt kind of nice.

"That sounds like a good plan," Raj said distractedly. "Now for our friend . . ." He floated through the table to wait in front of Jake who was still staring off into space with glazed over eyes. Raj looked like he was about to cry.

"How do we get him back?" he whispered. He shook Jake gently and said his name, but Jake didn't even seem to notice.

Gilbert floated forward hesitantly and said in a raspy voice, "Time."

"Time?" Raj asked earnestly. "Just give him time? Is there anything we can do to speed it up? We need him."

Gilbert shrugged and gestured to himself as if to imply that he obviously hadn't figured it out yet either. Then he disappeared. That's how wanderers are. Push them too hard and they completely clam up.

"There isn't any sense of time down there," my mom whispered, "but I don't think he's been like that very long. When I first got there, he was still . . . s-screaming." She broke down into tears again and Natalie floated over to hug her.

"The length of time as a wanderer definitely makes a difference," Sandra said quietly. "It's easier to bring them around if they're new." She gestured to the various wanderers in her apartment. "These guys have been with me for a very long time, but they aren't the only ones I've helped. I've worked with a lot of temporary wanderers who moved on very quickly."

I leaned closer to Jake. "Come on, man. Rugby. Star Wars. Cute girls. Fighting demons. Making fun of David."

There was almost a flicker of recognition in his eyes, and his glazed-over look seemed more defiant than before.

I grinned. "Okay, which of those things worked? Cute girls? Fighting demons?"

He blinked and leaned away.

"Probably the second," Sandra said quietly. "It's the negative stuff that tends to snap them out of it the fastest, but I wouldn't recommend—"

Daisy got up in Jake's face and shouted, "Malum! The Hurricane! That evil pit!"

"Daisy!" Ted scolded quietly.

Recognition sparked Jake's eyes. "*NO!*" He screamed, his face contorted in agony.

Natalie glared and punched Daisy in the arm. "Look what you did!"

"At least I'm trying something!" she shouted back.

Jake floated out of reach, covering his face with his

arms until his whole body went slack. His arms fell, his shoulders and head drooped, and all of a sudden that blank look was back. I'd seen this behavior in Bill, and while Bill seemed to be coming around, it wasn't heartening. It emphasized the fact that my best friend really was a wanderer now. He was out of reach, and no one knew if or when he'd ever return to us.

Sandra patted my hand. "He just needs time. This is his mind's way of protecting him. He's not ready to face it yet."

"Yet the longer he stays a wanderer, the more difficult it will be for him to return to us," William said.

Sandra nodded. "But you can't force it. You just need to be there for him. Talk to him. Give him some hope. Why would he want to return to this world of horrors unless he knew that he was going to be okay?"

I glared at Jake, part of me half expecting him to start laughing and say, "Just joshin', mate! You flamin' galah, you think I'd be wuss enough to let that happen to me? I'm a bloody hero!" I smiled a little, the imaginary Jake in my head sounding just like him. But it was in direct contrast to the Jake that floated before us, which wiped that smile off my face before it really even lived.

Mom came up behind me and Sandra and stared sadly at Jake for a while. "The boy needs a mother. How long has he been dead? Eleven years? That's too long to go without a mama, especially for one so young."

She gently placed her hand on his cheek and softly said

his name.

Jake blinked, but he shuttered, and his eyes glazed over again.

She put her other hand on his other cheek, so he had no choice but to look at her. "Jacob. You are needed, and you are loved. Come back to us."

I saw recognition in his eyes. He sucked in a breath and shook his head. "No!" he croaked, trying to back away from my mom. He covered his ears. "No! I can't! Don't make me!"

Mom let him go, but she floated after him. "It's okay," she said. "We're all here for you. You're not alone." She waited to see if he'd keep retreating, but he just froze, his lip and chin quivering, his arms curled around himself. Carefully she wrapped her arms around him, and Jake let out a single wrenching sob, clinging to her for dear life.

Then he pulled away with such suddenness, my mom wobbled in the air. Jake screwed up his face and shook his head until he'd shoved all his pain away. His face fell slack and his eyes stared at nothing.

"Jake?" Mom whispered.

He closed his eyes and disappeared.

We all stared at the empty space Jake had occupied just a second ago. No one could bring themselves to say or do anything.

"He'll be back," Sandra said quietly.

I sniffed and looked up, forcing myself not to cry. "Are

you sure?"

"No," she said. "But I hope he does. And if he returns, I'll take care of him just like I do all my other wanderers."

I had a sudden flashback to what Hermes had said about her. *She was needed in The Resting Place. She still is.* I hated to acknowledge it, but he was right. Sandra was a better angel than most of us, despite the fact that she was the only one present who'd never even been to the other side.

Of course, I couldn't just have a day to just enjoy the fact that I'd done something right for a change. The next morning, I woke up screaming from a nightmare that I was back in the Hurricane. And the nightmares just kept coming. The thing is, I didn't feel like anyone in particular was sending them to me. It was just me, remembering being down there in that pit. I would have become lost without Sheila. I'd have become like Jake. The pain was too much to even process. My team thought somehow that I was powerful or special because I saved them when no one else had. But I wasn't special. I was just as broken by the pit as anyone else, and I wouldn't have made my way out alone.

My dad was a little more wary of me the days following that. The night of prom was the second time I'd run out of the house frantically without explanation. I could see him struggling, trying to decide if he should push me to tell him what was up, or if he should just stay out of it. He hadn't pinned me down yet, but I could tell he was working up to it.

Luckily, it looked like Sheila was giving me a little break from the attacks. I wondered if it was her choice, or if somehow Malum learned about the jailbreak and was punishing her. I had no idea where I stood with her. I still hadn't forgiven her for all the despicable things she'd done, but—and maybe this was stupid of me—I didn't think she was my enemy. Malum was the real villain. Sheila was just his lackey that he tortured and forced to do his bidding. At least, that's what I'd gathered from her behavior. I could have been wrong.

chapter 33
LEFT BEHIND

"Happy Birthday, dear Rocco! Happy Birthday to you!"

The crowd of family standing around my dad's kitchen table cheered as Rocco blew out the birthday candles on his blue Paw Patrol cake. The whole family was here, except Sam. He had some important meeting to get to, so he had Jessica drop off the kids for him. Elena set Gloria down on the table and she immediately took a chunk of blue cake in her chubby hands and smooshed it onto her face while everyone laughed.

"*My* cake!" Rocco yelled.

"It's all right, buddy, we'll all get a piece," Dad said, scooping up the frosting covered baby and holding her at arm's length. She squirmed in his arms, trying to reach a purple balloon that had floated up to the ceiling.

Sandra smiled and grabbed my hand. Not to show me

the ghosts in the room, of which there were three, but just because she felt like it. My smile widened. There was still a lot that was wrong and needed to be fixed, especially poor Jake who was still wandering around Sandra's apartment, but at this moment, things felt pretty perfect. I had my family around me, living and dead, and Sandra next to me. What else could a guy ask for?

"What did you wish for, bud?" Charlie asked, pulling Rocco onto his lap.

"Cake!"

Ginny, standing next to them, folded her arms. "You already have cake; you're supposed to wish for something you don't have."

"David! Get your hands out of there!" Elena shouted.

I jumped and let go of Sandra's hand before I realized Elena was talking to Little David who was trying to scoop something out of the trash. Sandra snorted and elbowed me.

The sound of a car in the driveway stopped both of our laughs.

"Sam's early," Dad frowned.

"I'd hide if I were you," Charlie said. He frowned as the piece of cake fell off his fork onto Rocco's head. Baby Gloria laughed and clapped.

"Come on," I whispered, grabbing Sandra's wrist and pulling her after me. We sprinted down the hall to my dad's room, past the master bathroom, and into the walk-in closet. I shut the door, leaving the two of us in total darkness except for the tiny strip of light at the bottom of the door. We sat in silence for a moment, no sound but that of our breaths as we tried to slow down our breathing. Then Sandra started giggling.

"What?" I whispered.

"This," she said.

"What, the two of us hiding in my dad's closet from my brother? Is this not normal?"

She giggled harder.

"Shhh!" I tried not to let her laugh spread to me, but it was hard to control myself. I heard the front door open and close. "Be quiet or he'll hear us."

I didn't know what was happening to her, but the torrent of giggles would not end.

"If you don't stop, I'll just have to kiss you until you do."

Her only response was a snort, followed by louder giggles. So, I made good on my threat and took her face in my hands. I pulled her in for a kiss, but it didn't quite work right with her lips pulled tight in a smile. It was a bit ... toothy. Not exactly an adjective one wants to use when describing a kiss. Then she seemed to get a little excited, because this was literally the first time the two of us had truly been alone. At her apartment there was always an audience. She threw her arms around my neck and pulled me closer. At first, I was taken off guard, then I was fighting back a smile of my own. She'd never kissed me like this before. She laced her fingers through my hair, and I pulled her onto my lap as she wrapped her legs around me—"

"Excuse me?!"

The two of us pulled apart and Sandra scooted off my lap like I'd shocked her.

"Who was that?" I asked.

Sandra grabbed my hand.

"Your mother, that's who," my mom's voice said. "And Jake," she added as a side note.

"What did you bring him here for?" I asked.

"I'm not letting him out of my sight until he's better."

My mom had taken to dragging Jake around with her everywhere she went when she wasn't in The Resting Place. She'd taken responsibility for him as though he were her own son. My face heated in embarrassment at my predicament: alone with my girlfriend in a dark closet with my mother and best friend. Not that Jake would even be aware of what was going on. He just sort of stared off into the distance these days. It broke my heart.

"What do you two think you are doing?" Mom demanded.

"We were just hiding from Sam," I said. It was really weird talking to a ghost in the dark. While she looked different as an angel, her voice was exactly the same. Part of me could imagine that my mom was alive and physically here with us. That made it even weirder.

She harrumphed. "It seems like you were doing a little bit *more* than hiding."

"But—"

"No buts, young man! No kissing in the dark!"

"I'm twenty-seven, Mom. I think. It's not like—"

"You are *not* going to make out in my closet!"

My cheeks burned and I gulped. "Okay, okay. I promise we'll stop. I was just trying to get Sandra to shut up because she wouldn't stop giggling.

Sandra snorted and I heard her slap her hand over her mouth to stop another torrent of giggles.

"Go check on Sam, we promise to keep it PG," I said in dismissal.

I could hear the frown in her voice. "You'd better keep it G, boy, or so help me—"

"Fine, fine! Just stop talking to us. We're trying to be quiet."

After a silence I was pretty sure Mom had left. I sighed and leaned back against the wall. Sandra squeezed my hand, and I kissed it, just enjoying the nearness of her. I'm not sure what it is about the dark that somehow makes it easier to tell truths that are harder to say in the light of day, but a million things bubbled up to my lips, trying to fight their way out.

Before I could stop myself, I whispered, "I don't want to die anymore."

Sandra's grip tightened on my hand. "I'm sorry, *what*?"

"That came out wrong . . . I just meant that I don't

want to go back to The Resting Place anymore. I want to stay here with you. I love . . . being with you."

Sandra was quiet for a moment. "Do you think you're going to have to leave soon? I don't want you to go." I heard her struggle for words. "No one understands me the way you do."

I pulled her close until she rested her head on my shoulder. "I might have a choice in the matter," I whispered. "At least, Hermes said I would. I know what my choice will be though. My choice is you. And life. And maybe a life with you." Three little words bubbled to my lips, but I held them back, chickening out. Instead, I said, "You might be my favorite person in the whole world."

I could hear her hesitating. Did she want to say the words I was too cowardly to say myself? She sighed and settled for a substitution like I had.

"You make me happier than anyone I've ever met. When I'm not with you, I feel like something's missing. If something funny happens, I want to laugh about it with you. If something sad happens, I want to talk about it with you. Sometimes in class, a kid will do something stupid, and I turn my head to smirk at you across the room, forgetting you can't just float on in whenever you'd like anymore. I'm glad you can't though. I prefer you alive."

"I prefer me alive too," I grinned, kissing her forehead. "Don't worry, I'm not going anywhere. Not if I can help it."

After a day of playing hard with the crazy children at the party, we drove back to Sandra's place and decided to take a walk like an old couple. Sometimes two people just want to be alone, and that's kind of hard to come by when the guy lives with his dad and the girl's house is haunted.

It was almost nine, so the only light came from the dull, flickering streetlights. The scenery was a mixture of shadowed sidewalks, parked cars, and a stray cat that trotted across the street and into a garage that was open a crack. I jumped when a random wanderer floated through one house and into the next. It wasn't exactly what you'd call a romantic stroll, but neither of us really cared. When you understand the true gravity and suddenness of death you learn how to appreciate just being alive.

As we walked through the neighborhood behind her apartment complex, Sandra frowned and looked down at our hands.

"The problem with this is, how do I know if you're holding my hand because you want to or if it's just to see all the ghosts? For all I know you're just interested in me so you can cheat all the time."

I nodded. "You're right. I am one hundred percent using you. I don't care about you as a person at all. What's your name again?"

"Shut up," she said, trying to keep a straight face, but not succeeding. Her reluctant smile and eye roll were adorable.

I stopped walking and pulled her back by her hand until

she was facing me. "How about every time I'm holding your hand just because I want to, I'll squeeze it three times."

She smiled and pulled me behind her as we crossed the street. "That is so cheesy, and not even—"

Sandra gasped and clutched my arm.

My head snapped to the side, following her gaze.

Headlights. Screeching tires.

Panic.

Pain.

A terrifying thump to my left.

A car passing over me.

A metallic crash.

Brief blackness and a sudden awakening. I was disoriented, unable to process where I was. Streetlights glared down at me, and the asphalt dug into my back. Then I heard the sound of choked breathing and my mind caught up. Sandra. The car. We were hit.

Whimpering, I lifted my head from the asphalt. A cold shot of dread gave me the strength to roll over and crawl my way over to Sandra. Blood covered her body, broken and bent at horrifying angles.

"Sandra?" I whispered. Tears sprung to my eyes. This was the moment I'd been dreading. I just knew it.

She sucked in a strangled breath and looked at me in panic. Her eyes pleaded for me to fix her. I fumbled in my pockets with shaking hands, frantically searching for my phone to call 9-1-1, but it, too, lay next to me, as shattered as Sandra's body. I shook my head, clutching my hair.

Her eyes widened and she gasped. And then her eyes glazed over.

"No, no, no, no . . ."

I checked her pulse, but there was nothing. I tried CPR, but there was nothing. I kept trying, even though I knew deep down that there was nothing I could do. I knew enough about death to know the truth. Her body was dead, and her spirit had been ejected, forced out of the shell that had been hers for twenty-eight years. The shell that was now no more than a bloody, broken corpse.

I gripped her hand, foolishly praying that maybe if we touched I'd be able to see her spirit and . . . what? Put her back inside? There was nothing I could do. For a moment, I just stared at her, shaking, as the truth set in.

I was going to fall apart, but I had to hold it together for her, because if this was real, this was a crucial moment. Chin quivering and teeth chattering, I whispered in a broken voice the words I knew she'd need to hear if she was listening. Permission to leave. Closure. Encouragement to move on. I could not let her become another wanderer.

"You . . . You'll make a great angel, Sandra. Go with your aunt. I'll be okay."

I spoke to her body even though I knew that wasn't where she was. She'd be floating above me somewhere, watching as I had when my family found me dead.

I held off as long as I could, giving her time to leave before I fell apart. I didn't want her to witness my grief. When I couldn't hold it in any longer. I clutched my head and rocked back and forth as sobs tore through my throat. In the cruelest way possible, I finally learned what it was like to be left behind.

Sandra—my sweet friend, my almost love, my only connection to the other side—was gone.

chapter 34
THE HOSPITAL

I must have passed out, my body and mind unable to cope with the trauma, because I woke up to a jarring cacophony of sirens and flashing lights. I was being lifted into an ambulance again on a stretcher. I tried to lift my head, but someone pushed me back down.

"Don't move, son. You have a lot of injuries."

I could tell. I was starting to feel it now. I couldn't breathe. Every time I took a breath it felt like my insides were stabbing me. Not to mention the fact that every inch of my skin felt scraped raw.

"Sandra," I croaked. "Where's Sandra?" But no one heard me. The ambulance took off, sirens blaring, the smell of metal, bleach, and blood somehow reaching through the oxygen mask they shoved on my face.

I pulled it off as soon as I could make my arm work. "Is she gonna make it? Can you save her?" I asked, already knowing the answer.

The EMTs—a man and a woman—continued to talk over me, barely acknowledging me, despite the fact that it was me on the stretcher. The man briefly paused to say, "Just focus on you, son. You're gonna be okay—"

"Can you save her?" I demanded.

He shook his head mournfully. "The girl is dead. They couldn't restart her heart."

I let out a sob and dropped my head back on the stretcher, fresh tears snaking their way down the slides of my face into my hair. Crying physically hurt, my insides screaming at me to stop breathing so roughly. I tried to slow my breathing, but I couldn't. I started hyperventilating.

They shoved the oxygen mask back on my face and when I was breathing normally again, they started asking me questions like my blood type and if I had any allergies to medications and what was my level of pain. *Ten,* I wanted to tell them. *Sandra's dead. My pain is a ten.*

The rush to the ER was a blur. They'd clearly given me some kind of pain killer because my mind was fuzzy, and I couldn't focus. Either that or I had a concussion. Despite all of that, all I could think about was how none of this mattered anymore. I was done. I didn't want my injuries treated. I didn't want to get better. I wanted to go with Sandra and leave all the pain behind. At the same time, I felt like I deserved the pain. This was what I got for involving Sandra. For allowing her into my life. For falling in love with her. I was an idiot to think I could have ever deserved the brief happiness I felt. Life was pain, and naive former angels were not exempt. How could I have ever believed that things would work out? What kind of idiot holds on that stubbornly to such a foolish dream?

A detached part of me wondered how many demons were swarming me, putting those thoughts in my head. Or maybe it was just me, and Mom had already fought off all the demons. *Mom.* I wanted my mom so bad. For the first time it sunk in that my mom was *dead.* And that meant something now, because there was no more Sandra to connect us.

They called my dad as soon as I signed a HIPPA form with emergency contact information. The first responders probably would have called him off my phone if it hadn't been destroyed. I didn't want him to come. I didn't want the doctors to try and fix me. They could try to put me back together again, but they wouldn't succeed. My heart was in a million pieces, smooshed onto the street like roadkill. They couldn't fix that. It became an unspoken challenge in my head. I suddenly wanted them to try, just so I could prove to them that even when they healed me, I wouldn't be whole. I was broken, and always would be.

My dad came as fast as he could and found me glaring at the ceiling, listening to my heart monitor. I resented that beep. It meant that I was alive. I mentally willed it to flatten out so I could go back to The Resting Place. Life was overrated. Who would *want* this?

A wash of all different kinds of pain rolled over me, from dull aches, to sharper, more demanding agonies. I groaned and tried to will myself to sleep.

"David? Are you awake?"

I squeezed my eyes shut. I did not want to confront my dad.

"David?"

It was his broken voice that brought me back to the surface. I forced my eyes open. Even that simple act hurt my face. My face probably looked like a horror show. But not as bad as Sandra . . .

"Can you hear me?" Dad asked.

"Yeah," I croaked, staring straight up at the ceiling. I didn't want to look at him. He'd see how not okay I was, and I was starting to realize that my being hurt was also hurting him. I searched for something normal to say. Nothing came to mind.

"I talked to the doctor," he said quietly. "That car did a number on you. Broken ribs, internal bleeding, dislocated shoulder—but they said they fixed that already—concussion, and you're cut up and bruised all over. I bet the ribs hurt the most, huh?"

I didn't answer. The car did a number on *me*? I was barely scratched compared to Sandra.

"They said they want to monitor you overnight, but then you can come home to rest."

I closed my eyes again and gritted my teeth, suddenly angry about everything.

"Are you in pain?" Dad asked.

"What kind of stupid question is that?" I snapped, gracing him with a glare.

"Sorry, I . . ."

Regret washed over me, but I wouldn't take it back. It *was* a stupid question. Of course I was in pain. That's all I was. Body, heart, and soul.

"Do you need more painkillers?" he amended.

"I don't even care," I said, closing my eyes again. This was sort of a lie. My chest felt like I was being stabbed by knives every time I took a breath.

After a pause I quietly asked, "They couldn't save her?"

"No, son. There was nothing they could do."

I felt his hand on my shoulder and nodded once. "I want to be alone right now."

I opened my eyes when he didn't answer. The pain in his face seemed to mirror my own as he tenderly brushed my hair back against my head. "Oh, my boy . . ." Somehow, I knew he was remembering me as a little kid, happy and free, and comparing that image to this broken version of what I'd become. He gave me that *look* that a parent gives you when you're hurt, and they'd do anything to take it away. My eyes welled with tears, so I squeezed them shut. I didn't want to cry. If I started now, I'd never stop.

A nurse interrupted at that point and after grilling me

on how I felt, gave me some more drugs. They made me drowsy, and I thankfully fell back into blissful sleep.

They kept me overnight, and I was upset at Dad for calling Elena and Sam. Elena was hysterical, scared I was gonna die again, and Sam hung up once my name was mentioned. I'm not sure which bothered me more. Dad drove me home when we got the all clear and I was confused by how the world still looked the same. The roads, the neighborhood, the cars. The world just kept right on spinning as though nothing had happened. As we pulled in the driveway, the sun cheerfully shone down on the house, birds chirped in the trees, flowers in the yard swayed in the wind. One of the neighbors was mowing his lawn, while some kid chased her brother down the sidewalk, giggling. I hated it. I felt like the world should be on fire. What right did everyone and everything else have to just go on living their lives as though nothing had happened? How could they be so oblivious to the fact that everything was broken?

Dad helped me out of the car. Moving was ridiculously painful, and I breathed in short gasps, gritting my teeth. He unnecessarily kept his hand on my back to steady me as we made our way through the garage door into the living room. The first thing I saw was a blue sweater draped over the side of the couch. *Her* blue sweater. I picked it up, staring, but not really seeing. How could it be that she'd never put this on again? She used to struggle to take it off, embarrassed when her t-shirt underneath would come up as she pulled it off. It was cold and lifeless without her. I squeezed my eyes shut and clenched my jaw.

Dad came up behind me slowly and put a hand on my shoulder. "She's gone, son. She's gone, and it hurts. You need to let it out."

I shook my head, a tear already leaking down my cheek.

"Come here. Let it out." He put his arms around me and pulled my head onto his shoulder. My resolve broke. I threw my arms around him, suddenly bawling like a baby, clutching onto him for dear life. "It's not fair," I moaned. "It's not fair."

"It's not fair," he confirmed. "You're right. Death isn't fair."

I couldn't believe I'd ever been so cavalier about the concept of death. What a naive little jerk I used to be, to act like it's no big deal. I cheered when my mom died. I cheered! What right did I have to try and comfort mortals when I, myself, had never felt grief? I started crying so forcefully, Dad moved me over to the couch and I cried as I'd never cried before. I thought I knew pain and heartache. But that was like someone with a few stitches saying they understood a full amputation. The things I'd gone through before were not nothing, but they weren't like this.

When I finally ran out of tears, I pulled away and stared

at nothing, a numbness brought on not by lack of feeling but an overload. I tried to follow the rhythm of my dad's rising and falling chest, focusing on nothing other than just breathing. Strange that such an instinctive and simple process took actual concentration now. And it hurt.

"It doesn't fix the hurt, but she might be here right now," Dad whispered. He had one arm around my shoulders and another on my thigh, as though he could tell I would shatter into a million pieces if he let go. "You of all people know that. What would you say to her if she was here?"

"To go away," I said quietly, silent tears still streaming down my face. "I don't need her to see this."

"And what would you say if you were in her position?"

My face crumpled and I closed my eyes. It was hard to imagine, but I'd been in that situation before with my own family. I watched them grieve over me and my mom. I'd had no right to assume I could comfort them; I'd had no idea what this was like.

I gulped and took a breath, wiping my face. "I'd say that I would never go away. That I would always be there, no matter what, in any way that I could. I'd say something stupid like everything would be all right in the end. But I was an idiot, Dad. I didn't know what this was like. It all sounds so empty now."

"No, son. You were right. Maybe you can't process that right now. That's okay. You need to grieve. But eventually the pain will ebb. It won't go away completely, but you'll learn how to live again. Pain is the price we pay for loving people, but I've come to the conclusion that it's worth it. This probably isn't the right thing to say right now, but . . . if it hurts this much, you must have really loved her, and how *beautiful* is that? That you got to experience a love like that. That your heart was capable of that much love. That's how we know that we're not broken, because our hearts still love.

"I miss your mother," he said, his voice cracking. "I always will, but she's not the only one my heart loves. I love my children too, and my grandkids. I love *you*, David. I know this hasn't been easy for you, and if I could take all this pain away from you, I would. You may feel broken inside, but you're not. If you can feel this level of pain, then your heart still loves. Hold on to that. Don't let yourself become jaded. Hold on to the love that you feel, not just for her, but for everyone you care about."

After a long silence, I looked over at my dad with the long-buried eyes of *angel* David. The me that I'd almost forgotten. Dad had said it so much better than I ever had. He would be an amazing angel one day. Just like Sandra. They'd be better than I ever was.

"Let's get some food in you and get you in bed," Dad said, carefully extricating himself from me without jostling the couch. He turned on the TV to some show I didn't pay attention to, more likely to fill the silence than anything. Silence can be bad when one's mind is in a dark place. He set the remote on my lap and went to make me something to eat. After a few minutes he brought me some tomato soup and a grilled cheese on a TV tray. He cleaned up after me and helped me get ready for bed.

I was too numb to do any of it for myself. If I was any less numb, I'd have been grateful to him. Mainly all I could think about was how my dad never had anyone to do this for him when my mom died. That wasn't fair either.

chapter 35
THE INTERVIEW

After the funeral, I went to my room, kicked the door shut, and fell into my bed, not even bothering to take off my shoes or jacket. I stared at the wall with my eyes half open, not really seeing anything. My whole body ached as I released the tight muscles and clenched jaw I'd held for the past hour. Exhausted didn't even begin to cover how dead I felt. I'd spent the entire funeral forcing myself to not feel. I didn't listen to the speakers. I didn't talk to anyone, I just sat in the church pew and stared ahead. I refused to cry, because I knew that she would be there, and I knew from experience that moving on is so much harder when people cry for you. So, I turned off my mind and my heart and just sat in my own little bubble of misery.

I tried not to think about what would happen to all the wanderers she left behind at her apartment. Would Jake be okay? Would he ever find his way back? Maybe not, now that Sandra was gone. She had a way with lost souls that few could replicate. As lonely as she often had been in life, her funeral was packed with people whose lives she'd affected. People, like me, who would ache from her loss. I'm ashamed to say I was too distraught to introduce myself to her mom. I didn't speak to anyone at all. If I had, I'd have fallen apart, and I couldn't let Sandra see that and blame herself.

I tried to tell myself I shouldn't take it so hard. I, as a former angel, should have been happy for her. Angels welcome death because it means another good guy to add to their ranks. It's a new beginning without pain or fear or sorrow. The dead do not mind that they're dead. They're free. They're happy. They have purpose. It's just so much *better* there.

But that way of thinking was logical, and emotions don't heed logic. I was mortal now, and I thought like a mortal. Death was an end, not a beginning. I loved Sandra, and now I wouldn't see her again for a very long time. She was gone from me, just like my mom, and Raj, and Jake, my grandmas, my entire team. I was supposed to return to them quickly, but I had failed somehow, and now without Sandra, I couldn't even talk to them. I was slowly losing faith that I'd ever make it back to The Resting Place and I was almost to the point that I didn't even care.

PRAY.

I ignored that. Praying was the last thing I wanted to

do.

WHEN YOU DO NOT WANT TO PRAY, THAT IS WHEN YOU NEED IT MOST.

I growled and sat up. "Leave me alone!"

So, he did. I waited for him to prompt me again, but he was gone. Hermes doesn't force you to hear him—you have to choose to listen. I fell back on my bed and scowled at the ceiling, trying not to be hurt by his abandonment. As much as I didn't want to listen to Hermes, I wished he would have stuck around longer. That more than anything convinced me to reluctantly do as he'd said.

I was tempted to think I was just weak for taking this all so hard, but this was too much for anyone. I'd been hunted and attacked and manipulated. I'd been burned and broken and tortured. I'd simultaneously lost half the people I cared about and watched one of them mutilated before my eyes. This all barely happened in the space of a year. I knelt next to my bed, ready to rip into the Big Man and call him out on all the crap he'd put me through. But the minute I opened my mouth to really consider what to say, my chin trembled and all the pain I'd cooped up inside spilled out. I bent so low my head touched the floor. I couldn't find the words I wanted to say, so I asked the only question I had left.

"Why am I here?"

My mind took me back to another time I'd asked that question.

Fresh from death, I'd just recently walked through my door to The Resting Place. There wasn't a huge crowd for me, because most of my family was still alive. After awkward reunions with a few distant cousins and great uncles, my grandmas tugged me along. They took me to the front office, which is not far from the front desk where I ended up working. Most of that area behind the front desk is conference rooms, but there is a doorway to the right that opens to a narrow hallway that leads to another door.

"Right through there, *mijo*," Nana Maria said, squeezing my shoulder. "Then, after this, you'll meet with Hermes, and he'll give you your assignments."

"What's through there?" I asked. "And who's Hermes?" My head was spinning, I still didn't understand what was happening or where I was. I was frightened and shocked and confused.

Grandma Gertie smiled at me and patted my cheek. "It's all right, pumpkin. We've all been in your shoes. But you'll feel better after you talk to him. I promise."

"Who's him?" I asked.

Nana Maria gently shoved me through the door. I gasped and spun around. I'd never walked through anything before. I wanted to yell in fear and frustration— Why wouldn't anyone explain anything to me?—but I sensed another presence in the room.

Slowly, I turned around and I saw him. The minute our

eyes connected I knew which him she'd meant. He radiated holiness, power, and *love*. So much love I couldn't understand it. How could he feel that for *me*? It was incomprehensible, like someone loving a cockroach. I was so overwhelmed that I fell to my knees. Then, remembering my own foolishness and idiocy, I dropped my eyes, wishing I could disappear. I was not worthy to even be here. I knew that he knew all I had done, all the selfish thoughts I'd had, every mistake I wished I could cover up, and I wanted to sink into the floor. A small part of me wondered if I could literally sink into the floor if I tried.

He stepped closer and I bowed further, terrified that I was about to receive my deserved punishment for what I had done with my life, which was a big fat nothing. And then he knelt in front of me. Why should he get down on my level when he was so above me? He took my arm and gently urged me to stand. If I was still mortal, my legs wouldn't have held me, but being nothing but spirit, I did as he insisted.

"Please take a seat," he said softly.

I hadn't noticed anything about our surroundings yet. There was nothing in there but a bench and a chair facing each other. Literally nothing else. Even the walls looked insubstantial. He sat in the chair and gestured toward the bench in front of him.

As I walked to the front of the bench, I wasn't sure which side to sit on. Why a bench? Why not a chair? I considered sitting in the middle, but I like to sit by an arm. I went back and forth for a minute, my nerves making me indecisive.

"You may sit where you're most comfortable," he said, his eyes twinkling.

I gulped and plopped myself down on the right side.

He smiled at me in a way that made me very uncomfortable. Like he knew everything I was thinking. I waited under his penetrating gaze, but he seemed to be waiting for me to speak.

"So . . . I'm dead?" I asked, stating the obvious.

"Yes, David. You are dead." His voice sent a shiver throughout my body.

"You know my name."

"I know everything about you," he said softly. "Your past, present, and future. Your hopes, sorrows, and secret thoughts."

"So, what's the point of me even talking if you know everything I'm thinking?" I asked. Then, realizing just how disrespectful that probably sounded, I quickly tacked on a "L-Lord."

He smiled at me. "As with prayer, you don't speak to me for my benefit. This is for you."

"So . . ." I trailed off, not sure if I was supposed to lead this conversation or him. "They said this was an interview? Do you ask me questions, or . . ."

"Not at this time. I already know what is in your head

and your heart. As I said, this interview is for you. Do *you* have any questions for *me?*"

"Can I ask you whatever I want?" I asked.

"You may ask what you wish, though I cannot promise you all the answers."

"Oh. I thought in heaven we get all the answers. This is . . . heaven, right?"

"Not quite," he said. "This is just a stopping point."

"Did I do something wrong?" I asked, panicking that I was being held back for failing my life. Was I going to hell? I knew I wasn't a saint, but I never hurt anyone if I could help it.

"Technically everyone has done something wrong. That is why I came to earth. But that is not why you are here. Everyone who crosses over comes here first. This is just another step along the way."

"The way to where?"

"That depends on what you truly want," he said.

I frowned. How could I know I wanted something if I didn't know what it was?

"You will learn," he said, reading my thoughts. "That is part of why you are here: to learn. To finish up what you started on Earth."

I sat back in my chair and let out a breath, feeling completely overwhelmed. He just smiled and waited for me to get my bearings.

"Is there something you would like to ask me?" he prompted. I could tell from his expression that he already knew.

I considered saying no. I mean, why should I bother the king of the universe with my stupid, tiny little problems, no matter how earth-shattering they felt to me? But I found that I couldn't lie to him. I was still so raw from the nightmare of falling to my death and being ripped from my body and watching everyone mourn me and not being able to do anything about it.

"Why am I here? Why now?" I asked, feeling that awful tightness in my throat. "I mean, I'm grateful for the life I had, but it was kinda . . . short?" I swallowed. Even without a body I felt that heat behind my eyes and pressure in my nose as I tried with everything I had not to cry.

He stood up and sat next to me on the bench and put his arm around my shoulder. Tears sprung from my eyes like a dam giving way to a waterfall. I cried even harder when I saw that the tears just disappeared once they fell from my face, reminding me again that I didn't have a real body anymore because I was dead. You would think it would be weird, a stranger was hugging me while I angel-cried on his shoulder. But this wasn't a stranger. I knew him. I wasn't sure how I did—I wasn't super spiritual when I was alive—but I felt like I'd done this before. Maybe he'd been with me all along and I just didn't see him.

"Why now?" he repeated softly.

I pulled back and nodded, wiping my incorporeal boogers and tears from my insubstantial face.

He put a hand on my shoulder and said, "You are here because this is where I need you to be."

What did he need me for? Surely he was all-capable? I wanted to ask him that, but I didn't. For the first time since I'd died, I felt safe, and I didn't want to do or say anything to lose that feeling. I just nodded and said. "Okay. I trust you." And I meant it. I didn't understand what was happening, but I knew that he was on my side.

"This is not the end, young one," he said. "You will continue on, and you will find purpose and happiness in serving those around you. Just know that when you find yourself asking again, 'Why am I here?" the answer remains the same. I will place you where you are needed, but it is up to you to fulfill that need."

I nodded though I didn't quite understand. Another question was at the tip of my tongue, but I felt too stupid to ask it.

He put a hand on my cheek, gently lifting my face to look into his piercing eyes. He smiled softly. "Yes, David. I know you, I love you, and I want you. It brings me great joy to see you again."

I gulped. I had never felt so *seen* and *wanted*. Even more tears leaked from my eyes.

I looked down at the bench and came to a realization. "Oh. That's what the bench is for. I'm not the only one who's bawled his eyes out on you, am I?"

"No," he smiled. "They all do. Every single one."

I thought of how wet his shoulder must be from all the tears and had a really inappropriate image of him throwing a burp cloth over his shoulder every time a new person entered.

Knowing my thoughts, he chuckled. That's right. My brain is so weird, I made the Big Man laugh.

Back in the real world, I slumped against the wall. I still felt like hell. Alone and confused and heartbroken. I had just asked that question he had known I would ask again: "Why am I here?" He'd said he would place me where I was needed. But why was I needed here? What was it that I was supposed to do? And how was I supposed to do it when I felt like I was falling apart?

chapter 36
BROTHERS

I was in the pit again. The red mist swirled around me. Tortured souls screamed and clawed after me as I tried to get away. I closed my eyes, but it wouldn't go away, no matter what I did. A red-eyed demon latched onto my arm. "You belong with us!" it screeched.

"No!" I yelled, trying to pull away. "Let me go!"

Then all was Darkness. Total sensory deprivation. The only sensation was my racing heart.

A deep voice laughed at my distress.

"Leave me alone!" I cried.

"Why?" Sandra's voice asked.

I spun around. A reanimated corpse staggered toward me. It was Sandra, her body broken and decayed. Her eyes were empty sockets, the skin on her face ripped away on the left side to reveal her grinning skull. I vacillated between running from her and running to her.

Then a car fell from nowhere and crumpled her underneath.

"No!" I screamed.

I tried to run to her, but something caught my foot. A demonic zombie grinned up at me with my mother's face. I stumbled back, too horrified to even scream.

Hordes of my undead family and friends surrounded me on all sides, pulling me in every direction. Sam, gray-skinned and bleeding dead, brown blood, laughed as he yanked my arm. Elena, with half her arm missing, cried as she tore at my shirt. Dad growled softly as he grabbed me in a chokehold. The only ones not participating were my nieces and nephews, who stared dully as their parents, and grandparents ripped me apart.

"Make it stop!" I screamed as I struggled.

"No," a deep voice said, shattering me into a million pieces. The voice echoed and bounced around me. "You have failed me. This I cannot forgive . . . I cannot forgive . . . Cannot forgive. You are lost . . . lost . . . Cannot forgive! Lost . . . fallen too far . . . You belong here! Belong in Darkness . . . belong here . . . lost!"

"Wake up!" another voice said.

"I can't!"

"David, wake up!"

I sat up with a start, breathing heavily, covered with sweat. I tried to ground myself in reality. My hands went to my aching ribs. That's right, I was hurt. I was in an accident. Three days ago. An accident where Sandra . . . died. The renewed realization hit me all over again. My waking life wasn't much better than my nightmares now.

I looked around and nearly jumped out of my skin when I saw my dad sitting on my bed. His face was half lit from my lamp that I left on every night since returning from the pit. His eyebrows pinched upward, and his mouth parted.

"David," he whispered. "I know you had nightmares before the accident, but they seem to be getting worse."

I nodded and rubbed my face. The nightmares certainly were getting worse. That was no surprise. My subconscious had some very recent horrors to add to the selection.

"Maybe you should see someone," Dad said nervously.

"What are you talking about?" I slumped exhausted against my headboard.

"Like a professional," he said. "Son . . . you're not okay. You need help."

I shook my head and sighed. I couldn't talk to mortals about any of this afterlife stuff. I'd be put on antipsychotics for sure.

"I can't talk about it," I said heavily. "It's not just S-Sandra. There's . . . other side stuff I'm dealing with."

"Then pray, son," he said, patting my leg, "and don't stop. You know I'll be praying for you."

The next morning, I woke up to the sound of the doorbell. I groaned and rolled over. I hadn't slept well, and I didn't appreciate the wake-up call. I checked the time on my alarm clock and was surprised to see it read 10:00 am. The part of me that wasn't in emotional agony registered that I was supposed to work today. My shift started an hour ago and I never called in, but I couldn't have cared less. I laid back on my pillow and stared at the ceiling, unable to find the will to get up and start another day.

There was a knock at my door. "Hey, David. Someone's here to see you."

"Tell them to go away," I said.

"It's your boss."

"*Definitely* tell him to go away."

Dad opened the door. "It's up to you, son, but I think he might just be checking up on you. It's not good to shut people out."

He stood there waiting for my response. I closed my eyes and sighed. "Fine."

I groaned and sat up. I wasn't up for company, but I was curious what the heck Preston was doing here. Throwing on a shirt I found on the floor, I followed my dad to the door and frowned at Preston standing there tapping his foot uncomfortably.

"Hey," I said.

His eyes widened as he looked me over. "You look like *hell*."

"Thanks, Preston."

He wasn't wrong. I hadn't showered or shaved in days. My face and arms were covered in cuts and welts, bruises and bandages. The left side of my face from cheekbone to eyebrow was a dark purple bruise and the right side of my forehead had a jagged line of stitches. He couldn't see the giant bruises from my broken ribs, but I'm sure it was obvious from the way I held my hand there, slightly hunched. I also probably looked like I'd been crying and not sleeping well. Also true.

"Can I come in for a sec?" he asked uncertainly.

I simply held the door open and moved out of the way. I led him to the living room where he rested uneasily against the arm of the chair. I gingerly sat on the couch, wincing as I leaned back.

"I, uh, came by to give these to you," he said, holding out some flowers and a card. "Your dad told me what happened, and I told everyone else. The whole crew chipped in and signed the card. It was mostly Piper who put it all together. I know it doesn't mean much—flowers don't exactly bring back the dead—but we wanted you to know we were thinking about you."

"Thanks," I said, taking them from him. He was right. It was very sweet of them, and I was touched to know they were thinking of me, but I didn't feel any better for it. Flowers were just flowers. The card was filled with empty sympathies like, "everything will work out" and "time heals all wounds" and crap like that. I wanted to just throw it all in the garbage. I probably would once he left.

"Look, I, uh, kinda know a little bit of what you're going through," he said, staring down at the floor. "I lost my mom when I was ten. So, yeah, I know firsthand that nothing I say will really change anything. It sucks no matter how nice people are to you. I just wanted to let you know that you can have as much time off as you need. I'll cover your shifts and I'll clock in and out for you so you can still get paid. I mean, as long as *my* boss doesn't come by. Sorry, but I'm not gonna lose my job for you."

"Dude, with all the other crap you've done as manager, clocking in and out for an employee that isn't there is the least of your worries."

"That's true," he grinned. "I spent my entire first week smoking pot in my office and no one cared."

I blinked at him, expressionless. I could tell he was looking for a reaction. Hoping I'd fill in my regular role of being his emotional babysitter. But I was too dead inside to fake emotion.

He cleared his throat. "Just, uh . . . don't wait too long to come back, okay? You can't hide yourself away forever. You're gonna need people to get through this."

I raised an eyebrow and wondered what guardian angel was feeding him his little speech. It was actually wise.

"Who are you even?" I asked. "You're acting like a nice person."

He snorted. "Well ever since your stupid ass showed up, I can't stop thinking to myself, 'What would David do?' and it's freaking annoying. So, thanks for that, jerk."

I almost smiled. That sounded more like the Preston I knew. But improved. I was starting to realize that Preston might have some potential. Strange that the one person I disliked more than any other mortal was the one I'd actually had an impact on

"Thanks, I guess." I stood up like an old man and shuffled to the door. As nice as it was of him to come by, I was done with his company.

"Yeah, see you around," he said, walking out the door. He turned around again and said, "I'll tell the crew not to grill you with questions when you come back and just treat you like normal. It's obnoxious when everyone starts to treat you like you're made of glass or something. Harder to return to normal."

I gave him a half-hearted smile. "Stop being considerate, Preston, it's creepy."

He grimaced. "I know." Then he smiled and walked away.

The next week I went back to work. As much as I didn't want to deal with people, it was better than being alone with my dark thoughts. I tried to act normally for the sake of my worried dad. I got ready in the morning, I served pizza to children, I put away dishes after dinner, I went to sleep. But I was just going through the motions. My mind was a fuzzy cloud of numbness interspersed with brief moments of despair when the pain would break through. I had too much time on my hands, and that was not a coincidence. There were no more demon hunter meetings for me, and no more missions. No more Sandra. I was really just a regular old mortal with no purpose and no connection to the other side. I felt forsaken. Why wouldn't anyone tell me what I was supposed to be doing here?

Preston was creepily nice to me at work, and the rest of the crew treated me like a delicate flower, which actually made me feel more isolated than anything. I overheard Joanna telling Kendra, a new hire, about me. "Oh, David? Don't be offended if he doesn't talk to you or notice you. He's really depressed right now, but he's not normally like that. He's the sweetest guy ever. Honestly! But he's had a lot of bad things happen to him recently. He almost died in a fire, and then he was in a car accident and watched his girlfriend die in his arms." They gasped when they realized I was listening, then gave me pained smiles and asked if there was anything I needed help with. I forced a smile, shook my head, and walked away. I hated the way they treated me, but it was better than everyone treating me like crap, I suppose. I *was* a little delicate emotionally; they weren't wrong about that.

It was during one of my breaks that I got a text from Jessica saying that Sam had agreed to meet with me if I was up to it. I wondered over the timing. Likely she'd used my recent accident as a reason for him to be nice to me. I felt conflicted. On the one hand, I really didn't want to deal with Sam. On the other hand, I'd recently been reminded of the fragility of life, and it would be nice to have my brother back before one of us died. I sighed and closed my eyes.

"You okay?" Jorge asked. I jumped about a mile and opened my eyes to see the big guy standing in front of me with a mop. I hadn't heard him walk up. After a quick text to Jessica, I shoved my phone back in my pocket. I faked a half-hearted smile and said, "I'm great, how are you?"

He just nodded and walked off. Jorge was a man of few words. The fact that he'd asked if I was okay must have meant I wasn't fooling anyone with my fake smiles. I sighed and got back to clearing dirty dishes, stepping over a wad of gum on the floor, and wiping pizza sauce off a table while a kid across the room cried and ran away from Liam in the Chuck E. costume. At least I didn't have to wear the suit. Since the fire all those months ago, Preston still hadn't scheduled me to wear it. It wasn't technically fair or allowed—all employees have to take their turn— but I was weak enough without dealing with my embarrassing phobia of a human-sized rat.

I didn't want to, but when the time came for me to meet up with Sam, I went. I reminded myself that not everything was about me, and that I wasn't the only person in the world who'd ever felt pain. I'd been witness to Sam's pain for eleven years. It was part of why I didn't hate him, to be honest. It wasn't until I died that I realized how much he struggled, and I defy anyone to watch someone struggle like that without feeling some compassion toward them. I just wished he'd grant me the same courtesy.

We met at a coffee shop, which I thought would be better than lunch because we could end it at any time without worrying about the bill. I waited in my car for probably ten minutes before I had the courage to join him. He'd already sat down at a table and had twice gotten up to leave before turning around and going back to his table. My shaking hands struggled to pull my keys from the ignition. I didn't know why I was so terrified to face him. It might have had something to do with the fact that the last time I saw him he attacked me. That *might* have been a contributing factor.

I took a deep breath, left my car, and walked up to his table. He looked up sharply when my shadow fell over him and I lamely said, "Hi."

He didn't say anything, so I took this as an invitation to sit.

"How's it going?" I tried. My voice cracked, so I cleared my throat.

He scowled down at his coffee. "I'm not here to talk or 'make amends' or whatever. I just wanted to give you the chance to apologize."

"Me?" I asked incredulously. "Apologize for what?"

"For this load of crap," he said, tossing my letter on the table.

I barely held back an eye roll. I was *so* not in the mood

to deal with this right now. I shoved my hands through my hair and said, "Look, I don't know what you want from me, Sam. I'm trying so hard to fix things with us, but I can't do it alone."

"Why don't you stop with the lies, then?" he growled.

"Because you didn't believe me when I told you the truth!" I said. "It doesn't matter what I say, you've already decided that I'm the bad guy."

"Dude, you came to my house and talked to my girlfriend behind my back!"

"Because you wouldn't come out yourself! And unlike you, Jessica's a reasonable person."

"I don't have to deal with this," he muttered, shoving his chair back.

I wanted to just let him storm off, but in my mind's eye I saw him speed off getting into an accident and dying. I grabbed his arm with a flush of panic. "No! Sit down. Just give me a chance. Please." I saw Sam struggle as he looked at my pathetic face. He growled and threw himself back into his chair. He glared down at his coffee, and I stared down at my lap.

Thank you, Mom, I thought. I had no doubt it was her that convinced him to stay.

After a long, tense silence, Sam looked up at me and frowned. "You look terrible."

I looked away. I wasn't sure if he meant that emotionally, or just looking at my beat-up face. Most of the bruises were healing, but they were that greenish-yellow color that almost makes them look worse. My stitches were gone, but they left behind another scar to add to my collection. I really didn't want to talk about it, but Sam was tired of lies so I felt like I had to tell the truth. "I was in an accident and lost someone close to me."

He didn't look surprised, confirming my suspicion that Jessica already told him. She likely learned from Elena.

"I'm sorry," he said quietly.

I didn't say anything.

He hesitated. "Are you okay?"

I shrugged.

Sam looked thoughtful, almost empathetic.

I figured if I was trying to get through to him, one of us would have to make ourselves vulnerable. May as well be me. "It's just hard to go on without her."

He was quiet for a moment, then expression slowly darkened. "Yeah. It's not easy when people leave us, is it?"

I scowled. "What's that supposed to mean?"

"Well, that's what you did to all of us when you left. You made us believe you were gone, and you broke everything."

"Are you kidding me?" I blurted. "Are you seriously making this about you right now? I'm the one whose girlfriend just died in front of him!"

"Oh, and that was any less traumatic than when my brother faked splattering all over the ground?"

I flinched.

"You left us all to pick up the pieces!"

All my anger boiled up inside. I was so done with this guilt! I slammed my hands on the table and the words just exploded out of me. "It wasn't my fault. I'm sorry you were hurt when I died, but you know what, it hasn't exactly been a cake walk for me either! I'm sorry you felt abandoned, but I promise, I never left you! I have been with you the whole time. I was there when you drank yourself into oblivion after my funeral. I was there when you proposed to Chelsea on that rooftop. I was there when you visited my grave and decided to name your son after me. I was there when Chelsea left you. I've been with you in a more personal and intimate way than any living person could, and I've done nothing but try to help and support you. So don't *ever* accuse me of leaving you, because I've been here the whole time, you just couldn't see me."

He glared down at the table, looking chastened and defensive. "Well even if that was true—which it isn't because there is no afterlife—how was I supposed to know you were there?"

I sighed and leaned back. "I don't know, Sam. I guess you just sort of feel it, if you're paying attention. Sometimes it seemed like you could hear me when I was trying to talk you out of something. You ignored me most of the time though. It made me sad."

"Why?" he snapped. "What do you care what I do with my life?"

I forced myself to look him in the eye. "I care because I love you. I know that you never mean to hurt anyone and when you do you beat yourself up inside and I hate that. I was just trying to help. You deserve to be happy. You're amazing, Sam. I've watched you struggle through so much, and I'm so impressed with how far you've come. I just wish you wouldn't shove me away."

Sam's face contorted into so many struggling emotions, I couldn't tell if he was about to cry or throw things. "*Why* do you have to be like that?"

"Like what?" I demanded. "What have I ever done to you?"

"Nothing!" he said, throwing his hands up. "You've done nothing wrong. Ever. You've always been that stupid, annoying, perfect brother. And then you sit there and tell me you love me after I act like a total jackass! Can't you just give it back to me? Just once, so I don't have to feel like crap about it?"

I laughed in total bewilderment. He thought I was perfect? That was ludicrous. I was the biggest screw up that I knew. But, as I thought about it, I started to see where he was coming from. While my parents praised me, and my sister came to me for advice, he was constantly scolded and grounded. He was the one always letting people down—the constant disappointment. Which, I'm sure, only led him to more self-sabotaging behavior, perpetuating the cycle. I felt so foolish for watching over him for so long and never understanding why he acted the way he did. I hated disappointing people, but he'd dealt with that his entire life. He was never the person his family wanted him to be. And, at least in his head, I was.

He didn't hate me; he hated himself.

I leaned forward, trying to emphasize what I was saying. "I am *not* perfect. If you had any idea how badly I've screwed up, over and over again, you wouldn't be saying those things."

He shook his head and rolled his eyes. "Yeah, but you try. I just give up . . ."

"You don't always give up," I said, confused about how this conversation had turned to me comforting him. "You've grown so much. You're a really good dad, and you're great to Jessica. And you're here right now, which means that you're at least trying to get over whatever you have against me."

He sighed and rubbed his temples. "That's the worst part about it. I was an awful brother, and I know it. I was jealous, so I treated you like crap. And then you went and died before I had the chance to fix it! I had to move on knowing that my brother died thinking I hated him. I'm pretty sure the last thing I said to you was, 'Who the hell cares?' That's what you did to me when you died. You made me realize that I'm a terrible person and didn't even give me the chance to make amends. Do you know what that's like to have to live with guilt like that?"

"Dude, don't even talk to me about guilt," I muttered.

"The worst part about dying is knowing you messed everyone's life up."

Sam sighed and looked away. I stared down at my hands. I had no idea what to say. We'd both confessed more to each other than we ever had, but there was still a tense uncertainty between us. Did he hate or love me? Or was it a bit of both? And what did he want me to do, try less, so he would feel better about not trying more?

We were quiet for so long that it took me a while to notice my foot was tapping to the beat of the music the coffee shop was playing. A little bit of the old me came out and felt the need to say something awkward to relieve the tension. I pointed up at the speaker playing the early 2000's pop song Elena was obsessed with as a kid. "This song reminds me of that time Elena was dancing to this in the bathroom and I pushed her into the bathtub with all her clothes on." I was pretty sure it was Sam's old bath water. He always took the longest baths and forgot to drain the tub.

Sam's mouth twitched. "Didn't she have your Game Boy in her pocket?"

"Yes! I'm still mad thinking about it! It was totally ruined after that."

"And then I pushed you in with her and we ended up having a 'soap fight.' Whatever that is."

I snorted. "At least the bathroom smelled good for a while."

"Yeah, nice change from the burnt hair smell from Elena's mini curling iron."

I chuckled.

He gave me half of a hesitant smile that reminded me of all the good times as a kid I'd forgotten about. He wasn't a jerk *all* the time. Sometimes he was fun.

All I could think at that moment was that I loved my brother, and I didn't want to let him go. I couldn't go the rest of my life hiding from him. We butted heads sometimes, but he was family. There was a bond between us, and I found myself starving for connection.

"Do you want to start over?" I asked. "Just let go of all the bad stuff and move on?"

Sam studied me for a moment, his face hardening. "Are you back for good? Or are you gonna leave us again?"

"I'm back for now. I don't know how long, though. Please don't hate me if I have to leave. Not everything is in my control."

"I still don't believe this about you dying and coming back to life. But I saw you dead . . . and now you're alive. That's not possible. But this dumb story you made up about witnessing a crime and faking your death sounds just as stupid."

I shrugged. "Does it really matter? I'm giving you a chance to get rid of the guilt. Will you take it?"

He swallowed, then nodded quietly. "Just don't go behind my back to talk about me with my girlfriend anymore. How would you like it if I did that to you with *your* girlfriend?"

I winced at the sharp stab of pain in my chest. *My* girlfriend was dead. I'd almost forgotten for a moment. Flashes of her mangled body crossed my mind for the millionth time.

"You jackass," he mumbled to himself, covering his face with his hand. He shoved his hand through his hair. "See what I mean? Stuff like that just comes out when I'm around you. I'm so sorry, David. I didn't mean—"

"It's fine," I said quickly. I sniffed and looked up, willing my eyes not to water. Now was not the time to fall apart. "I promise not to go behind your back again." It was physical pain keeping the tears in. How was it that I still had any left?

Sam felt so guilty he paid for my coffee.

How odd that he'd feel so bad about a tiny slight like that, but not for literally attacking me just for showing my face. Maybe he did feel guilty about that. I had a feeling the poor guy was constantly beating himself up in his head, and his low self-esteem just led to more poor choices. Regardless, for the first time I felt like he was on my side. And I needed as many people on my side as I could get. Preston wasn't wrong—I needed people to help me through this.

chapter 37
I SEE DEAD PEOPLE

I was sitting in conference room nine at The Resting Place Headquarters. Eight empty metal chairs sat around in a circle. I looked down and I was wearing a glowing white robe. When I stood up, I floated.

"Sweet!"

I flew up through the ceiling and into the sky, closing my eyes as I floated among the clouds. I wasn't even cold because the water vapor didn't stick to me. I grinned and flew higher, wondering why I'd never tried to see how high I could go. Could I reach that distant star?

Down here, David. We don't have time for you to fly to space.

I startled and hurdled back down through the clouds and the ceiling until I was back in the conference room. Hermes was waiting for me. He stood in the middle of the room, tensed as though ready to leave at any moment.

"Hey, long time, no see!" I grinned, feeling lighter and happier than I'd felt in a long time. What had I been so upset about before?

I couldn't even remember.

"Focus, David. I need to deliver a message to you, but we don't have much time."

"Shoot," I said, taking a seat in the chair I'd vacated.

"It's time for you to return to your duties."

"What duties?"

"You're a demon hunter. You haven't been released from that."

I blinked and it all came flooding back. That's right. I was a demon hunter and a mortal. Sheila had been after me, and then I'd gone to the Hurricane to save my mom and Jake, and then . . . Oh . . . That's why I'd been so depressed.

I deflated as I slumped into my chair. "How, Hermes? What am I supposed to do? I can't even talk to my team without . . . S-Sandra. I mean, I guess I can do that leave-my-body thing again, but I can only do that two more times."

"No, that should be saved for emergencies. There is another solution, but you have to accept it."

"What?"

"Instead of you depending on a mortal medium, you become the medium."

I blinked. "Oh . . . Really? Like, the Big Man would just do something to me, and all of a sudden, I would see the dead?"

"Yes. It is a big responsibility and will very much complicate your life if you accept. But if you do accept, it could bring us one step closer to capturing Malum. What is your answer?"

"Yes!" I said immediately. Talk to the dead? Half of the people I loved were dead. This was the ideal situation.

"Good. I'll send an angel to explain the details when you wake. I must go."

He frowned, looking around as though he smelled something rotten.

"What?" I asked.

His expression darkened. "You have a nightmare coming. I'd stay and chase it off, but I must leave now."

"It's fine . . ." I sighed. "What's one more horror dream?"

Everything disappeared. I fell through the floor and into empty air again, speeding toward the rocks below me. I screamed just as I was about to make impact, but I fell right through it all into total nothingness. I continued to fall and fall, feeling like it would never end, when a hand caught hold of me.

I was hanging from the edge of the Hurricane, dangling over all the screaming spirits of the dead. Others fell past me, screaming in agony, and I tried to reach out and save them, but they were all just out of reach.

The hand holding me started to slip, so I gripped tighter. The mist cleared enough that I saw Sheila above me, holding my hand in two of hers.

"Don't let go!" I pleaded.

She smiled slowly, but when she spoke it was Malum's voice. "All right. I'll pull you back up." She yanked me up to her, grabbed me by the throat and kissed me. I struggled and tried to push her off, but she was too strong. She was feeding me Darkness by the mouth, filling me up with despair and fear. I finally pushed her face off me, and she tilted her head. "Oh? So you do want me to let go? Okay."

She released me, smiled, and waved as I fell into the pit, screaming. But my screams weren't loud enough to drown out the miserable wretches that screamed and laughed and clawed at me.

"Never enough . . ."

". . . failed . . ."

"Coward!"

"Pathetic . . . selfish . . ."

"Forsaken!"

"No escape!"

"Wake up, mate!"

"Make it stop!"

"It's a dream! Wake up!"

I jolted upright to see a glowing figure sitting on my bed.

I screamed and pulled up the covers. Sadly, I didn't have to worry about my dad hearing me and coming in to check. Since visiting the Hurricane, I usually woke up screaming. By now he'd stopped racing to my door every time it happened.

The figure grinned. "You see me? Like, you defo see me?"

My eyes widened and my mouth fell open. I rubbed my eyes to make sure I was seeing clearly. "Jake? Oh my gosh, Jake! You're okay! Why are you appearing to me? What happened with you?"

I launched myself at him, going for a hug, but I fell through him and rolled off my bed.

"You can't hug dead people, ya fruit loop," he laughed.

I staggered to my feet and clutched my stupid ribs that still hurt, grimacing. That was dumb. Carefully, I staggered back to my bed and sat, leaning against the headboard. "How long have you . . ." I gestured at him, unsure how to phrase it. He clearly wasn't a wanderer anymore. He was glowing Light and everything. "What happened? Last time I saw you, you were staring off into space. It was, like, the saddest thing I'd ever seen. What brought you back?"

"Well, that was your fault."

I snorted. "I've done absolutely nothing but mope and cry. I'm barely functioning."

"Yep. That did it."

I raised an eyebrow. "Come again?"

He sighed and rolled his eyes. "Fine, I'll spell it out for ya. So, when you're a wanderer, it's kinda like being in a big pool of water." He spread his hands out to indicate a watery expanse. I'd forgotten how much he talked with his hands. "You can't really see or hear anything going on above you. But sometimes you float a little closer to the surface and you start to hear things. Most of the time you just push yourself deeper into the water, because you don't want to surface, but you can't block out everything. Your mum was dragging me along with her, hoping that going through the motions of guarding you would help bring me back. Well, I was kinda close to the surface one day, when I heard you crying. And it made me . . . sad. I felt selfish for hiding in my bubble when you needed a friend. I mean, I was still dealing with my stuff, but that all happened to me in the past. Your crap was still happening, and you needed help."

"And you were just fine? Just like that?"

"No," he chuckled. "I was a mess. When everything comes rushing back at ya, it's pretty bad. Your poor mum. You were bawling and I was bawling, and she didn't know what to do with us. We were like two big crying babies."

"Fun stuff."

He grinned, and I was so happy to see him smiling again. "Anyway. the Big Man's helped me get back to myself a bit."

"Glad, you're back, man," I said with a genuine smile. I'd missed my friend. "Wait a minute," I said, sitting up straighter. "I'm glad you're here, but why are you *here*? Like, appearing to me. Is something wrong?"

"Yeah, mate. You're super depressed and it's bumming me out. But I'm not actually appearing to you. You're just seeing me on your own."

"You're not making any sense." I rubbed my eyes again. I was awake, right? Jake was definitely still there when I opened my eyes. "Am I dead? Did I die in my sleep?" I touched my face and arms. I was still covered in old bruises and cuts. The tender scar was still there in my forehead where my stitches came out. Definitely still mortal.

"Mate, you're not dead. No dead person could snore like that. Didn't Hermes give you a heads up?"

"Huh?" I blinked and then my mouth popped open. "Oh! Yeah, I did have a dream he showed up and told me I'd be able to see dead people. He said he'd send someone to explain it more. I'm guessing that's you. So, what? Are there rules? Limitations? Why wait until now?"

"Basically, you can see all spirits: angels, demons, and wanderers. You can also see our auras, unlike . . . uh . . . some people." The avoidance of Sandra's name still made me wince. "And the Big Man wasn't gonna throw that on you while you were still, you know, grieving. You needed time. And then you had to accept it and all. So yeah, that's the gist."

"Why even ask to accept?" I said. "He didn't ask if I wanted to be mortal again."

Jake shrugged. "Who knows. He's the Big Man. He has his reasons."

"I Iuh . . ." I said. I looked out the window as I tried to process. The sky was still the gray before dawn, but I could hear a bird twittering by my window. Without the sun shining through, the only light in the room came from my lamp and Jake himself. I looked back at him and frowned, thinking about what he'd said. So, the demon hunters still needed me? I was back on the team? This was all good news, right? Somehow, I was afraid to trust it.

"So, I'm a medium like S-Sandra was?" It was harder than it should have been to say Sandra's name. It was a word that was actively avoided in my house.

"Yep! It's gonna be sweet as! Though I think he called you a mediator, not a medium. Unlike Sandra, you can see Light and Darkness. See?" He turned off his Light and started radiating Darkness. He quickly flipped back to the Light. "Probably because there's a bunch of demons after you and you need to know which dead people are trying to kill you. We try, but your mum and I can't be with you every second of the day."

As if on cue, three demons flew through the wall and came at me snarling with fangs and claws and faces contorted into grotesque sneers. I screamed and crawled back against my headboard. Jake casually created a ball of Light the size of a beach ball, smashed it down to the size of a baseball and tossed it at the demons. The ball of Light exploded, and the demons scattered wailing in agony as they departed.

I breathed heavily, my hand on my heart. Since being mortal, I knew I'd frequently been assaulted by demons, but I'd never actually seen them. Well, other than that time Sheila revealed herself to me. It was ten times more terrifying being able to see them, and I think they knew that.

"What was that?" I asked when I could finally catch my breath. "Did you just make a Light *bomb*? How did you do that?"

"Old defender trick," Jake said with a shrug.

My mind returned to trying to catch up to all this new information, while simultaneously tunneling in on one very specific hope. "So . . . is S-Sandra around? Could I see her?" My throat tightened up and my heart beat faster. I was so afraid to hope. It was possible this was all just a dream, and if it was, it was going to crush me when I woke up.

Jake smiled ruefully. "I was wondering how long it would take you to ask. Yeah, she'll be here in a sec. We were arguing over who got to come debrief you, but then she got pulled into a Light training meeting, and I left without her." He chuckled. "She's pretty busy though. She's officially joined our demon hunter task force, but she's also a rescuer and she's really changin' things up. She started her own task force that focuses on rescuing demons. Crazy, right? Everyone thinks it's nuts, but we're also a little desperate, so no one cares."

My heart rate kicked up a notch. "She's trying to rescue *demons?* That sounds dangerous! She could get hurt!"

Jake shrugged. "She's already dead."

I winced at his phrasing. It still hurt.

"Sorry," he said quickly.

"I can think of something worse than death," I said darkly. "We've both been there."

Now Jake winced and I felt terrible for bringing it up. He'd spent much longer in the Hurricane than I had and had certainly suffered because of it. I noticed something in Jake's face I hadn't seen before. He had wrinkles. Not enough to make him look *old*, just older than the eighteen-year-old he'd always been. A few lines on his forehead, a crease between his eyes, the beginnings of crow's feet. I doubted it was a conscious thing. He felt older, so subconsciously he'd made his appearance match.

"Sorry for bringing up that place," I said quietly.

He sighed and frowned down at his feet. "There's all this talk about going back there to rescue the angels left behind—there were two you guys missed, and one more captured since then—but I just . . . I can't do it. I know it makes me a coward, but I'm never going back there again. Never." His face darkened, and for a second, I saw a hint of that lost wanderer from the pit.

"Then don't go," I said quickly. "That doesn't make you a coward, man. That place is . . . I don't think anyone who's been captured should go back there. I'll do it. I was only there for like a second."

Jake snorted humorlessly. "A second's enough. Your nightmares are proof of that."

"Yeah, but I wasn't actually captured," I said. "And I had help. From Sheila of all people . . ."

I remembered for a second how she said she was the one who set Malum free. I still couldn't figure out how that was possible. Jake's face hardened at the mention of her, and his aura flickered *Darkness*. He'd been protecting me from her from the beginning, but now it was personal.

"Sorry," I said quickly. "I shouldn't have mentioned—"

We were interrupted by someone floating through the ceiling and falling through the floor.

"Oops! Too far," said a muffled voice below my feet.

Jake's face thawed and he rolled his eyes. "She's revolutionizing The Resting Place, but she still doesn't know how to float."

"Shut up," Sandra said as she floated up through the carpet, glowing and wearing the typical angelic robe. She glared at Jake and held up her hands in annoyance. "We're supposed to be using the buddy system. Why'd you ditch me?"

Jake shrugged. "I wanted to see him first."

"Sandra!" I gasped, jumping to my feet. I forgot for a second that I was wearing nothing but my boxers, but I didn't care. My chin quivered and my eyes filled with tears. She looked amazing. Lighter and happier. Filled to the brim with hope. As I gazed at her floating above me and radiating Light, I knew she was always meant to be an angel. This was right, and I *hated* that. I knew that someday when I died, I could be with her again. But a lot can change with time. She might find someone new, and I was still secretly holding out for that long life and family Hermes mentioned. The hope of growing old with Sandra was as dead as she was.

"Hey, David," Sandra said with a sad smile, looking me over. "You haven't been doing so good, have you?"

"No, I haven't," I said, wiping away tears.

"I'm really sorry I died . . . I know it was totally horrific for both of us, but honestly, I'm okay. You're way more upset about it than I am."

I rolled my eyes and smiled. "That's such an angel thing to say. You guys act like death is no big deal, even though it sucks for us. But whatever. I love you, so I guess I'll forgive you."

Her jaw dropped and my face heated. I hadn't meant to say that.

Then she screeched and balled her hands into fists. "Are you kidding me! You say that *now?* After I'm *dead?*"

I rubbed my neck uncomfortably. "Sorry. But I mean, wasn't it kind of obvious?"

"It was pathetically obvious," Jake muttered in the background.

"I don't care," she said. "A girl has to be told these things! Ooh, if I could slap you, I'd slap you!"

She floated up to me and flapped her hand around trying to hit my face, which just made me laugh. The release was amazing. I hadn't laughed in so long, so I threw my head back and laughed harder. Sandra tried not to join in, but she was never good at keeping a straight face.

"I've missed you," I said, still fighting back lingering chuckles and somehow crying at the same time. I sighed. "I'm sorry I waited until you died to say I love you, but at least you know how I feel."

She smiled. "I love you too, dummy. Even though you

always wait for one of us to die before you actually do anything about it."

My heart ached just looking at her, but before we could say more, we were interrupted by eight more angels popping into existence, floating around my bed.

"Is now a good time?" Raj asked with a grin.

I spun in a circle to see them all, the corners of my mouth creeping up into an amazed grin. They stood in pairs with their partners, which seemed to have been shuffled around since the addition of Sandra. Raj and Ying Yue, Frederick and William, Jake and Sandra, Ted and Natalie, Daisy and—"

"Bill?" I gasped.

"At your service." He grinned and tipped an imaginary hat, his Light aura unmistakable.

"Oh my gosh, congratulations!"

I turned around again to look at all of their angelic faces. My team. My family. Here they were, smiling at me, just as happy as I was that we could now speak face to face.

I looked back at Raj. "A good time for what? A meeting?"

"Yeah, kid. We've been waiting for you."

I looked down and my face heated, remembering I was still in my underwear. I was sure my hair was sticking up in all directions and my breath smelled.

"Can I have a minute?" I asked, running a hand through my hair.

"What's the big deal?" Daisy asked. "We all check in on you every now and then. We've seen you in your boxers before."

"Daisy," Bill chided.

"It's true!"

"Let the lad go," Frederick said. "He wishes to be presentable. It would be inappropriate to expect him to participate in nothing but his undergarments."

"Enough about my underwear," I said, rushing through William to reach my dresser and pulling out some jeans and a t-shirt. I hurried to the door but spun around to glare at them all first. "Don't go away."

"We won't," Sandra promised.

Raj smiled in a very fatherly way. You know that look a guy has when he has a million burdens, but he throws on a smile for his kids that's part forced, part genuine? Raj looked at me like that as he said, "We never left, David. We've been with you the whole time."

I took in the scene one last time then raced to the bathroom. I splashed water on my face, brushed my teeth, and threw on my clothes. Though I was in a hurry, I paused when I finished, distracted by the guy in the mirror. He looked a little crazy, and a little beat up, but he had a look in his eyes that had been absent for a long time. Hope. I smiled and hurried back to my room.

After the meeting, everyone left but Raj. He gave me that

fatherly smile and leaned against the wall. "I've been meaning to talk to you."

"What's up?" I asked, sitting on the edge of my bed.

"You need help, kid," he said bluntly.

I sighed heavily, slumping back. "Yeah, it's been discussed. But the thing is, this crap I'm trying to work through isn't exactly stuff I can talk to a mortal about. I mean the Sandra stuff, maybe, but not the demon stuff. That . . . place did a number on me."

He nodded. "Well, I know someone you can talk to."

"Really?" I said skeptically. "Who would that be?"

He smiled. "Me."

I snorted. "What, are you a therapist or something?"

"Yeah, actually. That's what I did when I was alive." He transformed his robe into a light blue button up shirt, slacks, and shiny dress shoes, complete with glasses and a notepad. "Dr. Rajesh Asan. Nice to meet you. I'd shake your hand, but I'm dead."

I chuckled. "Are you serious?"

"Yes, I'm serious. I think you need this, but I won't force you into it."

"What about Jake?" I asked. "I mean . . . He was pretty messed up by the Hurricane too."

"Not that it's our business, but he's already got the best therapist there is. He meets with the Big Man almost every single day and it's done him wonders. Your mother does as well. So, what do you say, kid? I promise whatever you say will be kept in confidence. We'll be totally professional about it. I'll even dress like this if it helps."

"Weirdly, it kinda does . . ." I said with an awkward smile. I sighed and shook my head. "All right, fine."

"Perfect." He just kept looking at me and smiling.

"What?" I asked, self-consciously.

"I'm just proud of you."

I laughed loudly. "You're saying this to the guy that's so screwed up that you think he needs therapy?"

He rolled his eyes and shook his head, sitting next to me on the bed. "David, a hero isn't the guy that magically saves the day at no cost to himself. Real heroes suffer. They stumble, they fall, they make mistakes, and sometimes they want to give up. What makes them a hero is the fact that they do get back up, even when it hurts, even when it doesn't make sense, even when they feel like they're falling apart, because someone out there needs their help. I know you don't always believe in yourself, but you try. You care. And you always get back up. You're a hero, kid. How could I not be proud of you?"

I was so taken aback I didn't know how to respond. It made me uncomfortable and emotional at the same time. Even if I'd saved the entire world, I could never see myself as a hero. But if my mentor thought that of me, maybe I wasn't as much of a failure as I thought. And even if I was a failure and Raj was just lying for my benefit, he cared about me enough to be sitting next to me giving me hope.

chapter 37
COMPANY

During the demon hunter meeting, Sandra warned me that my life was about to get a lot more crowded and a lot more complicated. I learned on my way to work that morning that she was not wrong. Dead people were literally *everywhere*. I slammed on my brakes getting out of my driveway because a wanderer was just floating there in the middle of the street. I felt bad driving through her, but she wouldn't move. There were more like her, and they obviously didn't pay much attention to where they were. Some floated in trash cans or on rooftops. Others were more mischievous, making streetlights flicker or scaring pigeons. (I guess pigeons can see ghosts?)

I almost had a heart attack when my grandmas popped up out of nowhere, Grandma Gertie in the front seat, Nana Maria in the back.

"*Hijole!*" I yelled, almost swerving into the car next to me. The guy in the car honked and flipped me off.

"It's true!" Grandma sang. "He can see us!"

"How's it going, *mijo*?" Nana asked.

I took a few steadying breaths. "It's amazing to see you both, but can you not startle me like that? My gosh."

"We met your girl," Grandma said, trying to elbow me. "We love her! Nice work!"

I repressed an eye roll. "Grandma, tell me you didn't interrogate Sandra."

"I just asked her a few questions," she said innocently. "And I wanted you to know, I approve."

Nana Maria held her hands up defensively. "I was not part of this."

"You two are perfect for each other. Tell me you'll wait for her!" Grandma said.

I smiled and shook my head. "Grandma, you'd think any girl who even looks at me is perfect."

"Yes, because it means she has good taste!"

"*Ay caramba*, Gertrude!" Nana scolded. "Do not put it in their heads that they should wait for each other. David's a young man yet, and he won't die for a long time. He needs to move on with his life."

"Oh fine!" she grumbled. Then her face lit up. "We'll just have to find him a nice *living* girl. There are plenty of those."

I said, "Grandma!" just as Nana said, "Gertrude!"

Mom showed up in the back seat next to Nana, and I had another mini heart attack, almost running into the car in front of me that had stopped. "You guys are gonna be the death of me," I said in a weak voice, clutching my heart.

"Ladies," Mom said. "I think you're needed at the front desk."

"At the same time?" Grandma asked.

Nana took the hint. "Come on, Gertrude. It was good to see you, *mijo*!" She took Grandma's arm and they disappeared.

Mom floated up to the front seat and smiled at me. She just looked at me for a while, searching my face.

"Hey, Mom," I said a little tearfully.

"Hello, my boy. How are you doing?"

"I honestly don't even know, but I'm really happy to see you. I missed you."

"Well, you're gonna get sick of me pretty soon. I follow you around a lot. Me and Jacob."

The light turned green, and I forced myself to look away from her. "Just don't pop up out of nowhere, all right?"

"What do you want me to do? I can't knock first."

"Good point . . ." I sighed, resigning myself to the fact that people were going to be sneaking up on me for the rest of my life. Lovely. How did Sandra manage this?

"Do you want to talk?" Mom asked.

"Yes, very much."

I let her do most of the talking, because I was exhausted and a little raw from all the pain and healing my heart had gone through lately. I don't know how, but she knew all the right things to say, and I felt much better by the time I got to work.

Mom shadowed me all day, but she didn't bother me, which I appreciated. I didn't want to talk to her in public and look like a total crazy person. I was sure I already did, flinching whenever I saw a dead person in an unexpected place. They were seriously everywhere. There was this one wanderer in the dumpster out back. Like, this grown man was laying in the trash staring at nothing. I didn't even see him until I threw a bag of garbage in there. He startled me so much I fell on my butt. Seriously, who wants to spend their afterlife in a dumpster at Chuck E. Cheese? That's the most pathetic thing I could ever think of.

I found two other wanderers that followed the Chuck E. costume around all day. Of all the things they could haunt, why a rat costume? And then there was this little girl wanderer that kept trying to go down the slide. She couldn't figure out why she kept falling through it. It was funny and depressing and deeply weird.

Later I found a demon hiding in the Chuck E. closet who screamed and flew at my face. My mom took care of her quickly, but it set off a panic attack and I had to step outside for a minute to pull myself together. I had some trauma in that closet, and I was sure that stupid demon knew it. Jerk.

I guess I was acting a little twitchy, because it wasn't

long before Preston pulled me into his office looking nervous and concerned.

"Dude, you're acting weird," he said.

"Sorry," I said, distracted by the angel floating behind him. Preston obviously didn't know she was there, but he did seem a lot more relaxed than he normally did. Was that his mom? Was she one of the ones Sheila and I pulled out of the pit?

Preston looked back to see what I was looking at, but of course he saw nothing there. He raised an eyebrow and asked, "Dude, are you high?"

"No!"

Apparently, that wasn't the answer he was hoping for. Maybe because if I wasn't high, then I was just hallucinating on my own, and that's not a good sign. "Look, man . . . maybe you should take some more time off. You came back to work the week after your accident, and after what you went through, that was probably too soon."

Of course, everyone at work knew what happened to me and Sandra. Since then, they'd all been either overly nice to me, or avoided me like the plague. People just don't know how to approach someone who's grieving. A part of me kind of appreciated how Preston was still blunt and honest with me. At least one person wasn't scared to talk to me.

"I'm fine," I said. "I'm sorry I've been acting weird. I'm just a little jumpy. I'm . . . getting help."

He nodded thoughtfully. "Good. All right, well, if you're up to it, will you do inventory? Joanna totally screwed it up yesterday. She miscounted literally everything, and she screwed it up last week too. I think she just sucks at math, and I don't want to have to yell at her again and make her feel stupid."

I just smiled at him.

"What?" he asked.

"Look at you all worried about people's feelings."

"Shut up," he said, rolling his eyes. "Will you do it or not?"

I nodded and he got up, leaving me alone in his office.

As he walked away, the woman floating behind him smiled and floated up to me. She looked nothing like him. He was pale and freckly, and this woman had dark skin and glossy black hair. But the way she looked at him, I had no doubt she was his mother. "Thank you for being his guardian angel while I was away. You've done well with him. I know he's . . . difficult to handle."

I didn't know about guardian angel. Babysitter was more like it, but I didn't think she'd appreciate my complaining. I hesitated, then pulled my phone out, trying to pretend I was on the phone as I spoke to her. "Are you his mom? Were you there? In the Hurricane?"

She flinched at the mention of the name. "I was there for a long time. I can't thank you enough for saving me. For mine and Preston's sake."

Preston told me she'd died when he was ten. I had a moment of compassion for him. Maybe that was part of why he'd been such a jerk—he didn't have his mom around to teach him how to be a person. I frowned, wondering what his dad must be like for Preston to have turned out the way he did. I had a feeling the guy was a real piece of work.

It was a very long day, and it felt like it took just as long to fall asleep that night. For one thing, there was a lot to process. Seeing dead people, talking to Sandra, meeting with Raj . . . I felt like my head wasn't big enough to contain all the thoughts and emotions I was feeling.

For another thing, I was distracted by the fact that someone was watching me sleep . . . My mom was with me most of the day, but now it was Jake's turn. I felt bad he had the night shift, which was probably super boring, so I propped my phone up on my dresser and let him do whatever he wanted with it. My insomnia wasn't helped by Jake's loud snorts of laughter as he watched some Aussie TV show on my phone, but it was better than him floating by my bed. That was just awkward. Mortals always have an audience, but you're not supposed to *know* it.

Though it seemed excessive to have babysitters, with my new "second sight" I could see why my angel friends wanted me constantly watched over. I had been attacked by a lot of demons that day, and I had the feeling this was nothing new. Luckily none of them were Sheila's caliber, so they were simple for Mom and Jake to get rid of. If they weren't there, though, I knew I'd have been dragged down by it like I was when they were both captured.

It was too bright in the room with both my lamp on and Jake's aura, so I switched off the lamp and stared at the ceiling trying to process everything that was going on. I still had no idea what to think about all of this. I was happy I could see all of my friends again but seeing dead people definitely complicated things. I'd need to have a talk with Sandra and get some tips on how to manage it all. We also didn't really get to talk earlier about where we stood with each other. At the moment, I was still grieving the relationship we would likely never have, and I was sure it would be a while before I could see her without it tearing me apart. Seeing her wasn't the same as *being* with her. But I felt that with time I'd come to appreciate having her in my life, even if it was just as a close friend. I could love her without her being mine.

"Could you turn that down a little bit?" I asked Jake sleepily.

"Sorry. Am I too loud?" he asked.

"Too bright," I said. "Couldn't you just hang outside the door or in the closet?"

"If I'm in the closet, I can't see you," he said.

"Just pop your head through the door every now and then," I said. "Come on man, I'm tired and you glow in the dark."

He shrugged. "Fine, but I'm taking this." He concentrated and floated my phone across the room until he got to the closet. He must have forgotten that the phone was not as intangible as he was, because as he floated through the door the phone smacked against it and fell with a thump.

I snorted. "Nice." I opened the closet and tossed the phone in.

Then I flipped the lamp back on, which was a lot dimmer than Jake, and fell asleep almost instantly.

A bird chirping woke me up the next morning, and I became aware of the sun shining through my eyelids. The furnace kicked on, and I pulled my blanket closer, snuggling into the warmth. I felt rested and relaxed. Peaceful. I didn't want to open my eyes and lose that feeling. I couldn't remember the last time I wasn't woken up by a nightmare, but the dream I had . . . I couldn't remember it, but I felt like it was important. I'd suffered so much since becoming mortal, but for a moment, my burdens didn't seem so heavy. What was my dream?

It was like trying to catch smoke. The only thing I could remember was a feeling of immense comfort and a phrase that kept repeating in my mind, in direct contrast to my nightmares.

I took a deep breath and opened my eyes. I'd been swimming in pain and fear for so long, but at the moment, all I could think about was how wonderful life was. I had my family back. I got to play with my nieces and nephews and hug my sister. I hung out with my dad every night and was on my way to repairing my relationship with my brother. I had a job and friends, who were weirdly becoming like a second family to me. And all the other loved ones that death should have separated me from were now a part of my life again. I felt loved and supported, and that filled me to the brim with hope and determination. There was a reason I was here. There was something I had to do, and the Big Man needed me to do it. I would figure out what it was, and I would not let him down.

I shut my eyes, and I caught a little wisp of my dream. Words I mentally clung to and hoped I'd never forget.

"Fear not, David. I am with you always. You may turn away from me if you choose, but I will never forsake you. I love you, my son."

End of Book 2

Stay Tuned for Book 3:
I DON'T HAVE A TITLE YET

(That's not the title of the book; the author is just being indecisive.)

Acknowledgements

The following people have helped me with this book:

A fabulous librarian

A woman I've never met

The guy I married when I was five

My wife

April Ludgate

That girl that fell down the stairs in a sweater

A jiu jitsu mama

The queen of plants

A left-handed man that paints right-handed

And the only Arizonan that hates Monsoons

All you awesome weirdos have been a part of this book's journey, whether you knew it or not. It may have been intense feedback and editing, or maybe you're just so much of my story that you made your mark on David's as well. Regardless, I love you all!

About the Author

Kendra Pettit Photography

Anni Sezate is a Yale University graduate with an MA in literature (pronounced LIT-chruh-chu) and lives with her high school sweetheart, Henry Cavill, and their four beautiful children in the English countryside.

Just kidding, she's a teacher that lives alone with her cat. She would like to point out that while she and Henry never worked out, she does have a super cool family, loves her inhospitable Arizona desert, and has an awesome life full of books, plants, and children. So there ☺

Keep in touch!

AnniSezate.com
IG: @Anni_Sezate